RELATIONS

A NOVEL BY
ZSIGMOND MÓRICZ

ZSIGMOND MÓRICZ

RELATIONS

ᗒᗕ

TRANSLATED BY
BERNARD ADAMS

WITH AN INTRODUCTION
BY GEORGE F. CUSHING

CORVINA

Published in 2007 by Corvina Books Ltd.
1086 Budapest, Dankó utca 4–8, Hungary

Originally published in Hungarian under the title
Rokonok

On the cover: *Sunday Afternoon* by Sándor Bihari

Design by Judit Kállói

Second printing

ISBN 978 963 13 5524 6

ZSIGMOND MÓRICZ,
THE PASSIONATE OBSERVER

"If Hungary were to be completely destroyed and much later a Martian or a German social psychologist were to read this collection of stories, he would get to know from them the very essence of Hungary. Get to know it? He would feel it physically, visualize it and catch the smell of it, and it would pain him."[1] So wrote the critic György Bálint about *Barbarians* (Barbárok), an award-winning collection of Móricz's short stories that appeared in 1932, the same year as *Relations*. He might have added that the smell would be redolent of dunghills rather than roses. But his statement might have been applied to the whole of Móricz's work. He entered a literary tradition that expected writers to speak to the nation, to fulfil the role of critic, teacher and prophet; he accepted this role and fulfilled it admirably. His work is set almost entirely in contemporary Hungary. Born in 1879, he lived through a chequered period of Hungarian history and found a wealth of material at his disposal, from the millennial celebrations of 1896 through the horrors of the First World War, the experience of a short-lived republic and a flirtation with Communism, the utterly unexpected dismemberment of Hungary by the Treaty of Trianon in 1920 and a period of increasingly right-wing government, the rise of Fascism and the Second World War which saw his death in 1942. And throughout this long period there was the dark shadow of an unsolved problem: the plight of the peasantry, numerically by far the largest class in the country. They were disenfranchised and depended entirely on the whims of their landlords, most of whom treated them as chattels. They were not homogeneous; some of them were relatively wealthy, some possessed land, while others were landless and relied on seasonal work to scrape a living. Few voices were raised on their behalf and these were largely ignored; such unrest as there was brought swift and savage reprisals.

Móricz himself came from peasant stock. In childhood he experienced the vicissitudes of life in a large family reared by a hard-headed, well-read mother and an ambitious father, a contractor whose efforts at betterment kept ending in failure. So for a time there would be comparative comfort, then sudden descent into abject poverty which lasted while the father clawed

5

his way out of it again. So at an early age he experienced the often heartless reaction of relations to the family's plight. These years he recalled later in a highly unconventional autobiographical work, *The Novel of My Life* (Életem regénye, 1939), which describes only his first ten years, because "this was really the whole of my life. All that made me what I became happened during that time. More occurred to me up to the age of ten than during the following fifty years."[2] Yet he was well-educated; he attended the prestigious Calvinist colleges in Debrecen and Sárospatak where, shy and lonely, he found it difficult to find his place, and finally at Kisújszállás, where a sympathetic maternal uncle was headmaster. He settled down to become a good student; he had access to the staff library (he was an inveterate reader) and began to indulge in a lifelong passion for walking. He discovered that this was the best way of meeting people of all kinds, and people were his main interest in life, especially when they were willing to talk. Many of his stories are based on conversations, and typical photographs of him show him with a notebook recording some encounter. He was a keen observer and developed a fine ear for dialogue. When he bought a site for a country house at Leányfalu, north of Budapest, he employed builders who had a taste for talking.

Móricz's first attempts at writing appeared in Debrecen, where he studied first theology, to please his mother, and then law, at his father's request. He finished neither course, since in his heart of hearts he wanted to be a writer. He became dissatisfied with himself, for he could not find anything to write about. "I kept writing and writing, but each of my pieces was worse than the last. I did not know what I ought to be writing. Here was life and everyone spoke alike, in Hungarian; how could they be characterized and differentiated from each other? And what was it in human life that was worth describing and had to be described? I did not learn this for a long time; it was very late, after I was twenty-eight, when I realized that one can only describe what hurts, what wounds one. And what is revenge."[3] In his initial depression he contemplated suicide, but two events restored his confidence. The first was his marriage in 1905 to a young teacher, Janka Holics, who became his muse and one of his sternest critics. It was an unhappy partnership, for both of them were very demanding, yet it survived for twenty years and provided him with a theme which recurs again and again in his novels: the problem of the relationship between husband and wife. Yet he also declared that she was represented in every one of his female characters. Certainly this is true of *Relations*; she may be seen in the level-headed Lina who keeps warning her husband of the pitfalls that lie ahead if he allows himself to be involved in the doubtful schemes proposed by his new colleagues.

The second event that changed Móricz's life was a brief spell as a collector of folklore among the peasants of his own native region. He describes this activity as "the key which gave me access to their lives."[4] Here he could indulge his passion for walking and talking, and steep himself in a highly complex world that he had merely glimpsed as a child. No other Hungarian writer penetrated it so deeply or destroyed the nineteenth-century image of the operetta peasant so effectively, for he did not treat them with condescension, but regarded them as his equals. Here at last was the raw material for which he had been seeking.

It was in 1908 that he suddenly sprang to fame. The new journal *West* (Nyugat) published one of his short stories, *Seven Pennies* (Hét krajcár),[5] a simple but dramatic tale of a mother and her small son who spend a whole afternoon searching for seven pennies to buy soap; in the end it is a beggar who gives them the last penny – but by then it is dark and there is no money to buy oil for the lamp, so the whole search has been in vain. That story provided the title for a volume of short stories published in 1909; it was unreservedly acclaimed and determined his future. He now devoted himself to writing. He wrote some 36 novels, 600 short stories and numerous so-called reports, which are often indistinguishable from the stories; he also wrote a number of studies, some verse and dramas. Although he loved the stage and adapted several of his novels for it, he was a failure as a playwright. But in the rest of his work he described contemporary Hungarian society with the passion of a reformer, starting with the people he knew best, the peasants of the Great Plain, but gradually moving to the rural and small-town gentry and the slum-dwellers of Budapest.

His first novel, *Pure Gold* (Sárarany, 1911) introduces one of his favourite characters, the failed hero. In this case he is an ambitious peasant who tries hard to improve his prospects, but is stifled by the stagnation around him and ground down between a faithful wife and an attractive mistress. All his ideas, all his energies, go to waste and in the end he commits murder. At this stage Móricz appears to be a naturalist; his language is coarse and the erotic scenes overplayed. He certainly knew the

French naturalists and early in his career had translated some French novels. But this was only a passing phase. He soon realized that his innate gift for narrative and his natural use of dialogue, fired by moral indignation, needed no further embellishment. The failure of Dani Túri was to be repeated in many of his works, including *Relations*; Kopjáss too has ideas for reform, but they come to nothing in the morass of corruption that surrounds him.

By now, Móricz might have been classified merely as a peasant writer. But in *Behind God's Back* (Az Isten háta mögött, 1911) there are no peasant characters; it describes the increasingly desperate attempts of a young wife to obtain some excitement in the numbingly dull small town to which her elderly husband, a teacher, has brought her. But she fails, and in her misery tries to commit suicide by jumping out of a window. All that happens is that she lands in the mud. Her husband cannot understand her, and life goes on as before. This novel is obviously inspired by *Madame Bovary*; indeed, reference is made to it in the text, but the action is compressed into a mere forty-eight hours. Here we have a failed heroine, and her attempt to liberate herself from her troubles once again demonstrates links with *Relations*, except that in the latter novel the reader does not know whether Kopjáss succeeds or not. But in both books nothing has been achieved and nothing has changed. Móricz puts this even more clearly in his wartime novel *The Torch* (A fáklya, 1917), which tells of the fate of a young Calvinist minister who arrives in a village full of reforming zeal, only to be ensnared by the apathy around him. The would-be torch-bearer of civilization is himself a victim of a huge fire in the village; in helping to rescue others, he loses his own life. This scene is based on an actual occurrence: young people in the village of Ökörító in Móricz's home region held a dance in a huge barn whose doors were locked to prevent gate-crashers from entering. The barn caught fire, and the death-toll numbered 325; in addition ninety-nine were injured. Móricz wrote a highly emotional report on it, which was published in *West* in 1910, and the memory of it never left him. Fire in his works usually brings destruction rather than warmth and light. And the final sentence has a familiar ring: "It is finished [Christ's words from the Cross], but nothing is solved."

After the war, the new republic held out hope of reform, and Móricz welcomed it whole-heartedly. He wrote about the possibilities offered by land-reform and went to see for himself how

8

it was being implemented. He also visualized a new culture for new audiences, and saw himself as a torch-bearer in this congenial task. But this came to an end with the establishment of the government of Admiral Horthy, and those who had played any role in the previous regime were brought to book. Móricz himself suffered, and for a time withdrew from public life. His novels took on new motifs and themes. First came one of his most loved and most misunderstood works, *Be Faithful Unto Death* (Légy jó mindhalálig, 1921), ostensibly the tale of a young and innocent boy at the college in Debrecen, whose belief in adult integrity is shattered by various disturbing incidents. The only answer to the injustice and humiliation he suffers is to remain consistently good. It is a beautifully told, tender tale and can be read as an evocation of childhood, and that is how most Hungarians viewed it. But later Móricz made it clear that it was much deeper: his own reaction to the suffering he had endured not at school but after the overthrow of the Republic in 1919. He was surprised that the Hungarian public, generally so adept at reading between the lines, had missed the point. But normally Móricz did not write in coded language, so that the misunderstanding was not surprising. ,

After this he began to write about a different section of Hungarian society, the rural and small-town gentry, who had it in their power to initiate reform. In *Until Daybreak* (Kivilágos kivirradtig, 1926) he describes a past world which still affected the present. The scene is a drunken party at the turn of the century to celebrate the betrothal of the daughter of the house to a wealthy landowner. But the engagement falls through, as do all the hopes pinned on it; nevertheless all the participants continue to enjoy themselves because, as one of them remarks, the greatest blow that can befall a Hungarian gentleman is the loss of his good humour. The world outside did not count – and this applied not only to the older generation but to the younger folk as well. The theme is continued in *Gentlemen Having Fun* (Úri muri, 1928), which introduces a highly eccentric but progressive landlord who holds a huge party, at the height of which he sets fire to his property to provide more light for his guests and then commits suicide. Neither book makes grim reading; both are full of colour and anecdote, illuminating the various characters; not all is drowned in rural mud and dust, and there are many glimpses of real humour in them. But they both pose the question: can such people be trusted with the future of Hungariandom? Do their way of life and their morals offer any hope of worthwhile reform? Or are they an anachronism in the twentieth century?

The answers come in *Relations*. It is a novel of total disillusionment, with barely a glimmer of humour; only the rogue of an uncle, Berci, who tries to palm off coal from Hungary's best mine as his own, offers any relief. When he began to write it Móricz declared, "I postulated the idea that in every family there is one man, the rest are relations. By this I meant that there is a competent, strong personality to whom the many incompetent cling. And this strong man cannot achieve anything, because the network of relations enmeshes him and drags him into the depths."[6] But in its telling the story takes on a much wider significance. Kopjáss is another failed hero; he has ideas, but is no fighter. He is unexpectedly promoted from a minor post in the civic administration to a major one for which he is not qualified. The background is the large town of Debrecen, very thinly disguised, indeed some of the place-names are genuine, and the surrounding countryside is accurately portrayed. As news of his promotion spreads, relations, both close and very distant, begin to turn up on his doorstep demanding his patronage, much to his cool and hard-headed wife's annoyance. Throughout the novel, Lina personifies good sense and sobriety as she protests ever more vehemently against the involvement of her husband in schemes of doubtful morality. But this is not all ; the town administration in which he now has a key role is thoroughly corrupt and plays a part in numerous shady deals. Whatever his good intentions, Kopjáss is drawn into the net, soon realizing that he has been promoted not for his abilities, but as an easily-led accomplice. In the end he is so troubled by his conscience that he decides to commit suicide – but it is unlike Móricz's previous novel-endings; the reader does not know whether his attempt has succeeded. If not, the city fathers declare that he may yet prove useful to them, "because in all my long career I've scarcely met anybody who's picked up the threads so quickly and so very well." The novel, which spreads its net even wider, to the whole country, is a complete rejection of the idea that the gentry could ever initiate reform; all they are interested in is their own personal position and wealth (even when there is little or none of the latter to support them).

The bleak atmosphere of *Relations* is enhanced by the background against which it was written. The world was in the grip of an economic crisis which affected Hungary's own desperately weak economy very severely indeed. There are references in the book to the price of maize, one of her main exports. Móricz's own situation was grave. In 1925 his wife Janka had committed suicide, and in the following year he had embarked on a second marriage to the actress Mária Simonyi which was showing signs of strain. In 1929, following the death of Ernő Osvát, the brilliant editor of *West*, he had assumed its joint editorship with the poet and critic Mihály Babits; its finances were now in a frightful state and showed no signs of improvement, despite his efforts to obtain more subscribers. Moreover he was under attack for having visited the new state of Czechoslovakia and reported favourably on the democratic spirit of the Hungarian youth there. In a period when Hungary was making strenuous efforts to have her old frontiers restored, this was tantamount to treason. All these factors played their part in the background to the writing of *Relations*, which was published first in instalments and then, considerably enlarged, in book form in 1932.

Interestingly the novel not only poses problems, but also offers solutions to them. The musings of Kopjáss, for example, in the train after an unsatisfactory visit to Budapest and Parliament there (an almost word-for-word account of Móricz's own visit in 1927[7]) convey the thoughts of the author. As he dozes, looking at the Alispán, he thinks:

> *This was just a living human being, interested only in his own close circle of affairs. Who saw no farther than the County boundary, and even within that couldn't think anything through or arrange things properly. There was a kind of bureaucratic system according to which things had to be done, but how should he think, for instance, of something higher, such as how to find work for the thirty thousand unemployed in the County? Thirty thousand men, agricultural workers, marvellous material. The country could be built with these thirty thousand. Roads, houses, schools, museums. All it needed was somebody to set the thirty thousand to work. A will, a power aiming at a goal. The whole country could be re-organised with just these thirty thousand...*

And there is condemnation of the contemporary system, put into the mouth of the leader of the opposition on the City Council:

> *Let's stay with the State. It's a great mistake to believe that man is born to be independent. Mankind yearns for depen-*

dence. I'm not an individualist. I represent a mass of poor people, and I don't struggle to liberate their individual characters, because my individuals, the farm people, don't know what to do out there in the sea of mud with their famous characters. What are they to do, when they're stuck out there for six months on end and can't move: I'm thinking of a million and a half Hungarians, buried on the farms with their own free individual characters. I'm looking at the people of five million acres, who don't need independence because they don't know what to do with it. They live in nominal independence, but this independence, personal independence, is more like the independence of people condemned to death and locked in cells. Every farm's a prison. The leadership of the cities has locked them away there, and the powers that be only show their face when they want something from the farm people. When they need blood-donors or tax-payers, they're there. They're there for what they can get, but they never bring anything to the people. No roads, no protection, no enlightenment, no entertainment."

And at the end of the novel, as so often with Móricz, nothing has changed. But shortly after the publication of *Relations*, other writers began to warm to the theme of reform. Foremost among them was the poet Gyula Illyés, whose *People of the Pusztas* (Puszták népe, 1936)[8] described the life of the landless peasants on the large estates of Transdanubia. His work was followed by a series of sociographical works concerning the peasants in various regions of Hungary; they were factual, dispassionate and supported by statistics and photographs. The 'village researchers', as their authors were called, succeeded in alarming the government which banned some of their books and tried their authors. But at last there was general recognition of a long-ignored problem. In 1939 a National Peasant Party was formed; it played a distinctive role in the political scene immediately after the Second World War.

As for Móricz himself, he had delivered his last word on the gentry. He moved on to a number of different topics. Moreover, there was a distinct change in his style. After the ferociousness of *Relations* and the volume of short stories entitled *Barbarians* (Barbárok) that appeared in the same year, he adopted a gentler, but no less effective mode of writing. He completed a vast and meticulously researched trilogy *Transylvania* (Erdély, 1935), a theme that had occupied him for many years. It had undergone several revisions, and was a colourful panorama of seventeenth century Transylvania; the two main characters were the wayward visionary prince Gábor Báthory and his successor, the cool, calculating statesman Gábor Bethlen. But in it there were lessons to be drawn for contemporary Hungary and the recurrence of one of Móricz's favourite themes, the tension between husband and wife. Also in 1935 he published *The Happy Man* (A boldog ember), the carefully-edited tale recounted to him by a distant peasant relative who professes to have led a happy life by simply surviving. The only assets he possesses are his family; he has never owned any wealth, and yet he is happy. The story is gently told, and all the more powerful for the lightness of its touch. It was the product of a lesson that Móricz declared that he had learnt late in life that it was possible to write something that could give delight.[9] And in his survey of Hungarian society he moved on to the slum-dwellers of Budapest. He found a congenial informant in a young girl he called Chicken (Csibe) and wrote with sympathy and humour on this new topic. Much to his family's consternation, he adopted Csibe, who became his constant companion.

It is noteworthy that nobody offered a serious challenge to Móricz's exposure of the ills of Hungarian society. By the end of his life, he had painted a damaging picture of complacent gentry, lazy and corrupt civic administration and the continuing plight of the poor. No other writer had such a deep knowledge of his subject, and no other writer was so passionately devoted to reform. He loved his country dearly and wrote from the heart. The same ardent love can be seen in his contemporary, the poet Endre Ady. But where Móricz was factual and precise, like Gábor Bethlen in his *Transylvania*, Ady was a visionary, whose extravagant language and rhapsodical style tended to provoke controversy rather than discussion. Moreover he was bereft of humour, while Móricz almost always indulged his love of it in his works. He was always approachable; it is doubtful whether any other Hungarian author could count on so many friends as he travelled the country. He cannot really be compared with any other European writer on the peasantry. As the critic László Németh writes, "If we compare him with the great Eastern Europeans, with Tolstoy, Dostoyevsky or his Hungarian contemporary Endre Ady, the first thing that strikes us is that with him there is no religion, no gospel, no battle for salvation. He did not proscribe these as an atheist; he simply shrank from them."[10] This is not entirely true; he frequently referred to his Calvinist upbringing and was proud of it. It would be truer to

13

say that his method of writing was different from that generally employed by Hungarians; although he was well aware of the didactic tradition of Hungarian literature, he simply presented the case for reform as he saw it and left it to the reader to implement it. He did not preach, as László Németh, for example, who saw himself as the educator of the nation, invariably did in his own works. He treated his readership as adult and intelligent. Móricz's last years were busy. His second marriage broke down in 1937 and he retired to his country house. Having left the editorial board of *West* after only some three years, he took over *People of the East* (Kelet népe) in 1939 and used it as a vehicle for his ideas, prominent among which was the slogan "Stop playing politics – just build!". He suggested practical ways of bringing employment to the countryside, such as cottage industries, and attracted a number of writers with similar ideas for the future. *The Novel of My Life*, one of his most appealing books, appeared in the same year, and he started work on a new trilogy, on the life of the bandit leader and folk hero of 1848, Sándor Rózsa. It remained unfinished at the time of his death in 1942.

Móricz wrote comparatively little about his attitude to writing, but in a speech to a youthful audience in 1927 he declared, "To me writing signified all the riches of life, indeed life itself. Life with all its hills and valleys, its clouds and oceans, and human life with all its action, philosophy, folk tales and abstract sciences. I took in and gave out the whole of life and really absorbed it at all times in writing, from the sunlight to the darkness of the prison, from the happy suffering of the lonely heart to the turbulence of the masses. In reality I received a great deal from writing, for it was not just one life that I lived; I always felt that I lived a life of thousands and thousands of forms. I was given it, lived through it and passed it on... I feel that I am life's torch-bearer... I needed writing to become a human being."[11]

This confession helps to explain the amazingly rich tapestry that is Móricz's oeuvre. *Relations* shows only one aspect of it, one of its grimmer facets. György Bálint was quite right in his estimation of his work; Móricz paints a uniquely comprehensive picture of Hungarian society during his lifetime.

George F. Cushing

14

Notes

1. György Bálint, 'Barbárok'. In: *A toronyőr visszapillant*, Vol. I, Budapest, 1966, p. 118.
2. *Életem regénye*, Budapest, 1939, p. 372.
3. Virág Móricz, *Apám regénye*, Budapest, 1963, p. 34.
4. 'Vallomás az írásról'. In: *Tanulmányok*, Vol. I, Budapest, 1978, p. 776.
5. English translation in: *Seven Pennies and Other Short Stories*, Budapest, 1988, p. 25.
6. Cited in: Kálmán Vargha, *Móricz Zsigmond*, Budapest, 1971, p. 109.
7. 'Tisztelt Ház! 2'. In: *Riportok*, Vol. I, Budapest, 1989, p. 635.
8. English translation *People of the Puszta*, Budapest, 1979 (second edition).
9. Virág Móricz, *Apám regénye*, Budapest, 1963, p. 34.
10. László Németh, 'Móricz Zsigmondról, külföldieknek'. In: *Homályból homályba*, Vol. II, Budapest, 1977, p. 423.
11. 'Vallomás'. In: *Pesti Napló*, 25 May 1927, and *Tanulmányok*, Vol. I, Budapest, 1978, p. 543.

Acknowledgement

I must record my deepest gratitude to the late Professor George Cushing, both for contributing the introductory essay to this translation and for undertaking, of his own volition, the onerous task of reading the text and offering many suggestions for improvement. That he should do this even when his final illness was gaining the upper hand was typical of the warmth and generosity for which he will be so widely remembered.

Bernard Adams

1.

He woke to the sound of his wife telephoning from the next room.

"Juliska, my dear, what was in the sauce when you gave us hare the other day? Pista really did like it..."

A great, burning sensation of warmth and affection flooded his heart. Was that his wife? Telephoning, asking how to cook hare the way he'd like it?

Something very like a tear trickled between his eyelids.

When he'd been a prisoner of the Russians nobody had rung from one block to another, asking...

"My father's sent a hare... Poor old chap, he's got a lot to put up with, his people have been giving him a lot of trouble since the war, the whole world's changed and he's getting on... He would have liked Pista to take over the property... Well, you know how it is with Pista now... My dear, what a fuss they're making of him... Everybody wants him on their side... He's still asleep, because that civic banquet went on into the small hours..."

He propped himself up on one elbow in bed to listen carefully to his wife's voice: was there a hint in it of anything to beware of? Wasn't she criticising him, complaining of him, condemning him? Not a bit of it. Lina was being as sweet, as reassuring, as happy as he hadn't heard her for a very, very long time. All things can deceive, but not the tone of the voice; that can be trusted to reveal every feeling. Lina was bursting with a sort of maternal pride, speaking of him as she might of her eldest son of whom she was proud because he'd passed his exams with distinction, won his race, brought in money...

It seemed that Lina had noticed the open door and started to speak a little more quietly; talk turned to the sauce. He sank back astounded into his sweet half-sleep. It must be late, wonder what the time is? These early November mornings it's hard to judge.

The banquet had gone on a long time the previous evening; the masters of City Hall, or rather, his friends had given it in his honour to celebrate his election that morning by the City Council to the post of Town Clerk.[1]

It was like a dream. The election had been so unexpected,

for of course the Mayor[2] had only proposed him because they'd needed a third name on the ballot-sheet, and one that wouldn't affect the outcome. Makróczy... How had *he* slept last night? The post had been Makróczy's. Yesterday morning nobody would have foreseen his failing to be elected. Old Makróczy, the Assistant Town Clerk, had been running the city as he pleased for the past ten years. He went hunting with the Főispán,[3] was hand in glove with the Mayor, the most influential man in the city, a little king in the making; it was on the cards that he might well have been the next Mayor, for the Old Man was getting a bit senile and it was shocking the way he'd feathered his nest and it was time he went of his own accord and if he wouldn't the present generation wouldn't stand for him at the head because of his age, these old swindlers couldn't be allowed to go on ruining the city, a new world, a new spirit, a new, more energetic pace must come, for the boom[4] had suddenly collapsed and economic conditions...

He dozed on, stretching more comfortably down into the bed, and getting up never even crossed his mind. No need to hurry any more, no need to break his neck. He felt a certain thrill. Power had fallen into his hands, and one had to know how to use it. While he'd still been a mere Cultural Adviser, then yes, he'd had to get up early and dash about to show that he was alive. Had to make plans, countless futile plans, for he'd never been able to implement a single one.

A song flashed into his head, a popular song, and he blushed all over. He was absolutely terrified of this blushing. Sin sneaks a thought into you and immediately it floods out with the coursing of your blood... Last night he'd had that song played for a whole hour, and nobody had known why... for Magdaléna... Somebody'd mentioned Feri Boronkay, saying that 'he might have come, because if there's going to be an investigation into the affairs of the Pig Farm, he'd better start getting on the right side of the new Town Clerk.' Then too he'd blushed. It had struck him at once, thinking of Feri Boronkay, that he'd be able to get to know him better... Magdaléna... Magdaléna...

And when that name came into his mind in any remote, unlikely connection, then he blushed and his fingers started to tremble. Boronkay's wife, Magdaléna Szentkálnay... That song was a seven-year-old memory, nobody guessed, nobody even dreamed that there was such a memory... it wouldn't matter if it got to his wife, she'd have no idea what that song meant to him.

17

Now he was really stretched out in the bed, full length, eyes shut. There was something in this of rigor mortis and the stiffness of the ecstasy of sleeping-sickness. To hear, simply to hear the music, as if the whole of Nature were full of it...

Then he shook himself, hard, with manly resolve not to let this stupid feeling get the better of him.

So, whatever he'd done previously had been to no purpose, plans, programmes, nothing had come of it, he'd just had to show that he could do something; he'd had to be involved in everything so as somehow to stay afloat... And now here he was lying in bed... In a moment a man finds himself in the most exalted situation... Now, if they were waiting for him, let them wait, everybody knew there'd been a big banquet the previous evening and he was still asleep.

The door gave a tiny squeak, he realised that his wife was peeping in to see whether the telephone had woken him. He was in no hurry to open his eyes, but suddenly he wanted his wife, his mistress, and he gave a little cough.

"Good morning, you old bear," Lina purred into the room, hearing her husband move and cough. "You Teddy, you old Teddy... Have you had your sleep out, you drunken thing? Do you know what time you came home?"

He laughed, looked at his wife and, like a sleepy school-boy, went on pretending to be asleep. "Doe idea."

It sounded as if he had picked up a cold overnight.

"Doe?" she teased. "Don't you doe? I'll bet you don't, you were as drunk as a lord. My father's sent a hare."

"Didn't send any wine?"

"It came with a hamper."

"Who was that on the phone?"

"Nobody."

His wife sat by him on the bed, ran her fingers through his hair, left them on his forehead, her hot palm on his head.

"Hurt?"

"No... Doe," he said, laughing.

"Well, tell me about it."

He just looked at her.

She was completely rejuvenated. Her face was as happy, as fresh, as when she'd been a girl. He let his eyes linger on her, just absorbed what had happened to this woman; she seemed to have lost ten years. He opened his arms, partly to stretch, partly because he wasn't sure that she'd feel like it, so he just stretched as if to clear away his sleepiness. Linácska, however, was completely unpurturbed, sat happily beside him, bent over the bed, put her arms round him.

"You old so-and-so, you boozer, you drunk, you stink of wine, ugh, you disgust me," and she kissed him gently.

And he thought as he laughed that a couple of days previously, if he'd been late, or even this very day, if he'd stayed out late at Makróczy's celebration, then those words would have been pronounced very differently. Scathingly, harshly, face livid, eyes cold, scornfully indeed, insultingly... What had come over Linácska?

He put an arm round her waist and carefully drew her to him, and to his amazement she didn't protest. She allowed herself to be embraced and didn't worry about her dress, didn't say she was busy, leave me alone... she'd got a headache, don't be mad. And she didn't tear herself from his arms and run to shut the door... she'd probably shut the door to the other room already, and from this a rush of blood went to his head and he hugged her tight, almost to break her slender waist in two, and Lina let him, as if he were receiving her favours for the first time.

He'd found a whole new woman; he vaguely recalled that she could be like this, but for the last ten years there had been at his side a woman discontented, sour, wanting nothing, permitting nothing, satisfied with nothing.

"Well, that's all in the past," he said to himself as she lay beside him, still, relaxed and happy.

Then he laughed as Lina suddenly thought of something, jumped up and hurried out. What did she want?

A couple of minutes later she brought in breakfast.

Breakfast in bed. That had been the greatest luxury of his childhood. His mother, who had so spoiled her children, spoiled him most of all as eldest son; he had only to sigh and she'd bring breakfast to him in bed, and there he'd drink lovely coffee with whipped cream and eat a piece of fairy-cake. But Lina wouldn't stand for it, called him to order, looked down on him if ever he expressed a yearning for any such childish affectation. It would attract flies, fill the bed with crumbs, make a mess, set the children a bad example. Oh yes, he hadn't thought about the children, what had happened that Lina hadn't said a word about them before this? Of course, they must have gone to school some time ago, what ever time could it be?

"Well, go on, what was it like?"

And she gave him the lovely milky coffee with a fresh white roll on a nice big nickel-plated tray.

"Well, Lina, d'you know what I have to thank for this whole crazy election?"

"Well?"

"Because you've got to admit, it wasn't entirely on my personal merits," and he laughed maliciously at himself.

Lina didn't laugh. Did she really think that he had been elected because the whole city actually placed its trust in István Kopjáss? Tricky question, best not asked.

"Well, do you know?" The old fool said the wrong thing in the Council Chamber ante-room. He said '*zsé vé*'.

"What?"

"*Zsé vé.*"

"What's that?"

"That? A kind of assassin's bullet. *Zse ve*, that's what shot Makróczy down. That broke his neck, that was the noose."

He laughed out loud.

"It means first that everybody realised that Makróczy owed them an awful lot. Then, that they'd had enough of his riding roughshod over people. As he stood there, leaning on the mantelpiece with his red double chin and his fat belly, receiving good wishes, he was like a kind of tyrant, and what he said to his bosom pals, round the side of his cigar, was that this had been his life's ambition, and at last there followed – *zsé vé*."

"But what is it?"

"*Zsé vé*... That's what's stamped on every piece of civic furniture, everything the city owns, branded on the hide of every cow: *ZsV – Zsarátnok városa*, City of Zsarátnok... But everybody knows that when you're talking about the establishment it's usually taken to mean '*zsebre váglak*', 'into my pocket'."

Lina laughed.

"Stupid," she said cheerfully.

"Stupid enough. Because in a flash it was all round the Council what Makróczy had said. He wasn't thinking it seriously, it was rather the sort of joke you'd expect from him, you know his dry manner, but somehow the Council turned in a moment. There was a buzzing like a bee-hive. They didn't want Makróczy becoming the Doge of the Great Plain. Because since the Mayor was in his pocket – he'd really got him where he wanted him – now he was about to become the all-powerful master of the city... These tragic shifts of fortune have always occurred. This time it was Makróczy that Nemesis struck down at the pinnacle of his glory. They'd had enough of him... The very city limits shook, the winds too must have heard it, *zsé vé, zsé vé,* and whispered it out over the Great Plain... and the earth opened, my dear, and swallowed up Makróczy. Everybody crossed him off the ballot-paper, even the Főispán himself, they say."

Lina shuddered, because if they too always had secret enemies, never to be seen, who paid them scant attention, small as they were, from their own high and mighty positions, they were all the more conscious of how essential it was to be on guard lest their paths cross... No indeed... It was because Kopjáss the Adviser had lived so imperceptibly in that City Hall that Makróczy had agreed on his name for third on the ballot-sheet, there had been none among the eligible that he would have feared less. He had altogether ignored that name, as if it had not existed. Thanks to Lina's silent, obstinate, clever and enduring caution Pista had learnt to watch himself, so that since returning from Russian captivity and resuming his former post with the city he had never become involved in anything that could attract the unfavourable attention of those in power. He had had a fortunate post, too, because in recent years he had found himself at the head of the lowest, most insignificant department, that of Culture and Education. What was that? An office that had by law to be maintained. He could have the schools whitewashed, if he was voted the money, he could make plans for village schools, for the education of the illiterate, which had not produced a single person in the enormous region able to read and write, and the last two winters he had been permitted to allot the dole.

"My dear, powerful villains like him put together this big territory in Turkish times,[5] when the people of the small villages fled from the enemy into the shelter of the city. The refugees were made citizens and their land was annexed. The documents are there in the archives, but not so much as a fly gets to see them. Even today they can't be touched. It was the Makróczys who stole this enormous area over three hundred years. When the National Archive was established the government decreed that its staff should go over the material in municipal archives, because there was such chaos everywhere, including here, that you couldn't make head or tail of it. The Makróczys of the time sensed that trouble would come of that, and wouldn't let the State officials through the door. Kálmán Tisza[6] himself became involved so that nobody should disturb

she was going to be left behind. That was the one sure fact. And suddenly she felt a pang in her heart because he was growing too big for her to hold. She was already missing that nice, quiet lifestyle, because even if it had sometimes been hard to make his small salary go round – there was never anything to spare – at least she'd had the feeling of certainty, of the strength of the rock on which the little nest was built.

Meanwhile, however, Pista had half dressed and gone out into the dining-room. There the post was waiting for him, and just as he was, braces dangling, he started to open the letters. Nothing but congratulation. At every single name he laughed out loud and pointed. There were those that wanted something from him, in some cases – the teachers that had been his subordinates in his previous sphere of influence – he knew exactly what, and there were others which made him rather nervous, because he couldn't see clearly what they were after. He just leafed through these letters, glanced at them. Nothing but big words, bombastic expressions about true worth bringing its own reward... the glory of the city... worth and truth...

Some of the letters had already been opened. Lina had acquired, among others, the bad habit of opening all her husband's letters. She said that he had no secrets... Now, as he picked up an unobtrusive letter, Lina said:

"Don't look at that one, dear."

Whereupon he read it with all the closer attention.

It was from his Uncle Lajos, his mother's brother from the country. He hadn't written in ten years.

He wrote, 'My dear good nephew, I've just been reading in the Budapest papers what great good fortune has come your way, things are going very badly for me, but you're certainly doing well'. He congratulated Pista on behalf of the whole Kopjáss family and called down God's blessing upon him. Then he said that if he'd had some better clothes he'd have come in person to congratulate him, because he'd got things to see to in town, but he couldn't come because all his clothes were falling off his back, and if he'd got anything that he could do without he asked him for the love of God to take pity and send it with the man who'd brought the letter, because he couldn't move from the village but he'd like to embrace his dearest nephew in person, but, you see, the harshness of the times was wearing him out. His son Elemér, too, was in the situation that he'd finished at the Academy of Music but had no job, the poor boy was playing in a cafe, in a gentlemen's band, it was true, called a

26

quartet, but nonetheless a band, to hell with his passion for music-making, if Pista could possibly squeeze him into the Civic Conservatoire, for he'd got a lot of influence, God would bless him for it… 'Give this man something, my good nephew, and perhaps put twenty pengős in his pocket', for the little pigs were dying, such was the poverty in the country that he couldn't describe it, etc…

"Yes, Lajos bácsi," he said carefully.

He knew that his wife had a pack of relations, and he said it like that for her sake. But his heart was warmed that at least one relation had come up among the first letters, and pleasant memories of childhood came into his mind. This Lajos bácsi was his mother's youngest brother and had been very kind to him as a child, his greatest entertainer; he knew all sorts of stories and jokes, could whistle, act the fool, got up to all sorts of tricks. He knew everything except one thing – how to live. Pista wondered what clothes Lina wouldn't mind him sending, for by now she'd know if he gave him anything.

"Lajos bácsi finds out quickly," he added.

"Yes," said Lina.

With that he went into the bathroom and had a mighty wash. He splashed as much as possible and spent a long, relaxing time shaving.

"Is that man waiting?" he said, coming out of the bathroom.

"Oh yes. Waiting faithfully," said Lina.

"Dear oh dear, that Lajos bácsi. Well, what could we give him? My dear, tell me, have I in fact got anything that I can do without? I can't spare the old beige, my hunting jacket's a bit old, but that's what I need it for and I can't give him that…"

Linácska did not speak.

As he was getting his briefcase ready, looking to see what was in it and what he had to put in, he suddenly thought of something.

"I could give him that old frock-coat. He's quite slim, it hasn't fitted me for ten years, and it's not worth having a morning-coat made out of it because they've gone out of fashion. So it's just going to the moths."

"Give him that," said Lina with a sigh. "At least that'll make some room in the chest."

At that Pista immediately put down his briefcase, went into the front room and opened the big clothes chest which his wife had inherited from her great-aunt. It was very big and didn't match the modern furniture, but it was nice and roomy. He

27

took out the old frock-coat from the back left-hand corner. Oh, he could certainly give this away, because it hung on him like a dried sheepskin in the attic. He looked it over to make sure that there were no moth-holes and could see nothing wrong; indeed, war against moths was Lina's principal task in life.

"Where is that chap?"

He went out into the kitchen and there sat the messenger on the bench, very humbly.

"Well, my lad, you've come from the master?"

The man stood up. "Yuss."

"And how is the master?"

"Well, allroight, loike."

"Have you got a bag?"

"Well, not really."

"Then how're you going to take him this coat?"

"Well, dunno."

"Never mind, my lad, there's an old suitcase up in the loft. Just go up and get it."

He turned to his wife.

"That's something I've been keeping out of sentiment since my student days, and it's no use at all. I've never been anywhere with it because it's so tatty, so I can give it away."

He was very pleased that Lina made no comment, and he exclaimed, looking at the kitchen clock:

"What, is it really half past ten?"

He gave his wife a quick kiss and hurried out.

In the yard he thought once more what an old house this was. The yard was cobbled, and the waste water ran over the stones into the street.

2.

It was odd that Wagner, the Chief Clerk, hadn't been mentioned when he was talking to his wife about the ousting of Makróczy. Wagner had been brought down over just this, the drainage. He'd been involved in Belatiny's dubious affairs, and when he'd extricated himself everybody knew that his passion was for laying drains, and the city had still not replaced the old sewage system. The amount of money that had been spent on doing the main roads would have provided for the whole city, or at least the central area. So for this reason Wagner's name had been struck out on the ballot-paper, because everybody had been happy to be able to get rid of him. "An even greater thief than Makróczy".

Pista walked carefully, having to step over the stream pouring from every gateway. There were few spots where the waste water was even spanned by a bridge.

They'd have to move into the main road somewhere. They couldn't go on living in this tumble-down street.

It was curious how the street in which he'd lived peaceably until now had, in a moment, become ugly and foul. Of course, if they got that American loan things would be all right. The city would certainly do well out of it, as it wouldn't cost a lot... He smiled, tasting in his mouth the fine flavours of honesty and decency... In any case, it would cost less than what the Legal Department usually stole.

But drainage or no drainage, they would have to move out of this street. It was a very dirty, untidy street. He'd really like a little private house. The corner of the forest was being developed into plots for civic officers, and he'd already said at home that they ought to buy one. His father would help, and his father-in-law. Now he would buy one. How nice it would be to have his own garden, plant fruit-trees, graft them. A nice little three-roomed house. That was ideal. Not too much work for his wife, easy to run, not too expensive... Or maybe four rooms, so that he too could have his own, however tiny...

"Hello, hello, my dear chap," a loud voice rang out as he turned into the main road, the Ferenc József Ring.

He looked up from his thoughts, good Heavens, he was being greeted by the manager of the Savings Bank.

He received the greeting with his usual humble pleasure. Kardics was a very big man in the city, the greatest power in the realm of high finance, had a very big house where financial affairs were settled. He'd scarcely ever spoken to him, just a couple of times, perhaps, in City Hall. They didn't know each other well and the previous day he might well not have received a greeting. Least of all one accompanied by a delighted doffing of the hat.

He was very pleased that Kardics the banker shook his hand in so warm and friendly a fashion.

Indeed, he did not release it, but exclaimed:

"Look here, Pista, my wife tells me that her mother was a Kopjáss; d'you know about this?"

Pista looked at Kardics for a moment, surprised and

29

thoughtful. Of course he knew about it, Mrs. Kardics' mother had been the daughter of Ferdinánd Kopjáss...

As he said nothing, Kardics went on:

"Yes, yes, from Verebes, Ferdinánd Kopjáss..."

"Szidónia Kopjáss."

"My mother-in-law."

"Well, fancy that."

They looked at one another for a moment as if they had just discovered each other and realised that they were both human beings.

Ferdinánd Kopjáss... Hmm, Ferdinánd Kopjáss... The biggest landowner in the county, or one of them. A great gentleman, so great a gentleman, indeed, that he'd never be seen abroad without a carriage and four, and four gleaming white horses at that. So great a gentleman that they'd never spoken his name at home. He'd been a member of Parliament too, for a while, one of Kálmán Tisza's closest confidants. He'd been Főispán too for a while, but he was such a gentleman that he hadn't cared for it.

"Oh, Ferdinánd Kopjáss," he said, "Ferdinánd Kopjáss of Verebes."

He refrained from adding, although it all came into his head at once, that at home they'd never called him anything but 'the black villain'. Because, according to family tradition, after Pista's father's death Ferdinánd Kopjáss had lost no time in appearing at the house in person with his carriage and four and removing every document that was to be found... Everything by which their title to a share in the estate at Besztered[7] might have been proved. They'd never been able to extract anything further from him; when they went and asked they were met with the coldest of shoulders; it was impossible to go to law, as Grandmama had assigned everything without any written record - poor, incompetent Grandmama, who for the world couldn't have doubted the word of honour of a Ferdinánd Kopjáss. So Ferdinánd had pocketed their share too, such was the family belief. When Pista's father had died young, poor man, his mother had moved into town, next to the College, and had brought up her numerous children by taking in students. Thus they'd lived in honest poverty, while Ferdinánd Kopjáss' family, in ill-gotten wealth, had had their daughter Szidónia educated in Vienna and Paris and had married her to the son of one of the Főispáns, Miklovichy... Their daughter, Gizella Miklovichy, was the wife of old Kardics... That was how

Kardics the corn broker had become the greatest potentate in the city.

"So we're related," said Kardics, and he took his in-law's arm.

Thus they went arm-in-arm down the Ferenc József[8] Ring towards City Hall.

At the corner of Wesselényi Street they stopped, for there stood the imposing building of the Savings Bank. Quite a new building, which Kardics had built.

"We're having some people in on Thursday evening. We shall expect to see you there with your wife. It's really disgraceful, a bad business, that you've never even thought to call on us in your position as a relation by marriage, my dear Pista. Don't fail to be there, or I'll come for you and drag you out with six oxen, you difficult people. It's all very well living in hiding, you know. You left it for me to discover our relationship. But that's the way nowadays, the old Hungarian custom's dying out, but it's kept the country going for a thousand years, has tribal unity."

Once more he gripped his in-law's hand powerfully, then turned into the main door on Wesselényi Street.

Pista, however, smiling and happily contented, hurried on towards City Hall. There was a great warmth around his heart. The old, pillared building stood on the opposite side of the road. People were coming and going, someone said good morning, he looked round hastily, anxious not to fail to return the greeting. A fat, swarthy lawyer was doffing his hat, his name didn't come to mind, leader of the Opposition, the one with the big mouth. On his greasy face there was a smile both derisive and flattering. Oh yes, Dr. Martiny. He knew him from the Club, they were even on first-name terms, but they'd had little in common until now...

He acknowledged the greeting with a deep, expansive sweep of his hat, then turned in through the front door of City Hall

When the hajdú[9] on guard in his blue uniform with red piping saw him he stopped in his tracks, came to attention and saluted.

Goodness, that was something new. He'd been going into City Hall for sixteen years and he'd never been saluted before. This mark of distinction was reserved for the Mayor and the Főispán, the all-powerful masters of the city. Little things make you think, he said to himself.

The shortest way up to his old office, the way he had always gone previously, was through a glass door into the foyer, then up to the first floor by a side stair at the back on the right. The Cultural Adviser's department was next to the Rates, at the rear of the building. This time, however, he did not go to the glass door but went straight up the main staircase, wide and red-carpeted. He strode up the middle of the carpet to his floor, so as to pass the Mayor's door first on the way to his old office.

The Mayor's ante-room was marked by an imposing wall of glass.

As he was passing, someone suddenly came running after him. It was the Mayor's secretary, who caught him by the arm and said:

"I'm glad to have caught you, Town Clerk, would you mind, His Worship has asked several times whether you'd come in yet and told me to keep a look-out and the minute I knew you were in to run and fetch you, would you be so kind as to step inside, my dear sir, His Worship is waiting impatiently."

"Right away, I'll just put my briefcase down."

"*Oh la la*, don't worry, please, I'll see to it."

There could be no opposition to that, and he turned back and went into the Mayor's anteroom, where there stood hajdús who, as he entered, solemnly began to salute. They went into the reception room, where he had always felt a little out of place, because he would always be attending for an interview with a feeling of tension; the thought had always been in his mind, in what mood would he find His Worship, because he always had something to ask for, to beg, on behalf of the Education Board, and he could never reckon on being a welcome visitor because he never brought and always wanted to take. Being the champion of culture was quite a different thing to representing the men of the Legal Department, who served money...

The reception room was very big and extremely ill-lit, especially on this November day when so little daylight came in through the low, square windows. There were a lot of people there, as usual. Emissaries and petitioners, because, with its powerful administration, the city was the principal source of good to the whole population of the region. The eyes of all looked to it, every organisation had to come here in order to realise its plans. Private citizens too came, like priests to the altar, to pray down into their dreadfully shattered lives some drops of charity from the clouds of power. A daring young man immediately confronted the new Town Clerk and addressed him with impudent frankness.

"One moment, Town Clerk, if you wouldn't mind, I want to write a big article in the Zsarátnok News on the new Town Clerk's first day. This had never been done before. We're giving the front page to it, and I'd be very grateful if you could spare me a little time in private to dictate your programme."

Before Pista could utter, being without experience in deflecting people, the Mayor's secretary inserted himself between them and said:

"My dear Editor, please wait, if you'd be so kind, please be patient, His Worship is waiting for the Town Clerk."

"Really, it's most urgent."

"Yes, but surely you've got until the morning to do it, the paper comes out in the morning, doesn't it?... This way, please, Town Clerk, this way..."

With which he ushered him in through the green upholstered door.

Inside was another room, empty this time, and the secretary ran ahead, opened the door and announced:

"Town Clerk Kopjáss."

"In a moment," was heard from within.

Then he had to wait.

Wait. A dam had been placed across the flowing river, and he waited.

The new Town Clerk was somewhat disconcerted at having to wait so long. If he could have gone straight in he would still have been full of old Kardics' handshake, the leader of the Opposition's greeting, the hajdú's salute, the journalist's enthusiasm, the surprise of the secretary's chasing him. If he had gone straight in, perhaps he would have taken the Mayor in his stride, but as he had to wait and wait all this fervour gradually cooled and it seemed that gradually the blood began to run backwards in his veins; the pulsing, overheated blood slowly, gently, began to settle into the nervous, mute, hopeless flow that befitted the Cultural Adviser, for waiting is hard. Waiting grinds nerves, breaks horns and, most of all, shatters self-confidence. He had felt that he was the hero of the hour... Who could there be in there more important than himself, more famous, having more urgent business?

The secretary had run out to those waiting, to tell them what was happening and to reassure them. Perhaps he was saying "You must wait, must wait, must wait, because the new Town

33

Clerk is in there, you all saw him..." And he had that feeling that there was nobody in with the Mayor, he just wanted to keep him waiting to undermine his confidence... Oh, they are crafty... Politicians know how to break a man's hopes... Of all weapons, making people wait was the vilest. How proud he could be that could go straight in at any time, who just came and went, whoever might be in there, because he belonged, had permission, was allowed, had a special relationship... But waiting, and while waiting to feel the filth of every torment seep through one... For what now came into his mind... The Mayor was a friend of Makróczy. What if the resolution of the Council hadn't been ratified, what if an objection had been lodged, it had been annulled, then that would be the end of everything, he could return to impotence, leave the city. Then there'd be nothing for it but to accept his father-in-law's proposal, go and farm a hundred acres, drink the wine he made, for there'd be no selling it... Oh, but what did this Mayor want – and he began to pace the room with great strides. By one of the windows was hanging the plan of the new City Hall. This had been on the stocks for some time now, for the present one was old and cramped, the public rooms were insufficiently decorous, he tried to find the Mayor's office, reception rooms... became bored, broke off, sucked his teeth: he had been elected, he wasn't going to be offered the position... Other impossible thoughts came to him too; perhaps the Mayor was preparing him, by making him wait like this, to resign of his own accord. He'd show him, there was nothing he could do. He wasn't going to be at his beck and call. How could it be that a young man would just walk in and simply expect to take charge of the most delicate affairs? He knew that the Mayor had his favourites, arranged everything with them and didn't give a damn for the others, the majority of the advisers. No, that would be no kind of life, there would be no prospect of anything... But what in Heaven's name did he mean by keeping him waiting like this?

Now the secretary bustled in, opened the door and came out again.

"Won't be a moment," he nodded confidentially and left.

How that lad cheered one up! What an unpleasant type he was, too, Imrike Keék. The Keéks were one of the most distinguished city families, the school was always full of them, there'd been one in his class, Feri Keék, and then there was a lawyer, Duckó Keék, a real drunkard, he was with the County now, Chief Executive... They'd taken over the city, they were every-

34

where, really, it was terrible to wait so long. Now Imrike came back with a sheaf of documents and went inside, leaving the door ajar; voices could be heard inside.

This immediately calmed him, all his tension and sense of offendedness left him.

Of course, if there was someone in there, that was different.

In that case it was natural that the Mayor couldn't call him in. He wiped the drops of perspiration that stood on his forehead and began to think quite differently.

It was even better for him to be here, in the inner reception room, because outside everybody thought that he was in with the Old Man. It was in any case better than being outside among the waiting people, because then, he knew, he'd have been unable to escape questions and for the time being he knew nothing and must say nothing. God save him from getting into conversation with a journalist until he'd found out from the Mayor what he was to say.

Out came Imrike.

"They're just finishing."

He realised then that all the anxiety had been caused by the lad's failure to tell him who was in there. Nor, indeed, had he enquired. He was thinking of this as Imrike stood beside him talking of the previous evening's dinner. He too had been there, and had done some very amusing things. He'd drunk a glass of champagne standing, sitting and lying down without swallowing, merely pouring it into his throat and letting it trickle down, without choking.

He had a great future in the Administration.

A bell rang inside, Imrike went in and a moment later opened the door.

His heart thumping, Pista went in, as if into the lion's den.

"Ah, hello," said the Mayor.

3.

The Old Man was bearded, grey-headed, exquisitely groomed, a very elegant little old man. He was sitting at his desk behind heaps of papers. The desk was the size of a castle. Beside it stood a second desk with countless drawers and nothing to speak of on top. Only the day's letters, which he was about to sign and send out. In front of him was a row of bell-pushes.

35

"Ah, hello," he repeated, and his porcelain teeth sparkled.
"Pista remained standing while the Mayor rummaged for some time among the papers, then stood up.
"What, haven't you sat down? Here, have a cigar. I'm very glad you've looked in, I was hoping to see you."
"Terribly sorry, Your Worship, but Kardics caught me in the street and I was a bit late. We're related by marriage in a way..."
The Mayor raised his eyebrows. He had little, bushy eyebrows, not as elegant as his beard, more like little shaving-brushes.
"Kardics the Bank..."
"Yes."
"You're related by marriage?"
"Yes, his wife's the grand-daughter of Ferdinánd Kopjáss. To tell the truth it's just a Hungarian relationship, because Ferdinánd Kopjáss was a cousin of my father."
The Mayor came forward and said:
"But that's marvellous, marvellous," and patted Pista's shoulder as if congratulating him on some great stroke of luck. "Please, do sit down."
There were some exceptionally large leather armchairs in the wide room. It was a corner room, with a view of the street on two sides. Pista was already familiar with these armchairs, but when he sat in one this time it was as if he had never sat there before. Previously, when he'd been for an interview, he'd usually stood in front of the Mayor's desk, never in all his life had he sat like this, right back in the armchair, resting his back. It was a very pleasant sensation, he felt that this was really sitting. Previously the feeling had been one of tension and discomfort, he could scarcely wait to escape, but now this didn't even occur to him, but he chose a nice cigar and lit it carefully.
"Please, help yourself, go on... How did we sleep after last night's celebrations?... I'm sorry I had to leave early myself, but my wife's not too well, unfortunately, but I hear that it all went off very well and you all had a splendid time. You were even dancing."
"Me?" he said in amazement, for the dancing had taken place very late, it must have been the small hours, and he'd forgotten, it was when he didn't know what he was doing.
"Well, that's as it should be," said the Mayor, and his teeth gleamed whiter than ever. His old man's ashen complexion and his bright white teeth looked strange, almost ghostly. "Well, I just wanted to say, my dear boy, that the newspaper, that's the

36

first thing... the newspaper's always the first thing... because you've got to keep the public informed... so you've got to give them a programme, it's expected of you."

Pista was listening carefully to what the old man said. He spoke in so dull a tone, colourlessly, without intonation, greyly. To look at him one would think that he was an extremely witty man whose words would simply sparkle with intellect, at all events it was one's belief that he was exceptionally intelligent, that his mind was razor-sharp. But when he did speak one cooled, waited to see what he wanted, what he was driving at, where it was all leading, one always wanted to help him, put words into his mouth, lend him a hand, because he couldn't find the words that he wanted.

"You've got to be very careful. Not a word too much... you understand... But then, you're a very clever man, my dear chap."

So what was he to say? What must he say? But he said nothing, merely drew on his cigar, drew and sucked at it as if to block his mouth, as if the cigar was only there to prevent him saying what he wanted to. It was giving him a lot of trouble. He never used a holder, but was nibbling away at the cigar, which was becoming damp and ragged, bits of tobacco sticking to the sides of his mouth and clinging there as he failed to brush them off, drying up, further fragments collecting beside them, and by degrees his mouth was beginning to look like a black hole framing his freshly brushed teeth; one would have thought that the maid had cleaned them with scouring-powder, so white were they despite his smoking.

He spoke.

"The drains..."

He dared say no more, didn't even quite know why that had come to mind. Of course, this morning, as he'd left the house, he'd been thinking about drainage.

"Yes... that's very good... that's the bane of public life," said the Mayor. "Drainage... necessary... indeed, most necessary. We're behind the times, there's a very great deal to be done. The ground will have to be prepared... there'll be a lot of opposition... among the elderly... because naturally... they'll all be worried about the karst..."

Pista looked at him in surprise. The Mayor liked to lace his speech with the odd chosen word in local patois – *karst*. That's how he pronounced it – *karst*.

The Mayor shook his head.

"You'll have to tell 'em... tell 'em absolutely straight. It's intolerable for us in this day and age to have no deep drainage... only in the very centre... but until now it's been impossible to do anything about the road-surfaces... because the drainage has to be in place first and surfacing can only be done as it progresses, can't it?"

"Exactly, Your Worship."

"Please call me Béla. I'm very glad... that you're related to Kardics... you can't imagine how glad I am about that."

"We shall be at their place for dinner on Thursday. My wife and I," he added.

"Quite so... Thursday... Well, I'll see you there... Your wife...," he gave a little cough and flushed.

"What was your wife's maiden name?"

"Szentkálnay."

"Szentkálnay! She's a Szentkálnay?"

"Yes, Your Worship."

"Béla bácsi," and he placed his dry, withered hand on Pista's arm, "Béla, please. And then the re-organisation of the Legal Department, don't you think... You must say something about that, because the Legal Department isn't popular. It's got to be re-shuffled... whoever sat on the right must go to the left, and whoever sat on the left must go in the middle, don't you see, my dear boy."

Pista realised that the re-organisation was to be nominal rather than radical.

"I quite understand Your Worship's intention."

"You, as a *novus homo*, aren't bound by fear or favour, nothing... I'm very pleased with the Council's choice, because it must be admitted that there are a lot of anomalies here. Removing anomalies, don't you agree, my dear chap, is the new Town Clerk's first task... you must move people about, bring in new men, because an established man who's caught up in the system can't do it, but a new man... because the system grows into you, wraps round the man in charge like a spider's web... you see, my boy... On the contrary, you've got a free hand... a new broom in City Hall... That's very good, just the expression... a new broom... very good, just what's wanted, that says it all, my boy... a new broom, haha! Everything's going to be absolutely all right, my young friend... Nice phrase, eh, new broom?"

"Excellent, Your Worship, excellent."

"Hmm... Things are going to be..."

38

Pista smiled inwardly but was careful to keep a straight face, because he wasn't yet sure whether this was really aimed at Wagner.

"Are we going to get the American loan, Your Worship? That'll have to be applied to practical and profitable ventures... Investments..."

"Marvellous," said the Mayor. He took his cigar out of his mouth and looked at it for a long moment. His little insect eyes twinkled brightly and he repeated, "Marvellous... The Minister said the same... That he'd only allot funds for practical and profitable schemes when the... the American loan... Well, what do we need money for? Eh, my dear boy... What's the best investment today? Eh?"

Pista swiftly thought over the recent past; what had been most talked about? He wasn't really interested in such things, they'd not been his concern, but it dawned on him faintly that most talk had been about the Pig Farm scandal. This was fifty per cent a city enterprise, but it was facing bankruptcy. He burst out daringly:

"Economic planning... establishing businesses and setting them on their feet."

"Yes, yes."

"The city very much needs the Pig Farm."

"Ah, ah," said the Mayor rapturously.

He was so impressed that he got up from his chair and for a moment just stood there.

"That's very good," he said. "Not what I was thinking of, but very good."

Pista sensed that he'd succeeded in touching on the sorest of sore spots, slowly began to understand that this was the one thing to which not a krajcár must be given. He even perspired at the thought. He knew nothing about the Pig Farm except that Szentkálnay's son-in-law, Feri Boronkay... suddenly he began to blush... Magdaléna... That Boronkay had embezzled all the Pig Farm capital, had himself a villa built, so the Pig Farm was heading for bankruptcy... Now he began to think that it could be true...

He was cautious, didn't press the point.

"Well, that's very good, very good... very sound... you've hit the nail on the head... that was a good election, a very good little election, my dear chap...", and again the Mayor patted him on the knee.

"And to sort out the small-holders... I think, if Your

39

Worship..." Pista said suddenly, offering another programme item.

The Mayor raised a finger, at which Pista realised that he was marking not the point but the manner of address.

"With Your Worship's permission... Béla bátyám."

"That's better."

They said nothing and laughed. Laughed long, privately, for pleasure, Pista like a child, head down, with a flattered glance at the Mayor, the latter like an old uncle, teaching the child good manners, spoiling him at the same time...

"That's a tricky one," he said after a while, "that needs very careful thought."

The small-holder affair was the worst problem in the city. There were ten thousand of them, possibly more, and because of the unexpected collapse of the prices of produce the small-holders had sunk into the depths of poverty, but the city could make no concessions to them because that would have jeopardised the budget. They were the city's only source of income, because it made no money on the large tracts of land in private hands.

Pista, however, daredn't express his views, because until now he'd tended to the Opposition point of view. As champion of the village schools he was well aware of the small-holders' dreadful situation. They couldn't send their children to school, afford books, and he'd fought on behalf of the poor children, but he sensed that now, as Town Clerk, he was going to have to take the city's side, so he said nothing, just waited for a word of guidance from the Mayor.

He, however, didn't want to show his hand, but waited for the young Town Clerk to speak first. He stared at him and waited impatiently. Pista frowned a little and, against his convictions, said, to his own surprise:

"They want the goat to feast and to have cabbage left."

The effect of the old, worn, trite phrase was startling. The Mayor stared straight ahead, his eyes became as hard as his teeth, as if made of glass, then began laughing uproariously. A good thing, said this laughter, that this chap was so easily led. There'd be no problems with this one. He was like the rest. Well, to be sure, it was natural for him to be so, but the Old Man was always afraid, always anxious, that these new men might stir up trouble.

"Ha ha ha," he laughed, "well that's very good... isn't it, my dear chap. That's the best..."

Pista felt, beneath and behind his laughter, that it seemed that this was the worst thing that he could have said. He felt that he had betrayed something, that it was not right, not nice, to have said something at which this old villain was pleased. What if he was on that road, where would it lead him? Was he going to let them down?... and he despised himself when he looked with his inward eye at what was actually happening, things to which he was giving approval with his whole face, his whole body, his every word, with all that was external... but inwardly he was disgusted with himself... the former Cultural Adviser, who'd thought and spoken so much harsh criticism of these things, the former prisoner of war, who'd cherished in his heart ideals and dreams of doing something for people if ever he got home, before that the army officer who'd served four years in the front-line trenches and who'd felt it to be just his human duty, rather the champion of mankind, its soldier, its martyr, than... because first of all, in his youthful idealism, he'd built great cloud-castles, fabulous plans for leading mankind, and in particular those poor, broken, downtrodden Hungarians, into the right way...

And now...

And now, it was no good denying it, he was happy that the Mayor, His Worship, was laughing at what he'd said, because that way he was doing all right, getting on, doing his career no harm...

And he too was laughing with the same musical sound, the fanfare of *Schadenfreude*[10] trumpeting from the slit of his mouth, the golden bell of malice ringing, crafty cleverness, contrived, false humility, base toadying...

"My dear Béla bátyám, Your Worship... don't expect me to deliver you a lecture, when my main wish is to discover your intentions... I'm not yet *au fait* with things, I've got a lot of basic studying to do... I don't want to rush in like Balázs Hübele..."[11]

"Just carry on, carry on," exclaimed the Mayor sharply. "How did you put it? They want the goat to feast and to have cabbage left? Quite right. Do these wicked goats want cabbage?... My God, they're not the only ones in town... there are other people as well, more... There are ninety thousand in the city... the other eighty thousand have to live too, don't they, my dear chap?"

"An important matter, Your Worship: people must be made to like paying taxes."

"What?"

The Mayor was so flabbergasted that his face became quite caterpillar-like. His mouth was like a black gateway, and he said again:

"What?"

But Pista laughed. He was happy now to be able to produce such effects one after another with a couple of words.

"Paying taxes... because there is a problem in Hungary, a huge, great problem: in Hungary, people don't like paying taxes... Nobody does... I don't."

"You're telling me," said the Mayor.

"But the country will never become European until people come to like paying taxes... If they're unwilling to pay, it's the end of municipal life... We must love our city, it's ours. We must act in its best interests, and what the citizen can do is pay his taxes..."

He stopped and waited for the laughter, but the Mayor did not laugh, merely waited. So he went on:

"There are two postulations: the first is when people don't pay taxes. Such a state is always under despotic rule, because taxes have to be gathered, so bailiffs, policemen, soldiers and laws are needed to extract them... The other is when taxes are paid without coercion: such a state is a society of free, conscientious, self-aware citizens. There everybody knows what taxation is, what it's for, what its purpose is and what it's to be applied to, and the citizen body itself decides how much is needed in taxation..."

"Steady," said the Mayor, "don't go too far. This is beginning to sound a bit like Utopia... It's on the way to Utopian thinking..."

Pista was suddenly afraid that he'd revealed his true nature and allowed the Mayor a glimpse of his real thoughts, so he added in a cautious, regretful tone:

"Not a good idea, Mr. Mayor?"

"Well, yes and no. To a certain extent, but no more, d'you see, my dear chap."

"Payment of taxes is life insurance."

Once more the Mayor goggled.

"What on earth? Life insurance?... Very good!"

But he was not a bit amused.

"Those are just fine words. One lives to regret fine words. They're all very well, you know, but there cannot be any conviction behind them... What the Opposition's always writing, that's fine words, the Opposition press, that the authorities should give people a chance... Very simple... But let them try and sort it out. We don't have to discuss it... It makes a nice catch-phrase. The young are always able to come up with new catch-phrases... That's good. Because it's necessary for... Anyway, Thursday at Kardics's... That's good... Because of the City Council meeting on Fridays. We go over the agenda at dinner at Kardics's. Everybody's there on Thursday evenings that has business at next day's Council meeting, and there opinion is formed as to what the outcome will be... So don't waste your Thursdays, and try to be there every week if you can... It's the future, my young friend... The future... And now dictate your programme to the reporter, but don't forget to check the text, because you have to be very careful with reporters, they're exceptionally capable of silly mistakes. You must never let a single line go out that hasn't been approved... Never... because there can be a lot of recriminations."

They talked for another quarter of an hour about the current problems of the city. Then the Mayor called in the reporter and sat them down together in the little room on the left where, with much racking of brains and even more caution, Pista gave out his first programme.

4.

It was one o'clock when he returned once more to the Mayor's big ante-room.

Greatly to his surprise he found there the leader of the Opposition, the leading rouser of the small-holders.

Doctor Martiny.

Dr. Martiny was a somewhat younger man, about forty. He was that peculiar sort of person who could be recognised at a distance as a man that liked a fight. Now his eyes were piercing, penetrating, dissatisfied, and he was carrying his head on one side; he looked like a man charging from ambush.

"My deeply respected Town Clerk," he stood in front of Pista, "we have been waiting for Your Honour for an hour because we did not wish to forego the opportunity of appearing before you in the first hour of your holding office to draw your attention to that astounding anomaly which constitutes the hall-mark of this city. Let me introduce my friends András Csordás and Gáspár Veres, leaders of the small-holders."

43

Pista shook the two by the hand. Both their hands were big, rough from work. Both of them looked the sort who were unaccustomed to being in such a place, but he could sense nonetheless that they weren't overawed, and, indeed, that they'd been there possibly more often than he.

"Town Clerk, at this moment we have no hostile, provocative or recriminatory intentions. Sincere fellow-feeling has brought us to István Kopjáss, former Cultural Adviser, who has always been our choice among the civic officers, because we have always found in him help, good-will and understanding for the agricultural worker, helpless in the three-fold prison of illiteracy, ignorance and poverty. We wish to ask that, in your now elevated position, Your Honour will not forget these people, deserted by God, man and every official, this order of civic society, I might say, languishing in the most wretched circumstances, yet striving for all that is good and fine, the small-holders. We ask Your Honour for just a single word that may plant in us strength, hope and faith."

Pista had no taste for speech-making, and altogether disliked such a stylised, long-winded, oratorical tone on Hungarian lips. He took the peasants' hands, gripped them, the lawyer's too, and said simply and with a spontaneous wink:

"The main thing is for the goat to feast and for there to be cabbage left."

For a moment Dr. Martiny was silent, gaping.

Then he began to laugh. He had bad teeth. His few sound ones were black from smoke, because he was a heavy smoker, and he laughed in Pista's face.

"Of course, that's right. How on earth should it not be?"

And he began to laugh even louder.

"Did you hear, my friends?" He turned to the two peasants. "Did you understand?... He's our man, His Honour the Town Clerk's our man heart and soul. Let the goat feast... that means the noble city, and let there be cabbage left, that means the life and future of the people... Thank you, Town Clerk, that's good enough for us. We're reassured, and we shall go out into the farms and tell everybody about Your Honour's programme. Let the goat feast and let there be cabbage left. That sums it up."

They shook hands once more, and Pista hurried off to his old office.

He went down the corridor. There the staff had been waiting for him all morning, doing nothing. He handed the department over to Ványai, his deputy, and said to him:

"Well, this may please Dr. Martiny; the one department he's always fighting will have a lawyer in charge."

In this way he publicly revealed his hope that Ványai, who had been Inspector of Schools, would be promoted Cultural Adviser.

Everyone was delighted at this, they made a fuss of him, eyes were warm, faithful and grateful to him, and happy that he had remained so kind and close to them even in his new position of importance. Then off he went to the Legal Department, where almost the whole staff were awaiting him.

"Gentlemen," he said, "let's not stand on ceremony. I'm a man of deeds, not words. If the Council in its wisdom has honoured me with this position of great responsibility, it's my intention that everybody shall be satisfied and that the department shall discharge its functions well."

That was the end of his inaugural speech, and he immediately got down to work. He wanted to become acquainted with the organisation of the department and its most important business. But he made no great fuss about this, there would be plenty of time.

Isti Baday, the youngest member of the department, son of the great choreographer Lőrinc Baday, came up to him confidentially.

"Excuse me, sir, I saw you arm-in-arm with Kardics bácsi in the street, you didn't notice me, I took the liberty of saying good morning at the corner of Szent Margit Street."

Pista didn't remember this greeting, indeed, he thought it unlikely, he hadn't met Kardics by the time he reached Szent Margit Street, it had only been outside the Post Office, but never mind.

"The old gentleman and I are related by marriage," he said casually. Immediately he had to try to cover his blushing, for he was embarrassed to take advantage so often of this relationship, discovered as it had been only that morning.

"You were deep in conversation. It's a very great mark of favour for Kardics bátyám to take someone's arm in the street. He's quite a stand-offish old gentleman."

Pista didn't understand why the lad said that, but it was true. There were legends about whose arm Kardics would take. If he refused to shake hands with someone, that man was dead, so if he took someone by the arm, that man had arrived.

The staff were so pleasant that he almost forgot that he'd been feeling rather anxious about the reception that might be awaiting him in Makróczy's empire. Makróczy, of course, never came into the office again. He could not find it in him to come and take his leave. Someone said that he intended to retire.

The morning had passed off well, and when he went home at about two in the afternoon he was a completely different man from when he had left the house. He had realised that he was executive material.

5.

And how nice it was at home. There were flowers on the table. This he'd never been able to achieve, because by Lina's reckoning they couldn't afford it.

The children were excited and full of the news that the whole school knew about the *zs.v.* business. They'd all heard about the election, and they were saying in his son Berci's class that the City Fathers had wanted to punish Makróczy for the *zs.v.*, only Pista had defended him, saying 'Give the old chap some water'.

Not a word of this, of course, was true, but it amused him greatly that they had welcomed every teacher into class with "Give the old chap some water." There was in particular one elderly teacher who ought to have been retired long ago, as he could no longer maintain discipline, and for the whole lesson the boys had answered his every question with "Would you like a glass of water, sir?"

Well, being the Town Clerk's son was quite a novel experience.

After lunch he sat with Lina and told her all about everything. She became pensive.

"I haven't got a thing to wear, I don't know what I can do about Thursday. It's Saturday today, tomorrow's Sunday, I shan't be able to get anything made..."

"What I say is, my dear, go along to the dress-maker and order your dress, that's all you can do. She'll wait a little while."

"Oh dear, I'm not used to this," said Lina with a coy laugh, and went into the kitchen to bring her husband a nice cup of coffee. She had made it with fresh beans, specially.

The coffee was very good, and he regarded it as the crowning of his new position. He was very fond of good coffee, but for years had not been able to have it because Lina's all-pervading economy had not permitted there to be real coffee on the table except in minimal quantities.

After coffee, sleep overcame him, it had been a long time since he'd had such a late night and his body had been crying out for rest all day. He slept almost without interruption until next morning. He did not even know that there had been visitors. Lina guarded his sleep like a dragon.

6.

The following day he felt quite at home going to the office. He'd made himself familiar with the most urgent matters in hand. He was very pleased that he'd made no blunders. The newspaper interview had caused quite a stir. It was said to be such as ministers gave. He had expressed himself with the masterly superiority of a great politician, and there had been absolutely no trouble. Some of his remarks were being discussed everywhere, and the two catch-phrases in particular – that the small-holders' affair should proceed on the principle 'Let the goat feast and let there be cabbage left'; this old saying was taken up as if it had never been heard before, as if he had invented it himself. He couldn't understand what people liked so much about it, probably that it wasn't profound, and so they could interpret it any way they chose. In any case, it was amusing.

The second, however, they liked even more, that 'People should be inspired to pay their taxes'.

This really had become a sensation in the city, everyone was laughing about it.

This statement had made such an impression that all day people talked about nothing else but that the new Town Clerk wanted to inspire them to pay their taxes. What could be said more unexpected, more peculiar, in this country, where almost everyone lived by tax-evasion? The State was obliged to impose taxes double, triple, tenfold, in order to bring in anything at all. And even so everyone considered that whatever they paid was far too much, for in those days things were going very badly. After the Consolidation[12] Hungary was for a while a real Cloud-Cuckoo Land, stories were told of peasants having chests full of bank-notes that they could not count, and of special accountants doing the rounds in country areas working out the rich men's money. Those were the days when the wealthy peasant

47

Máté Pöthös went to town to order furniture for his daughter Juliska's dowry. When the cabinet-maker said that he could do it for three thousand new pengős, old Pöthös turned to his wife and said:

"Let's not waste our time here, Mother, we want better for our daughter."

The cabinet-maker was startled and began to work it out again, and said:

"Don't go, for five thousand I can make furniture that'll even surprise the priest."

"That doesn't mean much to us, we aren't beggars like the priest."

The cabinet-maker had a brainwave and said: "Well, if you want the real thing, have it made of rosewood, inside and out."

And he began to calculate and calculate and said:

"Look here, that'll come to twelve thousand, but even His Grace the Duke won't have anything better."

"Well, give us a piano as well, and that'll do."

So he got his piano for three thousand pengős instead of nine hundred and was satisfied.

Well, those days were past. Money had started to lose its value, because the price of wheat had fallen from thirty-two pengős to twenty. The price of boots had risen from twenty-two to forty. Cars too had been in vogue, there had not been a rich man that did not buy one, run it for a couple of years, did not understand it, had to pay the garage, and so, in short, once again there had struck the anxiety and terror that after a brief period of glory the agricultural worker was slipping back into straitened circumstances.

Now along came a new Town Clerk with the bright idea that people must be made to enjoy paying taxes.

Only that morning did it occur to Pista that he hadn't proof-read the reporter's article. But when he read it he could see that somebody must have done so, because the remark about payment of taxes stuck out like a fly in the soup. On the Saturday he'd lectured the reporter on the principles of economics and he had carefully written down why taxes had to be paid; because then the tax-payer had influence, had the State in his hand. He had a right to say how his taxes should be spent. Pista had cited examples. When the Bulgarians had entered the war, every last Bulgarian property owner had calculated what might be at risk and what might be gained through the war. This hadn't happened here, because the Hungarians had no developed national mentality, far be it from them to consider the requirements of the nation. They just paid money as ordered into the State coffers without the least notion of what would become of it... The Hungarian wasn't master in his own country, merely a tax-paying subject.

Someone had carefully removed all the higher political thought, leaving a lively and humorous account of the new Town Clerk's first day.

When he read the piece through, in his room with the door to the office closed, Pista was a little ashamed of himself, but at the same time quite pleased that it contained nothing difficult or compromising.

On Saturday, after talking to the Mayor, he'd found things to say in the course of conversation for which he was now delighted not to have to accept responsibility. So who could the charitable soul have been that had saved him from these weighty matters? He suspected that the Mayor himself had removed everything that went beyond the bounds of light-hearted chat and gaiety, for certainly, Pista thought to himself, if what he'd said were to have appeared he could have been labelled seditious.

Thank God it'd happened this way, and he blushed at the Mayor's intervention in his statement.

While he was pondering this a Bank official arrived. The Chief Cashier had sent round a representative. He needed a signature in some simple legal matter. There was an action in progress between the city and the Bank. Pista didn't sign, because he wasn't yet authorised to do so.

"It's not urgent, Town Clerk, sir, not at all urgent, I took the liberty of calling just for the sake of form, perhaps you'll be good enough to deal with it at your convenience."

"I'll have a word with His Worship the Mayor."

"Quite, quite... May I venture to say, sir, that your statement was magnificent. Magnificent it was, indeed, the Manager was delighted, he said 'This is a splendid man'. Splendid, sir, that's what he said."

Pista said nothing, smiled.

It would appear that that was what this man was saying, so it wasn't certain that the Manager had received it with such delight, he thought to himself.

"Excuse me, Town Clerk, sir, may I say another thing? Kardics úr, the Manager, asked me to invite your custom as a depositor."

49

"I have no dealings with the Bank."

"That's a quite ridiculous and intolerable situation. In the past year even peasants on the puszta[13] have been involved in share-dealing. Indeed, we've got one customer, a csikós,[14] who's been buying Kőszén and Rimamurányi.[15] And to such effect, what's more, that when he sold his holdings he bought a house on the Madas. Do you see, in that time everybody's built up portfolios, and there's only yourself that hasn't favoured us with even the tiniest bit of business."

In fact, it wasn't Pista's doing, Lina was so set against any form of speculation that he'd never been able to prevail on her to try their luck in the slightest.

"So, the Manager says that he attaches great importance to the Town Clerk's becoming a customer."

"How does Kardics bácsi imagine that?" he laughed at the omniscient bank-clerk.

"Very simple. If, for example, you needed to repay some small debt..."

"I have no debts. I've always had sufficient income to manage without borrowing anything at all."

"Yes, but that can't continue," said the bank-clerk. "From now on Your Honour will have to live in quite a different style, but I don't mean to exceed my brief. You may rest assured of our best attentions, sir."

"Very well. I'll have a word with the Manager. In any case, it's very kind of you."

He didn't know why he'd suddenly addressed a mere bank-clerk as *te*.

He shook him warmly by the hand and showed him cheerfully to the door.

When he turned round he said out loud:

"The first palm-greasing, the first, my dear chap, the first bribe..."

He was amused to catch himself repeating the words in exactly the Mayor's voice. This 'my dear chap', too, was the Mayor's favourite expression.

There was nothing in it, he said to cheer himself up, because naturally it'll never be possible to catch me doing anything underhand or illegal, and he looked at the paper and straight away underlined in red the emphatic words: 'I stand on a foundation of truth and law, and my sole aim is the defence of the interests of the people'.

50

The Mayor's secretary came over; His Worship was asking for him.

Quickly he took his hat, put his coat over his shoulders, holding the lapels together in front, and hurried out.

This time the Mayor saw him at once, did not keep him waiting at all, although there were a couple of people there having an interview.

"Excuse us a moment," said the Mayor to them, and they left the room.

"Well, how did you sleep?" asked the Mayor, seating him, in fact pressing him into an armchair.

"Excellently, Your Worship... You're looking quite rested too. Like a law-student."

"Ho ho," laughed the Mayor, "ho ho!"

"Really, Your Worship..."

"Oh dear, oh dear, but you've got a slow head, perhaps you've actually forgotten my name."

"Of course not, my dear Béla bátyám, I must thank you for being so good as to attend to that proof-reading on my behalf."

"What d'you mean, you didn't do it?"

"No, because I can't conceal the fact, I went to sleep and my wife didn't realise what an important matter it was for me and didn't want to wake me, you know how women are, so the proof went back just as it came."

"So..." said the Mayor inscrutably, "well, so much the better, then. But it's a rare stroke of luck that there should be no more damaging or worrying passages left in... just the one, perhaps."

"Really, Béla bátyám? What ever is that?"

"The expression itself isn't exactly bad, because a Town Clerk can do nothing but stand on a foundation of law and statute, but the emphasis on the word *truth* is, so to speak, a little... pointed... Because, d'you see, everybody stands on a foundation of truth, but if the Town Clerk emphasises law and statute in contrast to truth it might possibly arouse displeasure in certain circles and let the Opposition play games with the authorities, as if, hitherto, other people hadn't been standing on a foundation of truth... Truth only enters into it in so far as it's at one with law and statute. doesn't it?"

"Naturally."

The Mayor wasn't in such a good mood today as on the previous occasion.

He was making a tremendous fuss abut this word *truth*. There was no other possible explanation, he must be in a bad mood. Perhaps he wasn't very well. With such an old man the slightest change of mood showed in the face, the disposition.

Pista sat stunned in his chair and didn't dare say a word.

"Yes, we'll have to slip this past. I hope people won't notice it. Because you've got to learn that people are very fickle. As long as somebody's in their good books they'll put up with a lot from him. But once the mood changes, then they'll notice every little thing... The time will come when they'll say, when somebody blunders, that surely *truth* mattered a lot to him... and yet... Or they'll say that he used to be a nit-picker. He was a real speech for the prosecution against us... remember how he went on about truth in his very first statement... Yes, there's no harm done, because it was quite amusing, but letting a newspaper statement go out without checking... If you'd read it through in print you'd certainly have corrected it, because you'd have seen how it runs, how easy it is for the Opposition to make use of it, turn it against you, attack you... I don't like your not checking it..."

"Your Worship, I thought you'd be so good as to take a look at it, I told the reporter to be sure and send a draft to your private address."

"Well, yes, they'll do that in any case..." the Mayor gave himself away, "but I only took a few impossible things out. I left this in on purpose, to see whether you'd notice."

So. It had been a trap, after all. Would this happen all the time?

"Thank you very much," said Pista after a brief pause. "I really am most grateful for Your Worship's kindness."

"What's all this about the Bank? Kardics has been on the phone about your signature being required and you refusing."

"I wanted to have a word with you about that, I only said that I'd discuss it with you... that I wanted to wait for Your Worship's instructions, because I'm not yet familiar with this matter and I don't know what the city's standpoint is, because it's got something to do with the lawsuit taking place between the city and the Bank..."

"You'll have to sign," said the Mayor bluntly.

Then, however, he said more mildly and in a different tone:

"I hear you're a hunting man."

"Yes, but I'm not a member of any hunting club at present. I've got my licence, of course, but I usually just go after hares on my father-in-law's land. When I have the time."

"Ah, your father-in-law, Szentkálnay?"

52

"Yes."

"Where is his place?"

"Out at Kishegyes.[16]"

"How much land has he got?"

"He owns a hundred acres, but he rents a bit as well."

"Yes. Nowadays these hares are behaving a bit better. Of course, during the revolutions[17] the peasants persisted in destroying the game. They had ammunition left over from the war, and they even shot the crows."

He laughed, showing his false teeth right to the plate.

When the Old Man let Pista go he was somewhat confused. He didn't know what to say next.

"Well, excuse me, Your Worship," he took his leave.

"Yes, goodbye, goodbye, my dear chap."

As he left the Mayor's office he was so solemn that the little secretary winked at him confidentially.

"The Old Man's in a terrible mood today."

"I didn't notice," he said.

With that he returned to his office. His bad humour passed slowly off. He cheered himself up with the thought that it was hard for the Old Man to get used to him, he was a new man, bringing a new spirit, new words and a new purpose. He mustn't give way, he thought to himself. How fortunate that he he'd given a non-committal reply to Kardics's message. He wasn't going to sell himself.

It was an important point that his name wasn't on the books of the Bank. This fact alone gave him strength and assured his superiority.

Hmm, and how quickly Kardics had phoned about his refusal to sign. It would have been odd if he hadn't refused. How could he have given his signature straight away, on his first day, in a matter that he knew nothing about?

His first task was to look into the matter requiring his signature for the Bank.

Dr. Péterfi was the officer in charge of it. He came in.

"Tell me, what's this Macskási business?"

Dr. Péterfi was a slim, fair-haired, strongly-boned Székely,[18] and made his report with deep respect, bowing in the smooth manner which only Transylvanians have. The Bank held a small-holding in the forest, which had been sub-let to a man by the name of Macskási. He had felled the trees, but failed, as both the law and his lease required, to replant them, simply planting the land with maize. The case was about this re-

53

afforestation. Dr. Péterfi advised Pista that the Bank was completely in the wrong and had knowingly breached the regulations, and that the city had had to institute proceedings because the Forestry Department so directed. In order to escape responsibility they had to sue the Bank, and the Bank had to sue Macskási.

"So presumably the Forestry Department is right."

"Quite. They're in the right."

Pista didn't know what signature the Bank wanted. He'd been afraid that it was a question of some executive signature. For instance, one admitting on behalf of the city that there'd been some error in the drafting of the lease.

"Please, phone the Bank and find out what they want."

While this telephoning took place from his office, for there was only one telephone in the Legal Department, Pista studied the documents. He saw that the case had been going on for four years already, and was such an awkward one that even Makróczy had been unwilling to resolve it.

The Bank, however, simply replied that they only wished to confirm the date of receipt of a certain legal document from the court. The date of its arrival could only be established in the Legal Department.

Péterfi relayed this information, standing at the telephone.

"Tell them that there's no problem about that."

Péterfi passed on the message and replaced the receiver.

"Where are you from, Péterfi?"

Péterfi smiled.

"I, sir, if I may put it so, am a refugee civic officer. From Transylvania, Udvarhely county."

"Really. Very good."

Pista smiled to find himself speaking to this member of his staff, his equal in age, as the Mayor spoke to him.

Dr. Péterfi was an extremely clever man who was thoroughly versed in all matters in hand, and they talked all morning. Pista learned a lot that day.

7.

A couple of days later came confirmation of his appointment from the Minister for Home Affairs.

He was greatly relieved. Now he was firmly in the saddle. The Mayor had said that in the near future he had to go up and be presented to the Minister. They were only waiting for notification of when he could be received.

Lina's dress was ready by Wednesday. She tried it on and it suited her beautifully. Something altogether wonderful had happened to her. She was definitely younger and had regained her old girlish humour. She sang all the time and was so pleasant and lively as to be unrecognisable.

Pista and she had married during the war and had two children, Berci, who was in the fourth year at the Gymnasium, and Kálmuska, who was eleven and in the first year. They had kept it a secret, but Lina had refused to have more children.

True, she had had enough to do and enough expense with them, because she had brought them up and educated them very well. They had had a German nanny while they were small, but when the elder went to the Gymnasium they could no longer afford her, and because the boys needed their own room there was no longer one to spare for her. They had only three rooms altogether and Pista had been suggesting for a long time that they move to a bigger flat, but this one was so cheap that they were forced to stay there, and as the years went by they kept talking about moving, as if one day a house were going to spring up of itself for them, if they would but bide their time.

Pista was the sort of man that liked to speak his mind at home, and afterwards would not tell his secret thoughts to outsiders. He found in Lina a good helpmate, for she was the more sensible and could take a critical look at things that he would rush into. Now as the days went by, Lina felt that her husband was going to hold his own and not damage the distinguished position to which he had unexpectedly risen with outbursts of excessive idealism.

She did not tell him to humble himself, because she was essentially prouder than her husband, and indeed admired that capacity of his for fitting in, which she lacked, and for swallowing unexpected setbacks and hurtful minor difficulties. She was particularly pleased that he was capable of the arduous task of battling through the awkward period that everyone experiences on appointment to a new official position.

Oh, if only nothing went wrong! Most of all she was worried about this dinner on Thursday. As long as nobody offended her, for she couldn't swallow her pride. If she wasn't given her rightful place, if the lady of the house didn't treat her with the necessary respect, they could live a thousand years for all she cared, she wouldn't darken their door again. She thought about this a lot while doing the ironing and mending her sons' endlessly damaged clothes. But she couldn't imagine that there'd be any trouble. As they'd been invited they were obliged to dress up. When all was said and done, and she saw this, Pista was now in a position where the Manager of the Bank was compelled in his own interests to get on the right side of him. Yes indeed, this getting on the right side could always be strengthened through a man's wife. If they wanted her husband to be their ally, then they'd have to treat her as their ally's ally. Who could alienate the Town Clerk faster than his wife? They knew, and again she smiled a thin smile to herself, her lips pursed wryly, that no doubt she too would gain a certain influence. Good. She too, Lina Szentkálnay, would be somebody in the city.

She thought a lot, too about her cousin Magdaléna. Would she be there? What would she be wearing, how would she behave towards her? They were a younger couple than Pista and herself, but even so hadn't felt the need to pay a call on the Cultural Adviser and his wife. What did she know about culture, she said to herself. Magdaléna had a very bad name among the correct, the so-called respectable women. She didn't love her husband, they said, and on the other hand she had powerful ambitions. It was for her that he'd had the big villa built on the avenue. He was an industrial designer, an artist, and had himself planned and built the villa, furnished with unheard-of splendour, in the latest German style with a winter garden and plumbing, a car and a chauffeur, which, in a smallish town, naturally had a wild reputation. They hadn't met since they'd been children - not since then; she'd been to the Institute here in Zsarátnok, but Magdaléna had been to Budapest. She'd only come home for the vacations, and as her father had a big hardware business in the main square, which had somehow done very well during the war, they'd lived in fantastic wealth, and there was little likelihood of Lina and her coming into contact.

'Well, never mind, we shall see,' Lina said to herself, and her fingers searched on into the little pair of trousers for yet another hole.

'Magdaléna doesn't have this to do,' she smiled to herself. 'Simply because she has no children. She's infertile.' Women that have children feel very superior to those that have none. They look down on them as stigmatised. In a mother's eyes no earthly treasure can replace the treasure of children. Just let nothing untoward happen, then everything would be all right.

Such was Lina's agreement with herself, and she couldn't imagine anything of a disturbing nature that could possibly happen in so short a time.

And then, on the Wednesday afternoon, Pista's Uncle Berci arrived unexpectedly.

Lina felt as if a thunderbolt had struck.

8.

Ah, Berci bácsi, there was a remarkable man. Although he was a lawyer in a country practice he cultivated as magnificent appearance as a cattle-dealer.

"Hello everybody, here's Berci bácsi."

He opened the door to its fullest extent so that it creaked, they didn't usually open it so wide, and just stood there like a roast piglet at New Year, his face smiling and red, his eyes gleaming.

"*No, öcsém!*" And that said it all. Well, my boy! In this were congratulation, the delight of having such a nephew, the superiority of still being his uncle, older, wiser, from whom the children could expect all that was nice and good. And there was, too, the reminder that we're family, Kopjásses, and don't you forget it!

This '*No, öcsém*' dated from Kuruc[19] days or even earlier, from the depths of antiquity, from the miraculous world of tumult and affray, when the little Hungarian had been liberating himself from the enemy hordes and winning his homeland with an impudent, inflated self-awareness: *No, öcsém!*

But Lina knew this '*No, öcsém*' very well; its refrain went 'My boy, just a word... give me some money'.

She also knew that as long as she was in the room the stereotype phrase wouldn't trip forth, so she tried hard to stay to protect her husband if possible. Yes, but the lady of the house has

57

duties, if nothing else to find something to set before the guest, for the guest has had a long journey, he is always dying of hunger, for him restaurants do not exist, the possibility of eating outside the house has not been discovered, the guest always comes as if for all the world he has not eaten a crumb, for he does not want to spoil his appetite so as then to offend the lady of the house, his little sister, by refusing good food.

And so Lina listened for a while to Berci bácsi telling the tale, for great things happened to Berci bácsi, even on the road, on the train, whom did he not encounter, just imagine, in Füzesabony...

When she went out, Berci bácsi immediately dropped his voice to a conspiratorial level and sat closer to his nephew Pista.

"I want to tell you, öcsém, that there's a big deal in the offing. A big one, such as hasn't come our way since the Kopjásses fell on hard times. I've become a mine-owner."

"A mine!" said Pista, "What kind of mine, Berci bátyám?"

"A coal-mine, öcsém, a coal-mine..."

Pista laughed. Berci bácsi, who'd never got a pengő, owner of a coal-mine!

"It so happens, öcsém, that there's a very good little mine in Borsod county. At Kalács. It's called Kalácsbánya. Near Köleser...[20] Well, this young man comes to see me as a lawyer, tells me that his father's died, his father was a very honest, decent, hard-working master blacksmith, who'd set up this nice mine by an enormous amount of hard work and brains. Yes, but the poor chap had never had enough money, of course, to develop it in a business-like way, he'd simply done enough to keep it going from day to day, enough to prevent the Inspectorate of Mines from closing it. While he was alive it was all right after a fashion, because the old blacksmith was a real wheeler-dealer, and always scraped enough together to keep things going. He believed in his mine like in God. He knew it had a future, because there was coal like this in it, look here, I've brought a bit to show you."

And with that he took from his pocket a piece of newspaper and unwrapped a fine piece of black diamond.

"There you are, öcsém, I've brought that for you. That's my present. Put it on your desk and enjoy it, it's the light of our salvation. Look at it, see it shine? It belongs to the whole Kopjáss family. What veins of gold there are in it! Just look, how black it is, how hard and heavy. This bit compares with the best Prussian coal, but on average it's better than Salgótarján. Better than that. Yes, keep it and take a pride in it. Show it to everybody, öcsém, that knows about coal. Have it chemically analysed, burnt in test-tubes, vaporised, baked, cleaned, because I want to know what this coal is worth."

Pista looked at the coal, which was indeed a very fine piece, there was only one thing wrong with it: Berci bácsi.

If anyone else had shown it to him he'd have believed them, but from Berci bácsi's hand he took it nervously, examined it suspiciously and rigorously for a while, then put it on the table.

"Don't put it down, öcsém, don't put it down," exclaimed Berci bácsi, "Don't put it down, for the love of God. This is our salvation, öcsém, this must put the shine back on the Kopjáss name. Let me tell you a bit more... Anyway, this master blacksmith left six sons. He sent them to school, and not one of them became a craftsman, the one's a clerk, one's in the Land Registry, the third's a hajdú, in short, they're all educated men... so they've given up getting their hands black. Now then, there's this mine. The brothers can't agree how to divide it, and one of them came to me for legal advice."

He took out his handkerchief and mopped his brow.

"Well, that was all I needed. When I saw this lump of coal I said 'This is a piece of cake... and it's for us'. I asked all sorts of questions and found out all about it. I drew up a balance-sheet for it, then went to see my wife's brother Antal and had a word with him, he knows a lot about such things, having been in estate management all his life, anyway, we're all in it, the family... To cut a long story short, all I'll say for now is that a family company's been set up. We're going to buy the blacksmith's sons out for next to nothing and make the mine pay. We'll exhaust it, mine it out, my boy, thank God I've got a good head on my shoulders."

"That's marvellous, Berci bátyám, congratulations."

"You congratulate me! I congratulate you, öcsém. From the bottom of my heart I congratulate you, because you're the member of the family that's had the greatest success in the past hundred years. D'you know what that means? D'you realise who you are? Especially if you get to understand this coal, get to like it and take an interest in it... Nowadays towns are very worried about how to provide themselves with fuel. None of them is properly organised. They buy expensive coal and cartels are being set up and palming off the world's worst coal on them. Öcsém, the city of Zsarátnok itself is enough customers for me, until we get more..."

59

Pista looked straight ahead for a while in reluctance.

"It's nothing to do with me," he said quietly.

"It's nothing to do with you. Who then, if it's not you? It only takes a word from you. You speak to the city finance department. Just tell them to take a look at this coal. Let them order a sample from the mine. I'm prepared to give them a load for nothing, so that the city can see whether it'll do, say, for heating the theatre. If not, they needn't give me a single krajcár. Let 'em try it in all the municipal works. If they can use it, well and good, if not, I never said a word."

This was very awkward for Pista, who had never had anything to do with purchasing.

"I can't, Berci bátyám, I can't," he said decisively. "It's nothing to do with me, and I won't use my position to obtain business."

"Don't be a fool, öcsém!" exclaimed Berci, flabbergasted. "You're throwing away a fortune!... There's your own position, you've got children, you've got to think of them too. I'll give you twenty percent of whatever's ordered. If they order a hundred thousand pengős worth, that means twenty thousand for you. Clear profit. In your hand, ready money. How can you have it in you to throw away so much money, you young devil! I'll set your wife on you, and the whole family. We'd all be saved, because the way we see it is that for this we need to set up a family company, and this is the way we can do it."

"Just now you said you had."

"On paper. But to put it into practice we need an order, then we're off. In the present difficult climate money doesn't grow on trees, however wonderful a business may be. But if there's one order like that, then we've got it made. We shall have that much money to play with, we shan't know where to put it. You won't have to put a fillér in, my brother-in-law Antal and I will take the mine over and run it, you'll have nothing to do. You take your cut and off you go."

Pista listened to the old man with deep discomfort. All his life Berci had been full of ridiculous plans, and he was racking his brains for the right thing to say to put him off.

It was, however, his belief that members of the family should not be condemned, for who would take care of one if not they? That was the creed in which he had been brought up, his mother's belief. And now too it kept him dumb, while he heard out all that the old man had to say. It took all afternoon.

When Lina was in the room Berci bácsi immediately

changed the subject. He had plenty to say about the family, the relations, because he knew everyone, was in touch with everyone, and was full of gossip.

"Do you know, Berci bácsi, who was first to congratulate Pista?" said Lina with a thin smile. "Lajos bácsi."

"Which Lajos is that?"

"Lajos Bátay."

"Who's he?"

"Your brother, of course."

"Oh, good Heavens, you haven't had anything to do with him? Give him a pengő and tell him to push off. He's a nuisance, you know." Lina and Pista said nothing, smiling inwardly.

"And what was he after?" asked Berci bácsi, his mouth full.

"Clothes."

"You didn't give him any?"

"Why?"

"Lord, you'll never get rid of him. He'll put 'em on and be round your necks. What clothes did you give him?"

"My husband's old frock-coat."

"Then you did wrong. He'll be round to the Bishop tomorrow. That's just what he needed. He's got this mad idea that he should have been educated for the Church. We never dared give him anything black, because he'd immediately start dressing up and getting us into all sorts of trouble. My dear, you've got to watch the relations."

"This is the first time he's ever asked for anything," said Pista quietly. "He's never even asked for anything by letter."

"Why should he? He wouldn't expect anything…"

Pista gave Berci bácsi a sidelong glance. It had occurred to him that, as far as that went, Berci bácsi hadn't asked for anything before, either.

The old man had, furthermore, not the least intention of going and stayed to dinner. He sat with the children and played with them as if he too were an old child. He knew how to make himself liked in such a way that the boys flung their arms round his neck and perched on him like sparrows on a tree. He told the most marvellous stories, a lot had happened to him in the course of his life, and even Lina was forced to smile and to admit that he was a lovable old idiot.

Berci was leaving next day on the morning train and they took it in good part that he had no-one in town to visit, just stayed in and spent the time with them. He said no more about the mine, only when he was on the point of leaving he turned to Pista: "Öcsém, have you got twenty pengős?"

"Twenty pengős?"

"I've run out of cash, but if you haven't got any on you it doesn't matter, I'll get some somewhere, well... I'll just say, that mine business, give it some thought, I'll look in again next week, I'm coming in then, no need to rush things, but you mustn't let the grass grow... I mean, you're new in your job, but you might at least get this piece of coal analysed by the city. I'm very interested in getting an official opinion on it... If the verdict isn't bad, we can get something started... I mean, time's getting on, because here we are in November, a good planner will have seen to the winter stocks by this time, but we're living for the future, we shall want money then too... We have to prepare the ground."

Pista would very much have liked to give the old chap a bit of money, but he simply hadn't a fillér on him and he dared not ask Lina for any to give him, so he excused himself for his empty hands, made up some tale about his wife, you know... another time... He didn't know himself how things were for the time being...

"Well, I'll have that offer made official with the management of the mine and sent to you, öcsém."

"Management of the mine!" thought Pista, and was convinced that he wouldn't hear another word about Berci bácsi's coal.

"What did that old chatterbox want?" asked Lina once Berci bácsi had left.

"Nothing!" said Pista.

"What sort of nothing?"

"Well," Pista laughed awkwardly, "he'd come with one of his usual ideas. There's some coal-mine he's got a lot to do with. Probably an agent..."

"So what does he want?"

"He'd like an order from the city."

"Goodness, Pista, I hope you haven't got mixed up in it?"

"No way."

"Be careful, darling, be careful... He's a dear old villain. Don't take anything he says seriously."

Pista said nothing, and Lina realised that after all he was her husband's uncle, she didn't want to hurt his feelings.

"I'm saying nothing, I know nothing about it, but I do know that you can't just take Berci bácsi at his word..."

"Of course not... He's left this lump of coal for me to have analysed."

"I wonder where he got that? Picked it up on some railway station."

Lina herself laughed at what she said, but Pista thought that it wasn't very nice of her.

9.

Otherwise, the days began to come and go in routine fashion. Pista became accustomed, wherever he went and whoever spoke to him, to being addressed with distinct respect. He worked through the business in the office and was surprised that in three, four, five days he hadn't come upon any trace of scandal. He had, however, been prepared for quite a legacy of trouble after Makróczy.

At mid-day on the Wednesday, as he was going home from the office, he met Vadasi, the member of Parliament, who had been roughly his contemporary at school, just a couple of years his senior, and with whom he'd kept up acquaintance. He now greeted Pista with an unfamiliar affability, which was like a breath of fresh air.

"What's news *in politics?*" asked Pista.

The member of Parliament laughed. He flung back his oddly-shaped head and laughed harshly, his mouth wide.

"Things can't go on like this," he said, "Smooth smiling isn't government. The boss[21] just smiles at everything. The greatest affairs in the world may be taking place around him, he just smiles. It's all very well for him. And for others too, no doubt. God created him so that in hard times like these He should have a nice fat man to place at our head, who'd laugh down from the throne. He has no conception of what's wrong. There's never been any trouble in his life, he's never been hungry, how is he to know what hunger means?"

Vadasi laughed. Just like a bulldog in its prime, that too is confident, that too can laugh.

"If we talk to him about what's going on in the country, he smiles. He taps the ash off his cigar and smiles. People being exploited, people out of work, farm-workers that can't find jobs, thirty thousand unskilled manual workers unemployed, all this doesn't exist as far as he's concerned. He smiles, things have always been like this, the poor have to be there."

Pista didn't know the Prime Minister, except from pictures, and now this uncensored description startled him severely. He felt that it was appropriate, but was amazed that a member of the governing party should speak in this way. "He's popular," he replied.

"D'you know what popularity consists of?... Fifty per cent is power. This, as a form of popularity, is what any head of government can expect. Twenty-five per cent is personal charm; if a man in a high place hasn't yet had any scandals exposed, he's got a kindly personality and he's popular. The remaining twenty-five per cent... isn't needed. The nice chap that nobody objects to, there's something wrong with him... D'you know what the peasants tell us down our way? 'He's such a good man! As good as a slice of bread! So good that he isn't called anything any more'."

They both laughed heartily and looked at one another as if they understood one another perfectly.

With that they parted, and Pista reflected all the way home on how right the member of Parliament was. With an evil smile he drew for himself the conclusion which applied, it seemed, to himself as to anybody that occupied a position of power.

Never mind. If that was the case, so much the better. He was beginning to understand what power meant, and the reason why men struggled and competed for it.

But one had to know how to live with power. And he hadn't yet acquired that knack. He still retained certain fanciful notions from his student days, that power had only responsibilities and was not permitted privileges.

At home there was great excitement. Lina's dress had just come from the dressmaker and she was trying it on, as a result of which lunch was late. The whole family was looking at the dress, admiring it, the children were making a great fuss of their mother, how beautiful, how splendid, how marvellous. There wasn't another like her. Nobody had such a beautiful mother.

Pista too was delighted, truly, he hadn't realised what a lovely woman his wife was. As she stood there in her cocktail dress it seemed that a higher being had appeared in the little three-roomed flat. Previously she'd been like Cinderella, now it was as if the walls around her had vanished. The plain, smooth furniture, which had been in fashion when they'd married, looked shabbily at its beautiful mistress and rejoiced in her, the faded wallpaper, the poor, cheap flowers stuck on the walls by the decorator, paled in her presence and Pista felt that some dreadful injustice had been perpetrated all these years that this lovely Szentkálnay woman had lived, repressed and concealed, in that cramped and airless flat.

"Lina," he said, quite taken aback, "you're a very lovely woman."

Lina laughed, and how that little laugh suited her! With what charm her delicate, slender lips could smile! Her healthy little teeth, which scarcely used to gleam from behind the closed lips, now shone sweetly. Her dark eyes now opened wide, and then great desires blazed forth, now closed to mere slits, becoming even more enigmatic.

"My word, I didn't know that you were so beautiful. You'll be a triumph."

And at this Lina laughed in astonishment, for this was the one thing that she hadn't thought of.

She was annoyed, and realised that lunch wasn't on the table yet.

This made her irritable, and she began to pester the dress-maker, saying that the dress was tight in the shoulders, cut her under the arms, that she didn't feel right in it.

"But Madam, it fits as if Madam had been poured into it."

"No, I can't wear this. I'm not a tailor's dummy, to have clothes stretched onto me. I want to live in it. I can't move, look, I can't raise my arms."

"Madam has a wonderful figure," said the girl, "a lot of people would be jealous. You needn't hide anything, you can show it all."

"I don't want to show anything, I want to wear the dress, and I must be able to move in it."

She looked at her husband and said petulantly:

"I don't want to be a doll that can't move, it's no good to me if I've got to feel that I can't move because I'm in a shop window. I want the sort of dress that I can feel free in."

Pista laughed, but he wasn't pleased that his wife wanted the comfort and simplicity of everyday clothes from evening dress as well, which of course has quite a different purpose. He could see nothing in the dress to find fault with.

"Of course, because you're looking at the colour and the material. I chose that, but what they've done with it is awful."

The poor girl had to start it all over again, pinning up the places that were wrong. In effect, she had to re-make the dress, letting it out here, taking it in there, making it almost everywhere fuller and more comfortable. But this way the back looked tight, and to alter that now, at the last minute, was simply impossible. Lina had said that they were going out for lunch somewhere and that she needed the dress to be suitable for that, not just an evening dress, and wouldn't admit, while there was time, that there was still half a day for alterations to be made.

Then she was on the telephone, an irritable quarrel that led to tears.

"It's absolutely awful, useless, now what would I do if I were going to lunch? You're terrible, but at least do something about it..."

As the dressmaker, one of the staff of the best salon in the city, realised that the dress was needed for the evening, she immediately said that Lina would need an opera cloak as well, and to pacify the customer offered the loan of one for the evening.

Oh dear, there was no end to the quarrelling, arguing and weeping, because Lina, as was her custom, burst into tears. And in her stressed condition she would have liked to die.

"Oh, what d'you want me for?" she said angrily, her eyes red from weeping, "Perhaps I'd better change my skin to help my husband's career. Leave me alone, this is terrible, it's enough everybody worshipping you all of a sudden, I'm not going to change for your sake. Why do you put me through such torment, I'm no good to you the way I am, the way I've always been..."

Lunch took place in a very subdued atmosphere, the boys didn't speak, ate the soup (which was overcooked) and the meat (which was cremated) in silence; only with the sweet did the mood lighten.

To escape the excitement of the afternoon, Pista went into City Hall and buried himself in work. He had a lot to do to familiarise himself as quickly as possible with all the current business, previously so far removed from him; indeed, he'd never been concerned with the legal side of city business. Fortunately, Dr. Péterfi was a most useful man, who knew everything, had an opinion on everything, and made light work of explaining the most complex matters.

In the evening there was another crisis. The younger boy developed a sore throat, and his mother was almost beside herself. The child was lying sick, temperature thirty-nine, and she was off out enjoying herself like a step-mother.

66

And into the bargain the dress was no better, in fact, if that were possible, it was worse. Lina all but tore it off, and it was only with the greatest strength of nerve that Pista was able to force her, that is, persuade her, to put it on; to-morrow they'd take the whole thing back and have a new one made. Inwardly he decided to compensate the dressmaker, find the money somewhere... and he thought that it might be possible to arrange some business with the city for the salon, because for the time being he hadn't got the money... To complete the disaster, at the last minute Lajos bácsi arrived.

Lajos bácsi was a very pleasant man, full of smiles, in fact all the Kopjásses were; Lajos bácsi wasn't really a Kopjáss, but an uncle on Pista's mother's side, a Bátay, but in her anger Lina made him a Kopjáss... And, if you please, Lajos bácsi would stay the night, because they couldn't turn him away. How were they to make room for him? There was nothing for it, they'd have to put up the iron bed in the boys' room, he could sleep there, and that evening the elder boy wouldn't be able to do his prep, but would have to listen to that old chatterbox's drivel, and the little one would be dead by morning...

Finally they called a taxi. They couldn't go on foot, although it wasn't far. On another occasion Lina would have walked it ten times, but not in her suede shoes trimmed with silver, the street was muddy. And what was that going to cost, she didn't feel at all like going, she'd rather go to bed. And she had to give her husband money.

"Don't take me to places like this, Pista, don't make me into what I'm not. What a palaver it is for me to emerge from this rat-hole and show myself off to people. It's easy for women that've got six rooms and don't know what a family is... I'm not a society woman..."

Pista laughed. Now Lina was imagining herself as a woman about town!

At last they got into the taxi.

Lina was like a piece of wood. Pista felt very strange at being in a taxi with his wife. This had never happened before, and indeed, this taxi, with its worn silk upholstery, with the doll dangling in the rear window, might be taken for the ship of wonders carrying them from poverty to the flowery fields of wealth... He tried to give Lina a hug in her borrowed cloak, but met with icy rejection and dared venture no further.

Nor was there time, for now they were outside the Kardics

house. Kardics bácsi lived in the main square, occupying the whole first floor of his own block of flats. From below they could see the brightly-lit windows.

As they got out, Lina looked to see whether her husband would give a tip. She was annoyed because she couldn't see what he gave. She had the feeling that it was too much. This decrepit taxi had impressed him. Oh, this man!

10.

They went up the wide, well lit stairs on the taut red carpet and rang the bell.

A footman opened the door, helped them off with their coats. Pista looked at himself in the mirror, his dinner-jacket seemed unexceptionable, and Lina looked like an angel come to earth. He stared at her in amazement. Didn't she want a mirror?

Lina smiled.

There was an unusual brilliance in the ante-room, which led into yet another hall, where a huge mirror welcomed them. Here Lina glanced into the mirror, then calmly stood in front of it and looked herself over. She touched her hair, for women always have something to adjust in their hair. Hers was short, cut in quite a boyish style, and she liked it so for comfort, but now she eyed herself contentedly. He head was not as conventional as other women's.

Pista in his turn was pleased that Kardics bácsi himself came to greet them.

He shook them cordially by the hand and led them into the big drawing-room.

"Look who's here, my dear," he said quite loudly to his wife.

There was already a cluster of guests. They were happy to have arrived at the right time, neither too early nor late. Just after them came the Chairman of the Board of Magistrates, Ambrus Darkó, with his wife and two skinny daughters. They might have been pretty girls, but at the time Pista only noticed how thin they were.

The Alispán[22] was an old acquaintance and greeted them as such, and immediately expressed an interest in the Szentkálnay connection, because his son had married a Szentkálnay girl, so that straight away they established a relationship.

It was only now that they began to notice Mrs. Kardics. They'd been so ill at ease when they were introduced that they

68

hadn't exchanged a single word despite the fuss that Kardics bácsi'd made, and now it was bothering Lina a little that this pale, aloof, plain woman had so few words to spare for her. 'Terribly refined,' Pista said to himself, and he too felt somewhat less than comfortable with the lady of the house. He'd omitted to make the first visit, and it only now occurred to him that he ought to have called formally on the Kardicses before accepting the invitation to dinner.

It was no good, they weren't familiar with society ways.

He was worried, because he over-estimated the importance of this, and racked his brains for a way to rescue himself.

But then he overcame the problem. When all was said and done, it was not he that was invited, but the Town Clerk.

He sat down in a big armchair and lit a cigarette. He didn't want a cigar before the meal. Gradually he settled down and got his bearings. He looked at his wife, sitting so simply and with marvellous grace among the women, she must be feeling at home, and she was the most beautiful of all present.

It was a good feeling, suddenly to be among the cream of society. It was as if the water had cast up the drowning man, and he who had felt himself lost among the sea-weed found himself on a magic island surrounded by roses... Suddenly life was beautiful and there was nothing wrong.

A very fine company was gathering. There was a big lawyer, Boldizsár Kemény, one of the Transylvanian Kemény family, but not from the noble branch, although this meant nothing in Transylvanian terms. Therefore he cut quite a lordly figure, an imposing, powerful, tall man, a typical Transylvanian count, for Transylvanian counts are distinguishable from their Magyar counterparts in that they are not of degenerate appearance. And their little daughter was so outstandingly lovely that one's eye was brought to a standstill at the sight of her.

There was His Majesty's Regional Director of Education, a tall, distinguished-looking man. Pista had known him for a long time as Cultural Adviser, of course, and now he was surprised that they'd never called on one another. All present, generally speaking, were proud men, and even if they were small of stature nonetheless they held their heads high. Perhaps this was only because of their stiff collars, because among themselves they were thoroughly cheerful, good-humoured, could laugh like children, as if they were hiding nothing, neither age nor wealth nor power nor an impoverished country.

The bishop was there too. His enormous purple silk sash

was rather intimidating, for as Calvinists they were afraid of Catholic priests. This was a feeling that had been inculcated in them, they were aware that the Catholic clergy were a more privileged breed than the Protestant. They had that aura of great wealth, great power and, indeed, of a higher culture. All evening Pista scarcely dared speak in his presence, because he was afraid of perpetrating some vulgarity, whereas the prelate was like a Renaissance bishop, refined and distinguished, with a huge ring set with an enormous diamond, on his face an unchanging, forgiving, or at least disregarding, gentle smile. Whatever was said to him he received it with this smile.

The rest were all either business men or officials. The well-known names that the popular press liked to attack. And those heads of departments, terrors of the judicial bench, that sat where they really cracked down on people. Every tiniest place has its own upper class. Zsarátnok was a big enough city for there to be quite a gallery of wielders of power. It was a curious city of many contrasts, and none the less it was as if there were no contrast at all. It was like the Hungarian puszta, of staggering width and yet terrifyingly restricted.

Pista tried to find his level, just observing, and careful to sit with sufficient dignity yet in such a way as not to seem uncomfortable. This was no easy task among men of natural distinction, and he was very conscious that the stamp of yesterday marked him out, the stamp of the *nouveau venu*. Where had he been hitherto and how did he come to be there?

But he watched carefully those of whom he'd previously heard nothing but bad reports. The Chairman of the Board of Magistrates, who would pass merciless judgement on him if he came up before him... the Bank officials, who would never have put a fillér in his hand... the big businessmen, with whom he'd never had a thing in common... who even yesterday had looked through him like air.

Suddenly he heard a word, and at this a deathly pallor spread over his face, after which a fiery red burned to the very tips of his ears.

He was so startled that he thought that the room was spinning, and that he'd have to leave.

"Are we expecting Magdaléna?"

A question from one gentleman to another.

Was Magdaléna going to be here too?

He hadn't thought of that. He must have known that the

70

Boronkays were usually there. But the last few days had been so packed with incident that the thought had gone out of his head.

What would happen if he met Magdaléna in front of his wife?

Boronkay's presence at his inaugural dinner had been enough to set every drop of his blood on fire, and by the end of the meal he'd been quite mad. Now he'd suddenly sunk into the same giddiness. He was losing all his self-control and he glanced at Lina to see whether she'd noticed what was happening to him. If she'd seen him change colour it was all up, he'd never find a convincing explanation, and if Magdaléna were to appear, then the situation would be really fraught, because Lina'd be sure to see that with her there he couldn't control himself...

Apart from that he only felt an inward excitement. He was expecting them to arrive at any moment and had decided to exercise every precaution and not even to shake hands with her if he could avoid it. It would be terrible to feel her body; even a mere handshake...

Eventually dinner was announced and they went through into the dining-room. Pista waited to see what would happen, but Magdaléna was nowhere to be seen, nor was Boronkay, and they sat down without them.

Everyone took their named places and there wasn't a single empty chair left. Perhaps they weren't coming.

He relaxed, and was very pleased to see that he had been shown great honour. He was seated on his hostess' left; on her right was the bishop.

Mrs. Kardics was indeed a dignified lady. She never spoke, only looked, but in her look was revealed her assessment of everyone. Kardics bácsi, on the other hand, was mercurial in temperament, although he had no need to be, he had the reputation of infinite wealth and was, furthermore, by virtue of his position in the Bank, the real ruler of the city.

Lina was seated opposite her husband in the middle of the long table. She'd never been so far from him, and even now was not exactly opposite. It was always their custom, wherever they went, to sit together in friendly circles, but on this occasion, of course, there could be no question of that. Nor even of their eyes meeting much, because Pista was occupied in sweating blood to draw a faint smile from his hostess. Lina, however, was terribly ashamed of her hands. She'd only got one maid, and that a peasant girl, she had to do the cooking herself, and had

71

been trying in vain for the past few days to take care of her hands, and they were red when she finally had to take off her gloves.

Two servants were waiting at table. White-gloved, accomplished footmen, one serving on the right of the table, the other on the left, very clever at ensuring that no-one went without anything. Lina didn't stop worrying, why had she come here, if ever she had to return hospitality how could she give a dinner for people like these...

But apart from that they quite enjoyed themselves. Everyone was most kind to them, and at the end of the meal Pista was actually toasted. The Director of Education, of all people, stood up and made a very generous speech in which he referred to the enrichment of the life of the city by the arrival in the forefront of the person of the new Town Clerk. The Alispán, surprisingly, seconded this with a 'Hear, hear', and Lina almost burst into tears.

After the table was cleared little groups formed, and Pista was even further separated from his wife, they just met in the first movement as the diners spread out, and exchanged warm glances.

"How're you feeling, darling?"

Lina smiled, and in her smile Pista read 'quite bearably'.

"You're the most beautiful, you're gorgeous."

"Ssh," said Lina and closed her eyes. She was warning her husband not to disparage the other women present.

Pista laughed and was pleased that there was really nothing wrong.

Kardics bácsi came upon them just as they were exchanging a kiss.

"Oh, these young married people!" he exclaimed. "Well, my dear, you'll have to do without your husband today, because we're going to eat him."

Lina laughed.

"I've got enough of him left," she said.

"What's that?" asked Kardics bácsi provocatively.

"His bad temper stays mine," said Lina, and at this Kardics bácsi roared with laughter.

"Has he got one?"

But Lina spoke no more evil of her husband, because she was afraid for him. And she didn't like Kardics bácsi taking the liberty of calling her *te*.

"Wonderful little woman you've got," said Kardics bácsi,

and pinched Lina's cheek, at which she turned quite pale, so embarrassed was she.

Kardics didn't notice, held the little woman even more daringly, put his arm round her waist and kissed her. Lina didn't like to object but pulled away, stiffened and blushed deeply.

"Ah, ah," exclaimed Kardics bácsi, "the loveliest rose for the loveliest woman."

And with that he went to the table, took a long-stemmed rose and gave it to Lina.

"Now she's like a picture."

And this expression pleased him very much, he repeated another two or three times that she was like a real painting, a splendid old master. "Leonardo da Vinci," he said, and Pista could believe him, so beautiful was Lina in her delightful confusion.

The wife of the deputy clerk to the court, a little blonde woman whose husband was a member of one of the leading families of the city, which is why they were invited, put her arm through Lina's and led her off. Lina sensed that she too was a little out of place at this dinner, and felt comfortable with her.

The Gyöngyös wine was having a very stimulating effect on Pista, and as the great danger, the appearance of Magdaléna, had not materialised, he felt the happiness of his student days. It seemed as if he hadn't been married sixteen years but was a young bachelor. Now he gave free rein to that wit which he had abandoned in his youth. He circulated among the women, said to each that she was beautiful and youthful, and by so doing teased a smile to a number of faces.

It must be admitted that he was a success. He was no longer silent, as he had been at first, and he had found his feet in this company, had been accepted as if he had always been there. He even talked about the theatre and was amazed that these women knew the doings of the Budapest actresses better than the Bible. A certain beautiful prima donna was at the time in the middle of a scandal. When he'd read about it in the paper Pista had not supposed that it was such a great matter, now he was forced to admit that if he wanted to be a success among these women he'd have to learn the secrets of the theatrical world.

Nothing very remarkable happened except for one thing; Kardics bácsi chose a suitable moment to take him to a corner table and say:

"Look here, Pista, I'll tell you something."

"Go on, Kardics bátyám."

"There's a very nice villa on the Avenue that you'll have to buy."

Pista couldn't help laughing, thinking of the money in his pocket, carefully counted out. Lina had given him notes, silver and bronze in case anything happened, but she hadn't given him enough to buy a place on the Avenue.

"I'm not saying yet which one I'm thinking of, just that it's very nice and for sale. How many children have you got, Pista?"

"Two, two boys. One in the fourth form at the Gymnasium, the other in the first."

"Fine... it'll just do for you... You can get it well below its market value."

"It can't be enough below," he said with a laugh. But then he became serious, because one doesn't joke with the powerful, and if Kardics bácsi was offering something it could only be a good deal.

"You'll have to buy a villa, dear relative," said Kardics bácsi sagely. "Not only because your position requires you to live in your own little nest. A civic officer can't live in rented property."

They smiled at this, for Zsarátnok was famous for its citizens' refusal to regard a tenant as a human being. The landlord didn't invite his tenant to the pig-killing feast. He looked down on him for having no house yet.

"But also because, my dear Pista, you need to forestall gossip! If you buy a house a year from now, people will say 'Look at that, another one that's taken care of himself'. But if you buy now, you can safely say that you've moved what's left of your family fortune into bricks and mortar, and whose business is that? Quite. Our people only trust a man who owns something. When King Károly[23] was being crowned, I myself heard two peasants standing by the royal coaches say: 'Hey, even the spokes of this are gold... These Habsburgs, they're proper kings."

With this he left him and neither asked for an answer nor gave him an opportunity to object or make excuses. He left the newly appointed Town Clerk to come to terms with the idea. Pista couldn't feel happy any more. The tempter had put ideas in his head.

"I haven't accepted the bank-loan they were talking about," he said to himself, "but they know I'll have to."

He felt it humiliating that this offer meant at the same time that it was beneath their dignity to make a return visit to his present small flat, of which they must be aware. So he was no good to the city as he was. They wanted to transform him into their own image and likeness.

He remained by himself and smoked. He'd chosen the fattest cigar, and thought reflectively, as he listened to the chatter around him, that at the age of sixty-two Makróczy hadn't succeeded in becoming Town Clerk, whereas he had achieved this. But Makróczy had a big house on the square, a princely house. Here everybody had to buy big houses. He looked round at those present, counted them over, every one of them had such a big house that those who saw it were envious. Even the heads of departments tried to get six-room flats. As if a magistrate could hand down a stiffer sentence if he lived in a big flat and was up to his ears in debt, than if he lived within his income, calmly and quietly... Even the dread Chairman of the Bench lived in Makróczy's palace. It was a two-storey building with only upper-class residents. Was this how Makróczy'd acquired it? Pista was at once affronted because they weren't offering him a house on the square, but were anxious to push him out to the Avenue, to the outskirts, because the Avenue was built on an outlying site some distance from the city centre. How was he going to be able to get in from there? There were no big villas there except the Boronkays'. The rest were small houses to a German design, full of little holes... Which one had they in mind for him?... Well, they'd be disappointed, because he wouldn't be pushed into any old corner.

At five minutes to midnight the bishop rose and left without any leave-taking. Pista noticed his departure and was very surprised that nobody saw him out except their hostess, who soon returned. She was a Catholic, because her mother had been converted when she married, or perhaps she hadn't been converted but had just allowed her children to be brought up in that faith. It was odd that all evening she hadn't said a word about their relationship. There was a lot of Ferdinánd Kopjáss's blood in this woman. He'd been a tall, slim, distinguished figure like her. Always went about with a carriage and four... Ought *he* to keep a carriage and four? Or a car?... Anyway, how could he afford to?

Lina beckoned him, he got up and they went out, but they couldn't do so without discreetly taking leave of the Kardicses, and they were then surprised to see that the other guests didn't at all follow the bishop's example, but a series of fulsome exchanges took place. Some said good-bye as if they were off at once for America.

There was a taxi-rank outside the house and as it was trying to rain, a chilly, early November rain, they got into a car and had themselves taken home.

On arrival they both had the same thought.

Without speaking, they went into the flat, Lina hurried to look at her younger son, who had been ill, and was pleased to find him sleeping soundly.

How comfortable they'd been in this flat all this time. They'd been living here for at least seven or eight years. Of course, they'd come here when Pista became a clerk with the Council. At that time the children were beginning to walk, and there'd been no room in the previous small flat. That had been in the market square, but overlooking the yard. They'd lived in even worse conditions when Pista returned from the Russian prisoner of war camp, they couldn't get a flat and, as a soldier's family, squeezed into an awful little room and were happy to get even that. Then they'd moved here to Szent Katalin Street and now, Pista supposed, they must look for somewhere else.

'It's strange,' said Pista to himself, 'Are we going to move farther out of town?'

"It's all right for these rich people," he sighed at length, sitting in his dinner-jacket in the worn armchair, which had been completely kicked to bits by the children. The springs came through, the boys had grown up on it. They had liked to jump on it. He spoke only to save his wife expressing their joint feelings.

"Yes, it's easy for them," said Lina. "I couldn't count the rooms they've got. Is there another one behind the study?"

Pista would have liked to raise the subject of the villa purchase, but he held back. He waited to see what his wife would think... Because the one sure thing was that they couldn't stay as they were.

Lina said nothing, just looked straight ahead.

"What d'you think?" she asked after a while. "Are we going to have them back?"

Pista was silent. Well, yes, they'd have to... But he blushed to think of Mrs Kardics coming into their place. She'd behave as if she were visiting an office-boy. It would be an act of mercy.

"How did you feel?" he asked, changing the subject.

Lina said nothing for a moment.

"All right," she said, "It all went off very smoothly."

She was replying to herself, to her fears before setting out, that they'd be disregarded, insulted. That was what 'all right' meant. Pista realised that and smiled inwardly, but the smile did not reach his face, because there were so many whirlpools in his mind that the tiny feeling was swept away.

"It was a good meal," he said.

"They say their cook's a man."

Again they were silent. The excitement that had been aroused had left them so dizzy that they couldn't bring themselves to speak, because the old harmony between them was in abeyance. Another time, when they came home from the least important of dinners, they didn't cease talking over one another, everything just poured out of them to release the tension which they always felt as the result of the efforts of a friend or enemy in their own circle, for a dinner-party is always a trial of strength which the assembled guests judge as such. For the women it is a competition in house-keeping, for the men a contest in money-making. On this occasion, however, they couldn't talk about this, because it had so far surpassed what Lina could have given or Pista earned, they simply felt that it'd been a spectacle, like a big firework display, or as if they'd been to an ox-roast on St. Stephen's Day,[24] to which their own ambitions didn't extend.

"Relations," said Pista as he quickly undressed and got into bed.

He glanced at his wife, who was still silently getting ready, undressing carefully, taking off her expensive dress. She hung it on a hanger from the top window-catch so that the creases would fall out by morning.

As she reached up, her beloved figure was slender and willowy, and Pista wanted her.

"Hey, stop watching me," said Lina uncomfortably, and Pista made a show of shutting his eyes, and a moment later was looking again, admiring the way she folded her underwear, like a saleswoman in a shop who was anxious about things. Then he saw her sit down in front of the mirror, combing her hair and doing her toilet for a long time, all in silence. He almost went to sleep for a moment, but he didn't want to go to sleep, nor was he in the mood for talking. Loving, warm, yearning feelings were pulsing through him.

What ought he to do to shut out the strange influences around him, so that just the two of them might live out their lives? Now he was very much afraid that this pleasant, warmly domestic and yet sensual happiness in which he'd been until now was in jeopardy. He wouldn't have given his wife for the whole crowd, how beautiful she'd been all evening, how well-known and familiar, and yet unfamiliar, new, exciting. After the meal desire had arisen in him more than once to take her in his arms and thank her with love for being, and for being so sincere, true and uncomplicated. Like that, especially from behind, in half-profile, she looked like quite a young girl. It was amazing, sixteen years of marriage had left not a mark on her. She'd managed to keep her figure and her face despite all the work, all the child-rearing, so fresh, especially like this in the electric light.

Finally he woke to realise that she too was in bed. He stretched out an arm towards her and she let him stroke her.

"D'you know what Kardics bácsi said," he said quietly in the darkness, calmly, released from sleepiness, kissing his wife's shoulder with tiny kisses, "He said that there's a villa for sale on the Avenue, very cheap, well below market value, we could get it easily just now."

Lina lay there rigid. She stiffened, took fright at this remark, what was all this? She was immediately afraid, suspicion and alarm struck, wasn't someone plotting their downfall?

"Whose villa can that be?" she said quietly, at once huddling up like a child, hands clasped in front of her face, knees pulled up like a baby.

"I don't know," said Pista, stretching out and speaking more realistically. "I confess I'm afraid... afraid that that old villain will get me into his clutches... must be very carefulv"

"Oh, I do hope there's not going to be trouble," sighed Lina with a groan.

"Awkward business," he said out loud. "Difficult either way. To accept is difficult, not to accept is difficult... The Bank will buy the villa, that's all right. The rest we can manage. Furnishing and equipping. But I still don't know what's going on here in the city. It's really surprised me that I still can't find any shady deals after Makróczy, but I was prepared to be walking into an ants-nest; either it's been very cleverly done, or there isn't anything. That's impossible, perhaps he concentrated his efforts only on big affairs, and these haven't shown up so quickly. Now the Bank's being kind - because Kardics bácsi didn't acknowledge me as a relation for nothing; he needs me. Why, he alone knows. At present I don't know what position to adopt in the event of anything fishy. If I present myself as a purifier I might make myself offensive to the lot of 'em... I saw today, they're all linked together to such an extent, all connected by marriage. The Alispán's an in-law of this one and that, and a number of in-laws are in a kind of Mafia that I still can't penetrate... If, on the other hand, I look the other way, keep my head down, later on something will surely emerge."

Lina didn't reply. She was lying in such alarm that she'd almost fallen asleep. She was hiding from the terrors of the morrow under the warm folds of the duvet and her body was throbbing. She felt very well, satisfied in body and soul, and didn't want to think of anything unpleasant. She was rocking herself on the lake of sleep.

"The Chief Engineer said something good," said Pista and laughed. "He said that in a certain provincial town they were changing the post of Chief Engineer into that of Technical Adviser, and they'd invited someone from Budapest for interview, a technical expert from the Interior... The gentleman in question asked at the interview: 'Is there mains water?' 'Yes.' 'Are the roads surfaced?' 'Yes.' 'Well, has the gas-works been converted into a power-station?' 'All been seen to.' 'Well then,' said he, 'What is there for me to do in this town?' "

And he laughed again.

"Very good," he went on. "The men from the Ministry, the way they think of towns like this... Well, here you can still find something to do. We've got nothing, now we've got to lay watermains, surface the roads. One thing's been done, the electricity... Poor Belatiny, came a cropper over that... rather unlucky... when you look at the city..." and he laughed.

Lina woke a little and said:

"I say, Pista, it's not Belatiny's villa that's for sale?"

"Could be."

"His widow can't keep it up. No income, no need of it."

"That's right... A man struggles and fights, sticks at nothing... When he dies, the whole thing collapses like a balloon when the air leaks out... Do you suppose that when Kardics bácsi passes on, God forbid, his wife'll keep holding these big Thursday dinners? What for? It's only by way of business, I imagine that skinny woman is bored by the whole thing. But she doesn't have to strain herself, the staff do it all... The only thing is, how much energy that man has to put into it! The way he's always on the go! I'll never forget, in the street, when he picked up our relationship... Like a hunter, he always goes round with a loaded gun, and he doesn't miss the smallest game..."

He went on for a long time, but Lina was fast asleep.

He noticed his wife's profound silence, stopped talking, and listened to her quiet, even breathing, turned over with his back to her and, so aligned, they slept.

11.

Next morning they woke very heavy and tired. Pista hadn't dreamed of what to do, but felt as if his train had been hitched to a new engine, with an unknown driver at the controls, and was under way with him as a passenger, travelling into exile, being deported to some unknown world.

There was nothing wrong in the office. In fact he was met by an unexpected pleasure. The first contract. He got fifty pengős for it. He couldn't believe his eyes. He put the money away in the secret, never used, inner section of his wallet and went off to report to the Mayor.

The Mayor talked to him as if he were his son. The elegant little old man was like a magician, firmly on his feet amid the trickiest of affairs, effortlessly undoing knots so that everything should run without a hitch. He'd heard a very good report of yesterday evening's dinner. He excused his own absence, but Ministry people had come and he'd had them in to dinner, but Pista had to tell him everything in detail, which he hadn't expected. Finally even the question of the villa purchase came up. He asked for advice on how to take Kardics bácsi's remark.

"Kardics is a marvellous man," said the Old Man. "He's built up the Savings Bank from nothing, and today it's the leading bank on the Great Plain. If he says something's all right, you can accept it without a qualm."

Pista would have liked to ask how things stood with Makróczy. And he'd have liked the Mayor to confess whether Kardics bácsi used to do him similar favours. Whether his property deals too sprang from Kardics's head, and to what extent he was in the Bank's clutches, because he had a feeling that everybody here was caught in this web... But of course he couldn't shoot at this most distant of marks. Either people told one these things or they didn't. He wasn't yet secure enough to permit himself to allude to such secrets.

And so he asked whether the villa was Belatiny's.

"No, no," said the Mayor, "I don't think that's likely. There's a whole cluster of houses on the market in the Avenue, but the Belatiny business is quite another matter... The important thing is that your in-law Kardics is extremely well-disposed towards you. That much is certain. I've spoken to him more than once about you, and he's always said how much he's taken a liking to you, what a good thing it is for the city that, out of the blue, you've been given this appointment. On that you may rely."

"Thank you very much, Béla bátyám, very much indeed. I shall always do as you recommend."

He no longer needed to be reminded not so say 'Your Worship', but just 'Béla bátyám'... There seemed to be such a warmth and trust between them that he looked on the Mayor as if he were his uncle.

He felt as if he had really arrived, as if he were truly a member of that special social organisation which constituted the city, public life, power, reality. He felt that the city was in their hands lock, stock and barrel, with all its business and its interests, and that he'd always belonged there.

Now he went down the wide corridors of City Hall like a man in authority. It wasn't the office that gave him that feeling, because actually nothing had happened to require him to stand his ground, or that could have backfired on him, but this social strength raised his head high. It was this that straightened his back, it was the friendship of the powerful that inflated his self-consciousness. He sensed that the wealthy were behind him, felt the comradeship of those who knew how to rule.

Obviously, now that he had made fifty pengős out of his position... He wouldn't pass this money over to Lina, it would come in handy for official expenses. He'd think it over.

He ought always to have a bit of money. Cigarettes, a cigar, a tip, a beer...

Previously he'd always hurried across the courtyard of City Hall like a thief, an escapee, paying no attention to those around, like a colourless official; now he walked with self-assurance and slow steps, like one who means to continue to feel the goodness that is beaming upon him.

Even at home he went in through the gate serenely, graciously, his back straight; He almost failed to fit under the vaulted gateway, he seemed to have grown considerably. His head all but struck the gate-arch of the old-fashioned little house. There was a door to the flat under the arch, but that was kept locked, because it led into their bedroom and that wouldn't do for an entrance. One had to go into the yard and pick one's way over the cobbles to the entrance next to the kitchen.

There one went through a tiny hallway, just big enough for a cupboard, and doors were all the furniture it would take; they led into the dining-room, from where to the right was the boys' room and to the left their bedroom. These three rooms were the whole flat. Now, as he went in through the gate, he stopped and thought that this wasn't good enough. He ought to re-open the door under the arch and move the bedroom. Change it with the dining-room. They must have at least one room to take guests into.

Until now they'd only had the vet and his wife in, one or two teacher friends, a couple of country people, lesser landowners, who themselves lived in similar flats. Until now it had been acceptable. But now he had to consider in addition the prospect that if anybody came to see him the whole flat would lie open before them. Because if they were in the middle room it was inevitable that some member of the family would come through, as the other two rooms had no exit other than through the middle one.

Well, what would Lina have to say to that?

For the present he went in where he could; the kitchen door was open into the little hall, which reeked of onions.

He wrinkled his nose, hung his coat, hat and stick on the only peg and went into the dining-room.

Oh, it was an unpleasant dining-room, he felt deep down as if he'd been struck by lightning. How had he never realised this before? The table was laid. The cloth was nice and white, but the plates were of thick earthenware, like those in a cafe. Lina had made up the dinner service with these cheap pieces, as quite a lot had been broken.

The room was quite wide, there was space in it for an upright piano as well as the sideboard, and Lina used to play, but she wasn't a good pianist and played mostly exercises. She lacked the courage to play as much as folk-songs of her own accord. The boys gave the piano heavy use, but weren't keen on it, only banging out the official lesson, especially if their father wasn't at home. The younger had a fair ear and some inclination, but the elder had to be tied to the instrument with rope.

'Hmm,' said Pista to himself. 'If I move the dining-room to the room by the gate, the old problem will arise: there won't be room for the piano. If I bring the two wardrobes in here, there won't be room for it here either.' Now he recalled that it was when they bought the piano that they'd changed the two rooms round. With her usual genius, Lina had worked out that by changing the rooms space would be made for the piano. It was very important, because with this arrangement the flat became bigger and the piano could be played even if someone was asleep in the bedroom or sick in bed.

'There's nothing to be done,' he thought, and picked up the letters from the desk. There was room here even for this desk. Although there would be in the smaller room also... no problem about that.

As he picked up the letters his heart missed a beat. He recognised his younger sister's writing.

He'd broken with his sister Adélka ten years previously over her marriage. He held the letter in his hand for a while, looking at the torn edges. Evidently Lina had torn it open with her finger. It was a nasty habit, tearing everything open... He waited while memory trickled through his veins. How touching that Adélka too should have learned of his promotion and written to congratulate him...

Slowly he drew the letter from the envelope and started to read it, as he was, standing there. It was a terrible letter.

Suffering and sincerity poured from it. Her marriage had failed, she was obliged to say it and to turn for help to her brother, because her husband... After twelve years of marriage she had to admit that his bad qualities were beginning to show themselves and she couldn't stand him any longer... She couldn't endure life, she had to confess to her dear brother Pista that she stood at a critical point. Her husband was a completely useless man who'd failed to make anything of his life, he'd been out of work for two years now, and they'd been living on what she could earn. Often they had nothing to eat. Her five children... at this moment she didn't know what to give them for lunch.

He lowered the letter, couldn't bring himself to read on, such was the pain in his heart, and such fear had gripped him that he had to rest, to pause until he recovered somewhat.

He put the letter down and went across to the other side of the room, where there was a sofa and in front of it a little smoker's companion, a small, six-sided Turkish table with cigarettes on it. He lit a cigarette. Then he walked round the room. The boys were quarrelling in the room on the right, behind the closed door. This door had always to be closed, on Lina's orders, because the room was like a student's study, it was impossible to keep it tidy, and nonetheless somebody might call at any moment from whom it must be hidden that... Anyway, he was glad that the door was shut and that he didn't have to intervene in the racket the boys were making.

He picked up the letter again. He sat down at the desk, his back to the room, the desk stood between the two windows. And he read that Adélka said that it wasn't enough, all this trouble, her husband was chasing another woman. It wasn't enough that she'd taken on the two children of his first marriage in addition to the three that they'd had, and had treated them as her own, now he wanted another woman. He couldn't live in this hell, he said, he needed a bit of sunlight, which he couldn't find with his wife, so he found it with trash in the street, a painted harpy. And there he was, often away from home for a week, and now she was afraid that he was going to abandon her...

He threw the letter down again. He leapt up and paced the room with great strides. Adélka had been the darling of the family as a child, the sweetie, the charmer, for whom all the brothers would have laid down their lives. That wretched marriage. She'd fallen for the gentlemanly son of a ruined family. A drunken, idle nobody. How they had foreseen this! What had they not tried to save Adélka from him! How much heartache, how much unhappiness! And that villain had left his wife for Adélka, and this was poor little Adélka's life. How she'd struggled with the family for this man. Their mother had still been alive at the time. How she'd regretted demanding that they regard her chosen one as she did. Dreadful.

He read on.

There were two possibilities. Either she risked starvation for herself and her children, or she went on suffering this martyrdom. She was ashamed to say it, but she hadn't a krajcár and couldn't help, the father never brought a fillér home these days, he couldn't stand work and what could she earn with what she could do... They were living on potatoes and dry bread, and even that was in short supply. She'd hung on and on, beyond human endurance she'd hung on, but this couldn't go on for ever, she hadn't been able to send the children to school this term, here it was, November, and the poor little things were hanging around the house. They were growing up before her eyes like street urchins, and she had to ignore it... what would become of them, uneducated, with a bad example set them, never mind the filth that came in from the street... If he ever came to Pest, would he come and see her, see with his own eyes what was going on and advise her...

84

He flung down the letter and clenched his fists.

'Now she wants my advice. But when I could see it all coming...'

He felt a terrible pang of conscience. He couldn't relax and could scarcely wait for Lina to come in.

She came in happily, presented her face for a kiss and asked what was news in the office.

"You can ask that? When Adélka's letter's here?"

"Oh, Adélka. Yes, I suppose it's very sad."

Pista was astounded that his wife wasn't taking it as tragically as he.

"My God," said Lina, "it's her own fault. Everybody could see what would happen. Guszti Rába, what a one to fall for. Don't upset yourself, darling, you don't have to take what Adélka says as Gospel, she fantasises, and when she's depressed she scribbles it all down. Afterwards she's sorry."

"But they're starving."

"Huh, darling, people have their ups and downs... It was different when she turned her nose up at what I had to offer... When I was living, after the revolutions, in one miserable room that had been requisitioned for us, and she came to visit and saw that I was watching every penny and looked down on us. But I treated her properly, gave her something decent... I couldn't give them as much as they'd have liked, and however much money I'd had I wouldn't have given it to them, because there's no point in throwing money down the drain, and the Romanians[25] had requisitioned my father's last horse, his last grain of corn, there was half a kiló of bacon left in the pantry and they took that too... and she came to me with demands like that..."

Pista's head swam as he listened. He'd forgotten the whole business long ago, and was astonished that his wife could remember it all down to the last exchange of words as if it had happened yesterday and there'd been nothing since. He could only remember that on that occasion, against his better judgement, he'd taken his wife's side against his brother-in-law over something that he hadn't understood at the time, and they'd quarrelled so badly that for ten years they hadn't had anything to do with one another. But for him the whole thing was in the past, and he was simply filled with an unquenchable yearning for his sister, his little sister, whom he'd only known as a young girl at home, whom he conceived as extraordinarily lovely, honoured the beauty of her kind, and now that precious child was starving... Since then he'd just waited and waited for it to turn out just once that Adélka had been right... And now here was the opposite, but he couldn't fight it, because all he felt was that his little sister was starving... and her children...

"What does she want with five children?" said Lina decisively and with conviction, "If they can do that, then they can just look after them as well... Children? For somebody else to look after? And her own weren't enough, she has to take on her husband's bastards into the bargain."

With which she went out, evidently for the soup.

"My God, what am I to do?" he exclaimed, clutching his hands to his head.

This movement reminded him of his mother. She'd had this mannerism, poor thing. Did that mean he'd inherited his mother's mentality?

He sat down in his place, unfolded the white napkin and spread it on his lap.

Adélka was a qualified teacher. How often had he thought of inviting her to apply for a post in the city and getting her appointed, but the idea always foundered on the two women. On his wife, who wouldn't hear of such a thing, who'd rather leave him than live in the same town as her sister-in-law. And on Adélka too, who never did apply. Now what was he to do? Should he try to get her in? At the age of thirty-four, with five children? Where? And what could he do with her? And this time too, what would Lina have to say to the idea?

Family trouble is the worst of the lot.

Lina brought in the soup and called into the other room: "Lunch!"

The children could be heard banging about, knocking over chairs, but they opened the door timidly and came quietly in with laughing, shining faces, in the manner of frightened young animals, as they applied the brakes to their temperament. And their mother addressed them as such:

"Now then, what's going on? You're rushing around like a herd of pigs..."

The boys came to the table.

"Have you washed your hands?"

"Yes," they both replied in unison. They displayed their paws, on which signs of recent water and ink-stains were equally visible.

"All right, sit down!" commanded Lina, because although

she could see that the washing was less than perfect she didn't feel like saying anything about it.

The boys sat down.

"Dad," exclaimed Kálmuska, the younger, "is it true that at Kardics bácsi's you ate with gold knives and forks?"

"Where did you get that nonsense from?" asked Lina.

"In school they say that for big guests they always lay the table with gold. Didn't they do that for you?"

"Be quiet and eat your soup. Tuck your napkin in."

The boys sensed that there was a difficult mood and were silent. They just exchanged an occasional giggle.

"I won't let you sit with us if this goes on," said their mother. "You can't have the two of them in the same room. I'll lay for one in the shed and the other under the gateway."

The two boys were silent for a moment, a little later a great roar of laughter went up. So fantastic did their mother's idea seem, they couldn't repress it. Kálmuska choked on his soup and coughed and spluttered for some time, had to leave the table and go into the other room to finish laughing and coughing, then came back.

Pista gave them a stern look and began to eat. The soup was very good, and he was very fond of soups. But when he'd almost finished his helping, in absent-minded fashion, the spoon fell from his hand and he could eat no more. Here he was, eating marvellous food, because Lina was a wonderful cook, all his life he'd been getting the best... and there was his sister starving, with her five children... Who could say whether there was anything to eat in the house today...

"Aren't you having any more?"

"No, thanks."

Lina took his dish out.

While she was out of the room the boys perked up.

"Dad. It isn't true, is it, Kardics bácsi doesn't have gold cutlery," said Berci, the elder.

"Be quiet. Don't talk rubbish."

"Only the King eats with a golden spoon," said Kálmuska.

"Silly!" Berci chipped in. "The Queen's children are going hungry now, in Lequeitio.[26]"

Pista looked at the two boys, his eyes blazing.

"Are you going to be quiet?"

Lina brought in the main course. It was pasta with curds. With sour cream and crackling. The boys looked at it, electrified. Their favourite food.

"Dad," said Berci, "the Holubs had an American visitor, an American businessman, ever so rich. When they served pasta with curds for dinner he thought the crackling was raisins, that it was a sweet, and when he got his and tasted the pork fat he was so ill he threw up."

Pista laughed despite himself.

"Who tells you this stuff?"

And he went on laughing. It was so funny.

"Péter König said in class," said the boys, cheering up at making their father laugh.

Even Lina was laughing. With these children there you had to laugh. She gave her son's face an affectionate stroke, and was happy that he'd broken the mood. She didn't want her husband to be overcome with grief for Adélka.

"Those Americans know how to eat," she said, with house-wifely superiority.

"Actually, all they eat is out of tins. Everything's tinned over there."

"Even goulash?" laughed Pista.

"Not just goulash, Dad, all their food. They just tell the cook what they want and out she goes and buys it in tins, soup, meat, sauce, vegetables."

"That's what you think, you fathead," said his mother, and Pista started to laugh so much that he went bright red.

So lunch was rescued, and it was in quite a good mood that they listened to the boys arguing.

"Bring the dessert," said Lina to Berci.

The boy got up, went to the sideboard, on which the fruit-dish stood ready. There were apples in it which they'd got from the farm, from Grandfather. He put it on the table with great care so that none should fall off, and was very proud of succeeding.

They each took an apple, and with that lunch was over.

"You'll find out what's what if ever there's trouble," said Lina, moralising, "but now you're all right, because Daddy provides everything, but if you don't study and work you'll turn out to be useless layabouts."

After lunch Lina went out to direct the washing-up and to dry the things. The maid was a peasant girl, also from the farm, and had to be taught all the time, couldn't be trusted with the washing-up.

Pista took out from the desk a pink money-order form, addressed it to Adélka and made it out for fifty pengős. Then he carefully took his wallet from his back trouser pocket, extracted the bank note, the first money he'd earned as Town Clerk, and handed it to Berci.

"My boy, take this round to the post office and send it off. I can't let anyone else. We have to see to such things ourselves.

"They won't take it before two o'clock," said young Berci.

"All right, go at two o'clock, then."

With that he left the order conspicuously on the corner of the desk, so that Lina would see it if she came in, and lay down to doze for a bit if he could.

When Lina came in she saw it at once, went over and read it. Pista was glad that he'd written nothing on the chit except 'your dearly loving brother'.

Lina read it and threw it down. She left the room without saying a word.

He was relieved, however. He felt as if he'd redeemed himself with those fifty pengős. As if he'd paid a very irksome debt, one for which he wasn't being dunned, but which caused his soul all the more pain. Somehow the thought came to him of the decision of his student days always to be a member of the Assistance Board, which he'd founded, or rather re-organised, and he'd worked out whole plans of how much he meant to subscribe annually until the Board became so rich that every child, rich or poor, would have his school-books provided by it. This was a very fine and inspiring project, which he worked out in the course of his University studies, and he gave it many warm hours in the imaginings of his heart. But what had happened? War had broken out, he'd been called up. (Even then he'd gladly have sent something – if he hadn't had to help his mother...) Then he'd been captured. When he got back home he was pleased that on his meagre income he was able to support his wife and family. Never in his life had he spoken to anyone of this secret plan, and often only the knowledge that nobody knew of this beautiful concept had kept him from blushing secretly. It came to him that now he was Town Clerk he would do what he'd not been able to do as Cultural Adviser by way of helping the schools under him...

It was the same with his family obligations. It made him feel inexpressibly good that he'd acted today. Adélka would feel good. She'd be impressed and reassured that her letter had met with such a response. She'd see that blood hadn't turned to water. Nor could it be right that, at this time, when such awful consequences were imminent, they should evade their responsibilities towards the starving on the pretext that she had been told at the time that she'd do much better to marry a rich, reliable man...

So bang had gone the fifty pengős, he wasn't going to follow Makróczy's lead with that. Because Makróczy'd always pampered his faithful, every week held a dinner or some meal for them. He was a keen huntsman and picked his hunting companions from his supporters. He used to get them together at the fish restaurant on the Tisza embankment, and there they'd carouse with wine and gypsies. Therefore they were his men for life or death. Well, he'd wanted to set up a reserve fund like that or go out for a few beers occasionally... Now that plan had folded straight away. He wouldn't have told Lina about this fifty pengős. As Cultural Adviser he'd never had any outgoings of this sort, and Lina wouldn't have agreed. But he must do something. He was gradually getting into an awkward situation with people, remaining indebted to everybody...

Well, never mind. It would be much better if Adélka and the children were eating, poor things. He kept an eye on the clock, dared not sleep, stayed awake the whole time. When it struck two he called to Berci that he could go to the post office.

The boy went out and Pista heard Lina ask from the kitchen where he was going.

"To the post office," exclaimed Berci proudly.

He waited for Lina to say something. But he heard not a word. So he relaxed and went to sleep for a while.

He woke up to Lina coming in.

She came in making a lot of noise. She didn't speak, but there was a storm around her. She was carrying a little piece of paper and threw it onto the desk.

When she saw that he was awake she spoke.

"So you've sent it!"

He made no reply. Lina bustled about the room, straightened the chairs, cleared the table.

"Poor thing," he said at length, to calm his wife. "A drop in the ocean... She deserved it."

"Precisely," said Lina, and stopped, duster in hand. "Precisely. She deserved it... So now you'll be sending drops to the ocean?"

"I will not, I've done with it once and for all."

"What, once and for all? More likely that's just the beginning. Or is that to last them all their lives?"

"I can do no more. I'm not Croesus, and I'm not ruining myself on her account."

Lina wept, wiped her eyes.

"Look, Pista, you've set out on a very dangerous road. If you want to collect all your relations, the uncles, your own generation, the youngsters, then I don't know where it'll all end. Are you going to let the whole pack of blood-suckers feed off you?"

Pista jumped as if bitten by a snake. He stood up and placed himself in front of his wife.

"What did you say?" he shouted at her at the top of his voice. "Are the Kopjásses a pack of blood-suckers in your view? What in God's name is going on here? Is that the way to speak to me? Have you lost your head like this over fifty pengős? Did you give me that money? Was that Szentkálnay money? Did the Szentkálnays help me out of poverty with that? Have I lived sixteen years for your father to send a hare and a basket of rotten apples?"

"Rotten?" said Lina quietly. "Can you honestly say they're rotten? Doesn't my father pick out the best? You insult my father, who'd give his life for you? Who'd go without himself, so as to be able to end you the finest, the best?"

Pista realised that his tongue had run away with him, because he didn't care for his father-in-law, who looked down on him for not earning more, and endured having his daughter here as a cook and maid... But he had to admit that the old man put a lot of thought into always being gracious. But he couldn't unsay it, and his onslaught had put Lina's 'pack of blood-suckers' completely in the shade.

"You've never had a fillér-worth of trouble from any of my relations. Because even if they were rotten, at least they send them, and you guzzle them. I saw you take a bruised apple out of the basket at table, but now I know that you suspected my father even then of picking out the bad ones at home for you to gobble up. But you ate them all the same."

Pista had such a rush of blood that he couldn't reply. Lina went on:

"There they are, in your belly. You haven't brought them up. They'll make you fat. You'll be even fatter, you'll be able to hold your head up, because I've fed you on Szentkálnay apples. You may swell up and burst, you're such a great man. You think I can't see that you're too big for your skin... You come down the yard as if you were coming here to visit beggars... And you

91

chuck fifty pengő notes about... I didn't give it to you? Then where the hell did you get it? You didn't have a single krajcár last time we counted up. So either you nicked it off me and put it away so that I wouldn't know, or you've already started sucking blood like a mosquito, and you've stolen city money."

At this Pista staggered back like a butcher pole-axeing a bull.

"Nicked it be damned," he said, picking up his wife's word, although he didn't usually use such harsh, strong terms, nor did she, except when she lost her temper. "That was honestly earned. I got it in the office for a contract that I drew up. Steal from you? What? What I put in, I steal back. To hell with this whole..."

He straightened his tie, which he had loosened when he lay down, and got ready to go out.

Lina was on the point of saying something, but choked it back, and for a minute stared her husband out; he saw now, and was again horrified, that in a moment his wife had become terribly old. Her face had fallen, the skin hung slackly from her cheek-bones. Her eyes were black holes, blazing with hatred.

Line didn't speak but turned on her heel and went out.

At this he tidied himself and quickly, as if escaping, so as not to be stopped, ran out of the house.

For what was perhaps the first time, he left without a kiss.

12.

He strode wildly ahead, his eyes burning with tears.

He hurried away from the city. He couldn't have stood meeting anybody.

All of a sudden he saw his life as hopeless. What did it all matter if one stood alone and couldn't live by those principles that ruled one, that made life worth living? He really did love his brothers and sister more than words could tell. He didn't think of how much more able he was than his brothers, of how they were backward in comparison. But even if that were the case, wasn't one chick in a brood better than the others so as to help the rest in their misfortunes and weaknesses?

Here was this election. But surely it wasn't he that had brought it about? It wasn't his ability that Fate had rewarded with this, the whole thing was mere chance. An act of God. Had He acted in this way so that Lina Szentkálnay should triumph?

Had God arranged everything for the benefit of Lina Szent-kálnay? Might Adél Kopjáss not get so much as fifty pengős? Anyway. It would all come out in the wash. There'd be another fifty pengős to take their place. And a hundred. And a thousand. And ten thousand.

Because here there were fantastic possibilities. Lina Szent-kálnay didn't even dream what might yet be...

His head rang for an hour. The quarrel with his wife went on and on. Now, inwardly, he didn't refrain from using the harshest of words. She was a good woman, hard-working, thrifty, a house-keeper, cook, laundress, cleaner. What more could be want? She could do everything.

But he wanted as a life-partner not a maid-of-all-work but a kindred spirit. He wasn't going to achieve his aims with this woman. Because she'd drag him down into the mud.

Blood-suckers. She'd called them blood-suckers. So what's that? A species of slave?... Blood-suckers... Wasn't it she that sucked his blood? She'd sucked out all the idealism from his brain, all that was fine. Furthermore, he really need be nothing more than a farm-hand. Out on the estate – the ninety-acre estate – the only way to make a living would be by abasing themselves into dung-worms. He wouldn't agree to that.

Was this to be his partner on the upward path? She was going to be a drag on his career, a dead weight, and she'd never realise that the Cinderella days were over. Now she'd have to change into a new woman, a career-building woman.

But he had nobody. Because this woman blocked the way if he began to be friendly with anybody. She didn't need anything but a couple of stupid servant-girls like herself, the vet's wife, with whom she chatted on the phone about cooking hares.

If one wanted to take power into one's hands one needed allies. Who was his ally? Whom had he to sit with and discuss his plans? He didn't even consider her friends worth thinking of, but he thought of his young brother Menyhért.

He ought somehow to get him here at his side. Had he any better friends than Menyhért and Albert? Especially Menyhért. He was like a second self, so well did they understand one another. On the few occasions that they got together there was no end to the arguing that stimulated them both, and it was wonderful how they had ideas that were fundamentally the same, yet argued so much over details, it was a real clash of champions, as if they were standing on the piste, sword in hand, dazzled by one another's master-strokes, for both of them were adherents of the noble and gentle warfare of fencing.

There was no arguing with Lina. She, although a woman, argued like a prize-fighter intent on knocking his opponent cold. Pack of blood-suckers... How could she think such a thing? This was the first word with which she'd deigned to express her divergent view. But how could she pick the foulest, most disgusting of all withering, gnawing expressions. Follow that if you can!

Why had his thoughts bounced back to Lina in this way?... Because Lina and Menyhért were not friends... Why not?... Because Menyhért had once urged Lina into an unlucky bit of business which hadn't come off, so now Lina had every reason to hate Menyhért for the rest of her life. But Menyhért had thought the matter out very well... During the war soldiers had brought back a lot of works of art from the theatre of operations. Despite the strictest prohibitions from the military authorities the squaddies had cut out altar-pieces, stuffed them into their packs and brought them home. Or liturgical objects, gold and silver chalices, and the costly treasures of great houses. He'd been there. A grenade would effect an entrance. A shell would wreck a whole palace, and might not a soldier pick up a shining fragment from among the smouldering beams and put it in his pocket, something nice for the children to play with back home?

Well, Menyhért had the idea, as a museum man, of setting up a company for the rescuing of military plunder. By this means it would be possible to rescue art treasures for the museums, or in some cases to return them to their owners after the war, and at the same time to protect the poor soldiers, who would have booty which, although they didn't know it, was sometimes worth millions, from being plundered by unscrupulous sharks for a few fillérs. Lina had a trace of Armenian blood; the Szentkálnays had once been called Karaker, goodness knows how they acquired the name Szentkálnay, and so she too had business acumen. She soon realised that there could be money in this, and she sank the bit that she had from her father into Menyhért's business... Well, who was to blame when the military authorities refused to permit the business on the pretext that bad blood would be caused if legally permitted trading in war booty took place? So the money that had gone into the preliminaries was lost, whereas an astute Jew didn't bother with the military authorities, but just went ahead and made a packet out of the idea.

So Lina mourned the loss of those three hundred and seventy koronas that Menyhért had 'tricked her out of' in three instalments. First two hundred, then one hundred, finally another seventy. Now of course she remembered them as 'gold koronas', although recently she'd come across five mint-condition hundred-korona pieces between the pillow slips in a chest. She'd actually forgotten where she'd put them, and only rediscovered them after they were out of circulation. True, she'd cursed herself enough for such a loss, but she forgave herself this trifle, whereas she refused to have anything to do with Menyhért because of the three hundred and seventy.

He must persuade him to come to Zsarátnok.

An idea now dawned in Pista's mind like a stroke of genius. The city was in the process of building a museum. Menyhért must be invited to become its Director.

Actually, Pista had thought of this a long while previously, and as Cultural Adviser had been concerned with the construction of the museum, but there'd been no chance of saying anything because Makróczy's wife had some handicapped brother, a Gymnasium teacher or something, and they meant to make him Director despite his lack of museum experience. In those days, who would have ventured to cross swords with Makróczy over such a matter?

And on the subject of Makróczy, it occurred to Pista that if he was now Town Clerk it was his younger brother to whom the opportunities would come. Menyhért was obviously a first-class man, on the staff of the Department of Antiquities of the National Museum. He'd published articles and books. He'd worked on countless excavations. He had a good reputation, and the only reason that the Hungarian Academy of Sciences hadn't published his work on the tombs of the Conquest period[27] was that their capital had been tied up in war bonds...

This cheered him up completely. He'd write to Menyhért at once, tell him to come down. He should obtain testimonials from well-known lecturers, from the best sources, and then he couldn't fail to push his appointment through. And then he'd be saved, because he'd have a marvellous friend and helper, as Menyhért wasn't just a one-track theoretician, he was full of imagination – wasn't he a Kopjáss? – and if the two of them put their heads together they could create a whole new world in Zsarátnok.

He himself didn't know how far he'd walked on the outskirts of the city. He 'd been striding along the wide, flat roads like a whirlwind, passing an unending row of little peasant houses, hurrying past fathomless mud and puddles. At last he came to the villa estate.

Here he stopped and looked round.

It seemed fated; he'd been meaning to come here for a long time. He'd wanted to see this development, and now gazed around curiously, wondering which house was to be his.

There were a large number of villas here, brand new houses for civil servants.

He would have taken any of them. Well-built, pleasant houses with gardens, in each of which a family could settle comfortably. Nice, big, shining windows, verandas everywhere. Red roofs, covered with tiles and asbestos, these new asbestos sheets were good, as if the houses were roofed with sheets of patina-ed copper. He went slowly along. Someone greeted him, he replied politely, but didn't know who it was. He was coming to himself. The Town Clerk, yes, it was; the new Town Clerk, and that was he.

. He reached Nagyerdei Avenue. This was the edge of the estate. Here there were only big villas. He recognised Belatiny's.

He went slowly past, had a good look at it, and smiled to himself; what would he do with such a big house? Would this suit Lina, who wanted to do all the housework herself?

Why had he thought of the Belatiny villa for Lina, he asked himself. Of course, she too knew that this was a house like a castle. Perhaps there was something in Lina after all?... Could she imagine herself in a house like that?

Suddenly his feet grew roots.

A woman was walking in front of him. A tall, erect, slender woman, extremely elegant, in a light-coloured suit. No umbrella. A little hat, like a Viking helmet, on her head. This too very light in colour. The whole refinedly unsophisticated and yet refinedly upper-class...

Heavens, it was Magdaléna Szentkálnay.

For some seconds Pista couldn't catch his breath. He felt that he must turn and run, rush away, gallop off. Out of the world... And then he was frightened that she'd go away, that he'd lose sight of her, and he strode after her.

Magdaléna was walking at an even pace. There was something unusual about her as she walked on alone. It was as if a great sadness hung over her. He couldn't have said why he felt that she was sad. She wasn't hanging her head, but neither was she walking happily. There was a spring in her step, but a certain stiffness about her posture. Her arms were hanging dejectedly. Perhaps that was it...

Such was her effect on him, he stared at her as if bewitched. He ought to run to her, overtake her somehow... Say good afternoon... If she caught sight of him, would she recognise him? Heaven help him, he couldn't stand it, his heart was pounding so, its pumping was almost audible in his breathing.

Fate again... What did it want with him? Why had it brought this woman before him just now? His thinking stopped, nothing more came into his mind, he was transformed into a running engine, but he was terrified that he'd lose her... Why should he? There she went, she couldn't vanish like a ghost... She was a woman, walking along in her two little shoes, with steady, even steps. Why was she out alone?... Did she want to be alone?... Was she out for a walk or walking into town?... Or had she been visiting somewhere and was on the way home?

Anyway, of course they lived up there, and where was Feri Boronkay? Was it true that they didn't love one another? He'd heard rumours to that effect more than once. How could that be? Was it possible that her husband might not love such a woman?... And she her husband?... Then why were they together?

But he couldn't bear to think about it. If he came a little closer he was overcome by a kind of great heat, if he fell back, by dread. Why did she have so great an effect on him? Would he ever meet her? And if so...

Now Magdaléna had stopped at a gate and was ringing the bell.

She hadn't noticed him and he didn't know what to do next. If he hurried on he'd catch her up, and what would happen? If he stopped he'd draw attention to himself. He just went mechanically on.

Now he was level with her, three paces away. The gate was being opened to Magdaléna, but the passing man attracted her attention. He greeted her stiffly, raised his hat, Magdaléna looked at him. She acknowledged the greeting, nodded and smiled.

Then she went into the villa.

He glanced after her and hurried away. All that he'd been able to see inside were leafy trees. The gate was of wrought iron, and the whole gateway revealed to the onlooker a gravelled, yellow, gleaming, moist patch of garden. Magdaléna went in and under the glazed canopy to the steps...

This was a big villa.

That was his first thought, and as he hurried off he stopped at a distance and looked at the house.

It was a really lovely house. The sort one saw in the architectural magazines in the Golden Pheasant coffee-house.

He went slowly as far as the forest, then turned back. He crossed the road to the other side, took a good look at the villa. But he was anxious that Magdaléna might look out of a window, so he hurried past the house faster than he would have liked.

This was another world. Different from the one in which he lived. Could they meet here?...

No, this one would have to be besieged, taken by storm. He'd have to break in.

13.

As he went down the road, his eyes on the ground, someone spoke to him.

"Excuse me, Town Clerk," a thin man approached him, "Forgive my disturbing your thoughts. But I was so pleased to see the Town Clerk that I couldn't resist the urge to renew our former acquaintance just a little... You don't remember me? We were at school together. Well, of course, it's been seven years. I was a year below you, so I knew you better than you knew me."

"Yes, I know the face, really, but the name..."

"I'm Hollaky, little Jani Hollaky. We had a few good games together in the school yard. Children still knew how to play in those days. Football hadn't caught on then, we used to play tick... How idyllically beautiful school was in peacetime. In the good old days of peace, Town Clerk, the golden, precious, good world of peace."

Little Jani Hollaky had an extremely unpleasant voice. Pista wouldn't have been greatly disappointed if they hadn't met, if he hadn't recognised him, if he hadn't remembered everything, if he'd known how to get away. But it wasn't in his nature to be impolite, so he had to listen to little Jani Hollaky all the way to the Market Square, while he told him his whole life-story. From school up to the present. His failures, for everybody had it in for him something awful. Perhaps it was because of his voice... Pista at least became so irritated by that harsh, cawing voice, that tiresome, monotonous chatter, that he'd have had no compunction about kicking him to shut him up. At the Club he stretched out his hand just at the moment when Jani Hollaky was about to make his request... for a little *protekció*...[28]

Poor chap, he was left standing stock-still there in the street, looking at the Town Clerk's back as he hurried, almost fled, into the Club, where, it appeared, little Jani Hollaky was not admitted. He imagined what Hollaky must be thinking of him and felt a twinge of malicious pleasure, because through him he'd acquired a loathing for his former school-fellows.

He went up the stairs. The attendant quickly relieved him of his coat at the cloakroom. He looked at the attendant, who was wearing a brand-new uniform with an oak-sprig on the collar.

"Sir," said the attendant, "if you could spare a moment some time..."

"Why, what's the matter, Janikám?" he said, and left him.

It was only when he'd gone into the lounge that he realised that this wasn't Jani, that was Hollaky. He gave a laugh, because this chap too was presumably after *protekció*.

He hadn't been in the Club since the election. He looked round to see who was there. He saw the usual figures. Every gentlemen's club has its regulars who do the same things every day at the same time. There are those who read the papers, those who sprawl in the corner of the red settee, escaping the delights of home, where they would likewise sprawl, rather like cast-off clothing, but their nerves need the heavy atmosphere of the Club. He didn't feel at home in this big room with its head-high panelling, and very seldom came here.

"Hello, Pista," called a fat man with a wide, laughing face. "What're you doing here in the back of beyond?"

Pista had last met him in the army, where he'd been a major. He'd been at school with him too, but his senior by a year; Jani Hollaky was right, Pista knew him better.

"How was the harvest?" he asked, because it came back to him that this was the landowner Bálint Mándy.

"Haha," said Bálint with a loud laugh, "my dear boy, I don't have anything to do with oats these days. Unless I eat 'em myself. I'm not a peasant now, I'm a gentleman. Finished with the land."

"You don't say! What do you do with your time?"

"I keep occupied, dear boy, I keep occupied. As I've nothing else to do I keep an eye on the love affairs of the younger generation. Poor kids, they come to me with their great problems in the hope that I've never heard the like. Whereas *iam vidi ventos alienos*[29]."

He had a marvellous laugh. His healthy teeth filled his finely-shaped mouth, but when he laughed the good looks of his youth shone from his face once more. He'd been quite a lad, had turned the head of many a girl, been famous for it in his time.

Suddenly he took Pista by the arm and led him to a corner.

"Well, the kissing scandal's been taken care of!"

"What scandal?"

"Ye Gods, you haven't even heard about it... You know, these young fellows today are different from what we used to be at their age. When we were after a girl we were happy if she gave us a kindly smile. These chaps come straight to the point. They get bored with lengthy courtships, so at a party, when they were desperate for a kiss, three of 'em grabbed a girl. Two held her arms and the third held the beauty's mouth so she couldn't scream and they all gave the sweet young thing a good kissing."

He brayed his laughter, and was so happy, he could have been taken for the very model of health and good humour.

"But that's terrible," said Pista.

"Terrible enough," laughed Bálint, "Because it caused quite a stir. The girl naturally complained to her parents. The father's an ex-army officer, hundred per cent disabled, and having nothing else to do made a terrific fuss. They got up a court of honour and asked me to become president of it. So I gave the boys a bit of a shock. I listened to all they had to say, then I said to them: 'Well, lads, *status quo* is that as her father can't obtain satisfaction himself, due to injuries received in the service of his country... it becomes the duty of us members of this court of honour to take you on... As, however, you're still schoolboys, for the time being all we can do is to put the matter on record, and when you come of duelling age we'll call you out and shoot it out with you, according to the book, at twenty five paces. After each exchange of shots we advance five paces... so that in the end we're shooting from across a handkerchief... Won't bother us, you know. What's left of our lives is nothing to us. On the other hand, some of us are tough enough to do it, and we'd consider it a fitting end to fall on the field of battle for the honour of a lady."

He laughed again and said:

"Of course, the boys were scared, but especially because they could see that they were in unheard-of hot water with their people if the school found out about it. They were only poor boys. One was the son of a widow of a General, the second was a war orphan, the third was the son of some pensioner, on a scholarship, which he could easily have lost, because the school isn't as easy-going as it was in our time. Discipline there's as hard as in barracks... So, dear boy, that's how we pass the time..."

Pista looked at his friend as if he were dreaming. He lived for this, indeed, this was what kept him going. Strange world, strange people. It was as if a living fossil were smiling there in front of him.

A well-built, powerful, healthy, intelligent man, and he was spending his life amusing himself. Like fish in nice warm water, these men danced and played in that social current that carried them along. Everywhere they were the leaders, those that set the standard, the decision-takers. Everywhere there was a place where only the chosen might stop, sit, speak: these were they. And with clear heads, warm hearts, goodwill and cheerful happiness they basked in the exalted light, the good air, the warmth.

Around them the legion of mankind bore the yoke, toiling desperately, their brows furrowed with care, their necks bent low to the ground, on and mechanically on. They, fat and happy, spent their time in idle chatter and laughter.

The previous summer Pista had taken a mud-cure for the rheumatism that he'd developed in prison-camp. In the lake of warm water he'd noticed what Society was. There was one place in the big pool, where the spring came up, where people said the water was bottomless, so it must have been twenty-five or thirty metres deep, and here the pipes from the pump-room went down into it. Here the members of Society had set up camp. And here those that belonged to the common herd might not so much as show themselves. This was nowhere explicitly stated in the regulations, but it came about naturally, on the basis of the rules of life. The members of Society were all good swimmers, horsemen, sportsmen. The common herd, however, with their bad legs, in the grind of toil went without all those things that strengthen body and soul. They hadn't the time for them, nor the means. They watched from afar as the sons and daughters of Society ploughed about with powerful strokes above the spring. As they hung from the dangling metal hooks, sat on the piece of wood known as the chatter-bench, which was an essential part of the fabric.

If somebody not of their number strayed that way he felt out of place in no time, because he found out that he didn't belong. Here was assembled a company of friends, and nobody that didn't belong had any right to pry out its inner, private and confidential secrets.

But how did they manage to recognise one another? All the swimmers in the lake were only patients in the clinic, including them. This was no family outing, it wasn't the outcome of some casual arrangement for friends to go out together. And nevertheless it was as if they were members of a single family; those people seemed to have been brought up together all their lives, linked by common memories.

And so it was. This social stratum was one, united and homogeneous. If anybody appeared whom social threads joined to this Society, they recognised each other at once, and in an hour were accepted, spent the time together. Anybody that was not one of them couldn't have made the same progress in ten years as a child of the same class from any part of the country made in the first moment.

This was a powerful organisation. In its hands were the authority and governmental power of the whole country. All of them were in high positions, senior officers of the army, mighty landowners. Secret societies had no sign that bound their members together more surely than this class that had done well in life.

And they were all cheerful, good-humoured, happy souls. Even the sick, even those who were out of sorts, once they were at home in that private world, were stripped of life's every care and united there in warm, welcoming, understanding reassurance and conviviality.

But the material basis which had brought this social network into being was crumbling terribly. The salaries of senior officials were falling. This year they'd been cut three times. The landowners were losing their life-blood. Those that had a thousand acres were penniless, buried in a mass of debt. Those with five thousand acres were in debt for a million pengős or two, and were only kept afloat by the special decree for the protection of the farmer. All of them were landowners in name alone. The only reason that they didn't get rid of their properties was that they could find no purchaser at auction. There were those whose ancestral estates had come down in the form of mansions of sixty rooms, and they still clung to existence around the mansion while the hyenas of the salesrooms auctioned the clothes of one or another in the great Budapest town house.

The lands of the hereditary aristocracy, the Körtvélyessys, Cseresznyéssys and Meggyesis, were now in the hands of the Schwartzes and the Weiszes.

And if it was so with the highest, the grief and the poverty were even greater at lower levels. They had no money in their pockets nowadays. The salary of a district administrator[30] had fallen to a hundred and sixty, and on that small sum alone he often had to keep a number of children. He couldn't obtain a suitable home, such as befitted his position, and none the less even then he had the authority and dignity of his office. This produced such tragic conflicts that the cutting of the Gordian knot was more and more often being performed with a pistol-bullet. And then families were left behind, and they fell away to nothing. They were scattered over the earth like the meteorite fragments of shattered heavenly bodies, and the debris would lie worthless for as long as could be foreseen.

Pista thought of this as he listened to the good Major's chatter, and pondered the road to disaster.

By this time the clubs were the last refuge. Here, without the outlay of a single fillér, one could still remain a gentleman. For there were still institutions that came to one's aid. At all the resorts they swarmed over the official accommodation with the aid of doctors' notes, and ate the sternly prescribed diets; but that was why these were they that stayed up till morning on the terraces of club restaurants in the fine summer nights. With a glass of mineral water, if there was no champagne, how they could enjoy themselves, sing, delight in life as if there were still, as before, the coach and four standing under the planes, waiting for the card-playing gentlemen to finish their *ferbli*.[31]

Pista listened absent-mindedly as the Major talked and talked, but it truly grieved his heart to hear this lovable man, his soul rich in every good and fine quality, tell tragi-comic tales of the dismal circumstances of the final destruction of his property.

"Believe you me, dear boy, Hungarian law takes a draconian stand against the debtor. The old law-givers maintained that anybody that fell into debt was either a gambler or a drunkard. Both deserved all the punishment possible, so as to become a terrible example to others. Now, however, a new world has come along. The price of money has gone up, the price of produce has gone down. So if anybody's been a good farmer, he's finished. Because he'll have taken loans to put his land to rights after it's been wrecked and devastated in the revolutions and the

Romanian invasion. And if anybody borrowed a thousand pengős in the days of thirty-pengő wheat, these days he has to pay four times the interest now that wheat is at eight pengős, or rather, he's supposed to, but in fact he can't do it, he's scarcely making enough for bare essentials. An ox that cost a thousand will fetch a hundred and eighty today. Try living on that... And then, when you're staring ruin in the face, the bank turns sour. Everybody that sees the chance is entitled to declare you bankrupt. Your creditor is so frightened of this that he gives you further loans over and above what he should so that whatever happens you don't go under. Because in the event of bankruptcy, immediately the president of the court of some other town is appointed receiver, and his deputy is likewise some magistrate or other. If you hire a lawyer, that makes it worse still. There were three hearings over my farm, and the total costs equalled the value of the place..."

At this he suddenly stood up and looked at Pista.

"It's true, my boy, anyway, I congratulate you as a future villa-owner."

"Me?" said Pista, taken aback.

"Of course. It's a very nice villa. In the whole town there isn't another so perfect. It was built to go on show in the competition for the world's most beautiful villa."

"I don't know what you're talking about."

"The Boronkay villa, of course, Andris bácsi, the Alispán, told me that Kardics wants to let you have the Boronkay villa."

Pista was silent, and for two reasons. Firstly, it was the greatest possible surprise, and secondly, his blood was suffusing him as always, Magdaléna... indirectly perhaps, but Magdaléna had been mentioned... and it was Magdaléna's villa that they meant him to have...

"Feri Boronkay's going up as Secretary of State in the Ministry of Agriculture."

And the old soldier bowed his head and said gloomily:

"Well, that's the best thing for poor Feri... That way he may get by somehow... He's dreadfully in debt... Be careful they don't pile too much borrowing on you for this property, because then you'll never make anything on it... That Pig Farm's really done for them... Can't understand how they came to go in for it just when the bubble burst... Well, of course, it was Makróczy's fault. That's why they had to throw him out."

This was all news to Pista. Every word a spotlight shining on things that he hadn't previously been aware of.

So... Makróczy had had something else to answer for, not just the awful brick that he'd dropped in the Council antechamber about *zs.v.* That had merely come as a handy opportunity to move against him. Pista shuddered gently at this, for he could see his own fate foreshadowed. He must be careful not to commit any crime, for then anything he said could be used against him if they wanted to get rid of him.

"But if you're clever and strike a good bargain, it's a valuable property. All this'll pass. Nothing lasts for ever, even the impossible. If you can bring it off you'll be setting your children up well in that villa, my boy."

Strangers were approaching and they stopped speaking.

Pista was so excited that he couldn't stay there, he made some excuse and left them in the Club to their chatter and gossip.

He looked in at the office as well. There he found Dr. Péterfi, and he asked him directly what this business of the Pig Farm was all about.

He learnt some awful things. It was an absolute scandal. The Boronkay villa had been built with money trimmed from the Pig Farm. These trimmings had been the undoing of Boronkay, who'd been Director of the farm.

Pista didn't grasp the whole of the disturbing business at first hearing. But he was so chilled by it that he felt the need to run home to Lina... He yearned to be at home in the little flat, where they'd lived until now so securely and peacefully, and he hadn't dared to think that he'd have to enter this creaking, crumbling big world... It'd be better just to shelter in the little nest.

Oh, but he wouldn't have wished at this moment to go home to the Boronkay villa. How much better the little rented place was...

Bright, cold cleanliness, compared with the pleasant, warm, scruffy corner. But how was he to pacify Lina?

14.

By the time he reached home it was dark. The street-lamps were burning and tendrils of mist swirled around the flames.

All afternoon the horrid feeling of having gone out of the house because he'd upset Lina had been working inside him. Now he made himself enter the flat like a man diving head-first. He sensed that she was in the kitchen. As he took off his coat he opened the kitchen door. There she was, ironing. He went to her and, from behind, kissed her on the neck. Lina quivered but didn't speak.

He stood behind her for a while, then said quietly, in a gently joking voice:

"Still don't love the blood-sucker?"

Lina burst out with a violent sob that he hadn't expected.

"Go away, go away, leave me alone."

And she collapsed onto the kitchen stool, covered her face with her hands and wept.

He stood over her, not knowing what to do.

"Lina, oh Lina," he said, "my dear, my darling. Don't take things so hard."

"Don't come near me," said Lina. "I've done nothing to you. The only harm I do is to look after your interests. You can chuck your whole salary away for all I care."

He was silent, waited, then said:

"Look here, Lina... you really can't take what I did today amiss... My sister hasn't turned to me in ten years, hasn't asked for a thing, and under the influence of that terrible letter..."

"Hasn't asked for a thing... because I've been here..." Lina choked, and now whispered out dispassionately her well-prepared words, "but if I'm in the way I can go. Then I won't have to worry about whatever you get up to..."

He had no answer, just stood there. Then he went to her, bent and began to kiss her hair. He could smell the kitchen on it, washing, bacon, and was ashamed of noticing this while he kissed ever more warmly that hair, so full of dreary smells. God, poor woman, she too might go to pieces in that big villa, if her fate so decreed... here was where she could work for her husband, her children... she was a saint.

He hailed this saintliness with persistent kisses.

And he murmured slowly to her:

"You're the only one that's perfect. You've protected our lives in these awful, changeable times, with the whole world falling apart, and we've been able to live in it... I know this perfectly well, and I'm grateful to you."

He put his arms round her and Lina let him, wept on her husband's shoulder a while longer until slowly her tears dried up. She was well aware that he'd always made every effort to suppress his higher desires so as to be happy and content in this

106

narrow sphere, and she felt that something had happened to him, he'd calmed down, that he no longer wanted to fight...

"Go on in," she said after a while, pulling herself together. "Go on in, there's a relation waiting for you."

At this she gave a strange kind of laugh.

Pista, however, was startled. "A relation?... Who on earth is it this time?"

"Go on in and entertain..." And Lina laughed so that after crying her tears gained fresh strength from laughter.

Pista went into the sitting-room racking his brains, and there found, sitting on the settee in his usual place, his mother's younger cousin, Auntie Kati.

"Oh, Kati néni," he exclaimed in amazement, "What brings you here?"

"I've just dropped in, my boy," said Kati néni, springing nimbly up and falling on her dear nephew's neck.

"Goodness, it's been ages, how are you, Kati néni?" He patted the back of the thin, incredibly thin, creature, who seemed to have only sinews left in her body.

"If only Zsuzsika could see you, your dear mother," Kati néni wiped her eyes, "What a good relation she was, goodness me. Goodness me. But so am I. I can't let myself fail to help a relation, so I've come to see you, my dear, to be what help I can. I know you'll need help, now that you're going to buy this big house."

"Gracious, Kati néni, don't worry about that, just tell me, where've you been, how are you getting on, what have you been doing, how are you? Are you well?"

"I'm not too bad, my dear. You can see, I'm not too bad."

And weeping, laughing, she blew her nose, not disappointed in her nephew, she'd been so well received by him.

Lina couldn't deny herself the pleasure of seeing her husband exchanging small talk with Kati néni, came in, went through the room into the bedroom. She put an armful of ironed clothes into the cupboard and came back out.

"Look, Lina, here's Kati néni."

Lina laughed but said nothing.

"What can I do to help, my dear?" Kati néni almost shouted at her, "What can I do, I really want something to do."

"Just stay where you are, Kati néni, and keep my husband amused," said Lina, and went back into the kitchen.

"Oh, she's a wonderful, sweet creature... you can kiss the ground she walks on," Kati néni whispered in Pista's direction.

"Oh, how she works, she's not like the old-time ladies, they certainly had an easy life. The trouble is, if they'd been a bit more careful with their money they'd all be better off now."

Pista laughed, because the great ladies of old were usually spoken of as never-ending toilers. But of course, here was somebody that could testify about them, she'd actually known them.

"Really, Kati néni! Didn't they have anything to do?"

"Oh, my boy, in the old days there was so much showing off! Don't even mention it. Your great-grandmother used to drive herself into town with a team of four, and there was always a cigar that long in her mouth."

Pista began to laugh silently, afraid that Kati néni would be offended.

"It was a very bad time, my boy, in those days there was only *ferbli* and eating and drinking. Well, of course they had things to do, because there was the house to see to, but *they* didn't do the work, there was plenty of help, even in your mother's younger days there were so many out of work, the whole village sponged on her, but your poor father would keep up the old ways, with him things had to be just so. Anyway, let's leave that, I'm glad you've grown up so, you've become a man. You're a real man. Oh, if your poor mother could see, she would be pleased. You're Town Clerk, my boy... It's a big thing. You're putting some gold back on the old coat of arms..."

"Coat of arms, Kati néni! We haven't got one now. The old coat of arms means nothing today... Anyway, how are you? You don't look any different, you haven't changed at all."

"Well, my boy, time's gone by. I can't complain, because it's gone by pleasantly, people have been kind to me everywhere I've been, they've never wanted to get rid of me, even your poor uncle Andris and his family, they were all crying something awful when I came away, 'Don't go yet, Kati néni, you won't be as well off anywhere as with us'. But I couldn't stand seeing all that trouble."

"What trouble?"

"Well, it's no life in those parts now. In the Rima valley. The Czechs are in charge. Poor Andris. his life isn't worth living these days. It's terrible to live to see such times. The days of poverty."

"What d'you mean, hasn't Andris got anything?"

"Nothing, my boy, they can scarcely get enough to eat. Oh, if only you could do something for him. A job or something. He's such a good farmer, and such a *Hungarian* person. You should hear them all talk about him! Last year, when he went to Prague, he went into a shop to buy some little thing for the family, some souvenir of Prague. He couldn't understand what they said, because in his whole life he hasn't learnt a word of any other language. So he said 'Heavens, you've belonged to us these ten years, haven't you learnt to speak Hungarian yet?'"

Pista burst out laughing. His aunt had said this in such deadly earnest, it was as if she sympathised with Andris bácsi. "Well, my boy, there he is with his six sons, and not an acre of land left."

"Dear oh dear, that's terrible. And have the boys been studying?"

"What, my boy? Breathing? That's all. What can poor Hungarian children learn up there? They have to speak Slovak, and a real Hungarian like him can't stomach that. Going to school means learning in Czech. What a lesson to learn in such a real Hungarian's house... Their father said to them: 'Leave it, or I'll knock that book out of your hand. It's not a book if it's in Slovak'. So after that all his sons became some kind of labourers, working here and there. The youngest have learnt to speak good Czech, so maybe they'll get by, but the big ones must all be brought back to Hungary. Oh, if you could do something for them, God would bless you."

Pista became serious. András Takonyi, his land-owning uncle, at whose place he used to spend the summer before the war. In his eyes he was a model farmer. He used to have wonderful horses.

"They've all been in the army. Of his sons, Vilmos was an engineer and is now in the silk business, Peter used to be in local government and is now living off his father. Gábor is in the bank on a pittance, Béla and Endre, the way they're marking time is beyond description, and young Mátyás, the best dancer there is, dreams of being a professional dancer.

"Dear oh dear."

Bugle beads hung from the silk of the lampshade, casting their shadows on Kati néni's face, gleaming waxen, ghostly in the lamplight.

Was everybody going to be a bird of prey, wherever they came from?

So they sat opposite one another, as if the confident feelings of the first moments had been suspended. They'd become worlds apart.

Kati néni talked of this and that. She said things about tax-

109

collections which were sometimes like fantastic horror-stories, sometimes as comical as silly anecdotes. Then her fantasy would pick up the days of old once again. She could remember everything from the times when Pista was still a fair-haired child getting up to pranks. Last century.

It would have been nice to listen to all this, had there not lurked behind every word something pathetic and shocking; they oughtn't to have done this, they oughtn't to have done that.

Lina went on working in the kitchen and wouldn't come in. The boys were doing their prep in the other room and weren't allowed out until they'd finished. Their mother was very strict with them.

"Your poor mother, how she passed away, how she passed away... Her life was simply martyrdom, poor thing..."

Pista's blood ran cold as he thought of how he'd only been able to help his mother after she'd been widowed and had moved into town after the loss of the property. There she'd raised her sons by laboriously taking in students, with colossal efforts. He knew nothing of the ancient secrets.

"Martyrdom. Everybody that lives, their lives are martyrdom. Well, Zsuzsika's was. The trouble your poor father caused her with his honourable nature. Poor István."

He dared not pry, because he was afraid that this strange old lady would let out something as she sat there, so superior, in moral judgement, old maid that she was.

"One woman wasn't enough for him," Kati néni sighed the most painful words.

There's nothing in the world worse than a scandal-mongering woman. Pista looked in embarrassment at the old lady. It'd have been better if she hadn't turned up. Now she was putting her finger on the sore spot in his heart. When his spiritual balance could so easily be upset.

"Let's not discuss it, Kati néni," he said quietly. "Let's stick to nice, pleasant things."

"Oh, really, it was nothing, my boy, because your poor father, he had character. He simply suffered."

"My father?" he said, numbly.

Kati néni leant closer and whispered:

"Love, my boy, love isn't a disgrace, it's an accident... Whoever it happens to... I hope you haven't inherited his nature."

He could see now that there was no escape. There was something that he had to find out. Something of which he was terrified, and which could not be avoided, like an act of God. He could scarcely ask the question:

"Who was it?"

"Mrs. Koltay."

Pista stared at Kati néni. Was this why she'd come, to set fire to his whole life in the very first hour?

"He deceived my mother?"

"He only pined for her," breathed Kati néni. "In ten years he didn't so much as kiss her little finger. It's easier for a man like that than for that Berci bácsi of yours, is he still alive? He was just fickle, everyone he saw he was in love with. He had girls everywhere, but István, he had character. He only worshipped from afar., but his wife suffered through it, poor Zsuzsika, she had to see her husband withering away, and couldn't help him..."

"But this is terrible," exclaimed Pista and stood up.

Kati néni looked at him with rapture and delight. "But he was a handsome man. Fine figure of a man. Like you. You've got his forehead, his mouth, tears came quickly to his eyes too..."

Pista rushed out of the room.

He stopped in the hall. Was this old lady a devil or what, coming straight out with things like that?

He went into the kitchen to Lina.

But the girl was there and he couldn't say what he wanted to, that this Kati néni must be got out of the house as fast as possible. "Aren't we having supper, darling?"

"I'll lay the table in a minute."

"Can't the girl do it?"

"I'll do it straight away. Are you starving?"

He couldn't stay in the kitchen. He went out into the yard for a breath of air.

15.

He spent all morning in the office, examining the Pig Farm documents. It was a typically Hungarian development.

A lessee by the name of Kaiser had leased Szentkálnay's ten-acre farm by the railway halt for pig-breeding. This had been when the boom was at its height, in 1928. Having gained this foothold he had managed to enlist the support of the biggest and most credit-worthy names in the city, and embarked on a huge undertaking. Hordes of pigs and piles of maize were bought in. It was scarcely noticed what a sensational amount of credit he was using up, and when he decamped to America with as much as he could pocket the whole world gaped at the hundreds of thousands of pengős involved. He had swindled everyone that had so much as spoken to him.

So the enterprise had failed, but there was Szentkálnay, left with a magnificently equipped pig-breeding establishment, because Kaiser had not stinted, but had had pig-pens of American design with all the trimmings built by the most expensive builder in the city; his swindle had required everything to appear large-scale and reliable. So there remained a half-finished site and a big construction bill.

Old Szentkálnay, however, was nothing if not a businessman, and he decided on the spot to form a public company to bring in fresh money, and did it. He persuaded the city to come in, the Főispán, the Alispán, the big land-owners and a host of small farmers. The area is the best for maize production, so the small farmers paid for their shares in maize and pigs. It was cleverly thought out, and the cleverest thing of all was the appointment of his son-in-law, Ferenc Boronkay, as Managing Director.

After that the building really became extensive. A big office block went up, electricity, running water, store-houses, granaries. And a villa in the estate for Boronkay out of the spare cash.

Before, however, the establishment had a chance of going into production, the price of pigs went down and that of maize, up.

That was when the crash came.

In vain did Szentkálnay drive in the whole pig stock from his own farms – he had two thousand acres – and in vain did he enter them twice on the inventory by having them taken out at night and put back in the day-time, and the difference accounted for as losses by disease, in vain did he inflate his assets, in the end the whole business came to a terrible collapse.

Such was the situation when Makróczy, who had been the villain of the piece, lost the battle and the task of sorting it all out devolved upon Pista. The strange thing was that he had been Town Clerk for some weeks, but the Pig Farm affair was still dormant; he only discovered its full horror by chance and his own persistence.

Shock followed shock as he delved ever deeper into the labyrinth of false balances, creative accounting and manipulation of statistics.

His calculations went on for days, he became quite an accomplished book-keeper, at home he couldn't sleep, got up in the night and did more and more calculations. He still didn't know what to do, but was studying the matter with the same passion as the hunter follows his prey, its tracks, its movements, to catch the fox, the weasel, big game, wild boar, bear, for every animal has its ways and every thief his methods, which can be recognised and fully understood.

One afternoon the Mayor called him in and told him that he was to take the night train to Budapest, the Minister would see him at nine next morning.

A great occasion in his life. He'd be representing the city before the Minister.

The Mayor went over with him in detail and point by point what he should say, what he should hint at, the purpose being to convince the Minister of the necessity of making a big loan to the city.

"Well, my dear chap, you'll have a pleasant journey because the Alispán's taking the sleeper as well, and you're going with him. At least you don't have to worry about your compartment."

At home Pista prepared for the journey with some excitement. Lina too was excited, because she knew in advance that the first thing that Pista would do in Pest would be to look up his relations.

They didn't say much about this. If the Minister was seeing him at nine, he'd be able to catch the noon express back.

"I'll go into a hotel," said Pista.

Lina received this without enthusiasm, for she thought that a hotel was unnecessary. He could have washed and changed on the train. True, the sleeper got in at five o'clock, but there was no great problem in killing time from five to eight over coffee in some cafe. But when she saw that her husband showed little interest in such a student arrangement, she gave in, let him do as he pleased.

The train left at a quarter to midnight. They stayed up, although Lina would have preferred to go to bed earlier so as not to waste electricity.

"Ah, good evening, sir."

"Hello, Pista, hello," said Andris bácsi, shaking Pista's hand

113

warmly. "So we're to endure the night together in the national interest," he added with a laugh.

The stationmaster came in person to greet them and to report that he'd reserved them a special compartment, and as soon as they boarded the guard was waiting for them. The train was packed, the corridors crowded, but he opened a compartment marked 'Reserved' and let them into a two-berth sleeper. The Alispán at once took the seat facing the engine. He unpacked his night things and lay down comfortably.

"A good soldier can sleep on a frozen field," he said kindly. "Settle down, Pista, and get some sleep before we reach Budapest. Five hours' sleep in twenty four is little enough, curse it."

When they were settled Pista, who wasn't yet used to this reserved category of travel, thought with a twinge of conscience that there were people standing in the corridor. But that wasn't his fault. He'd got nothing else to do but enjoy the fact that this was the way for those in authority.

"It's amazing," said the Alispán before going to sleep, "the way life plays tricks on you. All my life I've hated having anything to do with the kitchen. And so, during the war I had to take charge of food supplies. For year after year I had to keep tally of how many hundredweight of flour there were, meat, bacon, coffee, goodness knows what else, whatever was needed, so that it should always be there. At home my wife moaned that you couldn't get this and that, whereas I was having to see to the housekeeping of the whole county, and so it is today."

He laughed, turned over and went to sleep.

Pista, however, couldn't sleep, lay still for a long time so as not to disturb the sleep of his host. 'They know how to live', he thought to himself. 'So that was why the food situation was always so bad – the Alispán had never liked having to deal with kitchen affairs'.

But there was no question of his doing his toilet in the washbasin in the compartment. The Alispán woke before they reached the capital and said:

"It'd be a good idea to go to a hotel for a bath. What about the Pannonia, Pista?"

"Certainly."

The Alispán took him in a taxi, but Pista paid. The way the situation had developed, he had to become courier, seeing to the Alispán's things, the porter, the hotel room. And the paying.

"You can claim your expenses," said the Alispán with a cheerful laugh.

114

But Pista didn't lie down, but went early to see his young brother Menyhért. He had no choice but to take a taxi to their place in outer Ferencváros. In fact he woke Menyhért up. He was received with great pleasure, breakfasted well, and then they walked into town. Pista told him everything. He was pleased at last to have somebody to whom he could unburden himself. He'd have liked to look up Adélka too, but Menyhért warned him off gravely. Adélka was herself just as responsible for what had happened as her husband.

Menyhért accompanied him all the way to the Castle[32] and they sat in a little cafe until it was time for Pista to go to see the Minister. "Hercules at the cross-roads," said Pista. "Today may decide whether I can stand my ground or whether I come unstuck..."

"Why should you come unstuck?" said Menyhért seriously. "The Minister's flesh and blood like anybody else. The fact that somebody's connections suddenly fall into place and he gets a job in the government doesn't make him the proverbial statesman, he remains just the same sort of pen-pusher that God made him. They don't understand a thing, and that's fortunate, because when a clever man comes among them he can influence them."

"Menyuska, how can we arrange for you to come down to Zsarátnok as Director of the Museum? If we two were together my position would be stronger straight away, I'd be freer, having somebody to talk things over with."

He told him how the Great Plain Museum business had been botched. In the market square there were still one-storey houses, and these were to have been compulsorily purchased, but the Misses Boldogh had objected to leaving their familiar little homes, and as the Boldoghs were one of the biggest families the authorities didn't feel it right to disturb the two old maids, members of the Főispán's wife's circle, in their idyllic peace. So the city's most beautiful building had had to be pushed up a corner.

"That won't matter," said Menyhért, "the Museum could be even better in a quiet place. It'll form a kind of island in the dingy, dusty city."

Pista was very glad to be given such a reassuring thought on this vexed question. He could use that.

But his heart was all the heavier when, at a quarter to nine, they parted, he to go and see the Minister, who had summoned him to such an early audience, Menyhért to his office.

The Minister was already in, but Pista had to wait until eleven o'clock, because first of all the daily briefings had to take place and then, when Pista's turn came, the Minister had suddenly to go into the House and Pista had to follow in the hope of catching him there.

It was an uncomfortable, turbulent day. All day he chased the Minister, they sent him here and there, until finally at six in the evening he succeeded in entering the presence.

He was worn out when he arrived to catch the nine o'clock express – but the Alispán too had been through similar tortures, and was likewise only just going home; they laughed together, to think that in this mad Pest everybody had the same fate.

Once more the train was packed, and yet once again there was the 'Reserved' compartment. But this time only a single-berth.

In this special compartment, seated side by side, as if there were only there were only the two of them in the world, floating bravely and freely through life, the Alispán and Pista felt that they were *urak*, real gentlemen.

The Alispán, it seemed, had had a bit to drink, because Pista had never known him so lively, so communicative.

"Where did you talk to the Minister?" asked the Alispán.

"It was very odd, first I waited for him in the Ministry, then I was sent over to the Parliament – while the Minister was there I listened to the debate – then I had to go back to the office, because when I looked round the Minister was nowhere in sight."

"You've been in the House?"

"Yes, sir."

"Were they quorate?"

The Alispán laughed.

"I really can't say, sir, I counted the people in the House when His Excellency was speaking, there were seventeen altogether."

They looked at one another and laughed.

"I don't know exactly how many members there are."

"Two hundred and forty-four, the two hundred and forty-fifth being subject to a by-election following the death of Unghy."

"So then, there were twohundred and twenty-seven missing. Seventeen inside, two hundred and twenty-seven outside."

They laughed again.

"Nowadays the Parliament isn't a workplace. We do the work, not the Parliament. All the load comes on local government these days," said the Alispán.

"But when the Minister spoke, even those went out. There were seven left in the Chamber."

"These days every member prefers to look after his constituency. There's bound to be an election in the summer, so they're protecting their own interests."

"I was there last year, and then there weren't more than twenty-three."

"These days the work of a member of Parliament isn't in the House, but in being out and about. You can't imagine how much running about there is to be done. Everybody in the constituency depends on the MP in their day-to-day business. They demand everything of him, expect everything of him. Every MP has his pocket full of things to see to. But, damn it all, the truth is that only the MP can see to things. He can go in anywhere and everybody's afraid of him. All those lawyers, they live here these days. And the engineers, both of them have a gold-mine in being an MP. Likewise the financial types and the commercials. It's not bad for land-owners, either, because they can get things that ordinary people can't lay their hands on."

"Yes, but, sir, is the House not in the national interest?"

"The government does the work. The House gets everything on a plate, just has to pass it."

"That must be quite a big job," said Pista falsely and with a little self-abasement. He didn't dare say a word in opposition, preferring to keep his council. He was afraid that the Alispán might form a bad opinion of him...

The latter, however, yawned and said in a bored voice:

"And how many were the Opposition?"

"Three or four."

"So you see, there isn't an Opposition either."

He waved his hand.

Pista, however, had been sitting in the press gallery, where his good opinion had suffered severe damage. If anybody spoke, there was comment at once. 'That chap left the United Party because he knew that he was being dropped, so he wants to earn himself a bit of popularity outside. Now he's going over to the Opposition...' 'This one's making a speech in favour of the government from the Opposition benches to save his seat. Perhaps they won't put anybody up against him.' 'This one's getting so

117

worked up because some piece of business in his line has been seen to without him, and he's made nothing out of it.' 'This one's attacking the Archduke because he's announced that he's standing in his constituency.'

He didn't feel inclined to talk about these matters to the Alispán, but kept quiet while his tongue itched to say what he would have liked to.

But he didn't say anything, and smiled contemptuously at himself. Well, what if he did speak? He'd be playing with his job.

He was beginning to understand how it was possible for the whole country to be bought.

Everybody depended, by some thread, in some way, on the government. He, as a municipal Town Clerk, was so much a government servant that he couldn't have a thought of his own. If only he were stronger... but how could he be?... Only in two ways: material independence and social independence. If he got his house and had enough money...

The Alispán spread his handkerchief over the plush seat-back, rested his head on it and began to doze.

Pista too tried to sleep but couldn't. His head buzzed with thoughts like a bee-hive.

It was a pity that he'd mentioned being in the House, and that he'd been critical of what he'd seen. People became suspicious so easily. It was nothing to do with him. Neither the government nor the Opposition were any of his concern, why worry his head?

The country was big, and for him his own city was his world. It was as if this city didn't belong to the country, so private was the life it led, so narrow in compass. He began to read the paper, quietly, without rustling, and came across the name of a Mayor in the region whom the Fóispán had summarily suspended. He read the list of charges. Some were of a material nature: the Mayor had behaved irregularly in the purchase of the municipal market-gardens... behaved irregularly in the building of the nursery school... behaved irregularly in the purchase of a plot for the Mayor's residence... The sixth charge accused him of using municipal staff to work in his own house... He had allowed unauthorised persons to use a car, property of the municipality... Insufficient stamp-duty had been paid in connection with payments to a number of contractual municipal undertakings, and thereby the State had been defrauded... He had bought a duplicating machine without official permission... There had been irregularities in building work done under the auspices of the foreign loan... And finally, the most serious accusation, that he had profited illicitly from the allotting of land...

Pista read these charges over and over in horror. There was not one of them that wouldn't have been valid in Zsarátnok, and not one for which any legal proceedings would have been viable. 'He'll get off', he thought to himself. 'It's a plot'.

It would be possible to suspend any mayor in such a fashion, because none of the charges would stand... They were gossip...

At that moment he felt like a wild animal, still roaming at large, for which a gun was being loaded somewhere.

Life was a jungle. Wild things lived there that tore and ate anybody that they could.

Here nobody really understood anything. Here the trouble was that everybody was in a position for which they were unprepared. And those that did understand anything were nowhere. The journalist who'd provided him with insights in the Parliament had been in his class at school. He knew everything, and now was going grey as a mere political reporter. He'd explained, *inter alia*, that abroad, before becoming a member of Parliament, one had to go through a real school of life. The selection of likely candidates began in the field of canvassing, where they learned to speak and acquired the scientific knowledge required for politics. For nowadays governing a country was indeed a science. These young people would be secretaries of Party organisations and branches, take the lead, and over a lengthy period would learn how to deal with people. Meanwhile, as they did this, the whole life of the State would be revealed to them. They'd get to know the people who held leading positions in the work of Parliament, they'd exercise definite judgement on whom to entrust with what, who held what views, who was entitled to play what role in the State... There, the office of member of Parliament was at the same time the highest qualification and one that could be obtained only at the price of long and assiduous toil. In Hungary, on the other hand, there was no process of selection. Here every member of Parliament received his office as a reward for his social standing or his services to the government. What mattered was dependability, not what one had to offer. Family connections were the surest touchstone of dependability. And the less anybody understood of political science, the more dependable he was. Here what was wanted were voting-machines. Here the citizen had never had any rights. At one time people were marched here in chains to vote. The council of Parliament was empty not only today, it was also empty when there took place theatrical sessions, and a packed House listened to the great leading spokesmen. And then there was no Opposition. An Opposition that was fit to govern had only appeared for the odd moment now and then, and if ever it happened that a coalition or Opposition party came into power that meant no change, because once again only those who understood nothing would come to the fore, bringing no fresh air to nation and State, but keeping things going on the same road as the outgoing government had left them...

So where could there be any change of direction in the life of this nation?

The journalist had said that the younger generation was beginning to take an interest in affairs, and when this younger generation became fit to govern it would know how to do things. But where was it now?

"Today," he said, "such is the strength of the currents of world politics that an international decision so sweeps aside economic forces, or channels them in such a direction, that a little country really hasn't as much control over its internal affairs as the domestic affairs of cities have influence in national politics. It doesn't matter what Parliament decides or decrees, the pace of life is ruled by international agreements... Parliamentarianism has lost the power to act, it's a local phenomenon. In that case, there's nothing for it but to hand over to the few men who stand at the head of the government and tie the small boat of State to this or that. The big tugs will pull the country somewhere."

Pista looked under his lashes at the Alispán's face. He saw to his surprise a typical rich man's face. Much hunting, much exercise in the open air, had made it rough, left the skin shot through with tiny blood-vessels... Had this man ever read a book?... Had he any views on literature? Or science? What did he know of recent intellectual developments? Nothing.

This was just a living human being, interested only in his own close circle of affairs. Who saw no farther than the County boundary, and even within that couldn't think anything through or arrange things properly. There was a kind of bureaucratic system according to which things had to be done, but how should he think, for instance, of something higher, such as how to find work for the thirty thousand unemployed in the County? Thirty thousand men, agricultural workers, marvellous material. The country could be built with these thirty thousand. Roads, houses, schools, museums. All it needed was somebody to set the thirty thousand to work. A will, a power aiming at a goal. The whole country could be re-organised with just these thirty thousand. The karst of the Pilis[33] could be dug up and planted with forests, the Hortobágy[34] could be ploughed and the alkaline soils made fertile. The country could be increased tenfold without crossing the frontier. The fatherland could be profoundly enriched and a Garden of Eden created on these desolate, barren plains. But where was the man with the strength of will to take in hand the fate of this nation?... The thirty thousand workers lay there in their wretched houses, spent the whole winter sitting in their *suba*[35] in unheated homes, smoking bad, contraband tobacco or the leaves of trees... They had no land, no stock, no cottage industries. Where there were any, they were futile. Did this Alispán have the slightest idea of proposing cottage industries, by means of which the poverty in his County might be alleviated? He knew nothing about it. Didn't want to know. Only when the great, needy spring came, and all the seed-corn and every morsel of food was gone, and when there was no defence left against mass rebellion, then he'd think about some kind of poor-relief; send five hundred cart-loads of potatoes to be distributed among the people together with six or seven fillérs, because if they didn't have at least that there'd be civil disturbances...

Pista squirmed uncomfortably, and would have liked not to think of such things. Why couldn't he be so fat and sleek, capable of sleeping peacefully when the far end of the house was ablaze, saying 'Perhaps it won't reach here'...

Perhaps his trouble was that he too had had a little wine to drink...

Or was it his head ringing with the poison that his old friend had dripped into it?...

"If a Parliamentary correspondent stands for election," the journalist had said, "you can depend on it, immediately some unknown landowner will be put up against him."

Everything was contained in those words. Bitterness, jealousy and truth. An unknown landowner is unknown to the journalist, but not to the constituency. There they know very well who he is. They'll say, he's got two thousand acres. So many people have an interest in two thousand acres, beginning with the gentry of the county, who'll pick some fool from their number to run the gauntlet of the election. He'll take on the cost of it and will so burden his property that he'll possibly never be able to pay it off in his lifetime... He'll take it on with the result that he'll neglect the management of his land... He'll become estranged from his family, because, cut off from the life that he knows, he'll live in greater luxury and freer morals... He'll have to dine out more in conspicuous places, the prospect of easy love-affairs will contaminate his thoughts... and when his term expires, there he is, penniless...

On the other hand, what prospect is there of his achieving anything? First of all, he knows nothing about it. He doesn't even know what he ought to do for himself. Of course, he's never been any good as a farmer, because he's always just been a Hungarian gentleman, proud of the fact that he's nobody's servant... By the time that he learns, to his cost, he's lost so much more than he might have gained... His property's mortgaged... Nowadays everybody's mortgaged for five hundred pengős an acre. And five hundred is twice what the land can be sold for.

But the creditor, the finance company, the bank, can do nothing. Let them try to sell. Who's going to buy?... If thirty landowners stand together and refuse to pay any more interest, every bank in the country towns will fail.

Then what can people in this situation do?

Pista had seen a friend of his in Parliament. Back at home he was a model farmer, all his cattle were in the stock-books. His land was well kept. One might have said of him, not that he was one hundred per cent a good farmer, but certainly eighty per cent. Whereas the neighbouring landowners were forty or thirty per cent respectable, if not ten. If one considered the common people, they were one per cent, because they didn't know how to farm. How should they? They were pitched into this rapacious business and they hadn't studied it. Pista had been round the schools in summer, after harvest. On all sides he'd seen unharvested fields, abandoned because they hadn't yielded the reapers' payment of forty kilos per acre. Even then this man's land had produced more than the national average. And now, following a sudden death, his friend had been hauled off to the House. The bank had foreclosed, and he owed them two hundred and forty thousand pengős. For six hundred acres. His only hope was to help himself as a member of Parliament.

And now what would happen to him? He was still a young member, so he considered it his duty to sit in the House and listen to the twaddle. At home he'd been first out of bed, had looked after every little pig, every time the cows were fed he'd been there. Now his hands did as they pleased. If he remained a member of Parliament for long, he'd go the same way as the rest. It was impossible for his listening in the House not to damage his farming. Of course, he didn't know how to speak. He was a practical man, who had his capacity for hard work and his careful farming to thank for the fact that he hadn't sunk in the mire of the new taxation the previous year like the rest. His land had even brought him in twenty pengős an acre, while the other landowners had made losses. Now he too had set off along this road, because nobody would risk taking on the parliamentary seat. Even the most modest campaign costs twenty thousand pengős. Who's going to throw away money like that on such a brief period of time? And even then one wasn't to know that there wouldn't be another election in three or four months' time. Another twenty thousand pengős?

But what if he might hope to be of service to his country?

Of course, it isn't the same thing at all. How can a farmer expect to know what's needed for a country? How can he have the first idea about the running of a country? And even if he had, he couldn't do anything. There his vote will be just one of many. The government will have one vote more, that's all. And the minute he disagrees, immediately he has to join the Opposition, and how does a big landowner join the Opposition? And even if he does, he still can't do anything, because the Opposition's so insignificant that it can never defeat any government proposal. Of the two hundred and forty-five, twenty-five are in opposition.

There's nothing for him to do but resign himself to what can't be altered.

The cart of State was rolling, rolling, Today it wasn't a cart but a motor. A lorry. Somebody was at the wheel, and the lorry went where he drove it...

So if it was rolling, all well and good. But why should it? It was standing in the garage. And was the driver sitting in a bar? or gone hunting? It made no difference.

The journey seemed very long, while the Alispán slept so soundly that his mouth fell open and he gradually began to snore.

Well, there was nothing he could do, that's for sure.

He, Pista, had only one duty, to ensure his prospects from the material point of view without delay. He carried a heavy burden, a wife, two children.

He couldn't sleep a wink. He marvelled at the Alispán, how

123

soundly he slept. He was like a child, without a care in the world, untroubled by ambition, everything had been as it should be all his life. He'd lived in wealth and peace from birth, as if some private guardian angel had watched over him. Certain positions of great responsibility, such as he'd been discharging this day, were meant for such as he. He was a gentleman.

"Well, Pista, we'll be there in a bit," said the Alispán, sitting up with a great yawn and stretching.

He was like a lion. The lion is unaware of being the king of beasts. He's just an animal like the rest, it's just that his shape, his strength, his voice, his appetite are different.

"We've still got time – let's get something to eat."

They went through to the dining-car.

By this time there were not many there. Dinner was finishing. Some foreigners were sitting at a little table, talking quietly in an unfamiliar language.

The Alispán ordered the roast, Pista an omelette with two eggs.

"What about a drop of wine."

And the Alispán ordered a decent bottle.

"I was talking to my brother in Pest," said Pista suddenly. "He's a senior curator in the National Museum. He said that it didn't matter if the Museum went into a side-street, it could even improve its character as a museum. But what's needed is for the policy of the Museum to be worked out as quickly as possible."

"Really? Your brother's a museum man?"

"The leading specialist in his field."

"Then you ought to get him to come down and run the Museum."

"I thought it was a fait accompli. I know the post of Director has been promised to somebody."

"Who's that?"

"Makróczy's brother-in-law."

"Oh, come on! Makróczy's least concern's more important that running about on behalf of his brother-in-law. He'll be happy if he can save his skin. He's really in hot water, and if he can earn your good-will by that it won't even occur to him that anybody might complain. That Pig Farm, you know, is a very shady business."

It seemed fantastic to Pista that the moment had come when Makróczy was counting on his indulgence. He was careful, however, not to give himself away. His first thought was, naturally, that he must guarantee Makróczy an unbiased attitude, and then who could help it if the turn of events demanded something else? He had to allow himself that much cunning if he was to achieve his aims.

"So, my advice to your brother is to get his application in at once, then we can start things moving."

He laughed and looked at Pista as if he'd have liked to rush him into something. How cleverly they can do things. Pista knew by this time that the Alispán had a considerable interest in the Pig Farm, and if he got away with it, it would do him some good.

When he said nothing the Alispán went on:

"In any case, Makróczy's brother-in-law or nephew or whatever he is, he's not a specialist, and what's more he's a sick man, and can't work."

"Aha."

"Furthermore, basically it's a question of who proposes a candidate. The Mayor thinks a lot of you, he was saying the other day that he's very pleased with you."

"Really?"

"Of course. He's very fond of you."

"Fond of me? What do you mean, fond of me?"

"He rang me yesterday and said we ought to travel together, and it was very kind of him, because I'm enjoying this little trip together, you're a very pleasant chap, very pleasant."

And he placed his hand on Pista's.

Pista couldn't help noticing how his heart thumped. It had of course been very good, this being together on the train. In this way they'd got to know one another, taken stock of one another. How could this have been achieved otherwise? It was an unexpected gift.

He beckoned the steward for the bill as they were approaching Zsarátnok and paid for them both.

"What's the matter, do you pay everywhere?" said the Alispán with a laugh.

He didn't waste another word on the subject. They got up and went back to their compartment. They took down their luggage. As the train ran in Pista lowered the window and called a porter.

"Get me a taxi," he ordered.

125

"No, no," said the Alispán. "The car'll be waiting for me, I'll drop you off."

They got into the big car, the County mace-bearer was sitting by the chauffeur.

In the car the Alispán just said:

"I'll have a word with the Mayor tomorrow. So, good-bye, good-bye."

"My compliments to your lady wife," said Pista, and jumped politely out of the car, because the way it was standing outside City Hall the Alispán would have had to climb over him, so he got out to help the older man out.

"Take the Town Clerk home," said the Alispán to the chauffeur, and with that he nodded once more and Pista got back in.

"Do you know where I live?"

"Of course, sir," said the chauffeur, and it made Pista feel good that the County chauffeur knew his address.

When the big car stopped in the little street he gave the chauffeur a handsome tip, which was accepted with a deep bow.

16.

They were still up. Lina was waiting for him and the children hadn't wanted to go to bed. Kati néni was a source of constant distraction, because the old lady wouldn't believe that her duties didn't include talking all the time.

When Lina heard the sound of the car she was delighted, mainly, that at last Kati néni would dry up.

She looked out of the window, then ran to open the gate. The girl was awake too, she hadn't let her go to bed, why should the slave sleep when the gentry still needed her. But none the less she put a scarf round her head and went out, thinking that by the time the girl had roused herself she'd have opened the gate herself.

"Goodness, you shouldn't have come out in this awful weather," said Pista, giving Lina a hug.

So, arms round each other, they went into the house. The maid was sleepily rubbing her eyes and shut the door behind them as they came in.

"Bring the supper in," Lina said to her, "and don't break anything."

"Darling," said Pista proudly, "I shook hands with the Minister. Is Kati néni still here?"

"She is. She wants to stay for the winter."

"Hello, Pista," Kati néni called cheerfully, getting up from her sewing. "Are you hungry?"

"Supper's just coming."

Kati néni's presence inhibited them. Pista couldn't say anything in front of her that he would have liked to say, so he just talked about details of the journey, how he'd gone with the Alispán, how the County car had brought him home; how he'd slept well the previous night, not stopped in a hotel, just spent some time there, then gone to see Menyhért and stayed with him until it was time to go and see the Minister. And so on and so forth.

"What's that you're sewing, Kati néni?" asked Lina suddenly. While she had been outside the old lady had found, goodness knows where, some ragged children's shirts, and was hard at work.

"I'm working, darning, saving money," said Kati néni, "when the family hasn't got much to live on that's what you have to do."

"Oh, bless you, at least don't spread them out like that, my husband'll think that's how his children go around dressed. Those are only fit for dusters."

"I thought I was helping, my dear."

"Goodness, off you go to bed, an old lady shouldn't wear herself out like that."

"I'll do some cooking tomorrow, I'll make something like his mother used to make for him, let him have a bit of something nice for once."

"He gets that, praise be," said Lina with a forced laugh, "why don't you go and lie down?" She really pushed the old lady out of the room into the tiny maid's room, which the maid never had, the kitchen was good enough for her. Pista set about eating the dried-up pieces of meat.

"I didn't know if you were ever coming. Why didn't you come on the mid-day train?"

"I couldn't, I had to hang about until six o'clock before I could get in to see the Minister. Fortunately Andris bácsi too only caught the nine o'clock."

"Who's Andris bácsi?"

"The Alispán."

"Oh, I see. I thought you meant some relation."

As they were going to bed Lina asked:

"What are Adélka's lot doing?"

"Didn't go to see them. Menyhért told me not to."

He said that to make his wife think better of Menyhért.

As he relaxed in bed he thought: if only Lina were a bit higher-minded. What a pity it is that she's so immersed in endless cooking and washing. That was all very well while we were poor, but now it's time she broke away from it. I can't really discuss anything with her, and that's simply because her mind's fully occupied with hatred for my relations.

"I want you to speak to the children," said Lina when she'd got into bed. "Since their father's become such a great gentleman they won't work. I really had a struggle with them this evening. They think they can just take things easy. Cheeky young devils, as soon as they feel things are a bit freer they take advantage. What's going to become of them? Do they want to turn out to be Kopjásses as well?"

"You can't just condemn the Kopjásses in general terms like that. Even Albert's made a career. I haven't seen him lately, but I hear he's quite well up in the investment department of the Bank of Budapest. That's quite something in the banking world, and he's done it all by himself. You can't mess about with money, if somebody isn't sound he gets his neck broken straight away."

"It's nothing to do with me, I'm just glad they're doing well, because then I don't see them. I wish them long life and prosperity, but the trouble is rather that a letter came today asking you to get him a position with the Zsarátnok Savings Bank."

Pista became silent. It was unpleasant, the way Lina always had a card up her sleeve.

He tried to go to sleep quickly. He woke in the night and lay awake for a long time, What the devil was he to do about his family, he couldn't find them all jobs. But it would be no bad thing if Kardics bácsi would give Albert a job. He'd have somebody he could trust in the Savings Bank.

In the morning he went to report to the Mayor.

"Ah, hello, hello, my dear chap," the Mayor greeted him, his face beaming. "Well, what's the news?"

He had to tell him all about it, every least little thing. What the Minister had said, what he had talked about, with what emphasis, which box he'd been offered a cigar from, the one on the right or that on the left. Had he sat him down in front of his desk or had he got up and taken him to the little suite that was in his office? And then, how did he look, hadn't he heard that

128

last time he was out hunting he broke his girth? How did he sit in his armchair, did he fidget a lot? Could he sit the red velvet?

Pista was very careful not to give away the fact that he wasn't used to talking to the mighty in so frank a manner; as a person of little consequence he regarded the highest men in the government as extraordinary and exceptional beings, and in fact was at first embarrassed... Then it flashed into his mind that the Minister's private secretary, with whom he'd spent two whole hours in the same room while hanging about, had said that the Minister used a... what was it? A roller, a roller, that was it, and he blurted out:

"He's using a roller nowadays."

"Hahaha," roared the Mayor, his porcelain teeth gleaming in their gold mountings, "well, I suppose he's putting on a bit in the middle. That's very good," and he tapped Pista in the midriff, "very good, he's using a roller now... Fact is, he's thickened up quite a bit of late, but he used to be very slim as a young man, and a great sportsman, So, we've got to the roller stage. It'd do you no harm, my dear chap."

But Pista was blushing, he'd almost revealed that he'd had no idea that this implement was, evidently, for slimming. But he could see that the Mayor was satisfied and very much impressed that the Town Clerk should have struck up so intimate an acquaintance with the Minister at their first meeting that he'd given away such a secret.

Only then did they get round to the report on the official business. The Mayor thought that possibly the Minister had used so confidential a tone with the young Town Clerk because he was leading up to something. It would be good if he did have something in mind for the city, because in that case it would be easier to get a few things out of him after all.

He said that he wouldn't advance money except for profitable investments. I said to him "Your Excellency, we're in the fortunate position that there isn't so much money in America that we couldn't invest it profitably. Because of course it's true that drainage doesn't earn immediate returns, but how can one live without it?" To that he replied: "Quite right, my boy, you can't say that a roller brings in interest, but it does have its uses."

"Hahaha," roared the Mayor, "hahaha," and he chuckled.

The door opened and in came Kardics, unannounced.

"Hello, I can hear you're by yourselves."

"Come in, come in, my dear chap," said the Mayor, laughing

as he shook hands with Kardics. "This Pista, he's a gem. Just imagine, the Minister uses a slimming roller."

"Hahaha," Kardics laughed too, it was as if something remarkable had been said, and he couldn't stop laughing. "I daresay Countess Cimbi makes him."

The two old men laughed and laughed like a couple of students, and in a few moments Pista was let into the secret that the Minister was having an affair with Countess Cimbi, who was now 'putting him to work'. He would never have done it for his wife, but for Countess Cimbi he did indeed.

So the morning passed in pleasant chatter.

"So Béni Tóth's been made a járásbíró.³⁶"

"You don't say."

"For Lepény."

"That's tremendous…" Kardics laughed again, nearly as much as at the roller. "Well, it's all right, then." And he turned to Pista, because he had to make quite certain to pass on this amusing incident. "Last winter he won so much at cards that he bought his brothers' estate. The old family estate, I mean, six hundred and forty acres, at such a price that he simply had to take it, because he wouldn't have got it from an outsider. But fortune's fickle, the money went the way it came, and he had to sell the wheat when it came into ear. And that's how the Tóth family of Sebes ceased to be one of the leading tax-payers of the County. The Tóths are finished in Sebes. They're ruined… What lovely times I had there when I was young. There was Áron bácsi, there was Micsky – his son was asking me the other day to give him a job as a clerk in the Bank – there were the Balassys, the Meleghs; the Meleghs may have a bit of land left… Anyway, that was Ödön Melegh's doing… Quite right too, people shouldn't desert their families while they can be of help to them."

"Clever piece of work," said the Mayor.

"Very," Kardics laughed again. "Very clever. Now that he's out of office, and a Minister is attacked in Parliament for calling his son an articled clerk. The other one said to the Manager of the Exchange Bank: 'I'll take your son on if you'll find mine a job…' But this Ödön Melegh, he's still somebody even today… He's managed to have his man appointed straight to járásbíró."

The Mayor laughed with such delight, it was as if he had just eaten some marvellous sweet.

"Naturally," he said, tartly but without hostility. "Béni has no qualifications as a judge, just as a lawyer, and he hasn't any experience as that."

"Unless you call playing cards with judges and lawyers experience."

There was a tinge of malice in their words, and Pista felt that even these cynical old men found these machinations in public life amoral. He too laughed. Laughed because he was afraid of giving away how depressing he considered this whole incident, and indeed everything that he'd heard, but he also laughed in order to further his own plans, the interests of his brothers.

So the afternoon went by in pleasant chatter. Pista was amazed to see how well he fitted in with this company. He hadn't realised how much scandal he'd picked up in Pest, but it just poured out of him. The journalist had provided him with it, and the funny thing was that when he was listening to him there in the Parliament he'd been annoyed with him, yet now, as he dribbled over into their ears what he'd retained, he felt pleased with him, and didn't know what he'd have done if he hadn't met such a scandal-dispensing machine.

Finally, all three of them gave a great sigh, such as one sighs after a heavy lunch, to stuff the food deeper into oneself, and Kardics said:

"Well, I'll take Pista away, I'm taking him to the estate. I've been asked round to Feri's, Andris will be there as well, he travelled with Pista and phoned to say that he was delighted with him, he wants me to take him out to see whether he likes the house."

At this they laughed again, but Pista was so excited that he was about to meet Magdaléna that he didn't notice them laughing, and laughing at him as at a child, 'whether he likes the house'. It was like asking a man dizzy with hunger whether he'd like a beautifully cooked dinner.

Then he sent for his coat from his own office and allowed Kardics to take him by the arm and so lead him down to his car.

It was only when they were seated that it crossed his mind:

"I haven't said anything to my wife, the idea was that we'd look at it together."

"No need for women to have a say in everything. In fact, it's better for a man to find out the facts and tell 'em. Best of all, of course, is for him to present a fait accompli. I've never asked my wife for advice, just told her... surprised her..."

Oh, what a nice thing a car is. In seven minutes they were

out there in the avenue. There they were standing in front of the houses. This time Pista recognised the one, his heart knew it, and he was as embarrassed as a student.

They rang. The gardener opened the gate. It wasn't locked, you just had to know how the handle worked.

They went along the cobbled path. It was dark by now, he couldn't see a thing. The street-lamps only gave a dim light. They went not to the front door – Kardics knew the way about – but round the side of the house and on the far side there was an entrance like that to a castle.

It was just like one of the niches in the Fisherman's Bastion,[37] made of ornately carved stone, gleaming white. As they went up Pista thought that he was being taken to prison. Stairs like that existed in ancient monuments.

At the top was a huge glazed door, one half of which was open. They went in, and Kardics's hand went in familiar fashion to the light-switch. At once there was a startling brilliance, and they were in an L-shaped entrance-hall with head-high wood panelling. To the left a wide wooden staircase of Hungarian pattern led up to the first floor, and under it were a number of smaller rooms and a whole row of doors, he couldn't count how many. A glazed door opposite gave a view into the sitting-room.

They left their hats, coats and sticks, tidied themselves in a full-length mirror, straightened their backs and shoulders like actors going under the lights, and opened the door into the softly lit big room.

His first impression was that the room was too big. Its proportions were excessive for a living-room. It would be hard to heat in winter.

His second impression was that here he was in the presence of Magdaléna.

She was sitting in an armchair almost directly in front of him, with her mother on her right, facing away from him. Mrs. Szentkálnay was dressed as if for a grand, formal reception. A black dress, silks, jewellery, a gold chain. Pista, why he didn't know, stared at her and went on staring at the old lady, as if she were the key to the whole mystery. How white her face was, how well-groomed she looked, soignée, but she had some physical disability, either her back wasn't straight or she had a game leg, she walked badly.

Magdaléna, on the other hand, was incredibly gracious, and how tall! Taller than Lina. He didn't know whether he'd ever stood facing her like this, and was surprised at her height. And she moved so smoothly that it seemed an exaggeration. She moved like a self-sufficient person, who'd had to look after herself, used to being on her guard and to giving orders, who worked and got on with things.

"Do sit down. How are you, Soma?"

Kardics, as was his custom, talked a lot and loudly, behaved as if he were very much at home here, and did not conceal the fact. Exactly like Berci bácsi at Pista's.

For quite some time Pista didn't hear a thing that was being said, he was simply looking at the room. The walls were covered with pictures. That surprised him. Never in his life had he seen so many pictures in a private house as there were here. All four walls, wherever there was space, were crammed to a line drawn below the ceiling with pictures. So crammed that the walls themselves were all but invisible.

Magdaléna noticed his amazement.

"Pictures aren't in these days, but I don't care about fashion. I'm very fond of my friends and I wouldn't part with their work for the world."

"You know them? The painters?"

"Well, yes, from exhibitions at least. But a lot of them have been here."

There was an elaborate, thick, brass-studded album on the table; she laid her long, slender hand on it and said:

"We started this book when we moved in here, take a look, everybody that's been here is in it. You'll like it, you'll find poems and drawings and all sort of famous names."

At this he felt saddened. Somehow he'd become aware that she wasn't the woman that he'd taken her for these ten years. Her volatile nature seemed to have solidified, the lava seemed to have cooled to stone. He found her very positive, very confident, very self-possessed. He hadn't dared hitherto, but now he could let his gaze remain on her, look at her as calmly as at a living statue. It seemed that he'd never again have to refrain from offending her with his glances. The spell was broken. In Magdaléna there was nothing uncertain, no fits and starts, she seemed incapable of feeling. Nothing in her was childish, playful, doubtful. She was as certain as the furniture, certain, indeed, self-aware and immutable as a picture which perpetuates the uncertain.

They stood up and went along the pictures. Magdaléna knew every one by name, like a shepherd his sheep. Pista, on the other hand, felt that he'd never have been capable of memorising all these pictures individually. The best of the younger painters were there, among the imposing works of the oldest classics. Undeniably, they were cleverly arranged, because the colourful blotches of the young relieved the severely painted figures of the old, as if they were moving among swirling clouds.

"This is Mother..." Pista looked at the picture and looked anxiously back at her mother, who was taking part in the conversation, apparently very sagely and decisively, but in the picture she was portrayed as a Dowager Empress, white hair towering, tiara, cold blue eyes looking out with forced good-will from the picture as in life. But what bothered him was that in the picture there was no sign of her bad leg.

"This is me..."

"Very bad," exclaimed Pista indignantly.

"I like it," said Magdaléna.

She liked it, so there must surely be something in it.

He looked at the picture. An ageing office-girl. She was looking stern, and was proud that there were no mistakes in her figures.

So much dissimulation... He daredn't look at the picture, because it was so true to life, but it pained him, as he now realised, that this woman was quite devoid of the disturbance of emotion... How charming Lina was in comparison, with her blushing lack of knowledge.

"And this is my husband."

He was like Svengali with his black beard. And now in a flash Pista realised that it was impossible for the two of them to understand one another. No. This Svengali was afraid of this woman... Look at his eyes, how they looked inward, as if their rays didn't shoot out toward the person facing but remained inside... He glanced back at the office-girl, then again at the ineffectual Svengali... Hmm... a strange couple. An inverted relationship. Svengali wasn't doing anything to Trilby, but the medium was forcing her cold will on the hypnotist.

A smaller room opened off this one, though still quite large; this was the dining-room... The waves of pictures continued on the walls here too, but he was dizzy now, like the crowd at an exhibition, at the sight of the pictures struggling one against the other. He noticed a couple of nice bronzes too, a lion, two gladiators fighting, a reclining female nude and a streamlined sideboard, like a store-cupboard. His eye rather lingered on this. Magdaléna said with a smile:

"I designed that."

"It's nice."

"I believe that one wants to live in a house. The furniture has to answer the purpose."

That, it seemed, said it all, but Pista had to ponder it. In fact it was like any commercially produced glazed cupboard with sliding doors. A beautiful, polished wooden shape, elaborate cut-glass panels, but for all that the simplest show-case in the world.

He smiled and looked at Magdaléna, and now, for the first time in his life, spoke to her at ease:

"Is everything around you so sure and transparent?"

She glanced at him like a bird taking flight.

"What I'm prepared to show people is."

And she turned away, but Pista felt that a chink had been opened, and was glad. Now he felt that he had the upper hand. Quite so. That was true. It was conceivable; there are things for display, and other things as well...

"There are another two rooms down here, the smoking-room and my husband's study. Would you like to see the garden?"

Magdaléna's question, coming at that moment, was torn from her, bleak and resolute. It was brought home to Pista that this wasn't just a visit that he was making, but the viewing of a house for sale. He almost blushed.

Magdaléna was by now putting on the light. It wasn't easy. She had to go back and fiddle for some time behind a curtain with the switch.

Meanwhile they had all gone out onto the verandah, a large, curved glazed area, and were looking out into the darkness. Outside it was pleasantly dusk. Day hadn't long ended, and the night wasn't yet really dark. Faint outlines could be seen in the twilight, and one could make out the garden, beautiful even on this late autumn day, and its leafy bushes.

But suddenly there was a blinding light, and outside a powerful flood-light had come on. It was high up in the middle, on an iron column, and in its light, as if by magic, a huge rose-bed sprang into being in front of the house. The leaves were faded by now, but a bush or two still bore roses, and so dazzling was this enormous circle, this solemn world of roses, this Rosarium, that Pista was deeply moved. This surpassed every beautiful

135

thing that he'd ever imagined. Silent, overcome, he gazed at the scene. The light seemed finely judged, it was just enough to supply the garden itself, it went no further, one couldn't see where the fence was, which way the neighbours were. The light was burning on an enchanted island, and in the light everything that was, was lovely.

"Not feeling the cold, my dear?" said Kardics bácsi, and Pista anxiously, nervously, looked at Magdaléna, and it hurt him a little that he hadn't noticed the chill and been concerned for her...

The light went out and they sat down again inside in the nice warm sitting-room.

"Right, we'll draw up a provisional contract," said Kardics bácsi, and took out his fountain pen.

"I'd rather like to see it again with my wife," said Pista, a little hesitantly.

"Well, so you shall," said Kardics bácsi with imperturbable gentleness, and continued to write the contract.

Pista didn't know what to say to that, because he was at fever pitch; paradise seemed to be overwhelming him, and he didn't know how the dream would end. While he waited for the price he hoped that he'd have to feel ill, jump up, run outside, escape. But when Kardics bácsi said the amount he was simply shattered, it seemed to him so little. He'd heard a price for which one could have bought an ordinary civil servant's house at the most... He looked at the two women... No expression on Magdaléna's face, she looked as if she'd known for a long time what was going on, but her mother was sitting stiff and motionless on her chair as if changed into a pillar of salt. Pista quickly looked away, couldn't bear to look at them. He was ashamed of himself. The amount must have been half of the building cost.

He signed. First, Magdaléna as vendor. Then Pista as purchaser. The two hearts together... Then Kardics bácsi as witness.

Today he was the blue-eyed boy, the Bank was working on his behalf. Yesterday, of course, it had been these people's relation, today it was his...

Kardics bácsi let the ink dry, then folded the paper up and put it in a big leather wallet in his inside pocket.

"Tomorrow, the day after tomorrow, call in at the Bank," he said, "and we'll sort it out."

Pista found the matter natural.

As they left he daredn't look round but crept away, like a

136

thief taking his booty without examining it; it can't be such that he won't make something on it... There were huge box-bushes in the garden. Where'd they been able to get evergreens that size for this new garden? And the aloes. Were those all his now, or would they dig them up and take them with them? Who'd be able to afford to plant new ones in their place?

Kardics bácsi took him home to his flat, the powerful tourer seeming to push the little houses apart.

He shook Kardics bácsi by the hand warmly, gratefully, but inside he had another feeling as well... He was no longer so much his inferior. Now he had a house where he could invite him and his whole crowd for a party of a Friday. He was gradually coming up to their level.

Gradually? Could he move any faster than this?

"Well, good-bye, old boy, good-bye, my dear fellow."

Warmly he clasped the old man's hand and waited while he swung back into his place in the car and left. He'd been careful to say a word of thanks, but he couldn't bring himself to leave the car and go in before it disappeared from the street.

17.

'I'm standing here like a servant,' passed through his head, and he went into the yard, frowning.

It would be nice to know, wouldn't it? Nice to know how he stood with these people. An inferior position, in any case.

He had no time to think about it, there he was in the door-way, opening the door into the hall. Lina was in the kitchen yet again. What was she up to there, it wasn't six o'clock yet. She spent all her time in that wretched kitchen.

"Hello, my angel," and he opened the kitchen door, and kissed the back of her neck as she busied herself with the supper things.

"Dreadful, these maids nowadays," said Lina instead of a greeting. "She can't even get the supper on now. She just can't learn that Berci mustn't have the top of the milk, and she makes his brother's weak, all white. This cow. It'd be quicker to teach a horse than this animal."

And the girl was standing there in the corner, head hanging in servile fashion, with a dogged, wild expression. She was a pleasant, quiet creature, he'd never paid her much attention, had nothing to do with her, perhaps she was a bit slow-witted or not interested or dreamy, mind on other things, homesick for her village, perhaps she felt out of her depth in the city, goodness knows what was the matter... His wife's harsh manner worried him. How could she speak like that to a servant? She wasn't afraid that... He couldn't tell what she ought to be afraid of, the girl had been sent into service with them, how could that quiet, simple girl help it, but he had become accustomed to looking respectfully on the mass of unknown, simple people and on every individual among them, for the individual represents the mass, and authority is what the mass expects... He'd had plenty of time to learn that lesson in the Russian prison camp, but the upper classes here at home, and the women in particular, hadn't been through that school and could still behave to isolated individuals with effortless superiority and tyrannical manners.

He didn't want Lina to say any more to the girl in front of him, because he didn't want to adopt that tone himself, nor could he ask his wife to speak differently, nor could he encourage the girl to think that he could do something to improve her standing in Madam's eyes.

"I'm being driven mad."

"Just come inside for a minute, darling," he said pleasantly, in a quiet, urgent voice, and led the way into the little hall and from there into the dining-room, and everywhere he put on the lights. Lina sensed that there was something in his tone and followed him, putting them out again. Of course, it would have been a good idea if it had been a question of whole series of halls and big rooms, he putting on the lights and his wife coming after and putting them out, but here there were only feeble little sixteen-watt bulbs. It showed what different views of life the two of them had.

This too irritated Lina. She stood at the open door and said:

"I don't understand, you can't go these two steps without putting the light on. You'll bang your nose on all that furniture or I don't know what." And with that she turned and went sourly back to the kitchen.

Pista sighed deeply and looked at his desk. His thoughts were miles away, but his mind was seething, lightning was flashing in it. He reached for the cigar-box and took one out. Lina disapproved of his smoking in the house. She couldn't open enough windows afterwards, but none the less he lit a cigar, because he had something big to accomplish. He drew the smoke of the heavy Britannica down into his lungs and didn't

138

know what to do next. He was going to explode, he'd never known such excitement as now...

He couldn't bear to think about it, because suddenly it was all there inside him, and nothing could come out because of all the tensions that were piling up.

"Aren't you hungry?"

"No... Thank you... I've bought the house."

Lina looked at him for a moment, then said:

"Coming in a minute."

With that she went out and shut the door behind her.

Pista was left there, leaned back and went on smoking his cigar.

The chair was uncomfortable, it had a low, rounded back that gave no support, one couldn't be settled. Lina'd bought it for a Christmas present. It was flashy, modern, but from that modern period when things that were flashy weren't yet practical. Perhaps its flashiness was meant to demonstrate its impracticality...

Why had that Lina gone out when he'd told her that he'd bought the house?

He had to struggle against unknown forces all the time. Whichever way he looked, whatever he dealt with, he always clashed with wills that were resolutely at variance with his own. Now, on looking back at everybody that he'd met in the last twenty four hours, there was nobody that hadn't stood against him like a determined and hostile wall... Except perhaps for Menyus, his brother...

He stood up and started to walk up and down the room. A sudden, huge disquiet floated up inside him. Like a storm bursting beneath a ship. Of course, it was a big thing that he'd done. He shouldn't have done it without Lina... Lina's tyrannical nature... and then, her shrewdness... he oughtn't to have gone against her, left her out of the calculations... She didn't even know what the house was like... and he couldn't tell her... But that didn't matter, he consoled himself... It was a gift, and as a gift it was even better if it was perfect... One had to take the tide at the flood...

But was it? It was as if he were dancing on top of a skyscraper. He was dizzy, didn't know where he was, what to do, what to-morrow would bring... Might it not be downfall? Who knew what that was? And all around everybody's lives were so wonderful. Everybody was in the cataract of unexpected events. Such a house-purchase? Had such a thing ever happened before? In five minutes?... On nothing, to no purpose... That was just it, there was so little certainty in what had happened, because it was contrary to the normal pattern of life, progress step by step; he must surely go mad with the strain, what kind of world was this, that one could move forward like this, could one stop? Or was it just a merry-go-round, a dizzy mirage?

If it was true, he'd got a bargain!

But was it true?

By now he was so anxious that he followed Lina out and said in a somewhat petulant tone:

"Do come in... darling."

Lina came in.

"I want to tell you everything."

"I'm just giving the boys their tea. Just wait one minute."

With that she went out to the kitchen, and Pista thought in amazement that in fact it'd been only a question of moments, really she hadn't had time to pour the coffee into the cups while he'd been getting impatient. It was strange that time flew, while minutes seemed ever so long... He filled the time with such inanities, because his heart was so crushed, he had to talk to himself constantly, keep himself company, so that the burden of time should not overwhelm him.

Finally Lina came in.

She'd fed the boys and stayed in the room.

"Kati néni's out visiting."

"Oh, Kati néni."

He really hadn't missed her, her existence hadn't crossed his mind.

He set about talking to Lina. He told her everything that had happened. What he'd said to the Mayor, how Kardics had turned up, how they'd chatted...

He talked, but all the time he felt that his words were empty, mere bubbles that emerged and burst, there was nothing in them. On the other hand, there was something in the background that he was afraid to reveal.

"Then Kardics bácsi just got up and said that it was the last chance to show me the house, because to-morrow Boronkay's off to Budapest and... Anyway, he took me by the arm, dragged me down to his car, put me in it... I was laughing. I said to the Mayor that I wasn't going, because I'd said to my wife that we'd look at it together if there was any question of buying... He said that that was what he always did. But there were exceptional instances, and if I took a look, then it would be easier for us to

have another look together... So the old men's tyranny won...
Well, the Boronkay villa, my dear. The biggest villa in the
whole estate. Absolutely modern. With an upper storey. And a
cellar. A big rose-garden. Fifteen hundred roses in a big display
in front of the house... I can't tell you, I was bowled over; its
own water-system, a generator, what else can I say, rooms as big
as in the new County Hall, central heating... And what d'you
think the price was? About the same as an ordinary suburban
house... What could I do? I signed the provisional contract with
the proviso that I'd take the final decision only with my wife."
    Lina stretched out a hand and beckoned with a finger.
    "Beg your pardon?"
    "Show me," she said.
    "What?"
    "The contract."
    "It's still only provisional."
    "So. Never mind."
    Now a kind of silent amazement arose within him. He had
to admit:
    "Oh, I haven't got it."
    "Well, where is it?"
    "Kardics bácsi pocketed it, for us to sign at the Bank to-
morrow."
    Lina looked at him in amazement.
    "You haven't got your copy?"
    "No."
    "Then you haven't got a contract."
    He was silent. There was something in this.
    Lina stood up and went slowly out of the room. It was all
right for her, she'd always got something important to do out of
the room. Pista, however, had to stay there, and began pacing to
and fro with great strides.
    He was very much taken aback that in this too Lina'd been
so clever, logical and tidy-minded. And how was it that Kardics
had put the provisional contract into his pocket so calmly, so
naturally... Of course... He'd had no right to ask for it... He
couldn't do anything... It wasn't his contract, it was more like a
deed of gift, which the donor hands over when he wishes...
How could he have said that he wanted it, demanded it... He'd
have been looked at askance... But it didn't matter, for now the
situation was the same as an hour previously, the whole thing
turned on Kardics's goodwill.
    Lina came back, her eyes red with crying.

141

"What's the matter?"

She didn't reply. After a while she said:

"There's something fishy about this."

"What's fishy?" he asked, likewise after a pause. "Is the trouble that they want to swindle somebody by pushing a fine house onto him free? The house is theirs. I'd never have dared to make such a low offer for it. It's half what it should be... If I wanted to sell it I'd be able to get double."

"Try."

"The garden alone is amazing. It all faces south. Great big box bushes, like in the city park."

"That's where they came from."

At that he was silent. It was possible, it was conceivable.

He thought as he walked. These people really did live as if city property and the personal property of the leaders were fully interchangeable. Even in the Mayor's flat there were ornamental plants which had been taken there because there was supposed to be a shortage of space in the greenhouse... It was possible that these city property box bushes were only at the Boronkays' as a favour; even that they were looking after them as a favour.

"That doesn't matter, that's not the point... If we need something we can have it, but if we don't we can return it. The house is there, and it's in his name... It's a house fit for a prince. Such a pleasant, even temperature everywhere inside, there's nothing like it in Zsarátnok. In comparison, City Hall's a tatty, draughty, howling gale..."

"What must it cost to heat," said Lina softly.

He said nothing for a moment, then:

"The city's got plenty of woodland."

And he laughed cynically. He was certain that Makróczy'd always had as much wood delivered to his yard as he'd wanted. There'd been one occasion when they hadn't been able to get wood to heat the schools, and then the city's heavy carts had been delivering loads of firewood for Makróczy. He hadn't even thought that he might some day be involved in such arrangements, but it had just occurred to him that...

Lina didn't say a word, but stood up and went out.

Pista, however, went on walking round the table, round and round.

The point constantly at issue here was, he said to himself, whether Lina and he, for the two of them indisputably constituted a single unit, were or were not capable of rising to and living in the style of the Establishment of the city. If they remained at the level of such small-time middle-class morality, then the greatest dangers would threaten them...

This time he was thinking not of how he should make certain of his share in, say, the privilege of firewood that Makróczy had enjoyed the previous year, but of how he, as Town Clerk, should view the morality of the matter. There was no question but that long-established custom came into effect here. The salaries of City Hall staff were poor; so were those of the senior officers. And so, in times past, they'd had somehow to improve their situation with payments in kind... True, this had been illegal in the past too, but if it was by now accepted practice, could it be helped... In any case, he'd take a look at the regulations concerning salaries to see, for example, how much wood and other perquisites were laid down... There arose, for instance, the question of the use of civic transport. There were some gentlemen who used the city cars constantly, treated them as their own. He'd never yet been in one. He'd not been offered one, whereas he remembered perfectly well that Makróczy used to go out hunting in one... So Makróczy'd had no right to use it, but had been abusing his position... One had to be in with Csoma, the Economics Adviser... He was always creeping around him, but Pista hadn't yet accepted his flattery... One thing in particular came to mind: when he'd given Berci bácsi's coal specimen to Csoma, he'd promised with the greatest pleasure to report back in the most favourable terms... To which Pista had replied that he just wanted to know what it was worth. It would be a good idea to find out if it was any good... Since then, not a word... Now it flashed into his mind that perhaps Csoma had taken that to mean that it wasn't important to him.

He even laughed as he explained the matter to himself.

He felt as if a huge stone had been thrown into the middle of a patch of seaweed. He had to pull it out because his interests demanded that, but as he pulled, every frond of the weed would stick to him, and wouldn't they pull him under?

Straight away he saw that it was quite a devilishly simple situation that he'd got into. For weeks he hadn't caught even a whiff of the remotest trace of swindling, and now it was as if black threads were woven all through his life, and he, like a fly in a spider's web, was beating his wings so as to become a spider and suck like the rest, or they would finally suck out his blood...

"To tell the truth, I don't need it. Up till now I've lived my own decent, simple life, and I can do that after this."

But it was in vain that he said that to himself, heatedly; his self-respect told him that it was not so. Things had changed.

He opened the door and could hear from outside his wife arguing with the maid again.

He went out and said pleadingly:

"Do come in, darling..."

A moment later Lina came in.

"Give that girl the sack if she's so useless."

Lina stared at him.

"Give her the sack? Very well, and where do I get another? Will another be any better?"

"Then don't wear your nerves out. Have patience."

"I might as well endure the wrath of God! At least it might not get on my nerves. But it's easy to be here in the sitting-room... what do you know about it?... Being messed about by an oaf like that... she disgusts me all the time, makes me sick. I turn my back and she's cleaning the table with a napkin... a napkin! Let's see you put up with it... Huh!"

With that she went back to the kitchen.

Pista pulled a wry face... There was no help to be had here.

Lina was becoming soured by this poor life, he couldn't talk to her. But it was also possible that she was running away to the kitchen quarrelling so as to escape the larger issues... It was easier to lose one's temper over a napkin than to suffer in the spiritual clinic of house-purchase.

Now he noticed an unopened letter on the desk.

He picked it up and was startled to recognise the writing of his brother Albert. He began to read it in haste, standing there, but soon sat down because he couldn't bear the weight of those lines.

In the letter Albert said that he was sitting at a cafe table, and as he'd nothing else to do he was writing again. He'd written the day before yesterday, but then hadn't had the spiritual strength to confess everything, but now, as he sat there, he hadn't even enough money to pay sixty fillérs for his coffee. The Bank had abolished his job in the spring. It wasn't true that he was an investment manager. That wasn't needed any more, not in any bank, because there was no market left. There were seventeen pieces of paper that the gentry kept circulating among themselves, but there was no outside money. There were no customers for the market any more, and it made no difference whether the Exchange was closed or open, it didn't count. So he was without hope of any employment, just as he had no hope of anyone paying for this coffee for him. When he'd been made redundant he'd received a severance payment, but that had long been spent, since when he'd used what little credit he had. Now he was deep in debt and couldn't raise another fillér anywhere. That wouldn't have mattered, but he had his blessed wife and four children in a one-room flat, and such was the condition of his blessed wife that he daredn't go home because he couldn't face the wretchedness. The flat was in the slums. The landlord had evicted them, found him a one-room flat in an area on the edge of the city and excused him the arrears of rent, only the authorities obliged him to repossess. Now they were living in that hole like rats. His blessed wife took in sewing and did all she could to earn money so that at least she could make hot soup for the children, but he was sitting penniless in this cafe and was thinking that he'd have no alternative but to kill his family, and the only thing that stopped him doing that was that his blessed wife couldn't bring herself to do it, and he couldn't do it if they couldn't agree.

He read this letter like a fantastic myth. The whole of life was a fantasy. This was a myth. Everything here was a myth; nowadays life was producing myths.

He went on to write that he wasn't asking for anything. His conscience rebelled against the thought of becoming in any way a burden on his brother, with whom he'd once lived in such warm, brotherly affection. Perhaps he'd face the great decision for himself alone, but he felt that that would be unmanly, because the loss of himself wouldn't ease things for his family. 'It would be a terrible blow for them if the papers said...'

The letter fell from his hand. But he quickly picked it up and put it in his pocket.

That was all he needed, having his name dragged into the papers.

But what was he to do? How could he undertake to support another family of six?

He took out his wallet and looked. He'd got ten pengős left.

He stood up to go out.

He had to be alone with these thoughts.

He even looked in on the boys, so as to establish an alibi with his wife, and had a chat with them. He stroked their heads and felt pleased that there were only two of them. In this, too, Lina had been right...

145

'But what'll happen if Kardics bácsi changes his mind overnight?... He can't have second thoughts now, he's got to see it through.'

He looked absently at the boys' faces, and none of his preoccupations came into the open. He smiled, and just as the younger was in the middle of saying something very interesting, he nodded and left them.

The boys didn't complain about this, they were used to the idea that their chatter didn't always interest their father, and they got straight back down to their prep.

Pista, however, put his coat on, and, hat in hand, called in to Lina:

"I promised the Mayor that I'd look in at the Club. Half past six, I'm afraid I'm going to be late."

Lina just said mockingly:

"So now you're off playing cards?"

"Well..."

"Why not? A gambler should try everything."

"I beg your pardon, I'm not a gambler."

"Shut the door, you're making the flat cold."

"You know perfectly well that I live just for you all, my family. I don't deserve you to laugh at me or insult me. I could do with some sympathy."

"Poor man."

"I'm not a poor man, nor a rich one."

"Why? You got your travel expenses today. Because you got the cost of the journey to Pest, or am I paying the noble city for that as well?"

He was startled. He hadn't thought how clever this Lina was. He hadn't yet spent all the money he'd taken for the trip. But there was another point. How could he calculate what he'd spent for the Alispán?

Now again he'd have liked to discuss things with Lina, but having said that he'd got to go to the Club he couldn't get out of it.

"We'll go on with this when I get back."

"Of course."

"Goodbye."

He shut the door behind him and left.

In the street he thought:

'Who am I, how have I offended Fate, that it treats me like this? Do I have to suffer for the sins of my ancestors? I've got a brother and a sister in such a state that if ever it comes out I'll

146

be condemned as a hard-hearted man who wouldn't help his own flesh and blood. But what can I do about them?'

Then he thought:

'At least they know where they are. Ruined, and that's that. They're at the bottom of the well, and if they don't die their situation can only improve. But where am I?... Unexpectedly lifted out of a state of dependable poverty, and I don't know what's happening to me. I'm floating in the air, like Muhammed's coffin... What is going to happen?'

He was passing the post office. He went in, and the close, dark, old building enveloped him like a symbol. This was the old Hungary. From here the ancient, famous Hungarian mails went out... These days post offices were being transformed into gleaming, imposing palaces, only Zsarátnok was still chugging along the ancient channel. Well, the post office didn't matter much; who here wrote letters?... In the gloom he made for a standing desk, dirty, torn, ink-stained, and spent some time choosing among the pens with broken nibs the solitary one with which to write: 'Enclosing this 10P so that you can pay for your coffee, but horrified though I am I don't know what I can do... Will try to think of something. Best wishes...'

When he read over what he'd written he thought it was no good, but could think of nothing better.

He posted the letter, tore his brother's into tiny scraps and threw it into the waste-paper basket.

He'd kept his hat on all the time so that nobody should see his face. As if he were doing something wrong. As if he were cheating, even in a good cause.

'I've got to help them,' he said to himself. 'I don't know, if only I can find the answer. I'm like a tug pulling a string of barges. I'll pull while I can. I've got to get them into harbour.'

18.

There were very few in the Club.

"Who's here?"

The 'huntsman', in his uniform with its green facings and silver oak sprigs, was very un-huntsmanlike in his deferential manner. His cringing disturbed Pista, because it wasn't politeness expressed by the swift, reliable and excellent performance of duty, but the infinite humility of a man broken and brought

147

up to servitude. The dog, faithful or faithless, wagging its tail and waiting for the command.

"Dr. Martiny's here... The gentlemen are playing cards."

Pista didn't catch the other names. Dr. Martiny, the most strident leader of the Opposition.

He went hesitantly into the card-room.

"Ah, here's the Town Clerk, so you can be off," Martiny excused one of his partners.

Dr. Martiny almost commanded him to the table. They were playing rummy, the one game that Pista was any good at. Nobody would play with him at home, least of all his wife, because he was ruthless at the game, incapable of stopping if he was winning.

As if it were a matter of the least importance, he began to arrange the cards that he held.

He lost the first hand. The second he won. He came out of the third without loss and won the fourth. In the end he won the rubber of seven, and picked up three pengős twenty fillérs.

"Well, what about another rubber?"

He would have liked to go home, because a rubber lasted about three quarters of an hour and it was already half past seven, but the others insisted and wouldn't let him go.

"Newcomer's luck," said Martiny, "you must give us our revenge. What's happening about the big loan?"

"That still remains to be seen," said Pista, playing a card.

"In other words, it's frozen," said Martiny, as if there were no importance attached to what one asked over cards. "Only for profitable investments," he added.

"Something of the sort."

"I thought as much. Drainage isn't profitable, rebuilding schools isn't profitable. Nothing's profitable except the AKT. Good name that, AKT... Autó Kereskedelmi Társulat... No, Közforgalmi... Autó Közforgalmi Társulat... AKT![38] His Excellency has a very good *act*. He's the main share-holder. So there, that won't ... When are they going to start building the Zsarátnok AKT?"

He didn't answer. He smiled.

"Because if it's started there'll be an international loan for it... Just in the nick of time to prevent us running out of scandals. I hear the Pig Farm's coming along nicely."

"Do so few come here these days?" Pista tried to change the subject.

"Makróczy's given it up, since when the coast's been clear...

We'll be in a mess if the new Town Clerk likewise comes in winning money... That'd be a tragedy. As it is the Administration takes every last penny off us."

Finally Pista accepted the bait. He answered back.

"The Administration? Strikes me the Administration's the full-time scapegoat of public life."

Martiny was on his hobby-horse. Here was his chance.

"It really boils down to who the world belongs to. Capital? Or the workers? Or the State? What's certain these days is that the State isn't organised for the benefit of the people. It enjoys an exceptional position, like the ancient oligarchies. In the eyes of the people the State is a mystic power. An end in itself. Human life isn't important, what matters is for the State to flourish. The State devours its children. It's a real Cronos. They say we live in a State. No: the State lives on us."

"It's the same with marriage. As long as there's no better institution for the purpose we're stuck with it."

"Let's leave the question of marriage aside for the moment and stay with the State. It's a great mistake to believe that man is born to be independent. Mankind yearns for dependence. I'm not an individualist. I represent a mass of poor people, and I don't struggle to liberate their individual characters, because my individuals, the farm people, don't know what to do out there in the sea of mud with their famous characters. What are they to do, when they're stuck out there for six months on end and can't move? I'm thinking of a million and a half Hungarians, buried on the farms with their own free individual characters. I'm looking at the people of five million acres, who don't need independence because they don't know what to do with it. They live in nominal independence, but this independence, personal independence, is more like the independence of people condemned to death and locked in cells. Every farm's a prison. The leadership of the cities has locked them away there, and the powers that be only show their face when they want something from the farm people. When they need blood-donors or tax-payers, they're there. They're there for what they can get, but they never bring anything to the people. No roads, no protection, no enlightenment, no entertainment."

"But I don't want to talk about the farm question at present. It'd take for ever. I want to raise a much more profound problem. Do people want to live in free competition or not?"

"Well, they don't. Only an exceptional individual needs individual freedom. The masses moan and groan to have the

149

burden of free competition taken from them. We can't stand it. For individuals to be able to face the responsibility that freedom lays upon them they're obliged to join forces, sell their freedom to one another, to unite, so that, lost in the common forest, they'll be able somehow to fight the thousand-headed monster, the free life."

"Here it seems that there's a contradiction, because man experienced redemption when he was freed from serfdom."

"Yes. We lived in serfdom for quite a long time. But serfdom was only evil because the bondsman couldn't exercise any influence over the level of supply. It was good, in that the serf was calm and peaceful. He didn't have to look after himself. The responsibility was on somebody else, and if he was dying of hunger all that it had to do with him was that he could die of hunger if he wasn't looked after."

"Nowadays people crave the sort of dependence under which subsistence is guaranteed, and at the same time there exists the possibility of progress in accordance with one's abilities."

"This life of today, unemployment, this can't be tolerated."

"The masses have no influence over enterprise and performance, and when they're hurled into existence on the one hand as free beings, on the other hand they're left to their own devices. How can they struggle when they've got nothing? What's their freedom worth, if capital can't be compelled to employ them? My friend Péter Kis Kovács is the freest man in the world, he just has to pay tax, interest, levies, everything that the official mind can think up against him, he has to pay for his family's clothes and food, and then he's free. Free to hand over his wheat for however much some authority that he doesn't know has decided that he shall. A sum that won't meet a tenth of his outgoings. What the hell sort of freedom is that? What can he do out there with such freedom? He can write a letter, but if he does he's got to take it sixteen kilometres to the post. He can get an answer, but if it comes they'll put it in the post office window and if he hasn't been for it in two weeks they'll return it to the sender."

"He can bid for city land to rent. What? He can offer twice as much as his friend, who's bidding as well. Then the city considers that he's a free man, like Rothschild."

"But when he can't live with that freedom of paying the rent due on the dot in full, then there's trouble. Then he's committed a crime, for which he has to be prosecuted."

The Town Clerk said uncomfortably:

"The people do enjoy a much higher standard of living today than a hundred years ago."

"It won't last long. Not for the people, nor for us. We're heading full speed back to poverty. When fifty or sixty thousand starving people are being fed every day all winter in Budapest, when the smallest village is riddled with unemployment, when the greatest investors are terrified because they're making no profit, then the final phase of depression is here. We're going back to the Balkans, we're going back to the Orient. No, I say, there's a lower level than that. I've seen bast sandals and crowds of men out of work and starving. But we're on the way. Our poor are spreading the most terrible of infectious diseases – poverty."

19.

He made his way home, his head ringing. These things were too much for one's mind to accept. One could talk about them until the end of the world and it'd be no good, because even the best idea couldn't be tried out. Mankind lived in accordance with such simple patterns, and one system had lasted so long, that there was absolutely no hope of any change being introduced.

And everybody was so very afraid of the consequences. An Opposition politician could at least say all that he wanted to, but a civic officer had to remain silent.

Nor did he enjoy abstract thought any more. His life was so crammed that he had to wait for everything to sort itself out. That day, too. He couldn't bring himself to think through the innumerable pressures that he'd had to endure that day.

"What's the matter, haven't you eaten yet?" he asked as he opened the door.

"How could we, without the man of the house?" said his wife, somewhat tartly.

He said nothing.

"You were a long time talking to the Mayor," Lina continued.

"Not to him, because he wasn't there, but to Dr. Martiny. One has to fight a constant battle with the Opposition."

"Where? Over the beer glasses?"

"Didn't have any beer," he said, and kissed his wife, "just a spriccer, that's all. Forty fillérs."

He sat down to dinner. Above the table hung a big chandelier, but only one bulb, the lowest, was burning. He happened to look up at the lamp and smiled. He'd bought it with his wife at the factory, very cheaply, ten years previously. Since then he'd always been pleased at how cheap it had been, almost nothing, but now he was thinking of the fine chandelier in Feri's villa.

They had a roast. The noodles were by now dried out and crinkly on the stove, and the potatoes had become waterlogged.

He wasted no words on the subject, but when they had eaten their helpings he said to his sons:

"Well, boys, Dad's bought a house."

His wife gave him a disapproving look. The two boys, however, burst out with shouts:

"A house! A house! Daddy's bought a house!"

"Where is it, Dad?" asked Berci. "I hope it's in the villa estate."

Pista smiled. He looked at his son. There was something distinguished about the boy. He was a very handsome lad and held himself well.

He made no reply, only smiled, but that smile said that the boy had guessed.

At that Berci ran to him in silent delight and kissed him again and again.

"What is going on!" exclaimed Lina, and the boy went back to his place.

"You'll know all about it in due course," said Pista.

But dinner had become disorderly in the extreme. Nothing could be done with the two boys, so their mother sent them out straight away to go and finish their prep and get to bed. Children should be asleep by ten o'clock.

Pista remained at the table and lit a cigarette. When his wife had seen to the children and come back in she found him there, lost in reverie, thinking of the good things in store. The afternoon had calmed him. He was basking in the naive feeling that luck was on his side and that only good could come.

"Now, don't you want to hear about the great event?" he asked, and was very pleased that at last Lina sat down arms folded, ready for anything. Her stern look did not soften, however, and when he'd told her about the house-purchase over and over again, in every detail, it looked as if she'd accepted everything.

"What were the relations writing about?" Lina asked suddenly.

"What relations?"

"I saw that you'd taken the letter."

"Oh," he said, "Just wanting, wanting, wanting. There's nothing easier. They're Kopjásses like me. I've never turned to anybody, and now, when my luck's in, a number want to latch on."

"Show me the letter."

"It doesn't exist now."

"Where is it?"

"Somewhere in a waste-paper basket. I tore it up."

She said nothing. She'd already been through the waste-paper basket, but there hadn't been a trace of that letter. She didn't want to make too much of it. If there was trouble it would come out.

"Was that Menyhért?"

"No. Albert."

"He's another first-class chap."

Why didn't these idiots write to him at the office? What stupidity; they must send such things to his home address. They ought to have more sense. He'd meant to tell them about it, but hesitated. He was careful, said nothing about the ten pengős or his win at cards.

"I still don't know how Kardics bácsi's looking at all this. Because I'll have to pay something soon, although I think that the whole house is the Bank's property because of the mortgage, and I think that the purchase price is fixed at what's owing to the Bank... Never mind, it'll soon be clear."

But Lina said nothing, remained painfully silent, and gradually his conversation became empty, false, contrived. He couldn't feel happy and couldn't cheer himself up any more. Lina hardly looked at him. She gazed straight ahead and her whole bearing was tired and despondent.

"Well, say something," said Pista quietly.

Lina raised her head but her eyes remained downcast. Her body was bent forward, she only straightened her neck and sat there, head half bowed, with an expression like the Virgin Mary.

"I don't understand," she said at length. "It may be that you're right. In any case, think it out carefully, because I'm having nothing to do with it, I'll accept no responsibility... Whatever the outcome, Pista, it won't be on my head."

"What should be on your head?"

Lina gave a slight shake of the head as if to throw off a painful feeling.

"Look Pista, you and Kardics and the rest are going to do

something very hasty, and there'll be no going back. But do you know what it means to a woman that's built up her life, to have it turned upside-down at a stroke? What you're doing means that everything that I've done until now doesn't count. It's null and void. I've been used to having a husband with a limited income, but who gave it to me down to the last fillér. I've worked very hard to keep a decent house on that small income. To provide for my husband, bring up two children properly, and keep myself so that you wouldn't be ashamed to be seen out with me. This hasn't been easy, Pista... Now you've been caught up by this sudden good luck, or misfortune. The shock's knocked you off the rails; the only sure thing is that the circle that you move in now is quite different from the one you were in before. Its ways are different, its morals, its atmosphere, everything is different. There you've got to use a lot of money to keep up. For fifteen years I haven't had time to read a book, haven't read a paper, paid attention to fashion or done any of the things that non-working women fill their time with. I was there at that dinner, and all evening I was on my guard, all I had to do was to keep quiet and be intelligent so that nobody should see that I didn't belong there. Why are you forcing me to move into an entirely new world? Why isn't natural progress good enough for you? Surely, if things stay as they have been, if everything goes well, if we gradually get some money together, then we can find the kind of home that'll do for us, for our requirements. Look at our friends, the women we know. Teachers, doctors, engineers. Do we have to give them all up? Are we suddenly to become *nouveaux riches*, worming our way into the highest social circles? You're a clever man, have you thought out what the end of all this is going to be? Can people be taken out of their old skins and given new ones? And even if you can get a new skin, can your soul be remade? Am I to move into a six-roomed villa? Do you think I don't know who these Boronkays are? They've been in all the top places. Mrs. Boronkay's a sister-in-law of the Alispán, she was sitting in the Főispán's box not long ago, just her and the Főispán's wife, do you imagine that the Főispán's wife is going to send me invitations now? And if she does, what have I in common with that stuckup, sour-faced woman, who has never in her life known the meaning of work and money? She's always had so much she couldn't spend it with both hands. I can't spend money. Where could I have learnt how? Am I now supposed to go and wear myself out in the Boronkay villa? Do the weeding with my own two hands? Or will you be able to keep a gardener for me? A gardener cum butler cum cook, who can produce great dinners? And will you get a maid? And perhaps a manservant? I can't take it on, Pista. I valued your old student frock-coat as I'd have valued your life, that truly respectable life that you used to live. I know how hard it was for you to buy that coat in those days, because you told me, and I've remembered your every word, how you paid by instalments over eight or nine months, for me that coat was the guarantee of your respectability, a real certificate of nobility, a monument to nobility of spirit. How could you slip so easily off the old way..."

Pista listened in horror to his wife's quiet words of wisdom. It had often surprised him how, in moments of danger, she could express her thoughts sensibly and cleverly, much more so than he, but now he was surprised. Indeed, in the depths of his soul he was obliged to admit that she was right about everything, and it pained his heart that she should have perceived through his words the deep moral crisis that he'd had to undergo in the past few days. He lit one cigarette from another.

"Look, this smoking as well. Previously you were a clean person; our flat was as clean as a mirror, clean and sweet-smelling. The cleanliness of ordinary, decent people. For years and years you never lit a cigarette in the house, still less a cigar, and this made me proud, because I said to myself that I had a husband who understood my way of life. You didn't make the flat into a club, and the people who came here were our sort of people. Now, these gentlemen with whom you're connected haven't returned your visit, have they? They're not inclined to lower themselves to visit us, to our standard of living. Yes, they'll come once you've moved into the new residence, the castle that you've snatched from the Boronkays. There they'll be able to live it up. There'll have to be suppers and dinners such as they're used to. So tell me, Pista, will that all be covered by your official salary? It won't, but it'll have to be paid for somehow. So what will pay for it?"

He said nothing, and his face began to flush red, he could see now what his wife was driving at, and it wasn't long coming.

"I'll tell you where it'll come from, Pista. The same place as theirs. I think that those gentlemen all live on money which is accounted for not under the heading of what they get it for, but falsely. There'll be business activities, yes, after which they'll pass some on to you. I don't know whether it'll be a lump sum or what. It'll be booked as one thing or another; it came to so

155

much more. Perhaps they'll persuade factory owners to sign excessive accounts, so that there'll be no legal means of distinguishing it. The electrician said that some time ago, when he was tendering for some work with the city, he got a bit of money and signed a big receipt. You can't trust anybody over anything. They're all thieves up there, the electrician said, because he couldn't get work except when the builder gave him some, and the builder swindled him, he only worked because without work he couldn't have lived. If he got the amounts that they quoted for one piece of work and another, he'd be able to buy a house, but as it was he and his family could scarcely live, he couldn't send the children to school... Is that the kind of money you want a share in?"

"You're being very hard," said Pista and hung his head, looking morosely at the ash-tray on the table.

"Look, Pista, I'm not interfering with anything, I'm just telling you so that you can't be caught out. Anyway, I don't want to insult you, I don't even know whether these rumours are true. I'm not familiar with this way of life, but one thing's certain, your family can't be shifted from one day to the next out of its decent, modest life-style into the decent wealthy world. Because there is decent wealth, but for that you have to have something under your feet and something behind you. And tell me, Pista, what have you got behind you? You've got your poor relations, that you want to burden yourself with. And that won't do. Fortune hasn't smiled on you so much that you can offer all your brothers and sisters the same kind of position that you've got yourself. Never mind your uncles into the bargain, and all the rest of your relations, whom you're going to get without fail."

"I can give them charity at least," said he gloomily.

"Yes, and it causes you grief. Look, today I got a letter as well... This is another of your relations, Róza néni, writing from Nagykároly.[39] Your reputation's got as far as that. The Romanians aren't paying her pension and she's keeping herself by taking in mending. She can't be seen in public, and she's asking if I have any clothes to spare, a great lady like me can't wear a dress for as long as a poor woman, will I send them to her. Well, what can I send her, Pista? I shall have to send some of my good dresses, not because I can't have people saying that her famous relation, the wife of the Town Clerk of Zsarátnok, goes about in such tatty clothes, but because she wants to show off with these dresses, I've been sent this and that, my God, what kind hearts these people have, they're not mean to their poor relations."

Pista said:

"You don't have to answer."

"That's easier said than done. Should I be the only bad one? Let it go round the relations that you're ever so kind, you sent Lajos bácsi your frock-coat, but your wife begrudges her poor relations even her rags; that she'd keep in touch if we were as rich as we used to be, and so on."

They sat for a while in silence, then Lina stood up.

"Ten o'clock, the boys must go to bed... Well, all I'm saying is, Pista, think the whole thing over very carefully."

And with that she went out.

Pista was left with agonising thoughts.

He was, however, of a positive disposition, not given to philosophising, in a couple of minutes he was full of practical ideas.

Kardics doubtless had an extreme need to bind Pista to him. It crossed his mind again, as he'd often thought, that he'd very soon sell himself to this villain, and that it would follow that he'd be at his mercy in some serious situation. For example, the Pig Farm question.

If Kardics was deeply involved in the Pig Farm, then it would be Pista that dictated the terms.

The house-purchase was a good thing. The Alispán hadn't turned up, therefore it was completely accepted that the Boronkays had been dropped. One could only make progress in life if one freed oneself of burdens, and that meant all of one's burdensome relations too. There was nothing else for it, one should keep only those likely to prove beneficial, and the wasters, of whom nothing could be made, must be left to their fate. Menyhért, he was all right. He was in a post at the Museum, he could be brought in, he'd be productive. He'd got some energy. But Albert, with that plan for killing his family... What could be done?... He couldn't kill off his children one after another. Oh, he was talking rubbish. Though of late there had been a rash of such incidents. One read of them all the time – 'Family slaughter in Liliom utca'. But that a man of education... and his brother, into the bargain... he couldn't be sure that this wasn't some sort of blackmail... he must give him some assistance, in any case, enough to keep him going. Some little job. That could be arranged. To find a hole somewhere so that they shouldn't starve, but not to bring them to the city. If he were so incapable

157

he could be a messenger or a collector. The Kopjásses loved their children much more than that... Kelemen the schoolmaster hadn't shown up yet, he could stay where he was.

So that was his brothers taken care of. The uncles, however, if they were still alive – beyond their time, in any case – would manage to survive.

He wouldn't take on any particular burdens. No. He'd got enough problems of his own. He too had a family, everybody could see that.

The main thing was to see things clearly. Kardics... He was the most important. There must be some urgent problem there, because otherwise how could it have happened that, on the very first morning, this man had discovered him in the street, who had never before even bothered to pass the time of day.

If Kardics had accepted the relationship, now he must stand firm. But the way to approach the matter wasn't through the house-purchase contract... Not that, but what was wrong with the Pig Farm. Next day, when he went to see the old man, he wouldn't begin, '*Kedves bátyám*, how do you think I can undertake the provisional contract', but '*Kedves bátyám*, there's something I don't like about the Pig Farm. The city can't become involved in such a business. It can't accept responsibility for Makróczy's deals'. That was the solution. Let him come up with some proposals, then perhaps they could talk.

Again and again he came back to this in his thoughts. He invented whole arguments. God hadn't got enough money for his name to be... For the interests of the city to be...

There he quickly thought, what if the Alispán were right, if the calculations were correct, the only trouble was that the price of maize had risen so that it was dearer than pork fat... Suppose something could be done about this. Let's suppose that the Pig Farm were a going concern, with only problems resulting from the boom. In that case the company could bear the loss, and the city could take it all over. They'd have to work out a cheap proposal on the same lines as the house-purchase, well below the investment price. Why? The Bank could still do well out of it. There was also the consideration of reputations to be saved. The Szentkálnays were deeply involved, as the Alispán had said. Suppose something could be blamed on them. The house of Szentkálnay had enough money... They'd hand a little over... What if there were a criminal aspect to the affair, and the Szentkálnays couldn't evade it...

He felt that his power was growing, becoming firmer.

158

'Not so, my friend,' he said to himself, almost aloud. 'If you all need me, let's look at what's what. I'm not going to allow myself to be pocketed just like that.' Naturally, should need arise, use could still be made of the fact that they wanted to win him over in this fashion. A provisional contract, that was nothing. That didn't bind him, only the vendor. He wasn't even a relation. Nothing in this caused him concern. He couldn't be mixed up in a shady deal. This wasn't what he'd issued his programme in the paper for, to shake up the affairs of the city and save it from every liability. What mattered was the interests of the people.

It was also suspicious that he hadn't heard a word so far about the Pig Farm. They must really be in a spot!

If the worst came to the worst he'd go up himself and see the Minister and tell him everything. Who could say, suppose the Mayor too were involved. In this day and age disciplinary proceedings against Mayors were not unknown.

Gradually the house-purchase business began to assume smaller proportions in his eyes.

What was more, so far it hadn't cost him a fillér, and he must be careful that it didn't. Might it not be possible to get the whole house free from entailments? After that it'd be up to him to see that the city didn't pay for the Pig Farm. It could become a good business, in which case the city could only be grateful to him.

He'd go out personally in the course of the following day and have a good look at it, make a full appraisal of it. He'd take the Clerk of Works with him, for after all he was now virtually in charge of the city. Everything was in the Town Clerk's hands. He didn't have executive power, but he could make proposals, pass judgements, set things in motion, First thing next morning, before the Mayor came in, because he was always on the late side, he'd go out with the Clerk of Works and the manager and have a report produced on the Pig Farm, look at the books, do a stock-take, and then he'd have the whole thing in his grasp.

What was there to lose? On the contrary, he stood only to gain. There was nothing for it but to sit down with Dr. Martiny and then, finally, he'd have the whole city on his side. Never before had there been such popularity, it was as if he were gaining control of a notable piece of business.

The historical side of the matter too began to clarify in his mind. As Cultural Adviser he'd had nothing to do with it, but

159

not so long ago there'd been talk about the Pig Farm everywhere.

So here was the source of the trouble. This was what was behind it all.

He looked around the room and noticed that there was an awful lot of smoke. He opened the windows. The little street was quiet, not a light in a single window. He looked at the clock. He hadn't realised it was eleven o'clock.

Calmly and happily he looked out on the provincial city. People were asleep. Citizens. They didn't even dream what anxiety the new Town Clerk had been through for the sake of their well-being and happiness, how many plans he'd been weaving in his head.

When he saw that the room had been ventilated as well as could be he shut the window and went into the bedroom.

Lina was fast asleep in bed.

He carefully undressed and lay down.

But he couldn't sleep. He listened to the clock as it musically chimed the quarters.

It was odd, he'd never, at least not for years, had a bad night. He'd always slept as peacefully as an innocent child. He just put his head down and he was off. His wife always went to bed later than he, because her domestic and maternal duties occupied her, and she'd lost the habit of going to bed early. Pista, on the other hand, became sleepy soon after dinner. Sometimes he'd do some Latin with his sons, which he enjoyed because it pleased him that he was still good at it. Sometimes, less enthusiastically, he'd try to do their Maths, because they didn't like it, and then he always had to study the lesson first so as to explain things to them really easily and lucidly. But if possible he avoided lessons, pleading that he did enough work in the office, and went to bed.

Nowadays he couldn't sleep and every night was a bad one. If he did get off to sleep, he woke early and tossed and turned in bed. Sometimes his wife woke and complained of his sleeplessness. Sometimes they even had a bit of an argument, then she'd doze off, as she was tired and healthy. Certainly he'd got enough to worry about. It was only now, in bed, that he became aware of the impossible responsibility that he'd undertaken. However cheaply the house was sold to him, it was still an awful lot of money; a few weeks ago he wouldn't have dreamed of it. How was it to be managed? Suppose the Bank bought it for him, none the less he'd have to pay them back one day. His official salary wouldn't even pay the interest. So where would he get the income from? Lina was right. They were treating him like a man of means like themselves, or at least as one to whom five or ten thousand pengős meant nothing. Was that just their manner? Was it possible that he'd have such an income?

After midnight, he couldn't even have guessed the time, Berci bácsi's coal-mine flashed into his thoughts. That was a legal matter, and the old chap had offered twenty thousand pengős as commission. The sure thing was that if he let the money reach Berci he'd never see that twenty thousand, but it was actually there to be taken. He'd simply have a word with the Clerk of Works and keep his due.

He set about calculating how much coal would have to be delivered for the family to make a hundred thousand pengős. He'd have liked to put the light on, but he didn't want to disturb Lina. This sharing a bedroom was not good, and he suddenly realised why husband and wife had separate bedrooms in rich people's houses. The reason was simple. In that world husbands could sleep neither by day nor night. Who could sleep with so much to worry about?

Next morning he woke, bruised and battered. There was a constant quivering in his insides, and a bitter taste in his mouth. His head was swimming. He felt really giddy and had no appetite.

When he reached the office his first action was to phone the city Clerk of Works, Bisztriczay. He offered to come round right away.

They didn't know each other very well, because they'd never had much contact except when Pista'd been Cultural Adviser and had had to call on Bisztriczay to attend to school buildings. The Clerk of Works was a very senior man, whom Pista'd had no right to command, but whose word he'd had to accept. If he said that there were no funds for repairs, that was final. A second storey had been built onto one school, and it transpired that the walls weren't strong enough, the ceilings cracked. With great ceremony the Clerk of Works came out to view the problem. Now that Pista knew more about it, the superior air had been to cover up incompetence. He should have known in advance whether the walls would take the extra weight. He claimed that they'd been given an order and had carried it out. Now a further order would have to be issued for the problem to be solved as cheaply as possible. What they did was to let beams into the walls and support them with iron columns. The school looked ridiculous, but the pupils were happy because they had a week's holiday, and they found it odd that the school-room looked like a castle. Pista, however, had remained dissatisfied and bitter at the defaced room. He didn't know what had happened, what the trouble was, but had the feeling that something was out of order. His bitterness was all the greater as Makróczy had treated him very rudely, objected to his suspicions, whereas he hadn't suspected anything and was only expressing an opinion.

While Bisztriczay was on his way over all this went through Pista's mind, and in the meantime he briefed himself on the Pig Farm.

The Clerk of Works found him immersed in the study of documents. He was extremely pleasant, smiling, so obliging that Pista hated him.

"What d'you make of this Pig Farm, if I might enquire?" he asked when they were alone.

"If I might say so, it's a great wild-cat scheme that has ended up as such an airy-fairy thing should."

"And how should that be?"

Bisztriczay laughed.

"The way it is."

Pista asked thoughtfully:

"What're the buildings like?"

"First class. Much more up-to-date than anything at Kőbánya. Everything's been built on the latest Danish lines. Spotlessly clean. Hygienic, economical. Nothing wrong with that, but it was overdone, and they didn't allow for market fluctuations. The problem was with the funding."

They continued their discussion for a long time. Pista had to learn as he learnt Maths with his sons.

He called in the Agricultural Adviser as well. The three of them spent the morning going over the paperwork.

There was a terrible deficit. The management had been so slap-dash that the criminal element of the question came more and more into prominence.

"Somebody's got to be held responsible for this," said Pista, banging the table.

"Responsible?" said the Agricultural Adviser. "Held responsible?"

He regretted it at once. Why beat the drum?

"Please call a car, we'll go out to the site and take a look."

The city had a car, but the Agricultural Adviser dealt only

162

with horses. He phoned and in a little while the hajdú reported that the carriage was outside.

They went out to the Harangos. Among other things there was the irregularity that the site was entirely on city property, and it wasn't formally established whether this was an easement, a gift or a purchase. As the same people had been running the whole business, they'd omitted to clarify the legal position with regard to the ownership of the site. Thus the whole confused affair must be in the hands of the city, and it depended entirely on how the Mayor regarded the matter.

The journey was very pleasant. It was a fine autumn day, a light mist lay over the Great Plain. The sun shone through it. Peasants were harvesting the maize and mightily piled wagons came toward them, carefully keeping to the side of the road as they caught sight of the city carriage.

"What a pity I haven't brought a gun with me," said Bisztriczay.

He'd certainly not seen the birds flying up, the hares leaping away.

At the Pig Farm it was quiet. The pigs had been moved out because there was no maize. They'd been sold off half-grown. The extensive site stood there, its concrete sties, runs and enormous yard like an accursed castle.

Not long before, scarcely six weeks ago, the wealth of Canada had been here, and now there was silence. Just a pig or two left, belonging to the staff. Above the maize stores and processors circled a horde of crows.

He looked and looked at the site, but to no purpose; he couldn't make head or tail of it.

"That's where Feri Boronkay wanted to move in," said the Clerk of Works with a laugh, pointing to the massive office block.

Nobody spoke.

"That reminds me, your uncle Berci's sent a telegram," said the Clerk of Works, "saying that the first two sample loads had left the mine at Köleser."

"What loads?"

"The coal, of course."

Pista was startled. He hadn't even known that this coal business was so far advanced.

"Be careful," he said.

"Of what?"

163

Pista didn't want to speak evil of his uncle, so after a pause he said:

"The old chap's a wonderful businessman, but you can't trust him over money. Be very careful only to pay for the amount that's delivered."

"But the old boy wants to contract to receive at least 120,000 pengős in advance, because it appears that he wants to finance the mine with it. That's not such a big deal, and if the coal's good quality there's no objection in principle."

Pista was flabbergasted. 120,000 pengős! He'd get 24,000 if his sums were right... "I'm just saying, check the coal very carefully. I can't accept any responsibility."

"Well, if you won't accept responsibility, Town Clerk, then I won't accept the coal. The contract isn't signed yet."

"Then what's he sending it for?"

"He wants to strengthen his position."

"Naturally, there's no cause for alarm, but now, seeing this wretched business, I certainly don't want to get into a similar situation."

"Discretion is the better part of valour," said Csoma, the Agricultural Adviser, who liked to use folksy phrases, and whose speech was always peppered with such proverbial wisdom.

Pista reached into his pocket for his handkerchief to wipe his eyes, which were watering in the cold wind.

When he pulled it out he found inside it a tiny woman's handkerchief.

He only looked at it when he'd dried his eyes. It was a very delicate little handkerchief, and an unfamiliar perfume came from it.

'What can this be, whose is this?' he thought, and stared at the small, white, lace-edged handkerchief.

He sniffed it once more. He didn't recognise the perfume. It wasn't his wife's. Lina used White Rose, and this was some alien, exciting, penetrating scent...

He couldn't imagine how it had come into his pocket. In any case, it wasn't in the pocket where he usually put his handkerchief, but in his right side pocket, where he never put such a thing, and now he couldn't understand, confused as he was, how he'd come to put a hand into that pocket. Presumably his hand had known that the handkerchief was there.

As his eyes stumbled across his companions' blank faces, his mind was only on the origin of the little handkerchief.

"What's the matter, Town Clerk? A crime?" asked the Clerk of Works.

"What makes you say that?"

"I can see you don't recognise the handkerchief. You've stolen it somewhere and you can't remember where."

Pista stood for a moment taken aback, then his face began to redden, and he blushed to such an extent that he could no longer conceal it.

The Clerk of Works laughed. "Think back, when were you last in a woman's drawing-room?"

"Oh, I'm mad," he mumbled, "it's my wife's."

"Oh yes, so that's why you don't recognise it," the Clerk of Works teased him.

As if it were nothing, he pushed the handkerchief back where he'd found it, the right-hand outside pocket of his coat. When he'd done that he changed his mind and put it in the left inside pocket. He gave a little smile, but he didn't realise what a dangerous thing he'd done. There, on his left side, the little handkerchief began to work. The perfume on it, or something, began to warm him, excite him, numb him. Something went to his heart. He couldn't concentrate, and suddenly the whole business for which he'd come out lost its meaning.

Something else had flared up. He knew now, he was very much aware, where he'd come by that handkerchief. It couldn't have come from anywhere else, only there... He couldn't bring himself to recall how he'd put it in his pocket, how he'd stolen it, taken it to himself... This was a secret, a mystery, for it could belong to nobody but Magdaléna. But he'd done nothing, and yet here was the handkerchief.

He remembered once in his student days stealing a little handkerchief like this. It had excited him for years. He hadn't met the girl for a long time, many years, but the stolen handkerchief had still given him a thrill. Lina had hidden it eventually and destroyed it, because it presumably was an meaningful souvenir, whereas it had been nothing of the sort, and the most that he'd done with that girl had been to steal her handkerchief. That, however, he'd wanted, planned, accomplished, and he'd no idea at all how this had happened... It could only have been an involuntary act. His subconscious had been at work. His hand had done it. Left hand or right? It could only have been the right, because of course he'd found it in his right-hand pocket.

He became completely immersed in his thoughts, and his

165

emotions began to seethe, bubble, throb, like a kettle when a fire is lit under it.

They got into the carriage and he said not another word to anyone.

He was so limp, he might have fainted. He let himself relax, and lay there helpless, his arms, his legs, his whole body, blazing inwardly.

'It's fantastic,' he said to himself, 'I thought I'd got over her... When we were together I felt absolutely nothing and I was very glad to have cooled towards her so... And if you please, all the time this wicked, thieving hand of mine was stealing. How was I to know what a low, cunning act my body was committing without my being aware, how it had discovered this little item that could be stolen, and carried out the theft? The length of time that's passed since then, and the fact that I had no idea that I had any souvenir of Magdaléna, just goes to show how unaware of it I was. And now that I do know, a coal of fire has been put in my pocket.'

He reached over towards his heart and deeply regretted putting the little handkerchief there. He couldn't explain that either, why had he put it there? Obviously, he'd wanted to put it close to his heart... But now he was in a terrifying whirlpool. He couldn't even accept responsibility for himself, if the self maintained a secret organisation, in that while his consciousness happily rejected the former problem, at a lower level, in some sort of hidden cavern, the masters of the underworld and their henchmen didn't flinch from the greatest evil by way of breaking in and stealing or whatever; let him acquire a souvenir, a souvenir that will then be of great value to them in besieging his heart.

The carriage dropped them off one by one as they reached their homes. Pista had the furthest to go, and was glad to be able to remain alone with his thoughts for a few minutes, with the mystery on his heart.

When they turned into his street he gave a great sigh. He had to summon up strength to face his wife, and so that Lina shouldn't notice that anything had happened.

As he took off his coat he smoothed the side of his jacket in case the handkerchief was pressing against the material and Lina might notice that there was something there.

They were waiting for him to start lunch, and in order to preclude any word of complaint he said, in too loud a voice:

166

"The neighbours were surprised to see me come home in a city carriage now."

He laughed, but his laughter was false, covering up.

"Lot going on today. Been out at the Pig Farm site. Never seen a dodgier business."

While he washed his hands Lina was standing at the door. "I'll tell you what those gentlemen have been doing. What they've been up to."

But he was very glad that Kati néni was there and that he mustn't say anything, nor could he, on the contrary he was right to keep quiet. To keep quiet and to laugh, while his face looked as if every muscle had stiffened in the cold wind and now was disfigured in a frozen smile.

Kati néni rattled on about the relations that she'd been looking up. Pista hadn't known anything for years about the distant relations. Lina wasn't one for keeping in touch with relations.

"That Verpeléti, that Verpeléti," said Kati néni, "what he doesn't know about horses, he's such a great expert, he lives and dies for horses."

"Really, I ought to get Verpeléti into the city... I've just been with Csoma, and he was saying that the city could do with a new foreman on the puszta."

"Oh, God bless your every step," Kati néni began at once, and he was startled at being so careless as to speak unguardedly. He mustn't do it. Because this Kati néni would soon pass the word and immediately let his relation loose on him.

Lina too was appalled and gave her husband a severe look. She reached across to Pista and took hold of his jacket by the button-holes.

Pista grabbed her hand in such terror for fear of what she might be after that Lina was quite taken aback.

"Hey, what's the matter? What're you afraid of?"

"Me? Why should I be afraid of anything?"

"So why so nervous?" and she looked to see what might be the cause of her husband's shy, edgy movement, in which there were prohibition and alarm. "What's in your pocket?" she asked thoughtfully.

"In my pocket?" said Pista, and opened his eyes wide. He patted the breast of his jacket with both hands as if to see whether there was anything inside, and indicated that it was completely empty. Not the slightest bulge showed that anything was hidden there.

Lina didn't press the matter, but neither did she forget.

167

"I'm on edge," said Pista, "because of the terrible time I've been having lately."

Lina gave him another disapproving look, warning him to be careful not to say anything indiscreet in front of Kati néni. He understood and changed the subject.

"It's terrible taking on a new job, because your head splits with thinking while you're learning all that you need to know."

"Yes," said Kati néni, "the Pig Farm's a great scandal. Well, Magdaléna Szentkálnay..."

Pista quickly looked down, drank some water to cover his blushing. But why blush?... And how was it, that if one had some slight injury or something to hide, everything struck that spot? Magdaléna Szentkálnay's name wasn't usually uttered in this house, and it had been the first word that Kati néni had spoken after this pocket business...

"I hear they're having to sell the house, because they've got to get out, and that's their greatest problem," aid Kati néni.

"Problem?" asked Lina.

"Yes. I hear that there isn't a brick in it that couldn't be the subject of legal action. So they're selling to get out of trouble, and then things can take their course."

"My dear," said Pista, "I'd very much like to take a nap. Would you mind?"

Kati néni immediately jumped up, because she felt that it was something to do with her, and with great enthusiasm recommended Pista to have a sleep in the afternoon, meanwhile she would explain to the boys...

"Don't bother explaining, néni," said Lina, "they've got to learn."

Pista could see that there'd be no sleeping in that room, or at least only with some inconvenience, because his wife and Kati néni would have to go into the kitchen if he wanted the dining-room to himself. So he went into the bedroom, and Lina followed and made the bed for him to lie down, because there was no room for a sofa.

But if he was to lie on the bed, then he had to take off his jacket so as not to cover it with fluff.

Carefully, while Lina's back was turned, he took the little handkerchief out of his left-hand pocket and stuffed it into his trouser pocket. Then he hung his jacket over the arm of a chair and lay down.

He stretched out, covered himself up, and pretended to go to sleep.

"Where are you taking my jacket?" he asked Lina suddenly.

"I'll see to this button, it's only held on by a prayer," said Lina in an indifferent tone.

When she'd gone out he laughed silently. It was a good thing he'd been so careful. And he'd had a bit of a shock, how awful it was that one should let out such a secret at once. Lina'd never even thought of suspecting the inside pocket, but now it was absolutely certain that she'd taken the jacket to search it. For the moment he was safe, but if things went on like this he was going to go mad...

While he was trying to doze off and was thinking of nothing, a further piece of black magic occurred to him. It seemed that secret rays must be emanating from the handkerchief. His trouser pocket was beginning to feel warm, as if it were full of hot coals.

With a sudden, convulsive movement he turned over in bed, and a wild, tempestuous surge of emotion burst upon him.

He awoke to Lina coming in and saying quietly:

"Kardics bácsi's sent an urgent letter, darling."

Lina was as sweet and gentle as he hadn't seen her in a long time.

He came to slowly and scratched his head. Then he got up and tidied himself. Kardics bácsi was asking him to call in at the Bank right away.

"Tell him I'm coming at once."

Lina moved as quickly as a young girl. She'd been very relieved at finding nothing at all in Pista's pockets, but little did she know that the tiny handkerchief was from then on the symbol of the heat and passion of great love...

It was very quiet at the Bank. The iron shutters were down, the street doors were shut. Pista had to go in across the yard, and then he was astonished to find every official sitting at his desk, working in deathly silence. It seemed that some sort of depression was in the air, even the messengers were coming and going in their uniforms as if they were undertakers.

Kardics bácsi was sitting in his office, and when Pista went in he sprang up so cheerfully and briskly that Pista was simply amazed, it was so out of keeping with the afternoon hush that permeated the whole building.

"Hello, my dear chap," he exclaimed, shaking both his hands.

"Are you really open in the afternoon?"

"Of course, of course. Haha, you're not in the city now, this is the Bank! Come on, sit down. Will you have a cigar? Go on, take one, it'll help our conversation."

Pista felt rather uncomfortable sitting there. The chairs were unusually large, leather-upholstered, and he was almost lost in them. He had the feeling that Kardics bácsi had bought such big furniture so as to intimidate his victims. Kardics himself was not a big man, but he was used to it and jumped about on the settee like a strange, dangerous animal.

"So you haven't been in the office this afternoon?"

"Actually, I was asleep."

"Ah, there you are, riding in carriages and fresh air take their toll! And the boss keeps an eye on things, of course," and he laughed so heartily that he choked.

'He's got false teeth as well', thought Pista to himself. 'But his are better than the Mayor's, not so porcelain white.'

"Well, my dear chap, it's an enormous business, the Pig Farm, enormous," said Kardics bácsi. "It's a gold-mine, you just have to view it in the right light. Here we are, in the middle of the Great Plain. Here in the homeland of maize. I remember when I was a boy bandits used to hide in the maize, and God didn't have enough policemen to find them. I've got a shepherd who met Sándor Rózsa[40] himself in the maize when he was a boy. Sándor Rózsa said to him 'Now my boy, off you go to town and bring me some bread and some bacon'. So off he went and came back with it. Of course, the bandit gave him the money for it. To this day he's sorry that he didn't hand him over to the police. Or goodness knows whether he's sorry or not. They belong together. The poor man and the bandit hang on the same rope. You can't tell 'em apart. If I tell him to do something he never does, whereas he would if a bandit told him to. It's pure romance. But do you realise how romance nourishes life? If romance stops, fantasy stops. Without a bit of romance there's no enterprise."

"I think there's too much romance in this."

"Where? In the Pig Farm? You're very much mistaken. It's a sound business, but it's only just becoming that."

The old man spoke so spiritedly, he simply glowed and seethed. He was happy, *joie de vivre* positively fizzed in the air.

"Look, here's this city. Here it is with its own mammoth property. And it loses money on everything. Grazing land. Thirty-two thousand acres left as grazing. Well, isn't that a sin against God in this day and age? All right, there's a lot of salt land there, but there's first-class land too. You've got to consider the area as a whole, get hold of the map and specify precisely which parts are worth cultivating. But then get to it and plant maize. Here's the autumn, this is the time for soil sampling. Get ten steam-ploughs for the future. By next autumn the city'll have enough maize to install ten thousand pigs. As soon as the calculations are done, immediately we contract with the farmers that this one is to produce a hundred piglets, that one three hundred. The money can stay at home. Not Balázs Hübele style, but rationally. The people get rich and so does the city. It's the end of the deficit. The Minister's announced that he'll only allot funds for profitable investments. If we've managed without piped water until now, we shall manage for another couple of years. What? We'll drink wine. We don't need water. We need money, my boy, money, my dear chap. You couldn't find a more popular thing for the Council."

His eyes sparkled and he fidgeted in his great armchair like a racoon.

"We can get the whole thing for next to nothing. And we won't have to put another krajcár into it. Well, what the hell. The concrete won't come to any harm. We'll need a watchman to keep an eye on it, a site-guard. Then when the time comes we'll simply move the herds in. The city of Zsarátnok won't need anybody. We'll run the whole pig establishment ourselves. All the citizens will bless the name of the new Town Clerk. By Christmas we'll be producing so many bacon pigs that we'll be able to sell them cheap. The marketing style of the future is dumping. That's what Canada's doing, that's what Russia's doing, and that's what we'll do too. Create a market. Then the future's ours. It wasn't foolishness that the Mayor wouldn't part with the land at the time, but allowed the whole installation to be built on city property. That's how he guaranteed himself the prerogative. Nobody'll ever be able to take it off us by legal means."

The Town Clerk was beginning to appreciate the marvellous nature of the undertaking. He trembled inwardly. But he had to admit that it was cleverly devised.

Now Kardics bácsi took out a file and spread out the documents.

He became livelier and livelier. Hundreds of thousands tripped off his tongue, and the whole thing because as simple a piece of business as if it were a question of ten pengős.

Pista kept looking at Kardics's teeth. Now he could see that on some of them there were gold rings. These must hold the

171

adjacent false teeth. He felt that he was looking into the mouth of a wolf.

Kardics laid before him the contract, now fully detailed, together with the Bank's loan agreement. A whole pile of bills lay beside the contract, and a monstrously long insurance policy.

"Just sign these, my dear boy. Nobody's ever done a better bit of business in this city."

Pista picked up the contract and began to read.

He sat there so despondently, but took care not to let it show.

At that moment in came a young man carrying some documents. Kardics bácsi took off his glasses and looked up at him.

"Give me those, my boy."

He put his glasses back on and said kindly as he signed the papers:

"That's very good, very good. Your superiors are satisfied with you, and it's arranged for your appointment to be made permanent."

The young man, a tall, pleasant boy, well-groomed hair, nice tie, blushed and said:

"That's very kind of you, sir."

Kardics bácsi smiled.

"I like this younger generation, their minds are fresher, they're more energetic, harder-working, than we were at their age. When I think back to my own youth, the young bank-staff of those days just spent their time dancing and chasing girls. We used to come in of a morning hung over, picking our nails clean. How could anyone make serious use of them? Things are different nowadays, anybody that wants to get on in life has to work hard."

With which he stood up and patted the young man on the shoulder. He was a head taller, a fine, athletic figure.

"It's very good to play games, swim, fence, box. This chap doesn't waste his muscles, he goes in for sport, not champagne, don't you?"

The young man looked at the floor and smiled.

"Well, this very afternoon you'll get your confirmation. What does your father do?"

"He's a type-setter, sir."

Kardics froze.

"A what?"

"A type-setter."

At this Kardics's features hardened.

172

"I don't understand, what's that?"

"He's been a type-setter at the Zsarátnok News for thirty-four years. He's a very decent, good man, lives only for his family, and he had me educated as I'm the eldest, I went through the Kollégium here as a scholarship boy, because I always had a very good report."

"Yes, yes, quite so," said the Manager, "off you go then, and get on with your work."

The young man bowed and went out.

Kardics bácsi strode up and down the deep carpet.

"They're so careless. It's quite absurd. Why don't they find out what's what in good time? Well, my philosophising was so much hot air. Our lads don't work at all. They drink, go out with girls. So it isn't happening all that fast, this change. I could never get my own children to work at school. We even had their teachers round for dinner to encourage them... Well, never mind, the apple doesn't fall far from the tree."

"Tell me, if you don't mind, am I square with you people now?" asked the Town Clerk, still immersed in the papers.

"Of course, my dear chap."

"As I see it, a certain proportion of the total amount is unentailed."

"Well, of course, that's all taken care of. Kardics bácsi sees to everything. Now, we'll open you a current account, and the whole amount will be drawn down to your credit, and the repayments will be made from the current account. The unentailed sum, I don't know what it comes to, fifteen thousand pengős or whatever, is naturally at your disposal."

"I see."

"I'll hope to see you in the morning, then we'll deal with the formalities."

"Yes."

"Signatures and so on."

"Yes."

And so Pista went out like a man who had lost his innocence.

When he was in the street he felt like a girl who'd been in a man's rooms for the first time; she'd gone in, pert and self-assured, where curiosity and the momentary over-riding of the will had robbed her of her strength, and now she felt torn and ragged...

He had a current account in the mighty Bank, where previously he couldn't have asked for a loan of three hundred pengős. Now there were fifteen thousand to his credit. He was sure to draw on that at some time.

There was a conflict within him between his former self and the present one. A sort of inner disquiet. He couldn't resolve it, and it was horrible, miserable. He just walked, walked ahead, didn't know himself where he was going. Now and then somebody would greet him and he'd reach quickly for his hat, without knowing whom he was greeting or how he should respond. He greeted everybody as effusively as he could, because he felt so little, insignificant, unhappy, the least person in the city.

He stopped on impulse outside the post office. After a little hesitation he went into the telegraph department, asked for a blank and sent a telegram to his younger brother asking him to come at once as he had to talk to him.

That'd be good, he was reassured. Menyhért was the only one he could talk to. He couldn't discuss these matters with Lina. He daredn't even go home.

He just went on down the street and then turned into a side-street. There he could breathe with greater confidence, and as the street grew narrower and narrower, winding its way past the Piarist convent, between rows of little houses towards the working-class quarter, he breathed more freely. Finally he found himself surrounded by quite tiny wooden houses. He stopped and looked them over. They should all be demolished and houses for workers built instead.

How this should and could be achieved he had no idea, but it reassured him. Now he was after peace and quiet at any price. He wanted to give. To give to others, to the poor, who, incomprehensibly, couldn't acquire anything, who didn't have Kardics bácsi at their disposal. That was why he wanted to make a success of the Pig Farm too, because there work could be found for a large number, who at present were out of work, facing the winter with lustreless eyes.

This thought lifted him somewhat, and his imagination began to work, ways in which he might help the poor. Fantastic plans flickered up within him. The drainage must be finished, everything that would provide work. He could see the roads being torn up as the horde of workers toiled with pick and shovel, came for their pay on Saturdays.

No, there'd be life here. There'd got to be, because this was why Fate'd given him this position, called him to the defence and support of the common people. There'd got to be a large central hospital too. That had been in the air for decades past, and the doctors never stopped complaining of the terrible state of the old hospitals. He wanted to talk urgently to those doctors: Dr. Mannheim was usually in the Club. He'd once given Pista a lecture about the state of the hospitals; he suddenly turned to go to the Club – Mannheim might be there now.

He went so quickly, something might have been driving him. He turned into the main street and hurried along to the Club.

The customary silence. With his usual courtesy the attendant took his hat and coat and he went into the card-room.

"Is Dr. Mannheim in the Club?"

"No, sir."

But Dr. Martiny was.

Naturally, they were playing cards. A place was immediately made for Pista, and as if that had been his intention he sat down and joined in the rummy.

But he played very absent-mindedly, discarding his best cards, altogether paying scant attention to what was played. He lost. Lost a second time. They laughed at him. Finally he woke up somewhat and pulled himself together. Won a hand. Nothing much, but it was a win.

"Well now, what're you going to do about the Pig Farm?" asked Dr. Martiny suddenly.

"The Pig Farm?... What is there to do about it?"

Martiny stood up from the card table and walked towards the lounge. Pista followed willy-nilly. It seemed his duty to hear out the thoughts of the Opposition.

"These Bakony[41] robbers ought to be taught a lesson. Here's a unique opportunity for the city to take it over, but of course what matters is not the city's interests but the robbers'. I can foresee that there'll be some pleading for help from the city. But they'll wait until they can pull 'em out of the mire at the expense of the citizens' skin. Did Feri Boronkay build a villa out of Pig Farm bricks? Just so. Just what you'd expect. We mean to prosecute the blighter. Here we have a snotty-nosed character, hiding behind the Alispán's back, having himself a magnificent palace built to cream off the profits in advance. We're looking into the history of that building. Feri Boronkay was penniless a couple of years back, he got the Bank to bail him out because he could have ended up in prison... I advise the Town Clerk to lose no time looking into this business and sequestrating the Boronkay house. Because it's to be expected of that villain that he'll make use of this couple of days to sell it while he can, and then the business will immediately become more complicated. I'm convinced that Boronkay is inclined to sell his villa for half what it's worth this very day, just to avoid a nasty fight... Now all the responsibility devolves on you, this rat at least must be caught in his hole. He should be drowned in the slime of the gutter. Villains like him mustn't be allowed to escape the arm of the law. If there's a law for small-time thieves there should be one for big-time ones too."

The Town Clerk turned pale as he listened. He'd have liked the earth to swallow him up. Should he tell him that Feri Boronkay had already sold his villa? And, what was more, to him, the Town Clerk? Who should have been putting in hand the investigation? According to public opinion.

"At that time you weren't involved, but I've tabled questions about the Boronkay affair twice. Everybody knows it only requires a mere complaint, and proceedings the like of which the city's never seen will commence against him. The facts are all there. All the documents are in my office at the practice; complaints, affidavits from workers, everything's carefully worked out. I don't want to make the complaint myself, because it's the responsibility of the Town Clerk. You're not in this Mafia yet, and Makróczy, friend of the Alispán and prime mover in the whole criminal syndicate, would never have done it. But a new man, elevated to this position by public confidence, can do it. It's got to be done. After this will come the whole avalanche, and I tell you in advance that if you take this courageous step, in the first place you'll be most popular as protector of the city, and secondly, you'll have the chance of getting the Pig Farm for the city free of charge. Only keep well clear of that wicked old man Kardics, because he's the leading poison-brewer. I hear that he's already been angling for you, and that you and your wife have been there to dinner."

"He's a relation of mine."

"Is that so," said Dr. Martiny, drawing hard on his cigar. "Is that so. In that case, I never said a word."

"Why? It's not my fault."

"Quite, quite."

"His wife's a daughter of Ferdinánd Kopjáss, and Ferdinánd Kopjáss was my grandfather's brother."

"Interesting. What was your wife's maiden name?"

"Szentkálnay."

"Szentkálnay! It's preposterous!"

"What's wrong with that?"

"Wrong? Nothing. I never said a word... I simply find the coincidence striking. Naturally, blood's thicker than water."

"That's an insinuation to which I object most strongly."

"Excuse me, I don't see where you find an insinuation in that, Town Clerk."

"In the suspicious tone of voice."

"Really, a thousand apologies. I was unaware of certain facts. That alters things to some extent."

"That's the way it is in Hungary, this is a small country, everybody's related. I think that it's likely that if we really looked into it deeply, we two would dig up some connection."

"Of course, your grandmother and mine were both women. Here in Hungary that's sufficient basis for a relationship, assuming that one's opinions and interests are the same. In this case our opinions, our views of the world, our ideas of life are not the same, so let's leave this examination of relations and family trees... I will confess, I did feel a certain sympathy for you, Town Clerk, whence the confidential tone. But if Kardics is your uncle and Szentkálnay, the leading evil-doer, is your father-in-law, it's certainly going to be hard for us to see eye to eye. Hungary's a dunghill of relationships and scandals. It's a swamp, and anything that is planted on it either becomes acclimatised or dies. Plants that like this damp soil put out enormous flowers, and those that don't like it are sucked under the mud. So if you don't mind, I really don't think there's much hope of finding that we're related."

"What was your mother's maiden name?"

"In the first place, I'm a Lutheran, my family's from the highlands of Szepes[42] county. So straight away I feel it's impossible for the threads to have woven in such a way as to join us to the Kopjáss and Szentkálnay clans. Anyway, my mother's name was Malatinszky."

"Malatinszky?" exclaimed the Town Clerk. "My mother was Zsuzsanna Bátay..."

"A Bátay from Vér in Szabolcs?[43]"

"No, the family's from Gömör[44] county. And her mother was an Éva Malatinszky."

"It's preposterous!"

"There you are, then, it's not so easy to get away from one another on this point. This is a small country, you see, even the old Hungary,[45] what we call Greater Hungary."

"My father was a furrier. Just a fur-dealer. He moved about following his trade, came to Zsarátnok and settled down. But he

177

went back home for his wife and brought her down here. Yes, my grandmother was the daughter of a weaver. Her family was one of the well-known weaving families of Podolin.[46] As far as I know the family's died out back there, or at least we've lost contact."

"A Malatinszky from Podolin?" Martiny laughed. "It's fantastic. My mother was one of them. Well, in that case perhaps we might actually be able to get on with saving the Pig Farm?"

"So you shouldn't blacken anybody on the basis of his family, nor whitewash him. When all's said and done, we're people, and a man's worth what he's worth."

Dr. Martiny became pensive.

"The outcome is going to be that I ought, by right as a relation, to buy Feri Boronkay's villa, and so put an end to all my public activity. Would you be so kind, my dear relation, as to support me a little in this?"

"I'm afraid you're a day too late."

"What d'you mean?"

"The villa's already sold, the contract was signed today."

"And who's bought it?"

"I have."

Martiny gaped as if struck by a thunderbolt, and his cigar fell from his mouth.

"And what did you give for it?"

"Well... considerably below market price... the sort of money that I've inherited couldn't possibly cover such an enormous sum. The Alispán offered to intercede and the deal was done."

"Very nice." Neither of them spoke for a while, they looked at one another and laughed, but both were in deadly earnest.

"But if you think I ought not to buy it I'll happily stand down in your favour."

"No, no, not at all, thank you."

"Why not? It's a very fine house."

"Simply because."

"I knew nothing about its origins, the house is in Boronkay's name, heavily mortgaged, and I've transferred the whole balance of my current account to Boronkay, there's hardly anything left. In fact, I've got so little left that I'm very worried, and I don't mind telling you that as far as I'm concerned the deal depends on my wife's agreement, because she doesn't want to go in for such a big property, she's not up to such a lavish

178

life-style. To tell the truth, at the moment I've only got a provisional contract, and if she won't sign then the sale's off."

"Is the account a joint one?"

"No, it's all Kopjáss property and moneys, but of course my wife and I hold everything jointly, so I can't do anything against her wishes, nor do I want to."

"You signed it today?"

"Yes."

Dr. Martiny began to pace agitatedly up and down.

"Damn, I'm late for everything. I should have told you yesterday what I've said today. If I'd told you beforehand it would have prevented you going in for such a purchase. My friend, in that villa there isn't a single brick that's not stolen. As Director of the Pig Farm, Feri Boronkay had it all built of their materials. I've got proof clearer than the day."

"Look here," said the Town Clerk, "tell me, how can the city achieve the repossession of the whole Pig Farm? I was out there today, took the Clerk of Works and the agent with me, made them show me everything. The building is first-class. If it were possible to contrive for the city to get it cheap, or even free of charge, it could be made into a large-scale civic business."

Dr. Martiny was lost in thought. It had flashed into his mind that this might be the opportunity, with the assistance of this well-meaning but ill-informed man, to gain influence over the city economy. He was the only man in the city with whom he'd managed to establish a blood relationship. Time was going by, the end of constantly being in Opposition must come sometime.

He heaved a deep sigh and said:

"I'm afraid I've got to be going now, not just because of my wife, I've got a meeting with some people I've asked to come and see me, and they'll be waiting for me... But if you'd care to drop in tomorrow evening I'll give you my views on the matter."

They said goodbye and Pista too went home.

As he was about to turn in from the street a telegram-boy on a bicycle was standing under the gateway.

"Can I help you?"

"Looking for Town Clerk Kopjáss."

"That's me."

He took the telegram and read it. It was from his brother, saying that he was coming on the nine o'clock train, arriving at half past eleven.

179

He tore the telegram into tiny pieces and scattered them. Then he went inside.

"There's a lot going on about the Pig Farm," he said to Lina, "I've been discussing it all afternoon. I'll tell you all about it over dinner. There's a meeting at eleven in City Hall."

"Tonight?"

"Yes, because tomorrow there'll probably be writs to issue. It's terrible what that Makróczy was up to."

With that he went to wash his hands, then sat down alone to dinner in the dining-room, and told Lina in detail, with some exaggeration, about the plan for bringing the business under civic control.

Time went by so quickly that Lina had to point out that it was a quarter to eleven.

"I'm terribly tired," he said, "I ought to be going to bed, but there it is, if you take a job on you've got to see it through."

Lina went with him as far as the little gate and kissed him warmly in the darkness, like a servant-girl saying goodbye to her boy-friend.

As he went down the street he felt that he was doing wrong, being dishonest, God forgive him, he'd never do it again.

He walked slowly, his footsteps ringing on the pavement, looking at the sleeping houses. Not a light anywhere, only in the cafes and restaurants. How strange to think that there were people who always had the night to steal from next day's work.

He looked at the city like a rich man at his property. The point was that people should sleep peacefully. He looked at the tall buildings one by one. In one were businesses, in another private flats. Everybody ought to live well and blossom. It took a lot of doing for somebody to achieve their own happiness and peace. Everybody's life was simple and smooth, but he was beginning to realise that the life of the leaders was stonier and thornier, and that he who took thought on behalf of the masses had to think differently from a private individual.

Menyhért arrived on the eleven thirty express. The powerful engine puffed and hissed, there lay before it a long journey. This train was going on, on beyond the near-by frontier toward distant parts of the great world, to the east. That was where Hungarian farm and industrial produce ought to go, but couldn't. That was because trade and the listless traveller were stopped at the frontier by the customs barrier, and wheat bread and manufactured goods alike remained at home. He wondered whether they were at work now, in the night hours, the men

180

who dealt with such great matters, the fate of the peoples of Europe.

Pista and Menyhért embraced.

"What's up?" asked Menyhért anxiously, but Pista'd been relieved of the main great stress of worry by his talk with Dr. Martiny, and smiled.

They went to a little pub near the station, where Menyhért ordered roast pork and a *spriccer*; Pista asked for a coffee, but couldn't drink it. Menyhért's train back went at one o'clock, so they had a good hour to talk.

"I asked you to come down because I thought I was going mad. I've got nobody in the city that I can really speak my mind to. I'm in a very strange position, my former friends have gone at a stroke, been left behind. They don't understand what's happening to me, I'd only make them jealous, I know in advance what they'd say. Just that I should stay where I was, and where they still are, but I can't do that, because Fate's thrown me into a new, higher, altogether different milieu, and I've got to establish myself in it. On the other hand, I haven't so far been able to find anybody at this level that I can really share my thoughts with, because they wouldn't understand either. They'd simply say that if I can't stand the pace I should resign and go back to my own quiet life. But I can't go back, there's no stopping in life, and I've no other choice. I either stand or fall."

And he started to speak, without inhibition, as candidly as if there were nothing in his mind but summing up the whole affair precisely and clearly. He was talking to himself. Only to his brother could he speak like this.

Menyhért, who had hitherto been as far removed from these things as Pista, listened seriously and intently. He was a Kopjáss just like Pista, and he too had suffered all his life from the problem that he hadn't been just an academic, deriving his total satisfaction from the exploratory pleasures of his science, but had constantly made the attempt to profit by what he discovered, which he felt had a commercial value. But he'd never been able to acquire sufficient capital to realise his plans, and in consequence all his initiatives had come to nothing.

Now he understood his elder brother's affairs and saw that he was right.

He approved of the house-purchase, he approved of his desire to live at a higher level, it couldn't be otherwise if he was to be outwardly worthy in the eyes of those with whom he wanted to work. He wouldn't have a contribution to make to

181

that society if he were perceived as low-calibre, he'd have lost the battle before it began. It was a rule of life, he said, that each social stratum had to be on a certain level, otherwise there would be gaps that couldn't be bridged.

He also approved of his conclusions in respect of the Pig Farm.

Pista had to act in this way, because in fact something would come of it only if he made it his personal concern. Nobody but the Town Clerk could do it, because it was inherent in his office to be virtually judge and jury rolled into one. Therefore these plans could only be realised if the Town Clerk took them up.

Menyhért approved of everything, thought well of everything, and Pista experienced that inner calm which he hadn't known for a very long time, now that somebody, another human being, accepted his existence without opposition. This was part and parcel of brotherly fellow-feeling. He looked with great affection at his brother, and was deeply grateful to him for the way in which his passivity strengthened his own active nature.

The time flew by like a single minute.

As he was taking Menyhért back to catch the train he had a sudden shock. He'd forgotten to bring any money with him, and he felt quickly and nervously through his pockets in the hope of at least being able to afford his brother's ticket home.

All he had was a twenty pengő note, no other money at all. He'd used up all his change paying in the pub, and hadn't thought at the time.

"Are you all right for money?" he asked his brother.

"Not really. All I've got is seven pengős."

"Doesn't matter, we can get your ticket and I've still got fifteen thousand in the Bank, so we can sort it out. When I get a spot of cash I'll send it on to you straight away."

"All right."

"Goodness, I've forgotten to mention the most important thing of all – Berci bácsi.

And he gave a hurried account of the family coal-mine business, how the old chap had entered into a contract with the city and sample loads were actually on their way. And out of the hundred thousand pengő advance payment, according to their agreement, twenty thousand were for him.

Menyhért looked at him apprehensively.

"Be careful of Berci bácsi! He's not to be trusted. He's been a liar all his life."

"Nothing can go wrong. I'm having the coal tested, I've told

182

the Clerk of Works to check it as rigorously as he can, that I'm not accepting any responsibility. And I've told him to withhold my commission, the twenty thousand, I'll have that paid into my account. Indeed, I'll go further, my plan is not to touch the fifteen thousand left over after the house purchase, just in case it has to be repaid. If I knew where from, I ought to raise a small personal loan, but I don't know whether I can do that. None of my friends has even a couple of hundred to spare. Anyway, something'll turn up. By the way, how're things with Albert?"

"That's one unhappy man. He hasn't been round for a year, but he turned up the other day saying he was on the verge of suicide."

"I know all about that, he wrote to me that he was thinking of killing his whole family. That's why I've got no money, I've had to send something to him and to Adélka, she's in a bad way as well. So we're well off for brothers and sisters."

By now the train was in and their words became more urgent.

"If you see Albert, tell him to just let things take their course, I'm not going to forget about him, I'll get him a job of some sort, in any case I'm thinking about it, although it's very difficult, one can't carry people about, and I can't work out how to get him in, I'll try and use my contacts in Pest to find him something temporary."

"Oh, do be careful, look out for these relations."

"Your job at the Museum looks cut and dried. Your problem, of course, is completely different. Just work out the plan and programme of the Museum organisation as soon as you can. Well, God bless, my dear Menyhért, thanks very much for your kindness, you can't imagine how it reassures me that I've got somebody in this life that I can at least make myself understood to."

Now the train was moving, Menyhért was standing on the step as they embraced once more, then he took out his handkerchief and waved it after the departing train as long as they could see one another, then wiped his eyes and blew his nose for a long time.

"Good morning, Town Clerk," someone greeted Pista, and he looked round in alarm.

It was a doctor, seeing someone off.

They shook hands.

The doctor looked at him amusedly.

183

"That was my young brother," said Pista without being asked, indeed, no explanation was called for.

"I've been seeing off relations as well," said the doctor. "Ye Gods, we've all got relations. The funny thing is, they're always hard up."

He laughed loudly, and it seemed that he was a little bit tipsy.

"A man would have to be very well off for his relations to be pleased with him."

"I can't complain," said the Town Clerk, thinking with a trace of self-mockery of Kardics bácsi. "There are bearable relations too."

"Oh yes," said the doctor, "relations are all bearable, but they do tend to lean on one. Because, d'you see, a relation isn't the man who's doing well, but the man who's doing badly. In the eyes of a well-to-do member of the family, I'm a relation. How can I put it, relationship only spreads downwards. It's like a net; a man gets into it, his relations pull the ropes. They want to catch the big fish. Perhaps I've got hold of the rope of such a net, by virtue of some connection or other, only I can't catch a big relation. On the other hand, it's amazing how the little relations can catch me."

They went out to the front of the station. The doctor went on:

"If, for example, the Town Clerk happened to be a relation of mine, how nice that would be for me. I'd be very pleased to be offered some official medical appointment. Medical officer or the like. But I've got no relation to turn to for *protekció*."

"You don't need *protekció* for a thing like that," said the Town Clerk unkindly, "you need ability and aptitude."

The doctor was alarmed that in his self-assuredness he'd forfeited the sympathy of the Town Clerk.

"Quite, quite, I assure you, and I have these, because I've been in the city fourteen years; I've got a flourishing practice, and I've applied for the post any number of times, but God knows there's never been anybody to give my candidature a helping hand. It's not to be wondered at, there are such a lot of doctors in the city, not everybody can make good."

He realised that the Town Clerk wasn't seizing the opportunity, in the small hours, of offering his *protekció*, so he recovered his good humour and said:

"Well, never mind, next time round I'll try and choose my parents better. Good night, Town Clerk.

184

The Town Clerk felt that it befitted his position, because of the doctor, to take a taxi. It was only when he was seated in it and it had moved off that he remembered that he'd got no money on him, what on earth was he to do? He couldn't pay. He couldn't wake Lina to get one pengő fifty in a hurry. He was very anxious about how to handle the situation.

When the car stopped outside the house, and he was searching for the right words about how he'd settle up with the driver in the office next day, the latter jumped out of his seat and very politely opened the door.

With feigned nonchalance Pista felt in his pocket for money, but the driver spoke:

"Don't you recognise me, sir? I'm Pap bácsi, the carter, who lived next-door to you in Bácskai Street. I'd very much like to ask a favour of the Town Clerk, if you won't take it amiss. Please have pity on me, you see, I've got four children and I can't get a job as a carter with the city. I've written in, but I've got no *protekció*, and then your application's just thrown out."

"What did you want?"

"If you please, sir," the driver enthused, "as a local citizen I ought to have a right to get work with the logging, but you see, it's them with *protekció* as gets it all."

"What was your name?"

"Vendel Pap."

"Come and see me in my office in the morning and I'll see what I can do."

"Very good, Your Honour."

"I'm not 'Your Honour'."

"Very good."

"I'm a man of the people. With me there's no *protekció*. I look at merit. A native of the city has priority."

"Very good."

"Good night."

"I wish you a peaceful night."

When 'His Honour' had closed the gate behind him, the 'native of the city' said:

"Devil take you, you're a man of the people but you don't pay your fare. You're just like the rest, I'm sorry I spoke."

The Town Clerk tip-toed into the flat, took off his shoes in the hall, undressed in his study and went cautiously into the bedroom. The street-lamp was shining in and there was no need to put the light on. When he got into bed Lina stirred but did not wake. She was becoming accustomed to his coming home late.

He stretched out stiffly, clenched his hands together and began to say the prayer which his mother had taught him as a child.

Then it crossed his mind that he was related to Dr. Martiny through his grandmother, he smiled and fell asleep.

When he woke in the morning the children had already gone to school. It was quiet.

Later Lina opened the door, saw that her husband was up and came in.

"Terrible the pressure you're under," she said, "is this going to go on?"

"For the time being."

"Don't let yourself be put upon so much. You're not used to it. If you work yourself to death, what then?"

"Just let me get over this, then my authority'll be established and everything will go the way I want it. Just imagine, your relations being ruined. As I see it all the Szentkálnay property won't be enough to fill the great hole they've dug."

Lina sat down on the edge of the bed and he told her all there was to tell about the Pig Farm.

"They've had it coming, they've always been bad relations," said Lina. "They've never lifted a finger for us."

20.

He dressed and went to the office.

The Clerk of Works was there waiting for him. He was sitting by his desk, immersed in some papers, making notes in his note-book.

"What's the matter, my dear chap?"

That was an expression he'd picked up from the Mayor.

"I'm looking over these tenders," said the Clerk of Works.

"What tenders?"

"A bundle came in this morning. Tomorrow's the last day for tenders, and quite a few are in already."

With which he gathered the papers together and put them to one side on the desk.

"Oh yes, the iron bridge."

Just outside the city was a little stream, which was, nevertheless, quite a nuisance, because in spring and autumn, when

186

there were heavy rains, it would flood a wide area. The city had invited tenders for an iron bridge to replace the decrepit old wooden one.

Pista sat down at his desk and waited for the Clerk of Works to say what he wanted.

The latter, however, had nothing to report, and started to chat.

Pista listened boredly

"By the way, yesterday I was talking to Ráczkevey bácsi. The Főispán's promised him that he'd have a word with the Ministry of Finance about the mansion."

"What mansion?"

He'd like the Minister to buy his mansion for a tax-office."

"Ráczkevey?"

"Yes."

"First I've heard of it."

"Anyway, it's all in order, except that the mansion's a bit out of town, on the Nyomárka road."

"The Nyomárka road? That's well outside city limits."

"Yes, that's the problem. It's a long way. Because if it were in the city area there'd be no difficulty. It's a lovely house, very nicely built, good for centuries. It's a historical monument too, because in '48 Nagy-Sándor[47] had his headquarters there, so the city has a certain reverence for it. And the Ráczkeveys have always been big names in the city, a number of them have been főbíró[48] in years gone by, they've had an Alispán or two, in other words, the only bit of a problem is that it's rather a way from the centre."

"That's quite a problem, the tax office needs to be handy, so that people can get to it easily. It's hard enough getting them to pay their dues without making them go another couple of kilometres."

"It's no more than two kilometres," said the Clerk of Works.

Pista began to work it out, and reached the conclusion that it was surely further. At least three.

"Anyway, the point is," said the Clerk of Works, "if the city recommends it, the State'll buy it, and we've also got an undertaking that we shall also get the County Revenue Office. Zsarátnok's much more central than where they are now."

"Oh, you surely couldn't put the County Revenue Office out of town."

"Why not, it's an ideal position. There's a beautiful park,

ancient trees, marvellous air. No dust about. Every revenue officer will try to get here, the place is an absolute paradise."

"And is this currently taking place?"

"Of course, the whole thing's arranged. Ráczkevey's uncle's a Secretary of State in the Ministry of Finance."

"I'll have a word with the Mayor about it."

"Would you mind if I took the iron bridge estimates for a few hours? I ought to study them in good time so as not to be unprepared."

"Don't worry, you'll get them the minute the deadline passes. Naturally, it's nothing to do with me, it's up to you to express a professional opinion."

"Exactly, that's just what I mean. I've got a lot on in the next few days and I'd like to make a start."

"I think the regulations forbid it."

"What regulations?" shouted the Clerk of Works, bursting with rage.

"You don't imagine that I've got any interest in looking at the estimates before the closing date? It's all the same to me, you can do what you like without me."

He grabbed his hat in a fury and left.

Pista was quite taken aback by this outburst. Until then the idea of anything irregular hadn't occurred to him, but now he began to wonder whether in fact the Clerk of Works had no interest in seeing the designs that had been submitted before the deadline expired.

The Clerk of Works had by now suppressed his anger and was leaving quite quietly, because he'd already made notes of the most essential data; he would, however, have liked to copy out the statistical material so as to inform the firm of Holub and Company.

The Town Clerk took the whole sheaf of papers and locked them in the big filing cabinet. Then he called in the secretary, Dr. Péterfi, and asked for the Pig Farm file.

The Pig Farm had been set up in 1925 with a capital of 1.5 million koronas. When the coinage had changed to pengős that equalled 120,000 pengős, but by then the capital had vanished. Kaiser had expanded the project, and the capital had been raised to 400,000 pengős. The previous year a further share-issue had raised this to 600,000 pengős.

"Why did you tell me that the paid-up capital was 1.5 million?"

"That's what the Opposition say. They don't tell you that it was koronas."

"Right."

"And in fact, only the first 1.5 million koronas were fully paid up. Nowadays the losses are approaching 1.5 million pengős."

"Yes, I understand."

"Bills. The builders still have an enormous outstanding account. Purchases. Debts for maize and pigs. Investments. Steam-ploughs."

"How is it that even today the land hasn't been transferred to the Pig Farm?"

"The Minister for the Interior still hasn't ratified the Council's decision."

"Right."

All this was new to Pista. Only now was he beginning to understand the affair just a little.

"How did they run up all those debts?"

"The management soon reached the point where the capital was exhausted. But it was in the nature of the business that they had to go on expanding and developing. There were a number of attacks of swine-fever. Inoculations and veterinary fees came to huge amounts. And they plugged the gaps with more gaps. Old Szentkálnay's answer to everything was 'I'm here'. He signed things. Bills. Accounts. He did it quite irresponsibly. Then the price of maize shot up and it was all over."

By this time the history of the Pig Farm had been reduced to memorandum form and it was easy to go over it.

While they were in the middle of the documents the Mayor's secretary came, His Worship was asking for the Town Clerk.

Pista went straight away.

"Ah, hello, hello, my dear chap," said the Mayor, rising and advancing to meet him.

They sat down in the armchairs and the Mayor slapped him on the knee.

"Now then, I hear we're getting on very well, isn't that so? How're you doing with the Pig Farm?"

"Actually, your Worship," said Pista seriously, "I'm not quite clear about it all yet, but I have the feeling that the city will still be able to profit by it."

"So tell me, dear boy, tell me."

And so Pista told him what he'd heard the previous day

from Kardics. He avoided mentioning what he'd learnt that morning. The Mayor listened with close attention, and the only disturbing thing was the way that his eyes never ceased boring into him, which bothered Pista a little, and when he should have expressed the view that in his opinion the original share-holders were greatly responsible, he said nothing.

"It's got to be done," said the Mayor. "I hear you've been talking to Dr. Martiny, my dear chap."

"Well, I didn't tell him all about it, just as much as he could be told. I was very cautious."

"Yes, yes," said the Mayor. "We have to talk to the Opposition."

"And what I told him, it seemed to me, was to his liking. As a matter of fact he said the same. The whole thing ought to be preserved for the city, and placed under civic management. I'm convinced that this will be the first piece of business that the Opposition will have no grounds for objecting to."

"Oh, the Opposition," the Mayor gave a delicate wink. "The Opposition is necessary. If there's no Opposition nobody will believe that everything's in order."

And he laughed loudly.

"If the Opposition like it, the cat's eaten it."

Pista listened uncertainly and would have liked to know what the Mayor really thought.

But the Mayor had embarked on an anecdote about Ferenc Deák.[49] It had happened in his youth, because he'd known Deák, well, slightly, because he'd been old and sick by then and didn't take a very active part in affairs. But it so happened that in the course of a general election campaign he'd gone to see him in the Queen of England[50] as a member of a deputation – "My dear chap, the great man lived like an absolute lodger. We had to hang about in the corridor until we could get in to see him. Eventually Menyhért Lónyay[51] came out and in we went. Of course, at that time we were in opposition. Everybody's in opposition when they're young, and anybody that still is after the age of forty isn't going to get anywhere... But anybody that hasn't been in opposition before he's thirty isn't going to either. Kálmán Tisza was in opposition until he was thirty eight... So in we went to see the old gentleman. There he was, sitting in his big chair, didn't even get up. We stood in front of him like so many schoolboys. He listened to our statement and said 'Keep it short, my boy, because life is short, like the tape in your

190

underpants. You're always losing the end when you don't want to'.

He laughed and laughed, and it was so odd, in his presence you forgot that today too life was running out, you got a glimpse of a forgotten world.

Then he said that anybody that wasn't good-looking by twenty, wise by thirty or rich by forty wouldn't get anywhere. How old are you, my dear chap?"

"Forty-five."

"Prime of life. Tell me though, why didn't you give that poor Clerk of Works what he wanted?"

The Town Clerk was startled.

"Your Worship, I can't release the tenders to the Clerk until the competition's closed."

"Of course, of course, well, just give them to him; he's going to be terribly busy next week. I'll accept responsibility, and let's have no more 'Your Worship', I've told you before, you're *kedves öcsém* to me and I'm *bátyám* to you, unless you've some objection, my dear chap??"

"But... my dear *bátyám*."

"Then we'll have another word about this Pig Farm, it's very good, what you've told me, only thing that worries me is how to go about it. But let Dr. Martiny carry on being the Opposition, we really need a bit of Opposition terror, they compel us to get things done. If there's no Opposition, everything's dead. You have to give the Opposition their due... Ferenc Deák said that too. Anyway, how do you come to be friendly with the worthy Dr. Martiny?"

"We're related."

"Related?" exclaimed the Mayor.

There was such sincere amazement in his voice that he might have been told that Dr. Martiny had been appointed Főispán.

"Related?" he repeated. "How does that come about?"

The Town Clerk smiled.

"Well, his grandmother and mine were both old women."

But at this moment the Mayor wasn't in the mood for jokes. He looked stiff and somewhat suspicious, so Pista had to explain in detail.

"My grandfather, István Kopjáss (the same name as my father and myself), brought a wife from Gömör county. Her maiden name was Eva Malatinszky, one of the Malatinskys of Podolin. And Dr. Martiny's grandmother too was a Malatinszky

191

from Podolin. Hence the connection. It's very remote, it can be there or not as I want, it's up to you, *bátyám*."

"Hmm, hmm," hummed the Mayor, "disastrous, disastrous."

"That's why, according to Dr. Martiny, he's never found anybody in the city with whom he has any relationship, because he comes from the highlands on both his parents' sides. I think that's why he's so stubborn, why he's been leader of the Opposition for so long. He's had no point of contact."

"But you see, you see," said the Mayor, tugging at his beard. "Come back here, let's sit down and talk this over. This is not unimportant, not unimportant... And what does he want, this man... with this relationship... What does he want? What's he expecting to get? What's he got to say?"

The Town Clerk felt alarmed. As he sat down it crossed his mind that these *urak* really conceived being related to someone as implying an established right to be cut in on any rackets that were going.

"I don't know what he wants," he said cautiously. "He hasn't shown his colours yet."

"That's just it: he'll try... One has to be very careful. Round here people can't just pretend to be high and mighty, then when the hard times are over worm their way into city affairs where they have no business. Anybody can be in opposition. All that calls for is attacking and criticising. It's all very well for such nonentities, and I knew the time would come when he'd announce that he was related... Just look at him... This means he's arrived... You can't pick everybody up."

The Town Clerk was on the point of finding fault with Dr. Martiny, of saying that he hadn't a shirt or collar to his name, that he had no time for him, but then he thought that possibly he wouldn't be believed, and the Mayor would only think that he was disguising his purposes, that he was up to something with Martiny. So after a pause he said:

"Your Worship, I'm going to speak to him this evening in the Club, because he asked me to be there, and I'll see. I'll flush the hare out of the undergrowth. Let him show his true colours."

The Mayor's slender, bony fingers drummed on the table.

"I don't like this showing of colours, never mind him showing his colours, let him just remain in opposition. A nice, harmless opposition... What the devil is this relationship to you?"

"I can't help what my grandfather did."

"But you let it out... He's got a terribly big mouth..."

"So he'll have to be shut up."

"Him?... He's a very hungry man... Nothing goes right for him... His practice isn't worth anything. He makes money with Opposition tricks like this and he hasn't got any clients."

"Quite so. This is a serious matter, bátyám, a serious matter... Anyway, I'll sound him out. I'll know more tomorrow."

The Mayor's secretary appeared and announced that people were waiting outside. The Town Clerk bowed and left.

He was still smiling in the corridor. He was pleased at how adroit and clever he'd been. It was no bad thing to put the *urak* in check for a while. At least, until he was clear about everything that he needed to deal with.

The Clerk of Works was waiting in his office; Pista felt in his ease of manner that he was confident about the matter and knew that he was going to be given the documents that he wanted. Well, at least he'd kept him waiting a little.

Pista took the initiative.

"Well, my dear chap," he said graciously, "I'm glad you're here, I've been talking to the Mayor about the Pig Farm. Do sit down for a moment and let's look into this a bit."

"Yes, but I'm terribly busy."

"I know, I know, but this is extremely urgent. My dear Dr. Péterfi," he called into the other room, "would you mind bringing in the Pig Farm. Can you just tell us how much the establishment owes to Holub and Company?"

"I don't really know, the bills are there."

"In any case, quite a lot?"

"Yes."

"They did all the building work?"

"Naturally."

"And the installations?"

"What installations?"

"I'm thinking of electrical plant, machinery."

"No, Szentkálnay's did that."

"Right. So they have a mechanical agency as well."

"He's an ironmonger. It's his line of business, and it must have been cheaper to do it himself than to employ an agent."

Dr. Péterfi brought in the thick file. There was a big table in the centre of the room, and he put the main books on it and stacked the documents at the side.

The Clerk of Works looked at the preparations suspiciously and uncomfortably.

"Look here, old chap, I simply can't spare a quarter of an

hour for this today, I'm badly behind already and it's almost mid-day. I've got to do a report for the Mayor by then."

Pista looked thoughtfully ahead, decided not to pull the strings any tighter and released the Clerk of Works. He still didn't know enough about the business.

Without a word he handed over the tenders and smiled disapprovingly as Bisztriczay took them.

Even when the Clerk of Works had left, Pista couldn't recover his composure. He felt as if a robbery had been committed. What were these people planning, wanting, doing? There were going to be changes once he'd learnt the ropes.

Dr. Péterfi was standing in front of him, waiting.

"My dear Péterfi, I understand this business less and less. You know it so very well, would you give me a down-to-earth historical account of the whole thing?"

"As you wish, Town Clerk."

"I've got to have a first-class grasp of it, and quickly. As I see it, it'd be a matter of a few hours work to sort out the principles, and I can't face the *urak* without knowing the facts. In the interests of the case, and for my own sake, I must know everything clearly and at once."

"No trouble at all, Town Clerk…"

"Please sit down. Just a moment, allow me to ask you something very odd."

"Go on."

"Where are you from?"

"Me? I'm from Erdély. A Transylvanian refugee."

"Right. And your wife?"

"The same."

"In other words, you're not a Great Plain man, you have no relations here?"

"I'm afraid not."

"So how do you get on here among strangers?"

"To tell you the truth, with some difficulty. You've put your finger on it, the only people that get any help around here are those who get it from relations."

"In fact, the people of Zsarátnok think so little of 'incomers' that the landlord, for example, makes a point of showing us that we're here-today-gone-tomorrow. But we're used to it now, to not being asked to name-day celebrations, to pig-killings, even the least little thing, if they're cutting down a bit of tree, say, they treat us as if we weren't Hungarians but God knows what kind of alien intruders. We've just been having a bit of trouble, actually heard people running us down behind our backs, what sort of people were these 'incomers', turning others out of their own homes, but that was just because we wanted a cellar to store furniture, potatoes, barley for the winter, because my wife had acquired a pig, and they were most rude about throwing it in our faces that there'd been nothing in the lease, when we took the flat, about keeping pigs. The landlord's got plenty of sties, and they're empty, because he rents his property out, as they do round here, to his children, so that the old people have some income, and they only keep enough pigs for their own requirements; there's room for at least another sixteen, and they wouldn't spare a pen for our piglets because they weren't in use yet. This is a very hard town to live in. Things are quite different at home. There farmers are more considerate and kinder, and the way they keep on the right side of the *urak* is a delight. But we've got to put up with it."

The Town Clerk was reassured. He'd only wanted to know whether Dr. Péterfi was an 'impartial' witness or not. An impartial witness, who was totally disinterested. Now he felt that this man just happened to be there. He had not, and had never had, any relationship with anyone, and so one could believe his remarks and what he told one.

"How did this Pig Farm start?"

"That was before my time. I only came to the city in 1927. By that time the Pig Farm was in its second flowering. As I believe, the whole thing started after the revolution. There was a pig-dealer here by the name of Devecseri, and it was his idea. In 1921 or 22 he called a meeting of shareholders, and as they couldn't form a company he brought in Makróczy's tenant, and it was all set up with a capital of 1.5 million koronas. But then, because of the financial crisis, that small capital was destroyed, so that no business at all could be started and Devecseri went bankrupt. So did Makróczy's tenant, he lost his lease, and Kaiser got the whole share-issue free of charge and made the most of it. Then he went bankrupt and got out, went to America. Szentkálnay married off his daughter, then the whole thing was revived and it was decided to make a go of it with help from the city. It was then that people realised that Szentkálnay's former sphere of business influence had ceased because of the frontier. He had had an enormous trade with the Balkans and Turkey, but because of the new customs barrier he couldn't do that any more, and he had to find something else. Obviously, in this city there was money to be made out of breeding pigs.

There was a public demand for them. The civic enterprises were immediately available as customers. That in itself was a big item. But even more important was the fact that farmers couldn't sell their pigs. A company had to be formed to acquire the surplus. Thus at once the Szentkálnay farm was doing better that the rest, because it was able to create a steady customer for itself in the Pig Farm. Szentkálnay owns about two thousand acres and rents more, so that today he's got about three thousand acres. All the gentlemen are landowners. The Alispán has six hundred acres, the Mayor eight hundred. The three of them together were powerful enough to provide a high proportion of the business, and they didn't have to worry about the market. They hoped to supply the necessary maize themselves, so they were very well placed. No hassle with pig-dealers or grain-suppliers. Young pigs, maize, barley, oats, marrows, everything, in fact, was committed to the Pig Farm."

"Do these contracts exist?"

"Of course, they're here on file."

"Therefore these contracts were the Pig Farm's collateral."

"Yes. This is what was used to obtain a grant from the city. They found a very nice site by the railway halt, fourteen acres in area, absolutely free, in perpetuity. Or at least, for as long as the Pig Farm remained active and in production."

"It isn't active these days."

"No, excuse me, it is in business. There are about two dozen pigs on the premises."

Pista considered. He had in fact seen a number of pigs, but he'd thought that they were the property of some of the staff that were still being employed there.

"I see."

"So the city gave them a fourteen acre plot free and a further six hundred acres at a peppercorn rent. This also is, of course, for as long as the company's in business."

The Town Clerk was astonished at all this; he took it in but didn't smile, he was listening intently.

"In return for this the city received a thirty-three per cent minority holding of shares. At the time of the introduction of the pengő the capital was re-assessed at four hundred thousand. Therefore one third of that belongs to the city, fifty-two per cant to Szentkálnay and fifteen per cent to small shareholders, farmers. Such as received a share or two for their pigs."

The matter was beginning to make sense.

"Here's the first year. 1926. Just look at the balance sheet.

On the one side we have the share capital at eighty thousand pengős, on the other debtors of thirty-two thousand. So the shareholders had only paid up sixty per cent... And look at this: here's the rent for Tatárdomb.[52] This is a city property, so it's over-valued, God knows what kind of rack-rent this is. Buildings, stock and materials in hand. A purely fictitious amount... On the other hand, here's the first loan from the city of eighty thousand pengős and one from the Bank of forty thousand. Holub's bill, two hundred thousand. The turnover for the first year is four hundred and sixteen thousand six hundred and fifty-three pengős; when the shareholders had put in forty eight thousand, they'd managed to spend, or should we say invest, almost ten times as much."

"How much did you say Holub's bill was?"

"Two hundred thousand at the first year-end."

"Is Holub a rich man?"

"He used to be. He married well, Schlesinger and Wurmfeld. He married Ella Wurmfeld, only daughter, lot of property. Especially as it's in her own name. They say she's worth several million. But of course, there's not much liquidity there, because nowadays there's a lot of trouble. It's said that they're divorcing."

"Is this Holub Jewish?"

"No, not at all, very much the young gentleman. A very decent man, finished his education abroad, a lot of German influence, a very refined, artistic man, he's got a library better than any in the city, a collection of modern paintings. He was to have married the Kadicha girl, as I understand, but her parents wouldn't hear of it, so he married a Jewish girl. But of course these days he's in with the right people."

The Town Clerk smiled. That was why he had had so urgently to give the tenders to the Clerk of Works. Holub and Company.

Dr. Péterfi sensed that the Town Clerk was prejudiced against the Pig Farm, so he allowed his scorn freer rein.

"The deluge came, Town Clerk, with the buildings. Work began at the end of 1926, at such a rate that in three months Holub and Company presented a bill, and a demand, for two hundred thousand. This explains everything. It was lucky that frost set in and halted building work, otherwise the whole undertaking would have been wound up."

"And what did they pay the builders with?"

"Bills of exchange. And they gave them further orders. In

197

the meantime they reorganised the whole company. The basic capital was raised to four hundred thousand pengős. Then the city got the big loan, out of which they advanced another four hundred thousand, which simply gave the green light for development on an American scale. Suddenly the whole city began to believe and trust. Countless small farmers bought shares. They were quoted on the Exchange, but of course were unobtainable, and so their value went up and up. There were just enough shares on the market to beat the price up. The establishment was expanded to fatten six thousand pigs twice a year. So they meant to produce twelve thousand pigs annually. Now that year, anticipating the Christmas trade, they had in fact bought in five thousand. That cost about three hundred thousand pengős. Completion of the buildings, the machine-house, machinery, wells, electric motors, piping, sprinklers, sundry equipment, first-aid boxes, medicines etc. – one hundred and fifty thousand. Six thousand *mázsa*[53] of maize at twenty five pengős, one hundred and fifty thousand. In other words, in the second end-of-year balance the losses reached the million mark."

The Town Clerk suddenly looked up in consternation. Dr. Péterfi, although it was a lot, seemed to know everything precisely, like a prosecuting counsel in court. Why did he need to know all this? There are always men who enjoy going fiercely into the affairs of others, these are just the men who would be thought so quiet and pallid in their lives as not to hurt a fly. Perhaps they wouldn't hurt anyone, but act out the struggle taking place within themselves by means of this obdurate and thorough interest.

"There is no doubt," Dr. Péterfi continued his monologue, "that everything was built most perfectly. The Pig Farm site is fit for an exhibition, it's a spectacle. Those little houses thatched with reeds, because according to the latest theory that's the most suitable roofing material for pig-fattening, individual sties roofed with straw, perfectly cut, beautiful; nice swags at the ends, it's a delight. All of concrete, floored with slag cement, not even tried before, but a Hungarian invention, and allegedly the best and cheapest. As the accounts show, that's true."

"It's lovely, no two ways about it, lovely," said the Town Clerk.

"It's a little bit too lovely," Dr. Péterfi laughed.

"When the small farmers saw it they were so angry I can't describe it. What the devil, they said, here the pig-man's floor is boarded, while ours are earth! My wife paints the room herself, while here the pig-man lives like a lord! And when they saw the sties, three metres high! The pigs live in them as if they were just for show. The sties are like a labyrinth. And the piped water, jets playing like in some market-garden. Electric light. You really couldn't say it wasn't lovely, but everybody thought that it was a bit over the top."

"It'll be a good thing if the problems can be resolved and a new company takes it over."

"In that case, yes. But they couldn't do it, even at the first through-put there were only five thousand pigs, and the word is that there weren't that many. There were supposed to be herds that were entered in the books twice. And of course it didn't concern anybody if that was how they wanted it. And then the second through-put. That certainly shows only a thousand, one thousand, pigs. Indeed, that was a total failure. It was by then a complete sham. By then they were laying people off. They had to let a whole crowd of people go, because there'd been officials and staff galore..."

He closed the ledger, took another, and said cheerfully:

"There was a manager, a deputy-manager, office staff, a chief clerk and three young ladies, a secretary. a storeman, two graduate farmers, fifty pig-keeping experts, the monthly costs were like those of City Hall. And the interest?... They intended to produce 1.5 million kilogrammes of pig-meat a year, but we shall never know what they did in fact produce. The best of it all was that the farmers all sent their mouldy maize here, and the pigs wouldn't eat it. It was no good explaining to them that it had been grown by the shareholders. But the purchases of maize were more and more expensive. Maize reached thirty pengős, but the Mangalicas[54] wouldn't eat it, their teeth wore out on it. And the maize gave out. That year the corn crop failed everywhere, and it had to be bought in from Transdanubia... But the worst thing was that the price of pigs was driven up. The small farmers wouldn't sell them. They couldn't get them at market, because suddenly there was such demand for pigs that they could only get the first five thousand together by paying over the odds for every single one... There was the boom between January and March 1927, and that was when they set up the business and thought that that was just the beginning, it was going to go on growing at a similar rate."

"And then there was swine fever."

"Of course, and for that reason there was a lot of sudden

slaughtering, selling below market price. When they started the price of pork was a hundred and thirteen, and by Christmas it had dropped to eighty-four eighty. In fact it went even lower, down to seventy-four. A bit of cholera, a lot of terror. That's how it went. Because in principle they should only have bought stock that had survived it, but under the circumstances controls were waived for the time being."

"But surely, the Pig Farm won prizes at the agricultural show?"

"Rumour has it – and I venture to repeat this without being able to substantiate it – that Szentkálnay lent his own pigs for this purpose, because it was of vital interest that the Pig Farm should win. In this way he accepted ever greater responsibility. In fact, they say, the Pig Farm was the medicine for the bit of cholera. If the vet said that there were still twenty-four hours to go, they simply brought them in, weighed them, paid for them, and next day it was the Pig Farm's bad luck if he had in fact forecast correctly, although obviously the vet can't see into the future."

"Just a moment, I don't understand that. So all they did was to make a hole in one pocket and stuff it with problems from the other?"

"That's exactly how it was, you've seen that very clearly."

"Who was on the board?"

"Old Szentkálnay was chairman. The members were Kardics the Bank, Feri Boronkay, Makróczy, the Alispán was on it and the Mayor's son-in-law, but they never attended meetings."

"Buried their heads in the sand like ostriches?"

"Yes... The chairman of the management committee was the deputy Town Clerk, with the headmaster of the Kollégium and the Archdeacon. Big names at all events, but in any case here in Hungary a management committee has rights and responsibilities of management only on paper. The law ascribes to it the greatest responsibility, but there has never been an instance of a general meeting failing to back up a management committee."

The Town Clerk became pensive.

"It's a tunnel. This is really the Kellerman Tunnel.[55] You could write a book about this business."

"Yes, a tunnel bored through air," Dr. Péterfi smiled scornfully.

"Well, let's take a bit of a closer look at it," said the Town Clerk. "I'll try to make some notes."

So they sat down to work and went over the history of those two years in detail from the beginning. They worked all morning and Pista would see no-one.

It occurred to him at half past eleven that he had to go over and see Kardics. He'd promised the day before. He was getting tired of figures, and put the job aside for the day. By this time he was seeing things a little differently from the previous day. Kardics bácsi wouldn't be able to pull the wool over his eyes with big talk about a paid-up capital of a million and a half.

"Can you tell me, by the way," he asked Dr. Péterfi as he was washing his hands, "why are these books here in City Hall?"

"The reason is that the city is re-organising its finances, and the books have been deposited. I must point out that these are insufficient for a full investigation, because all the receipts aren't here. If, for example, one wanted to put in an auditor to make a thorough investigation, one would have to go to the Pig Farm records and go right through all the documents, because the balance sheets were never prepared on a factual basis, but as need dictated. In the interests of the company. A good accountant will arrange the data so as to produce the desired result."

"Of course, of course."

But if he wanted to go and see Kardics bácsi, he must go. Mustn't keep the old man waiting. In an hour's time he'd have fifteen thousand pengős.

At this, it crossed his mind that he hadn't got a single one on him. Not a fillér. That morning he hadn't liked to ask Lina for any money, because he'd have had to explain where it had gone. Lina knew in advance exactly every last fillér in his pocket. In general, Lina had a wonderful sense of reality and was infinitely precise and thrifty. Previously, in the early days of their marriage, he'd had to go over his expenditure to the last fillér on the first of every month, and Lina would give him something back. This had been something of a labour of love, because Pista, who'd never been well off, and had scrounged small amounts from his mother as a student, was happy when he had a sweet little wife and set her above himself as a mother and governing authority. Then it had cost him a protracted effort, years of assiduous guile, to regain something of his human rights, because his wife had learnt how to keep her husband on a tight rein.

The previous evening it had entered his head to send over the office messenger and ask Lina for five pengős.

201

Now that the time came to do this he hesitated to make such use of the messenger, indeed, he couldn't, because the messenger was a new man and Lina wouldn't have trusted him. So he sat down and wrote a note as follows:

> *Lina, my love, please let me have five pengős. This is the new office messenger, be so kind as to put it in an envelope and send it with him.*
> *Love, Pista.*

He rang for the messenger but no-one came. He looked outside but he wasn't there.

Oh good Heavens, where was the man?

Before he turned up it occurred to Pista that five pengős was very little. Who could say whether he'd have to pay for a stamp or a draft in the Bank, and it would be awkward to ask Lina for more because she'd have none left either. So he tore up the note and wrote another:

> *Linácska, my love, let me have twenty pengős, my dear. This is the new office messenger, a trustworthy man, it's safe to give it to him.*
> *Love, Pista.*

The messenger came hurrying in. He must have been chatting down the corridor.

"Where ever have you been? Just run round to my flat, will you, and give this note to my wife. You'll be bringing back twenty pengős. But hurry, please, hurry, I've got to go out."

The messenger took the note and hurried out.

Would Lina give it to him? By the standards of her housekeeping twenty pengős was big money. She was likely to let him have less. He oughtn't to have told the messenger how much it would be, just that 'the lady would give him some money'.

And it was terrible that he was without money to such an extent. It wasn't right. A man without money was like a man without arms and legs. Lina had about seven hundred pengős in the post office. He'd ask her for a hundred.

That was no good either. One must gain the greatest possible rights. He didn't want to reveal that he'd bought the house until everything was settled, but he didn't mean to touch that fifteen thousand because that would demean him. Just let it stay there untouched for a few months. Then, however, he'd have to have some money, and he wouldn't have to keep asking Lina for it and explaining.

That, of course, couldn't be arranged through a messenger, he'd definitely have to say it himself, and make it seem plausible that he was withdrawing the money for the sake of the family. He'd think of something. He walked up and down his office, pondering and contemplating, until the messenger returned. Meanwhile he thought of phoning Kardics bácsi to say that he was on his way, but he didn't feel like doing that until there was money in his pocket.

Blast that money! A man without money wasn't a man. He really must get some money from somewhere that he could rely on. The taxi-driver might come in at any moment, and he'd have to pay him last night's fare.

At last the messenger came back and handed him an envelope. He tore it open and inside were twenty pengős and a note.

He took out the money so that the messenger should see that it was there and only then nodded his dismissal.

Lina had written:

Dear Pista, I am appalled that you should take half the house-keeping. For God's sake be careful, my dear.

Love, Lina.

He looked at the note for a long time. Once, if ever he saw his wife's writing, he became so excited that his whole body quivered ecstatically. Now he felt embarrassed and puzzled.

Well, anyway, such was life; the greatest love fades with time.

He put the money in his wallet and with that regained his peace of mind and manliness. He picked up the phone.

Cheerfully he called the Bank and Kardics bácsi.

To his extreme surprise the operator said that the Manager was out.

"Out?" he repeated. "This is István Kopjáss, Town Clerk."

"At your service, sir, the Manager was in for a short while but he's had to go out."

"Who's his assistant, please?"

"Neuszidler úr."

"May I speak to him?"

"Certainly."

A ringing sound. A man's voice answered.

"Hello, Neuszidler here. What can I do for you, Town Clerk?"

"Tell me, has the Manager left a message for me?"

"No, Town Clerk."

"Nothing?"

"Nothing."

"And... where's he gone?"

"He didn't say, I'm afraid."

"It's impossible, do you see, it was agreed that I should call in now, and he's expecting me."

"He didn't say anything."

"Will he be back?"

"I don't expect so. In fact, he said he wasn't likely to be back."

"He said he wasn't coming back, and he's left no message for me?"

"I'm extremely sorry, Town Clerk."

"Well... thank you."

Pista put down the handset. He had the feeling that Kardics bácsi wanted to show him who he was, how great a man he was in comparison.

A blazing rage was beginning to rise inside him. After the scene of the previous day it was the most natural thing in the world that the manager of the Bank should always be at his disposal in future... He hadn't wanted it, such a thing would never have crossed his mind. But when Kardics had started it, had established a relationship between them, Pista wasn't going to accept that things should change so abruptly.

What was the meaning of this? Was Kardics regretting that he'd been so obliging? To hell with the old scoundrel! And now he had the nerve to treat him like this. To go out and say he wouldn't be back, and not to leave a message of any sort. This could only be a calculated insult. This was a grandiose gesture, and he wasn't going to stand for it. Did Kardics think he'd bought him? That he could push him about? Oh yes! What a good thing he hadn't been depending on that fifteen thousand! A good thing he'd said nothing to Lina about it! What would have happened if he'd speculated, gone in for something? It had looked dead certain the day before, he might have done it, promised Menyuska or somebody something. He'd be in a real mess now... This was a shameless piece of work.

He strode up and down his office, becoming more and more angry.

"Péterfi, would you come in?" he called into the other room.

"Coming, Town Clerk."

"Look here, how much is the Bank involved in the Pig Farm?"

"I can't say exactly, because all that's in the books is how much the Bank has loaned to the Pig Farm, and that's not much. On the first occasion they lent them forty thousand, then twenty and then a further ten. So that's seventy thousand altogether in a total of a million and a half. After that they dealt in fictitious bills. But in any case, Szentkálnay was the guarantor, so it's quite likely that they're in for more than a hundred thousand, only surely they'll have had the sense to secure these contracts on Szentkálnay's property, not the Pig Farm."

"Would you send round straight away to the Land Registry and have Szentkálnay's charges register copied in full. We'll see how much the Bank's mortgage has increased since the Pig Farm was set up."

"I'll go myself. It'll be easier to do that in person."

"Quite right, thank you. And would you mind at the same time copying Feri Borinkay's C register, and Makróczy's, while you're at it."

"Yes."

"And think this through. The question is, at what point did the management of the Pig Farm become criminal."

"That happened a long time ago. At the moment when the shareholders couldn't fail to see that the management was unrealistic, that there was no cover, and still continued to accept the conduct of affairs and to invest. It's quite remarkable that the Commercial Court licensed the business."

"Yes. Well, that's what we need."

Dr. Péterfi caught the Town Clerk's purpose, put on his coat and went out very quickly.

Pista went on pacing up and down; and again, silent rage and desire for vengeance began to rise within him. Now to teach them a sharp lesson!

Suddenly he took his hat, put his coat over his shoulders and went to the farther wing of the building, the Works Department.

"Where's the Clerk?"

"Which clerk, Town Clerk?"

"Bisztriczay, the Clerk of Works."

"He's out, I'm afraid."

"Where is he?"

"I don't know, he took his coat and went out. I think he's left the building."

"Oh... He's got a very urgent job here. I gave him the tenders for the bridge competition, he's supposed to be working on them."

"Yes, we're doing that, Town Clerk."

"Where are the documents?"

205

"Here."

He opened a door into the other room, where a young man was standing at the big tracing table, carefully working at documents which Pista immediately recognised. He was making drawings, and a whole heap of notes were in front of him, already finished.

"What's going on? Who on earth are you?"

The young man blushed.

"Éliás Sáfár."

"An engineer?"

"Yes."

"Who do you work for?"

The young man made no reply.

"Tell me at once, who do you work for?"

"Holub and Company."

"How do you come to be looking at the tenders?"

The young man said nothing.

"Stop at once, if you please, and leave the premises. Everything is to remain here. Go away at once."

The young man turned blue and green, looked round a couple of times in confusion, found his hat and coat and went.

"Pack all this up, if you please, and bring it to my office."

The Works Department staff scurried frantically about and in a couple of minutes were running to the Town Clerk's office with the documents.

He had them put on his desk and sent the Works people away. They slunk out like beaten dogs.

Now he'd taken the first major step. He was very aroused, because he was aware of the significance of what he'd done.

He lit a cigarette and sat down. Then he got up, walked round, sat down again.

'Never heard of anything like it,' he said to himself. 'What swinishness. Well, what will be will be. Never mind what those confounded villains think of me.'

He went on pacing the room.

'I'll bring you into the open. I'll find out what's going on here. I'm not mixed up in anything. I've never received anything. I'm still in the clear.'

Lina's letter came into his mind. 'For God's sake be careful, my dear.' Lina was right. One couldn't sell oneself. There was a Mafia at work here. That was why the city was going nowhere. The people were being subjected to bare-faced robbery.

The messenger came in and announced that a taxi-driver had arrived.

"Show him in."

The driver of the previous evening came in, took off his cap very politely.

"What can I do for you?"

"Town Clerk, sir, as you left me last night..."

"Oh yes. Now, you didn't tell me the fare last night. What was on the meter?"

"It doesn't matter, sir."

"What d'you mean, doesn't matter?" Pista looked at him, eyes gleaming. "Are you trying to bribe me?! What d'you mean, doesn't matter. How dare you! How much was on the clock?"

"One pengő twenty fillérs."

"I'll have the change."

He took out the twenty pengő note from his wallet and tossed it on the desk in front of the man.

The driver stuffed it into his pocket and took out a handful of money – notes, silver and bronze. Slowly he counted out the change.

"What a thing, really, that a rate-payer, a citizen of Zsarátnok, should behave like that! You all want to live by racketeering. You want a job here? I'm not sure whether you have any entitlement or not. We'll look into it and if you have, naturally, residents will have first call on city jobs. But you've got to put an end to this, the way everybody reckons, depends, on getting patronage from somewhere, if all else fails, by giving favours to civic officials, by bribing them and other illegitimate means. We need decent behaviour, otherwise the whole city's going to be ruined."

"Town Clerk, sir..."

"I won't hear another word, that'll do. Have you been given your fare?"

"Yes."

"What's your number?"

The driver took out his purse, extracted a slip of paper. He laid it on the desk in front of the Town Clerk.

Pista wrote the number down and gave the slip back.

"I'll look into it and see what the position is. I'll let you know. God bless you."

The man bowed his head, muttered something, then left unhappily.

As he went out he said to himself:

'Damn you, there must be something wrong, and because you're on the spot you take it out on a poor man. I wish I'd never set foot in your City Hall."

The Town Clerk dropped into his chair and picked up the papers that lay in front of him. The documents formed quite a tidy pile, all similar minor cases, only the names varied. They were stereotypes. The city had made quite a lot of its territory into smallholdings, and now a large proportion of the smallholders were unable to pay their rent. In the severe frosts of the previous year everything in the sandy soil had been ruined. Then there had been a distribution of grain to the needy, and now that ought to have been paid for by now. Meanwhile, however, the price of grain had fallen by half, and the State was demanding just the same price as the year before. Even if there'd been a bumper harvest they wouldn't have been able to pay, but in fact the yield had been very poor. In the Kose region hardship was rife. Two hundred and seventy court orders had been made against people who were more than three years in arrears. He looked again and again at the documents. Mass hardship. What was to be done? It was everywhere; he knew the area vaguely, because two years previously he'd had to travel round it on the illiteracy programme. In those days he'd seen things with different eyes, argued the people's case in his heart, but now he'd got to see things as a lawyer, think with the mind of the city. He had to find a way of bringing in all those arrears, which were as much a State concern as a city one.

What ever was to be done? They set the dogs on bailiffs. What about the rural police? There were hardly any of them, and they were helpless against the smallholders, because a whole world can't be dealt with by the police.

'The whole Great Plain farming system's in a bad way,' thought Pista to himself. They must set up 'bush-farms', such as he'd seen around Nyíregyháza,[56] where he'd been visiting schools on one occasion. Each farm was in the form of a 'bush'; it had a little cultural community, a central point, children could go to school easily, the elderly could reach the doctor. The authorities too could easily contact them. At the time he'd made a report to the city, essentially on the school problem, but expanding also to cover the social question, and he'd proposed that Zsarátnok too should institute the 'bush-farm' system, but only now could he see how useful it would have been to the city. Let it try to move the poverty-stricken little families off the two- or three-acre plots. Where was it to put them? Out in the open? It was inhuman to have the police evict them at this time, with winter approaching, when there was no transport to bring them and their belongings into town. Now if 'bush-farms' had been set up they'd all have been in one place, and it would have been possible to move out the crowd of dilatory payers and replace them with others. In that way the setting-up of farm villages would have been worthwhile.

He looked at the mass of papers. How much proof of hardship was there.

But then, how were they to make ends meet out there? Time and money had been wasted in building farm schools. How were the children to get to them? The schools stood empty all winter, for the children had no boots or shoes. It was good if a family had a single pair of children's boots, and the children took turns to wear them, so that one child wore them to school one day, another the next. And the colds, chills, sore throats and the thousand other maladies. The whole education programme was hopeless. In summer parents didn't send their children to school because they needed them at home. They had to see to the geese, the pigs, the calves. They had to help on the farms instead of being brought up to become useful, because their poor parents couldn't manage by themselves.

It was terrible, the mistakes the administration had made in permitting the farm-plots. It had squandered resources, really set the people back into antiquity. God forbid that anyone in a family should be sick... Where was there a doctor, a chemist, a midwife? The neighbouring women would help at a birth, if, that is, there were any and if they could be summoned in time. Infantile mortality was shocking.

Pista looked beyond the papers into the far reaches of the puszta. His heart sank to see his beloved Hungarian people so repressed, so sunk in ruin. But who would have put in hand the social measures? The Makróczys? Had they ever had any trace of social conscience?

There was nothing for it, now he had to go through with the re-settlements at the eleventh hour. Groupings, farm-villages. But how, with whom? The State had no funds.

But now perhaps the question was capable of some sort of resolution. The new leases must only be so drawn up as to require new smallholders to build on adjacent specified plots. It might be possible to do something on those lines if he emphasised the difficulty of collecting rents and rates under the current system. This way something might be achieved. If social arguments failed, this would have the desired effect. He couldn't make a single stroke of the pen. Should he write on a document that it was to be enforced? What was the good? Who was to enforce it and what would be the consequences of evicting hundreds of families?

Dr. Péterfi came back. He was excited and his face was glowing.

"Here you are, Town Clerk, it's all in order, now we'll be able to take a closer look at the business. Here it is, I've written out all the information we need. Since the establishment of the Pig Farm, Szentkálnay's outstanding mortgage has gone up by six hundred and fifty thousand pengős. I can't understand why the Bank should make such a large further advance on one thousand two hundred and forty acres. The whole property's mortgaged above its value. If you add the moneys due to the Pig Farm, it's the end of the whole Szentkálnay estate."

While they were examining the real-estate positions of the leading men in the Pig Farm, Clerk of Works Bisztriczay arrived back in his office and learnt what had taken place.

The Clerk of Works turned white with rage.

His first thought was to run to the Mayor and report the Town Clerk as he'd done that morning. Now, however, the situation had changed, now he felt that the Town Clerk had him at his mercy, because the presence of the engineer from Holub and Company gave him ammunition that couldn't be deflected.

So he took his hat and ran round to Holub's.

The architect was a tall, extremely elegant young man. He was sitting there in his ornately furnished office, smoking a cigarette.

He couldn't do anything, neither think nor plan ahead, he was just sitting and smoking. When Bisztriczay came in he didn't so much as turn his head.

"Look here, this man's gone mad. He needs his throat torn out."

Holub said nothing. The cigarette dangled from the edge of his lip, almost falling from his mouth, he was staring tiredly, languidly, lethargically ahead at some unspecific point. He was weary of life, which brought him so little pleasure. His wife was weary of all the trouble and the increasing expense, and amused herself with constant flirtations. Holub was deeply in love with her, and precisely because of the racial difference between them could not remain her husband. A young banker had opened a branch in the city the previous year, Béla Greizinger, a son of the great Greizinger family, the greatest name nationwide in the grain trade. This was perhaps the only company not yet affected by the collapse of prices. They had colossal holdings of land in the region, some twenty thousand acres. And fortunately they were able to go on and on opening new branches. The previous evening there had been a big party at their place, and young Greizinger had been talking about putting six hundred acres under rice. There was some place where the peasants cultivated hayfields by flooding them. A fertile flat plain, where all the dikes were already built, and which could be transformed into paddy-fields with practically no outlay. Through some detail of a contract this land had now come into his hands, and he, recognising its possibilities, had it ploughed up at once and put it to rice. In the very first year things had gone brilliantly. The rice hadn't been good quality, but there'd been plenty of it. It hadn't been suitable for commercial purposes because it'd been yellow and not shiny enough. But he'd smiled at these objections, and among the chatter had let fall that he'd wanted the rice, not to put on the market, but because in spring he was going in for duck-breeding. He'd revealed excellent and feasible plans for making a million pengős next year out of ducks alone.

Holub had to compete with people like that. He, who was up to his ears in debt. The Pig Farm had taken everything.

And so there he sat, like Marius among the ruins of Carthage.

That was why he hadn't even drawn the plans for the bridge competition. He'd no energy left, no strength, his inspiration had failed. He needed this competition terribly, and as was his way he had to compile his own entry quickly from the plans. Then had come the unexpected election result, the fall of Makróczy. Kardics bácsi had assured him, and Bisztriczay had guaranteed, that there'd be no problem. Such conditions were attached to the bridge construction, such huge sub-structures were demanded of the tenderers, that it was considered from the outset that the contractor selected, that is, himself, would be released from them, at the end of the day they wouldn't be required. In this way he'd be able to establish guaranteed prices with which he could beat the rest of the competition. Up with the cost of the superstructure, down with that of foundations. But he hadn't completed the plans, the statistical calculations were lacking. And now this peasant had interfered. But Bisztriczay'd done well to devise the plan of not bringing the plans out of City Hall, but of having the necessary calculations copied there.

Now here was scandal. Every level of the city despised and hated the monopoly of Holub and Company, and the Budapest firms, as if they could sense what went on here, had delayed submitting their tenders until the very last day.

Now it would be wiser not to enter.

And so he just listened, listened to the Clerk of Works' fulminations, and smoked his cigarette. He could see that this was the end, there was nothing left but a revolver bullet.

Those who were left could close the door. He didn't have to worry about his two children, they were being well looked after, better than with him around, because he'd not got the energy to cope with them. His whole life had ended in failure.

Suddenly in came Kardics bácsi. Cheerful and lively as ever. "Hello, my dear fellows."

They didn't answer.

"Whatever's the matter?"

It was painful to tell him.

Finally, Bisztriczay explained what had happened. Kardics bácsi was thunderstruck.

"What the devil!"

As a man of swift action, he immediately took his hat and set off to see the Mayor.

Holub hadn't moved. The cigarette-end burned beneath his small English moustache, not a muscle quivered on his handsome, marble-smooth face. He half closed his eyes with their long lashes and sat there like the statue of a life exalted above, or lacking interest in, everything.

21.

Off they went.

There was some deputation calling on the Mayor, but that made no difference, little Imrike the secretary went in and the Mayor immediately finished with the petitioners. He simply left out the routine Ferenc Deák anecdote, promised them everything, shook hands warmly with the members of the deputation and let them go, taking with them the feeling that they should keep up the good work and not give in.[57]

Kardics bácsi stormed in. He was laughing in sinister fashion and swearing most dreadfully.

Clerk of Works Bisztriczay explained what it was all about. The Mayor looked at them for a while with his fishy eyes, then said very graciously:

"Well, yes... of course, you're right... only things don't go quite so smoothly, my dear chap... Cleaning up is the hardest of tasks, but the finest, it's true... Lack of discipline, of course," he added thoughtfully.

Then he picked up a brownish railway docket from his desk. "What's this... this... coal business, Clerk of Works? This tender from the Köleser mine?... Somebody by the name of Bertalan Bátay."

The pupils fell out of Bisztriczay's eyes. He was astounded. He hadn't thought of that. How could he have failed to... This was marvellous. Everything was saved. Berci bácsi's coal...

Jubilantly, he gave a full account of the matter.

"Yes, Your Worship. That's right. You can imagine the sort of coal that the worthy Berci bácsi's going to send."

The Mayor said, boredly:

"What d'you mean, my dear chap, 'going to send'?" and putting on his pince-nez he looked more closely at the delivery note, "when it's already here?"

"The coal, Your Worship?"

"Yes."

"I know nothing about it, Your Worship."

"I think that's what this chit's about."

The Clerk of Works looked like a careless schoolboy who'd got the date of the Treaty of Westphalia[58] wrong and wouldn't believe the teacher who'd corrected him. He took the note and looked at it.

"May I use your telephone, Your Worship?"

He picked up the receiver and asked for the Goods Inward Department.

"Hello, that you, Máté?... What about this coal?... It's here?"

"Yes, and?... Excellent?... That's very good... So it's first class... So he's sent top-quality Salgótarján coal..."

A high-pitched laugh was heard from the receiver.

"All right, Máté, don't touch it. If it's top-quality stuff, that's all right, I just wanted to know... Don't let anybody touch that first-class coal. Get it?... Don't even let the birds mess on it. Mustn't spoil first-class coal."

He put the phone down and looked at the Mayor, beaming with delight. "Your Worship, we've never caught a fox so easily."

Kardics laughed loudly.

213

"And what a brain my man Máté's got," said the Clerk of Works. "A couple of days ago he said to me 'Boss, there's something I'd like to say... We ought to check that mine this Berci bácsi's going to send that coal from... I've heard rumours about it. It's not the first time he's tried it on. There's no coal there, just a kind of tufa that won't burn, it'll just clog up the flues and we'll have a cleaning job on our hands. I wouldn't dare stoke up with the coal he's likely to send, boss, just let me go to the mine and see for myself what coal the old robber wants to unload on us'."

The Mayor pressed the bell-push on his desk.

"Terrible, these relations," he said. "No good comes of them, relations. I really hate them."

They all laughed.

"And the numbers there are of them. And you have to bear in them in mind, they won't let you forget them. It's the same with people you went to school with. It eventually turns out that you were in the same class as everybody that wants something or has some problem. Especially those with problems. They catch you in the street, at lunch, at dinner, in the theatre, in the lavatory..."

The secretary came in.

"Imri, my lad, I'd like a word with the Town Clerk."

"Very good, Your Worship."

And Imrike took over the smile that beamed at him from the Mayor's face, exaggerated it and took it with him to the Town Clerk's office.

"Nice boy, every time I see him he reminds me of his grandmother. What a delightful, charming girl she was. Yes, well, of course, these children have taken over our roles... they even know... they know... in women's language. Ah, Soma, we had our days... Anyway, Clerk of Works, I'll call for you if I need you... I'll send for you, my dear chap..."

At that point the Clerk of Works got up and left.

"You're still quite a young man, though," the Mayor fingered one of Kardics's buttons, "I hear, this morning... you've been round to your young lady's?... Don't you have any other time?... You *are* a busy man..."

Kardics bácsi laughed.

"When I think back, if I hadn't been a little bit cautious I'd have been completely in his hands," he changed the subject to what was preoccupying him more than anything. "He hasn't got even a provisional contract. And if he had... He can't buy it

214

without the Bank... He hasn't got a fillér. I don't think he's got two pengős in his pocket... His wife gives him spending-money."

"Has she got any money?"

"Of course. Seven hundred and twenty in the post office."

They laughed.

They drew on their cigars, thoughtfully. They would have hesitated to discuss the matter with one another, the final decision, but they felt that the situation had not yet reached the ultimate step. At present the Town Clerk was in the ascendancy, because he had on his side the matter of the revelation of the tenders, which would evoke sympathy. Another move was needed before checkmate...

"I say!" said the Mayor.

Kardics understood.

"We must keep Wagner available."

"Of course."

And they could see that tomorrow the Town Clerk would resign, and that at the next election Wagner would be chosen, the original heir apparent... Wagner, their own man, the long-standing City Hall expert, friend and faithful servant.

At last it was evident to them that the career of István Kopjáss was at an end. These were two tough, tenacious old men, what they decided on had to happen.

Imrike came in and announced the Town Clerk.

"Yes," the Mayor nodded.

A second later Kopjáss was in the room.

"Ah, hello... take a seat."

Pista remained standing for a moment, then sat down. He was very agitated. He was ready for anything.

"Look here," said the Mayor, "look here, my dear chap, that Bisztriczay, he's an old fathead... You don't know him yet, but you'll find out when you've had a bit to do with him... As an engineer, yes, he's fine... but otherwise... simply unpredictable. I can never make out what he's after... What's been the matter? What's been going on here all day?"

Pista knew that they knew everything, that they were involved in everything, but he couldn't avoid going over it all in detail... So he talked, but as he did so he became sick of it... Once more he was having to talk about things that were super-fluous...

"Holub told me a couple of months ago that he didn't mean to tender for the iron bridge. He'd got enough losses on in the

215

city," the Mayor turned to Kardics. "This Bisztriczay's gone mad. I'll give him a piece of my mind. Why do such a stupid thing? It's a disciplinary matter. I've a good mind to take official action."

"He's gone too far."

"But Your Worship, a Holub employee was on the premises, and it was he that was copying the statistical calculations."

"Never, really, can you believe such a stupid trick? You've still got a lot to get used to, my dear boy. Working with people like that... But let's not spoil our appetites with it, you've had your invitation for Sunday evening?"

"Where to, Your Worship?"

"The Boronkays'."

"No."

"Goodness, they're about as bad. They're holding a farewell party on Sunday evening, and half the city's invited. They probably haven't sent an invitation yet because they mean to call with it in person."

"Yes, that'll be right," said Kardics bácsi, "Feri told me that they were going round to Pista's. By the way, my dear Pista, I'm very sorry that I had to discuss the big English loan today, and I had to go out... Did you go to the Bank?"

"No, bátyám, I just phoned."

"And I'd left by then?"

"Yes."

"Never mind. At least your wife will see the house. One ought to see the business running."

And he laughed loudly.

22.

Pista was very disturbed, and the two days passed in complete gloom. He couldn't find out anything about the Mayor and his cronies. He'd been feeling that everything was cut and dried, but now he had to think that nothing had changed, that it had all been a hallucination.

When he went home for lunch he told Lina that they were invited to the Boronkays' for Sunday evening.

Lina's face fell when she heard that the Boronkays intended to call, obviously for a special visit, and there could be no alternative, so Sunday morning... What was she to do? She couldn't

216

make the flat bigger, nor more beautiful. They'd have to take them as they found them.

At noon on Saturday Berci bácsi arrived. The old man was quiet, it was as if the sounds he made were unreal.

He reported to Pista that he'd sent two sample wagons of coal and would give him no peace until he rang Csoma, the Economic Adviser, who expressed approval of the coal. It could be sent.

At this Berci bácsi became heated and launched an attack.

"Look, Pista," he said, "why do you sound so uninterested in this business? You see, they themselves are all in favour of it. They've got the best coal they could possibly have. You have to think of business all the time, not half-heartedly, but with fire and enthusiasm. Business warms your heart day and night. You don't have Sundays, no office hours, no big deals and little deals, only business... Yes, I want to warm people with the fire there is inside me. Central heating for the whole world. My heart is that mine, which could heat all your offices, and the corridors. Every place where there are people, even the market-square and the stall-keepers."

"You haven't got that much coal, Berci bácsi."

"Never mind that, my boy. There's enough fire deep down in the earth. When the coal runs out, we'll go down to the centre of the earth."

"Volcanoes will erupt."

"So what, my boy, just let the fire come up the holes like electricity comes along wires. Boiling water will circulate all round the world. We'll heat all the houses with boiling water, all the factories. Mankind won't be able to make enough use of the hot water there is in the earth, we've just got to tap it... Limitless supplies of hot water at our disposal."

Pista considered this and realised that the old man was right. If the small amount of coal that remained from the ruins of buried forests had been sufficient for a hundred years, what about the heat from inside the earth? There was no way of measuring how much greater it was then the coal deposits. One day in the future mankind would succeed in storing the heat of the sun, and until then there was boiling water in the depths... The whole of the interior of the earth was a reservoir of boiling water at a uniform depth everywhere. He was simply intoxicated by the possibilities. There was nothing to do but lay the pipes...

Kati néni came in. She spent very little time in the house,

217

because the whole city was expecting her. She was out visiting all the time. Relations and friends. If anyone had any claim to acquaintance with the Kopjásses, round she went. Sometimes she did not come home for a couple of days, because they kept her for lunch, dinner, overnight.

"Berci!" she exclaimed as she came in.

Berci bácsi looked up in embarrassment at his former fiancee.

"Who's this scarecrow?" he exclaimed.

"Bercikém, don't you know me? See, it's me, Kati."

"Are you still alive? Why?"

"You haven't changed, how could you, good Heavens."

Berci bácsi stood up and put his arms round her.

"See, Pista, this is how she was two hundred years ago. Just as ugly. Well, give me a kiss."

Kati néni and Berci kissed.

"You even smell the same," said Berci bácsi, "you smell of mint. Where are you living?"

"I'm here, with my dear kind nephew. He's got such a sweet little gem of a wife."

"Well, she'll soon have you out. She's a very clever woman."

"Like the Czechs threw me out of Rimaszombat[59] for being such a good Hungarian."

"In other words, they'd got to know you too... Pista, I don't suppose you've got a drop of brandy? I'd like to wash the smell of this Kati away."

Pista went off in search of brandy and could hear the old couple engrossed in discussion of family affairs. It was depressing to hear how good things had been in the past, how the great family had fallen on hard times.

When Berci finally realised that Lina wasn't going to come in while he was there, he decided to leave. Before he went he beckoned to Pista.

"Öcsém, could I have a word?"

"What is it, Berci bácsi?"

"Could you just let me have twenty pengős?"

"I haven't got a fillér on me, bátyám."

"I'm in a bit of a spot because I spent my last cent on that sample coal. I could scarcely afford the railway charges, They wouldn't take it cash on delivery... Well, never mind. What's that Kati here for? You want to watch her! She's just a gossip! I don't know how often I've told you, don't collect so many relations round you. You've got to be careful about relations."

218

Pista considered this. Berci bácsi was right. But could he tell Kati néni to go away? Is there any means and possibility at all of escaping somebody that won't leave you?

"You must let me have twenty pengős, my boy," said Berci bácsi a moment later, "even if you haven't got it. I can't go out of the house like this, penniless, when you've got twenty thousand pengős commission coming to you the minute the city pays up."

Pista frowned and felt as if the house were on fire. In his gentlemanly, unmaterialistic life, commission was something that had never come his way. The very word set him on fire. He shuddered from head to foot, and thought that this one word was enough to wreck his career.

"Why, my boy? Commission's good money. It's a mark of esteem to those who get it. They're valuable people, who put deals together... Any fool can go down a mine. All that takes is for there to be coal under the ground and for somebody to know about digging... But selling... That's the art... There's so much on sale these days, everybody's trying to do everybody else down; anybody who can make money out of muck, out of raw materials, deserves what he earns. So first of all comes payment of commission. Because one good turn deserves another, especially between relations."

Pista stood up and began to walk nervously round the room.

"Let's have no false modesty," Berci bácsi went on, chewing at his cigar. "Why did I offer you that first twenty thousand share? Because you're a relation of mine... Why did you put through that first deal for me? Because I'm a relation of yours."

"That's not so," said Pista unkindly. "As Cultural Adviser I had no end of problems over coal. Every coal-merchant's a villain."

"That's true."

"They all do business on commission, to rake it in. And the backers are only in it in order to get commission themselves... I regard it as my duty to see, if I possibly can, that I procure good coal... There's nobody in the world that I trust more than my mother's brother. You're going to produce good coal, Berci bátyám, I know... And as for the commission... Certainly, I'm prepared to accept the money that's coming to me as it would go to anybody else... But I don't want to do that for my own sake, but because I've got great and unselfish ambitions... I want to set up something on the lines of a family company with it... You understand? I want to create the possibility of helping

219

the active and healthy members of our family to find employment and prospects, and so to speak to raise an army to serve the common good."

Berci bácsi listened in surprise.

"Who do you want a job for, then?"

Pista was silent for a moment. He didn't want to reveal his plans, nor was there any purpose in so doing, and it came to him that things were as yet undecided. Everything was in an embryonic state in his mind.

"I want to get András Taksony in as manager of the Pig Farm."

"András?"

"Yes."

"I know him. He was always a very nice, amusing chap. He once played a very clever trick on that Kardics, who's such a big noise here nowadays... In those days he was just a bit of a lad, travelling in grain, and one day András put him on a horse, that was a bit of all right... Wouldn't be a bad thing today either to make a horse play him up, that great bladder, that money-bags."

"That's just what I mean. Instead of those who've taken the leading positions by force, I want to place decent, honest men at the head of society, and what's more my own flesh and blood... I can trust myself, therefore I can trust my relations."

"I don't begrudge András his good fortune, but I will say one thing. Couldn't you get the city to buy my mine? They'd do much better if they bought it themselves... The coal's first-class, just like Salgótarján... Nobody can tell the difference... It's just that I'm short on operating capital. I'd let the city have it very cheap, I'd almost give it away, if they'd give me the job of manager and a salary."

"Let's come to that later, the main thing is to get the first deal through. Then if the coal's good enough we'll take it over and you too, Berci bátyám. It's important that I should be able to rely on you."

"That you certainly can. The cathedral will collapse before I'll let you down. Are you sure you haven't got ten pengős?"

Pista felt in his pocket and gave Berci ten of the twenty he'd had from Lina.

"My boy, your official salary's irrelevant. Anybody that doesn't have an extra income is down the drain, he lives out of his wife's shopping-bag."

With which he stood up to go. Lina came in and looked at him sourly.

"I'm just telling your husband how much faith I have in you... Look, Lina, don't let that Kati stay here."

"She said the same about Berci bácsi."

"But you see," snorted Berci, "wherever she pokes her nose in, there's trouble. My girl, you must love your relations, but you must be careful. The only relation to love is the one that's of use to you."

"I've heard that from Berci bácsi before, but he's never said what use we are to be to one another."

"You'll see... I'm looking forward to letting you have the first twenty per cent."

"What? What twenty per cent?"

"Berci bácsi's joking," said Pista quickly.

"Just a joke, my dear, just a joke," laughed Berci bácsi; he made much of kissing Lina's hand and left.

"What was he talking about?" asked Lina when they were alone.

"He's a wind-bag," said Pista. "He wants me to do some business with him... As if I were interested."

"Pista," Lina looked at him solemnly, "promise me that you won't do anything behind my back."

Pista pulled Lina to him and kissed her.

"What about organising the visit to the Boronkays'?"

"Oh, it'd be better if we didn't have to..."

"Yes, but we've got to. The Mayor himself made a point of saying that we've got to turn up. Everybody'll be there. We can't stay away."

Lina sat down tiredly like all housewives that spend all their day on their feet, at work. When they sit down, they collapse.

"I don't know, Pista, but I'm afraid, very much afraid of that life... We can't compete with these people..."

23.

The Főispán's wife gave Magdaléna a hug and patted her heartily on the back.

"You must be feeling very pleased, Magdaléna, the evening's been a great success."

"I'm glad, Szidi néni."

At that moment Pista looked across and his glance connected with Magdaléna's, the glass of champagne in his hand started to shake and a little spilled onto his shirt-front.

221

Lina looked, saw the shirt had suffered damage and was horrified.

Magdaléna was disturbed by Pista's look, turned away with the Főispán's wife and went into the big room.

The weather was beautiful outside. The big flood-light was blazing in the garden, the autumn night was wonderfully clear and soft.

Now Dr. Péterfi came up and took Pista aside.

"Excuse me, Town Clerk, sensational news... But be careful, don't let anybody overhear... The accountant says that a man from the Ministry's turned up and wants to see the Pig Farm documents this very night. It seems there's some serious complaint against Boronkay and presumably Makróczy, who's not here – and the Minister wants it looked into discreetly and at once... I advise you to look out, the Mayor's sure to send for you..."

Pista looked firmly to his front. This was good news. So they were in his hands...

Péterfi, so as not to arouse suspicion, turned away laughing.

Pista stood there for some moments, listening to the pulsing of his blood.

'Quite a detective story,' he said to himself, and there was a gleam of victory on his face.

"Oh my word," Lina came up, "you do look a happy man."

"Aren't you happy? Why not?"

"Are you happy? Why?"

Some ladies came out onto the glazed verandah.

"Madness, the way people dance these days," said a magistrate's wife to Pista.

"The supper csárdás[60] wasn't too bad," he replied. "I once danced a csárdás that lasted two whole hours!"

"When was that?"

"In the good old war days."

"Good old war?... You're right," laughed the wife of a big businessman. The ladies laughed and passed on. Lina had been listening in silence, hadn't joined in, didn't even know them.

"I asked you why you weren't happy?" repeated Pista.

"And I asked you what you were happy about?"

"Good evening, very well thank you."

Pista had addressed the Chief Inspector of Schools, then said to Lina:

"About all this, my dear."

"Am I to be happy because my husband's showing off like a

bird of Paradise? You're standing in the most conspicuous place, flashing your shirt-front."

"Ssh..."

"At least you needn't have spilt things on it."

"I won't be wearing it again."

"Naturally, if you don't look after it."

"Nobody's ever worn a dress-shirt twice."

"It'd have been all right with a jacket."

The Mayor's secretary came hurrying up, he'd been looking everywhere for Pista and took him by the arm.

"Town Clerk, the Mayor would like a word."

"Coming right away, Imrike."

"Yes, he's inside, in the card-room. Good evening, Madam."

Pista stayed because Berci bácsi was approaching, and he didn't want to leave him with Lina.

"Öcsém, could I have a word?"

Lina said sharply: "Let's have none of this 'word' rubbish."

"You are funny... I don't want to ask for money... There's nothing to pay for here. Only a tip for the footman."

Lina took out her little purse and felt in it for money.

"Don't make it too obvious," said Pista.

Berci bácsi took the small change with a laugh, as if it were a very good joke, looked at it and stared in amazement.

"Forty fillérs?"

"That's plenty for a footman. There's enough stealing round here as it is."

Berci bácsi's mouth opened and stayed open. He slipped the coins into his pocket and wandered off, a chastened man.

It took Pista a little while to recover his composure.

"That really was disgraceful, giving my uncle forty fillérs."

"He didn't give it back."

"And what am I to tip the servant?... Here am I, in evening dress, like the Prince of Wales, and I haven't got a bean."

He was just going to see the Mayor when Boronkay, his father-in-law, old Szentkálnay, and Kardics came out onto the verandah.

"Ah, the love-birds," said Kardics, "taking the chance for a kiss here as well?"

Pista felt that there was something insolent in Kardics's behaviour and looked at him, thinking *'zsé vé... zsebre váglak,* but now you're in my pocket... There's a great deal of difference between the last dinner-party and this one...'

"Well, do you like the house, my dear?" asked Szentkálnay.

223

Lina blushed.

"It's too high, too wide and too big for us," she said simply.

"Well, certainly, the youngsters were very extravagant," said the old ironmonger with equal simplicity and some conviction. The two of them understood one another. All the frippery of the modern age meant nothing to them. Lina was sorry for the old man, what pain it must cause him that in this harsh world all the fruits of his hard-working life were at risk.

"Öcsém, can I just have a word?" said Kardics bácsi, and Lina turned as if stung by a bee. He whole body was rigid. She had to compose herself for a moment, of course it wasn't anything to be afraid of, it was amusing that Kardics bácsi should address Pista with that phrase. It was, however, certain that the phrase meant the same in both contexts. What ever could a Kardics want from Pista?

"Your wife doesn't like it much," said Kardics bácsi.

"Far from it..."

Kardics thought for a moment.

"If you like, we can sign the contract. Right away."

Pista's eyes flashed brightly. But then he looked down, so that the other shouldn't see. He could sign the contract. The reason for that would be... It seemed that Péterfi was right: the auditor was here...

"I've just got to run along and see the Mayor. Béla bátyám has sent me a message and I have to dash."

"Never mind, I've come from him to look for you. He's left it to me to sort things out with you, and then we can go and see him together."

"Really?... Very well."

They sat down in silence in the farthest corner of the big picture-room. There was no-one to spy on them except the many pictures.

"Is the man from the Ministry going back again tonight?"

Kardics gave Pista a guarded look.

"Man from the Ministry?"

"In other words, is the inspection taking place tonight?" he asked hoarsely, because, after all, the news wasn't definite, it could be a mistake.

Kardics bácsi thought for a moment; then he laughed.

"Oh, yes. The man from the Ministry, well, of course."

There was a long silence. Pista lit a cigarette. The box was in front of them on the little table, full of fat English cigarettes. He took one, crackled it in silence. He didn't want to say anything, he was waiting to see what would happen.

Kardics was occupied with his cigar. He didn't know how this man could have found out. The Mayor had told him that he knew nothing. What did he know, and how much?

"Well, goodness," he said, "that'll take a quarter of an hour."

Pista said nothing.

"There's something wrong with the vouchers," he said cautiously, "the receipts and the order forms show everywhere the purpose to which material was applied, the villa or the Pig Farm site..."

"Quite."

Eventually Kardics said:

"And where are these vouchers?"

Pista didn't answer. He said evasively:

"Now, the bookkeeping is more cleverly done. It doesn't say anywhere whether a consignment was used for one administrative building or another..."

"What d'you mean by that?"

Pista crushed out his cigarette on the ashtray.

"I haven't introduced my young brother to you yet, have I, Kardics bátyám?"

"Well, I don't know, I don't think so."

"A very clever chap... He used to be an investment manager with the Bank of Budapest..."

"I thought he was something in the Museum Service. I've heard a bit about him."

"That's my other brother. He's Head Keeper in the Antiquities Section of the National Museum... I'd like to recommend him for the Directorship of the city Museum."

"Yes, yes, that's what I've heard. Andris told me, the Alispán."

"Yes, Andris bátyám was so kind, when he was advising me to buy this house, as to give me to understand that he'd have Menyhért invited to take the post... so he could be invited."

"That's a very sound idea."

Now Pista looked Kardics in the eye.

"So, I'd like to recommend Menyus for the Museum and my brother Albert for the Bank..."

"Albert," said Kardics, "Albert... Berci... Ah, Berci. This is that brother of yours whose coal the city... who's sending..."

"No. That's my uncle. He's got a little mine at Köleser, in Borsod county, the coal's similar in quality to Salgótarján...

Excellent coal... but he has no operating capital, and I'd think that one ought not just to get coal from him, but actually to buy the mine. The city'd have a much better deal."

"So, if he... your uncle, is he, Berci?... if he would undertake, what shall we say, to stay on as manager of the mine?..."

Pista fell into the trap for a moment, and it showed on his face, his pleasure shone forth... But straight away, he suspected that it might be irony, or, worse, might Berci bácsi have been sounding off about it himself?

"That's a matter for discussion, whatever seems best," he replied.

The important thing was that today it was they that needed him. There were a few more matters that he could bring up, Andris bácsi for manager of the Pig Farm, Elemér, Lajos bácsi's son, for the city orchestra... Adélka as a schoolmistress... But he said not a word, the opportunity would present itself, just let these go through... He was already regretting that one, his brother Albert... He wasn't a sufficiently serious person... It was a mistake to go on, it would have been enough in the first place to talk about Menyhért... One thing at a time... And it had worried him greatly to have to tell Kardics... It seemed that Kardics knew about Berci bácsi's coal... Indeed, he knew about Menyhért... So he'd have had to bring up those matters... Perhaps the occasion would have arisen in any case, but he'd brought it forward.

This was no shabby deal. He was offering the city outstanding ability. Menyhért ought to have been invited even if he hadn't been his brother. There was nobody to hold a candle to him. Local man, expert, good reputation... Albert was different, he oughtn't to have mentioned him...

Lina came in with Szentkálnay. She didn't speak but just smiled in their direction and went into the other room, she'd seen somebody she knew. Szentkálnay, however, came over to them and sat down.

"Excuse me," said Kardics, "you stay here, I'll go and have a word with the Old Man and come straight back to you."

'Go and present your report,' said Pista inwardly, a bitter taste in his mouth.

"Well, öcsém," said Szentkálnay, "are we going to be able to get out of this somehow? Out of this Pig Farm business?"

"Of course, bátyám, of course."

"But how?... How d'you think, my boy?"

"I don't know yet... It's a million and a half in the red.

These days that's an awful lot... When the price of land's two or three hundred pengős an acre... And it was a thousand in '28 or '29, when these liabilities were incurred... The only thing is to hope for outside help."

"Quite."

"It's fortunate that the city definitely needs it... If they acquire it in a sensible way it'll be a blessing for the whole population. Even the former owners won't have to lose everything."

"What d'you mean, everything?" asked Szentkálnay, and his white moustache twitched. He'd been beginning to feel pleased at what the Town Clerk was saying, but this had startled him and he asked again: "What d'you mean, everything?"

"Some losses are inevitable, that's for sure... The former owner always makes a loss on a bad deal."

"This isn't a bad deal," Szentkálnay exclaimed, "only the boom collapsed."

"One has to accept the consequences of that."

The old man's face was full of tiny blood-vessels. His nose was a network of blue and purple veins, as farmers' noses usually are. Now he was having a rush of blood. No-one had ever dared tell him, even hint, what this whipper-snapper of a Town Clerk was gibbering about... that he must lose, must be prepared for losses... Of course he'd known, but he'd kept it even from himself, because he'd been afraid that it would damage his health, and now here was this man saying straight out that he had to accept the consequences of the collapse of the boom... The fellow must be mad, one couldn't talk to him.

But then he thought that he was deceiving himself, and that he would at least find out what he daredn't calculate for himself, how much he stood to lose.

So he spoke his thoughts straight out:

"And how much will the loss be, in your view?"

"A lot... A lot, but not everything... The situation is such that one must be glad of every fillér that can be salvaged..."

Szentkálnay's chin dropped. He wanted to say something, but didn't even say 'Oh damn'... He took a deep breath and began:

"I've really tired myself today... I was out hunting and became separated from my party... so I walked a good six kilometres. As I was going through a copse I met an old keeper... I said to him 'Don't suppose you've seen my party?...' We had a bit of a chat. He was a man of about my age... In the end he said: 'What's going to happen, sir? Will there be an election?'"

227

He laughed.

Pista just stared at him. In a moment he'd wiped away the former pain. Now he could tell stories, get his pipe out and fill it.

"I realised at one that he was thinking of the election of a king...[61] 'Oh,' he said, 'How they've ruined everything...' The old chap meant, by the war, because he went on and complained: 'All that land we used to have, and how beautiful it was... if we could have stuck to dealing with ourselves then, we'd be all right now'..."

"But do you see," Pista interrupted, "how wise the old peasant was? 'If we could have stuck to dealing with ourselves'. It's the same with this... But people aren't wise enough, they don't learn from the misfortunes of others... Do you see what I mean?"

"What?"

"We must stick to dealing with ourselves; the same goes for your family... Let me explain..."

"You can't explain that to me," grunted old Szentkálnay, "I won't understand even then... That's what you young men are for, to take the burden off our shoulders... All my life I've worked, built, and now to lose the fruits of a life's work. What use has my life been, eh?... What have I done to deserve this?"

"Quite."

"I'm not royalty! This wasn't an inheritance, it's what I've earned myself. It's my rightful property."

"Look, I'll do what I can to prevent you losing everything."

"Everything!" the old gentleman lost his temper. "Everything! What mad talk is this? Why everything? Nothing, my dear fellow, nothing! That's how I would see it..."

Magdaléna saw from the other room that her father was becoming agitated and hurried over.

"Anything I can get you, Daddy?" she laid a hand on his shoulder.

"No."

Pista lowered his eyes and didn't look at Magdaléna. He looked at her shoes, her knees in the thin silk, how they moved as she embraced the tall, powerful old man. Slowly his gaze rose, from her shoes to her hips, her waist, her breasts, her bare arms and slender neck, her hair... As his eyes rose so did his blood, as if fire were driving up a thermometer.

Now Magdaléna looked down at him, seemed to be pleading with him not to upset her poor father. Their eyes met and Magdaléna began to be disturbed. She looked away nervously, as if she had encountered some unexpected force. Her fine, delicate mouth remained open, and for some moments she was not in control of herself.

Pista, however, was left quite giddy. It was as if the earth had opened and swallowed him, the world had become dazzling, as when one has a high fever.

"Won't you stay a while?" he said with grave formality, and Magdaléna left her father, who wandered off muttering something, stayed out of a slight, curious, sense of risk and sat down facing Pista.

"Oh, with the greatest of pleasure," she said, "I'm glad that we've met at last."

"Yes."

"I didn't know we were related."

"I've known... for a long time."

"Really?"

"Yes..." and he looked straight ahead with a certain smile. He looked up with a sudden drunken lack of inhibition. "A ball. Do you remember a ball, when you wore a green dress?..."

"Green?"

"Yes, green, the colour of new grass... You were as slender as a ray of light with the green of springtime all round it."

Magdaléna laughed.

"I did have a green dress once," she said thoughtfully.

"Yes, at that ball."

"Did we dance?"

"No... I wasn't dancing at the time..."

"Why?"

"An oath... You know, I'd spent four years at the front – two as a prisoner of war – then I'd come home, just when the troubles were dying down... I'd wanted to take some great oath... When one suffers one becomes childish and romantic... at first I was going to grow a beard, then I realised that it was out of fashion."

"Were you so rational in your romanticism?"

"Yes... I'm romantic and rational... I was afraid that stubble on my face would damage my career... so I just swore not to dance..."

"What were you doing at the ball, in that case?"

"Line of duty... I'd just been appointed Cultural Adviser, and the ball was something in aid of the education system."

"I remember," said Magdaléna, "I was quite a young woman in those days."

Pista said, with a hesitant smile:

"And I wasn't an old husband yet."

"I remember. Now I come to think of it, I remember you too. They said you'd learnt nine languages in the prison camp."

"And I've forgotten ten since."

Lina came over with old Szentkálnay, who could be seen at a distance praising the house to its purchaser.

"It's very well built," he was saying.

Magdaléna got up and put an arm round Lina. She bent towards her.

"I'm very glad you're having it."

"Oh, it isn't settled."

"Oh, go on!"

"How are we to take on this... Oh... My father's unhappy that we aren't taking over his house free of charge... Oh, that's a rambling house, the rooms are dark, intimate... This one's like a dream to me... which I couldn't dream... it's not my dream... How am I to live in somebody else's dream?"

Pista listened to his wife's voice in amazement, it sounded like music, and her thoughts were like poetry.

"You mustn't torment people..." said Magdaléna, and completed the sentence properly, as she probably did everything that she started, "torment people with such ideas. One says: this is life, and then one believes that it really is. Doesn't one?"

As Lina was in no mood to understand, she looked at Pista with her cold, grey eyes. He started and said: "Yes".

And now once again he couldn't see those eyes, was just aware of Magdaléna's presence, and he felt a kind of perverse delight in seeing the two women together, embracing, and a wild, unrestrained joy surged up within him, he half closed his eyes and looked at Magdaléna's silken knees again, and the wine was having its effect on him, the champagne...

Magdaléna looked at him and her eyes lingered, looked at him in alarm, enquiringly, saw the bloom of joy on his face and looked at him nervously, fearfully.

And Lina saw nothing because she'd closed her eyes and was engrossed in her private feelings.

Kardics bácsi came up with much fuss as usual.

"It's all arranged, young Pista, the Mayor said 'That Pista's got to be given everything'.

"Let me show you round the house," said Magdaléna to

Lina, "and I'll convince you that everything here is simply everyday life and reality. It can't be anything else, I planned it myself, and I'm no poet."

Her every word, her voice, her cool, restrained manner, were pure rationality, but their effect on Pista was to stimulate his senses.

Szentkálnay too came over and went slowly off with the two young women.

"It's built of the best bricks," he said, "and there's no problem with damp."

Pista gave a sigh, pulled himself together, collected his thoughts. The woman had been his, his for a minute... And she'd gone, left him. And he felt hatred: for him, she was not to be won...

"I was saying to the old man," he said hoarsely, inviting trouble.

"What?" asked Kardics bácsi.

"That he'd have to lose something."

"Lose? What?"

"The city can't take it on. You'd never get it past the Council."

"You're still on about that?... Well, of course... You've even been discussing it with the Opposition."

Pista woke up. There was hostility in that comment, and it cleared his head somewhat.

"Is he related to you?" asked Kardics. "Martiny?"

"Distantly."

"So let him come and help."

"He's the Opposition."

"Let him arrange for Opposition demands to match what we want..."

"That's why I've arranged for the former shareholders to stand some loss as well."

"How much? Well, what does Dr. Martiny think?"

"This isn't Martiny's idea, it's mine... And now I know a very great deal about the whole business, and the vouchers are in a safe place."

"And? How do you propose to rehabilitate the Pig Farm?"

"Very simple. The city can't have anything to do with a failed business. That would give the Opposition a very big target to attack... So we'll set up a syndicate which will take the whole thing over..."

Kardics stared, he hadn't been expecting this.

231

"A three-man syndicate will take a controlling interest and offer it to the city."

"Genius. And they'll sell off the controlling interest?"

"What else?... They won't be able to raise any new loans. The city'll be able to get new money for it..."

"Tremendous... A simple device... And will you have funds for it? For the syndicate? Because you'll be a member."

"Of course."

Kardics was completely silent. He didn't know quite how to take that 'of course'... Did it refer to the money or to the being a member? He couldn't sit still.

"Excuse me, I'll be right back."

'Go and tell the Mayor,' thought Pista.

And with that he lay back in the armchair, looking drunkenly straight ahead, his brain reeling.

Silent, alone, forlorn, Lina appeared beside him and sat down.

"This is a different way of life, Pista," she said quietly. "There are no children here... And the way this house is arranged. It's just for show. They don't love one another. Even their bedrooms are a long way apart... His is on the north side, which gets no sun ever, and hers is at the other end. How can this woman not be worried to death about her husband?"

"You wouldn't organise it like this."

"The place could be made a paradise... but it would need somebody else... But people don't come into such a freezing house. Ugh, these dreadful draughts."

Pista picked up a glass of champagne which the footman had already filled.

"Everybody's delighted with it."

"What does that matter to me?... They're simply people who have nothing in common... Look around. See how they're standing facing each other, they're just avoiding one another, and especially me."

"You have to find your niche in life. Here everybody wants you to be happy today, you just have to give them the chance to show it."

"Me, happy? You're very much mistaken, Pista. Nobody's wanted that all evening."

"You're like a thorny flower. Do you see how they run after me?"

"Who? Pista! They run after you like people run after a dangerous dog, they make up to it for fear it'll bite them. None of our friends are here. Walter isn't, nor those nice Lesnyás. I can't understand how there are so many people in this city that we've never seen. This is a different city, you know, from the one we live in. These are all strangers, enemies."

"You're talking rubbish."

"And leave me out of it. I don't understand it at all. I've said time and again that I don't. I've built up my own little life, of which I'm proud, and now I have to see that it's nothing... I'm not used to this. Champagne doesn't flow at my table. I'm used to a husband that doesn't even go out for a beer, and I respect him for it, and he doesn't have lovers, like these do..."

"How does that come into it?"

"This dress is burning my body. It's not my dress, I'd like to tear the wretched thing off, because it's not my skin, but theirs, these people here that turn their backs on me. If it were my dress, then I'd belong among them, and we'd have been friends for ages. Then I'd have sat with them on the sofa gossiping... But I don't belong here, and you forget that you married Lina Szentkálnay, not Magdaléna. And now nothing will be any good in future, because you've had a taste and your ancestral blood has come out... Chance has thrown you out of your place, and now you want to compete with these fools that you've got among."

"I want to be a leader among them, to give the orders."

"How dare you do that?... Do you know anything about it? Can you keep in step with them?... Their ways are different, their morals, their tone. If ever a friend's come to my house she's come in and been happy to sit at my table. She doesn't send in a visiting-card like they did this mid-day, then dash off in the car as if she were avoiding lepers. And when I come here like a fool, for my husband's sake, she says one word to me and goes off..."

"Because you stomp around like a queen in a huff."

"Because that's what I am. Because I've got a soul, and these haven't, or rather they have got one, and it's money... Here you've got to be able to compete, my dear, you can't come here on foot, you have to come by car, and the bigger the better. Why did you marry me while you were poor? You should have waited! You shouldn't have ruined me... What have you done to me? I never have time to read a book, I scarcely look at a paper, I don't follow fashion, I don't know the witty remarks these stylish women have to decorate their lives with...

Magdaléna... Perhaps she too would've been like me, but life's been too good to her..."

"Don't keep on insulting her."

Up to this point their conversation had proceeded as if they had just been discussing the company before them, swaying to the loud jazz, perfumed, crowded. Now Lina sat up straight in agitation and Pista, even in his drunken state, became alarmed, because he knew his wife, and when she lost her temper she didn't care about appearances.

"Why shouldn't I? She really impresses me. All the Pig Farm money went on her showing off, because when a woman's being spoiled there isn't enough money in the world... Do you want me to become what she is? Just buy this house then, and a car and a chauffeur to go with it, and a fur coat for the chauffeur and a gardener and everything. You think I don't know how to spend more than three hundred and forty-six pengős a month? What am I, then? Am I so short of ideas? Couldn't I get through thirty thousand? Every month?... Come on then... It's pathetic... you've got five pengős of mine in your pocket and your head full of dreams. You want a cheque-book and a bank account. Will you get that? Where from? On what? You want to be in with the big-time thieves?... Mind you don't get swallowed... Because I don't know whether they'll be prepared to give you a share... There are enough of them already... They don't need the Kopjáss army... they can already spend what small change there still is in the city themselves."

"Lina... You're a marvel... should you be tormenting me with such things when I'm taking on a world? For the sake of honesty... so that there shall be no more swindling here... Now, when the villains are racking their brains out there as to what to do next? I haven't bought the house yet because they want me to take it as blood-money... so that I shall help shift the great burden onto the people... and here are you, chattering like a sparrow..."

He beckoned the footman and had his glass filled.

"Pista, my love, don't drink, angel, my dear, you're worked up enough without that... don't over-do it."

"I'm having to deal with the powers of Hell here..."

"I won't let you, you shan't drink... Put that glass down or..."

Kardics bácsi surprised them.

"Kissing one minute, quarrelling the next," he said.

Pista looked at him sleepily. What was this man to him?

What was the matter? Wasn't he going to say anything? Was he going to remain silent? Was he going to continue their conversation?

"Can I go in and see the Mayor now?"

"What's the good?" said Kardics bácsi easily. "He's playing cards."

"He did send for me."

"Well, in that case. If he sent for you, all right."

Pista stood up, kissed Lina's hand to make a public end to the recent disagreement.

Lina smiled wearily. She realised that once more she was a minority of one, and in this she was not mistaken.

Pista went through the assembled company. A lot of people were beginning to leave. Several spoke to him, but he went straight on to the card-room.

He went in and stood behind the Mayor's back, but took care that he should notice him. He watched the play.

They were playing tarot.

"I'm very fond of modern youth," the Mayor was saying.

"You're a young man, Béla my lad, you're the youngest present," said the Alispán.

"No, I'm getting on, and I'm looking for somebody to take my place. That's always the main problem, who is to step into our shoes. Modern youth always seems to me as if they weren't our children. Their way of thinking is quite different, their tastes, their idea of patriotism... If they've got any... I don't know whether they have... Pure patriotism has gone out of fashion... But as long as we're here, Andris, don't you think, we'll maintain the standard..."

Then, when there was a moment's pause, he went on:

"Everything these days is to do with people's interests. Whoever heard, in our time, of the poor being treated according to their interests? The people need fine thoughts, inspiration... We must educate them... provide flags, ribbons, draperies in national colours for Christmas... bring in the schools and have them recite those fine patriotic poems. Make Christmas a regular national festival. The Italians have so many festivals that there's a national occasion every week, sometimes two or three. That's what's wanted. That's the only way to keep patriotic inspiration awake."

"The Italians also provide shoes for poor children."

Everybody looked up in shock at the Town Clerk's face.

But Pista had been unable to hold back his comment. It

235

offended him greatly that a moment previously Kardics bácsi'd come and sat down beside him as if there hadn't been the least disagreement between them. What was the matter? Were they dropping him?...

"What d'you mean, Pista öcsém?" said the Alispán with a cheerful laugh.

Pista was silent for a moment. Then he said: "The Italians don't know what winter is like on the Hungarian Great Plain. They should come here and try holding three festivals a week, going from farm to farm. In knee-deep mud. Or when it's freezing, with a howling wind in their faces. Indeed, whatever we like to say, the finest ribbon in national colours is no protection against mud and cold."

The tarot players paid close attention to their hands. They'd never heard such a thing in their lives. This was completely beyond comprehension. Who was this man? An *agent provocateur*?... A communist...

"Is that what they teach people in Russia? Really, Pista!" said the Alispán good-humouredly. "How long were you a prisoner of war there?"

"Nobody's taught me," said Pista, deeply upset. It was bothering him greatly now that he'd said such a thing under the influence of the wine, the champagne. "All I mean to say is that our ancestor Árpád[62] would have done better to ride a bit farther and not to stop until he reached Italy, where at least they don't have to provide heating. But here? People burn horse dung."

No-one laughed. But now Pista was trying to be funny.

"You don't really care for this land flowing with milk and honey," said the Alispán, who at least was replying. Because the rest, the Mayor and the Chairman of the Bench, weren't even taking any notice.

"For myself?... I'm ready to give my life for it any time."

"Well, that's very nice," said the Mayor, picking up his hand.

"It's just that you didn't approve, a moment ago, of the policies of our ancestor Árpád."

"That was only a joke."

"A nice little joke... And what about the rags in national colours, eh? Was that a joke?"

"I didn't say rags."

"You said ribbons. Red, white and green tapes, that's what you said."

236

"Who said that if they mended the holes in their shoes with red, white and green tapes they'd still let in water?"

Pista said "That wasn't me."

"Don't upset my lad Pista," said the Mayor, "he's an excellent, decent chap, who only wants to be of service to the city. A bit inclined to the Opposition, the shock-headed Opposition, but then Ferenc Deák used to say 'I like the Opposition when it's hairy, but not when it's bald'."

Pista considered for a moment who the bald Opposition might be, because Dr. Martiny had a good head of hair.

"Your Worship sent for me a while ago?"

The Mayor looked up, almost smiled, then returned to sorting out his hand.

"Ace of spades."

He looked at him again a moment later.

"Relax... I've got a lot to talk to you about."

Pista stayed there at the cards and watched for a whole hour. Then it crossed his mind that Lina wouldn't come in there. He thought of Berci bácsi too, and made his escape uneasily into the big room.

Now there were very few there, young people whispering in the corners, girls sprawling with boys on the couches by the standard lamps. He thought of that curious orgy-scene that his friend had depicted in the Club, and his imagination was stirred, how the youth of today lived!

He was quite relieved when the music started again and people began to dance.

That weary yet persistently turbulent mood of the small hours was in the air, which no-one can endure that lacks fire in the heart. Amorous desire and excitement make one forget the lateness of the hour, but anyone that works or carries responsibility all day can no longer stand the frantic pace. Lina was truly asleep. She was sitting there, eyes open, but she was so sleepy that it was an effort to stay awake, allowing the minutes to trickle past, not noticing them lengthening into hours.

Pista sat by his wife for a while, but he was neither sleepy nor tired. There was an irresistible turmoil inside him, because he'd had a nasty shock at the fear that they'd abandoned the negotiations with him, which had begun so splendidly. Kardics was no longer acting the go-between and old Szentkálnay wasn't angry. The Mayor had snubbed him, and with ceaseless dizziness Pista was hurtling downwards, what would happen in the morning?

237

He rubbed shoulders with the political groups, listened to passionate arguments, but all that he could think of was what blazed up from within: the Pig Farm, like something in a dream, was slipping away from him. Even at the beginning of the evening he could grasp it and dictate terms on it, now it was beginning to change into a wraith, a rainbow, something unattainable.

At one point he found himself spending a quarter of an hour pacing up and down the side of a room. Like a lunatic in his cell he was taking an endless walk. He was ashamed of himself, and was afraid that his shaken spiritual condition would be noticed, and their purpose achieved.

No, there was nothing to be done at this stage but to hold on. The weapon of truth was in his hands, and with this he could prevail. He scrutinised himself and his actions until then, and he could say that so far he'd committed no criminal act. Right up to the present he was untainted and innocent. His only mistake had been that under the influence of the first glass of champagne he'd regarded the matter as too easy, had revealed his intentions to the old man. That had been an error... Not a crime, because there had been no offence in it, but an error, because he'd shown his hand... They knew his every card, and he'd played his last trump, but he knew nothing of what they wanted...

There was anxiety in his heart, as if the morrow promised some grave danger. A deadly danger.

And he couldn't conceive of what it might be.

That he wouldn't get the house?... That was no danger, because Lina didn't want it in any case. Lina was afraid of this terrible burden.

Praise be! What then could they take from him? He wasn't involved in anything. He had his salary... His income was still adequate for his former life-style... There was therefore nothing for him to worry about... Truth was on his side. Therefore the weapon was in his hands. It was for them to be frightened of him. They'd given him an undertaking, but he hadn't yet put in writing anything that might compromise him...

Magdaléna was standing in front of him. A footman held a big silver tray of cool drinks.

"Offering me ice when I'm on fire?"

Magdaléna smiled with that peculiar, superior look that characterised her.

"Can you spare me a moment?" she asked.

"With pleasure."

They sat down in a corner.

Pista felt his head spin. He didn't know what she was about to say, but Lina wasn't in the room and there was something that he had to get off his chest.

"Tell me," and he spoke with the confidence of the whirling mood of the small hours, "aren't you surprised that here is somebody that remembers a green dress so clearly after seven years, a green dream?"

Magdaléna smiled delicately and looked curiously at Pista, but her eyes were so clear, so completely disinterested was she, it was as if she were listening just out of politeness. And he went on.

"And who, in seven years, never found the opportunity of saying that he remembered it to the one it concerned?"

Magdaléna laughed. She had very beautiful teeth, and could laugh sincerely.

"There are Don Juans and anti-Don Juans," said Pista, "the Don Juan runs through fire and flood and overwhelms the woman until he conquers her. The other remains dumb and can eat himself away with faithfulness for years and years."

Magdaléna was afraid that he was going to go too far and asked in a kindly voice:

"Are you going to buy the house, Kopjáss?"

"Excuse me," said Pista, cooling down; and after a lengthy pause he said hoarsely, "courtesy of His Worship, I believe..."

"It's not the Mayor that's selling it," said Magdaléna with a smile.

Pista was silent a moment.

"Marriages are made in Heaven, but house-purchases are often made in high political circles."

"Very interesting."

Pista now sat as if he wanted to assert his superiority by behaving as if he were confident in her presence. He crossed his legs and rocked the one on the other, looking confidently down on the woman, who suddenly said:

"I'd be very glad if you did buy it, because then I'd be sure that nice people were enjoying my great achievement."

The pain of seven daggers cut through Pista's heart. Could he exercise no influence over this woman at all? She was as far removed from him as if a world separated them. He slowly began to blush, he felt ashamed of himself. She was in an armoured tower as far as he was concerned, and he'd never be able to get near her. Why, oh why, had he declared himself to her...

Both of them became silent. He had nothing more to say, she even less.

Now it flashed through his mind that he was the captain of mercenaries, in love with the lady of the castle, but whatever he might do she would remain the lady of the castle whereas he, even if he resorted to the use of force, would only be a captain of mercenaries.

And so he looked and his face smiled, but now once more he was thinking not of what he had risen to, but that he had evidently been totally and finally dropped... The Mayor had spoken, and he had to be ejected... Magdaléna too had been different when they'd spoken previously. Now she was distant, as if she knew that he'd been dropped...

Ah, these people weren't like him. Why did he bother with them? There was nothing here for him... He couldn't blend in with them. Nothing would come of it. He was on his own if he remained opposed to them and they regarded him as dangerous.

He went on smiling, and his eyes devoured the beautiful woman, a little jaded at this late hour, as he smoked a cigarette. His eyes devoured her, but didn't know that she wasn't his and never would be... In that instant he no longer felt any fire or flame. He found her soul empty, and in fact she had the superiority, the frank look in her eyes, of a calm office-girl. How often had he reproached himself in the past for imagining her when he couldn't see her, and for falling back into the giddiness of love? And what had that love been? Nothing but physical desire? Did he want a child from a woman like this?... Impossible, what mattered to him were a colourful temperament, warmth of heart... So what did he want from this empty-hearted beauty?

They sat facing one another in silence, both smiling. His smile, however, indicated a wrestling contest, hers – nothing. For her, he didn't count. For her, he was nothing to worry about.

"Have you seen the new Chaplin film?" Magdaléna asked suddenly.

"No. I don't like the cinema."

"Yes, but Chaplin?"

"Him, yes."

"Entertaining, don't you think?"

"Yes. Very entertaining. And with him there's always a moral problem…"

"Is it true that the city's taking over both the cinemas?"

"First I've heard of it."

"It'll be a good piece of business. They can be open three days each."

"It'd be simpler for one to be open six days."

"Well, that's true," and Magdaléna laughed.

Then she saw someone that she immediately had to speak to. "Will you excuse me?" she said and floated away to discharge her duties as lady of the house there too.

Pista started to whistle, so quietly as to make no sound. Perhaps he'd had a lot to drink that evening, he felt so dizzy. He would really like there to be an end to it all.

"Pista, my love, shall we go home?"

Lina was standing there, looking down at him. Once more he glanced at Magdaléna. Tall, slender, beautiful, she stood there elegant and courteous. All these goings-on must be boring her terribly, but she was thoroughly accustomed to keeping late nights. Who knew what purposes she was achieving by talking so pleasantly to the infinitely ugly wife of the High Court Judge? What had she been talking to him about? Something to do with a double cinema programme?

But as they were about to leave, Kardics bácsi caught them and hung onto them so dreadfully that they couldn't get away. Pista really had the feeling that Kardics was very worried. But why?

"Going, my dear Pista? We haven't discussed anything yet. You know Béla bátyám, once he starts playing cards you can't talk to him, but he remembers, and he was just saying 'Be careful, don't let that Pista wander off until we've got things straight'."

So they had to stay.

And where did it get him? The quarter-hours passed and Pista just came, went, lounged, yawned, ate, drank, talked, waited. Nobody came to him, nothing happened, time went by, suddenly the mist outside started to lighten.

Then along came Imrike Keék, the Mayor's secretary, went into the card-room and out came the Mayor a few minutes later, with his head like an old jewel carved in silver, and left without a word.

This was the signal for leave-taking, and suddenly everyone was going.

Carriages and cars were standing outside, but somehow no-one had a place for them. They were by now so spoiled that they hadn't arranged for a car. Fortunately, a number of cabs had spent the night outside the villa because of the big party, so they didn't have to walk home.

Since the horse couldn't go through the mud of the side-streets, they had to cross the Market Square to reach Katalin utca. As they were passing City Hall Pista looked up. There was a light in the Mayor's window.

"Who can that be?"

"Cleaners," said Lina pensively. "It's morning."

24.

He took a cold shower and they went to bed, but he was infinitely ill at ease. He didn't get a wink of sleep.

He couldn't understand this day. What had happened and what was going to happen?

'A good thing it's turned out the way it has,' he said to himself, slowly, exhaustedly collecting his thoughts. 'I don't want the crooked road, villainy, dishonesty... I want one road in life: the straight and narrow. The road of truth and goodness.'

These wicked old men, these fat, greasy flatterers. This whole world filled him with something akin to disgust. How inane his night had been. What futile things everybody had talked about that had spoken to him... Magdaléna... The cinema, last of all. A fine way to spend the evening.

But at least he'd seen them all *en masse*. Those were the men of power. We're in their hands... So should a new order not come in? Should this mob of the old order not be replaced, which had been born to power, grown up and lived in it?

His thoughts were very bitter and very destructive.

'Perhaps it's the hangover,' he thought, 'If you've got an upset stomach you become a great moraliser.'

But on the other hand he was very curious about this day. How were they going to face one another today in the office...

By eight o'clock he was on the way to City Hall.

There was no-one in yet when he sat down at his desk. He was almost sorry to be there so early.

'I shouldn't be here,' he thought, 'What is there that I can do?'

He sat there, so incapable of action that he didn't feel like picking up a piece of paper.

Dr. Péterfi arrived. He said good morning, Pista smiled and looked at him, said nothing, just went on sitting in his chair.

He was tired, his thoughts drifted to and fro.

Suddenly Dr. Péterfi came in, his face flushed.

"Town Clerk, sir, somebody's been in here in the night."

Pista looked at him in consternation.

"How can you tell?"

"Everything's upside down, everything's been turned over."

Pista looked at the safe. There it stood, firmly locked.

What was this? Had somebody broken in? He daredn't think further.

His desk was tidy, but he could see at a glance that his papers weren't in the places where he'd put them the day before. What had been on the left side had been moved to the right... But the documents on the right were affairs that were settled, those on the left were those in progress...

Suddenly he stood up and took out the safe keys. He opened the door and looked inside. No money was kept in the safe, only certain important documents.

He lifted out the bundle of Pig Farm papers.

It had been opened and undone.

"The books have been gone through too," said Dr. Péterfi. "These calculations here have been left, these tiny jottings."

Pista went pale. The audit had taken place last night. That was why he hadn't been allowed to leave the Boronkays'. That was why Kardics had been agitated... He'd had to wait for Imre Keék to come back... When they'd finished in his office they'd continued in the Mayor's... That was why there'd been a light on when...

He felt dizzy, blood rushed to his head. Breaking and entering. Theft. Abuse of authority. Violence. Force. Theft. Burglary.

And the vouchers were in his flat, he'd taken them home to study for the indictment... Therefore from Boronkay's point of view the examination had gone smoothly, because there'd been nothing compromising that could be identified in the books... So Boronkay had escaped... The Minister would receive a favourable report on him...

He reeled against his desk. They'd played him a dirty trick.

He stared and stared at the safe.

"And what on earth is this revolver? Did they leave it here?" and he picked up the pistol from the bottom of the safe. There were five rounds in it. He shuddered – what was this? Were they even prepared to kill?

Péterfi looked at it.

"No, I think that's Town Clerk Makróczy's revolver. He's left it here."

Pista put it back.

"Now what are we to do?"

Dr. Péterfi said nothing. He pulled a wry face.

"Against unknown intruders?"

But they weren't unknown... He knew very well against whom...

"But how is it possible?" Pista said quietly. "I hold the keys."

Péterfi was completely silent.

"Well, all right... An outsider can't have been here, there's no sign of forced entry... In any case, I'll report it... At once."

He was so tense every nerve was quivering.

But he wasn't left hesitating for long. The Mayor sent for him. A hajdú came to say that His Worship was calling for him.

"Right, now for the showdown."

The Mayor's reception room was full of a delegation. Two hundred poor farmers were standing there, Martiny in their midst.

He immediately hurried over to Pista and said that they'd already seen the Mayor, but the poor men wouldn't go away until they'd received their rent moratorium in writing.

The secretary bustled in.

"My dear chap," said the Mayor, "we must sort out these people's business somehow or other."

Pista looked at the man. How cool, how calm, how ordered he was.

"How can we collect these arrears? Hmm. How *can* we do it?"

"This would be a good opportunity," said Pista huskily, "for the city to introduce the 'bush-farm' system. Then they would-n't live scattered over twenty square kilometres, but close together by the railway line. Then you'd be able to catch them."

But how could he sit there so calmly? Wasn't he dreading that Pista's first question might be what had happened in the night?

"Explain, my dear chap, explain, go on, do."

"This plan has been put forward on several occasions, but

244

the Council has never seen the point of requiring the smallholders to occupy 'bush-farm' sites, because the matter's always been badly presented. It's always been shown how much this reorganisation would cost, without reference to the advantages to be gained by the city... The point is, Your Worship, there just aren't enough police and wardens and bailiffs to bring in the arrears, nor is it possible for the city to obtain satisfaction by eviction. Because how are these people to be evicted? Are they to be piled in the fields? Not to mention that in such an event a socialist revolution would break out which would stir up the Budapest press and show the city up before the whole country in the worst possible light, and compel the government to become involved... But let's assume that a 'bush-farm' system were to be introduced; in that case it would be child's play to solve the problem. In the first place they'd be permanently under our control, it wouldn't be possible for them to fall years behind with rent, and even mass re-settlement would become a simple matter."

"Ah, ah..."

"If the smallholders weren't spread over twenty square kilometres, but, let's say, were transferred to ten bush-farms, then we'd have ten sites to deal with, and people could be moved on from one day to the next. If all else failed, they could be moved into town, put into Council accommodation, and replaced in the shortest possible time by another couple of hundred families, there's no shortage of applicants."

"Not bad, not bad. Look here..."

The Mayor stood up, came to Pista and patted him on the shoulder.

"That's very clever. And, you see, that would make your name... Naturally, of course, the utilitarian aspect mustn't be emphasised. I think it's very sound, if a trifle complicated. It would have to be linked with the local railway, don't you think? As the railway's built it could be arranged for these 'bushes', or whatever you call them, to be built along the line, isn't that the idea."

"In that case the problem of transport is solved as well."

"You see, nobody ever thought of that before. The poor bailiffs really can't handle the work, and the city can't meet the cost of all that transport. And how pleasant the puszta will look when farm-villages seem to spring from the ground along the railway line."

"And every village will have to have a farm office, a system of agricultural supervision, to keep an eye on the activity of individual tenants and to be responsible for the collection of rents and taxes."

"But what's all this going to cost?"

"Nothing, because the costs can be passed on to the plot-holders."

"Quite, quite."

He looked passively straight ahead.

"We'll have to have a word with the Alispán's uncle..."

He picked up from his desk a graph showing railway freight charges, looked at it, then started to speak, slowly, syllabically.

"Hmm, hmm. The whole world consists of relations, just relations. Nothing but relations everywhere. Everybody's got a poor relation who has to be found a job, and then, when they're in jobs, they do nothing, have no thoughts, no ideas, no industry any more... I'm dead against relations. They're the bane of Hungarian life... They've been nothing but trouble to me ever since I've been sitting in this chair... It'd be possible to manage perfectly well if there weren't all these relations. And everybody's somebody's relation, everybody's got relations. Well, tell me, I don't know everything... And my officers' children grow up and I'm supposed to know who's married whom, who's married his daughter to whom. They have children, these children start to grow, go through their illnesses, start school, something's got to be done about the school, if they don't get on very well with their studies you've got to help. Then these in their turn start to get married and the relations go on multiplying. Because a single marriage unleashes upon us one new family after another. You've got to know them all. An officer comes to see me and start talking about Mariska and Juliska, well, I'm supposed to know them, he's told me before, they've had a grant for them, so I know. What can I say about Janika's musical ability, he ought to have a scholarship, Péterke must get into the military academy, Palika's been embezzling, we've got to get him off... I'm expected to listen to all this, because I'm interested in this and that... and how I'm interested..."

The Town Clerk listened in surprise.

"Why are you laughing?" said the Mayor. "Everybody gets into this situation. I hear your relations get round to you all right." And he studied the graph.

The Town Clerk was startled. The Mayor went on:

"Along comes Jani bácsi: '*Édes öcsém*, I hear that God's given you good fortune, help me, because I'm in such a spot...' Kati néni comes: '*Édes fiam*, I hear that God's given you good fortune, help me...' Berci bácsi comes along, turns up first of all, '*Édes fiam*, I was always close to your dear father, poor chap, we were the best of friends, here's my coal-mine, buy it, it'll be so good for the city...'

The Town Clerk was beginning to realise that something was about to happen and listened in alarm...

"Well, the coal's good, the coal's good, that's not the point. And up to now the Town Clerk's relation has delivered. The Town Clerk's changed, the relation hasn't. His relation'll continue to deliver, what's more. Different dog, same collar. But what'll happen about Kati néni?"

"Kati néni too?" exclaimed the Town Clerk in horror.

The Mayor laughed.

"Well, you see, there's a Kati néni in every family. And every Kati néni's got nine grand-children. So you can't be too hard. You can't tell your relations to drop dead. You've got to have a heart. Especially here in Hungary, here the whole of life stands on a foundation of tribal co-operation. At the Honfoglalás our ancestor Árpád divided up the country between his relations and their relations, and since then the only thing that's counted has been blood relationship. There's no greater sin than for a relation to fall from power... But therefore, my dear chap, sometimes one has to concede a point to an outsider too..."

The Town Clerk's face was ablaze with shame, but he couldn't see where this was leading.

However, the Mayor did not leave him in uncertainty for long, he explained nicely, smoothly, kindly, good-humouredly.

"Just look, my dear chap, I'll tell you a secret. I've been sitting in this old City Hall now for thirty-eight years, in this chair. Today I'm the oldest Mayor in the country, and it does you young chaps no harm to understand why it's possible to have this long term of office... Why have I never been defeated? My dear chap, you can check the whole list of the officers of the city, in all that time I've never appointed my relations. I've always been good to my relations, when I've been able I've taken care of the less well-off, given them money, got them jobs, but in thirty years nobody's been able to throw in my face that a relation of mine's become Town Clerk, Deputy Town Clerk, an adviser, anything in the city. No. Never. I've never done business with the city, nor have my brothers, my uncles, my in-laws, not one of them."

"Your Worship, if Berci bátyám has appeared with this coal, I hereby withdraw my support, which..."

"Whatever for? The coal's perfectly all right. And as long as the coal's good it doesn't matter who delivers it. So that takes care of that. It wouldn't be honourable or logical or profitable, because of course you yourself aren't doing badly out of it."

The Town Clerk blushed so much this time that now his ears were burning too. The Mayor was alluding to his getting twenty per cent from Berci bácsi... That of the first hundred thousand, twenty thousand were going to him...

"You aren't Mayor, your job's much simpler. Nobody's going to call you to account as long as the coal's good, I'm not against the relation business, I just don't like it for myself, that's all. I respect and look after my officers' relations. I hate having to know everybody, and that it's so natural and so taken for granted that I should look after them, but I have no objection to recognising Berci bácsi instead of Samu bácsi..."

"Your Worship..."

"Wait a minute, you can have your say in a moment, my dear chap, just let me finish. All I have to say is this, and no more, that relations have to live, but for that reason so do non-relations. When all's said and done, there are people in the city who aren't relations... In fact, they're the majority. Because there are ninety-six thousand people here, aren't there? Not all the ninety-six thousand are related to anybody, and you can't deprive them of the right to a living just because they haven't got any relations."

The Town Clerk said nothing.

"What about that poor Holub? Just because he's not my relation, and one doesn't have as much regard for people's affairs when they're not relations?"

The Town Clerk exploded as if struck by lightning. So this was about the Holub business. The Mayor wanted to have it out with him about the stolen plans.

"Your Worship..."

He stopped, because all of a sudden he couldn't express himself precisely. He was also worried that the Mayor too was saying nothing and seemed to be waiting for his reply.

"Your Worship, I don't want poor Holub and Company to be ruined. I know that the Pig Farm owes him six hundred thousand pengős. If he got that money he'd have no problem, he can't get it because there's none to give him, whereas the Szentkálnay property's over-mortgaged, and in the event of a bank-

248

ruptcy the whole Szentkálnay firm will go under, a hundred-year old business will vanish, its members will need the charity of the city or the State... I'm not anxious, because the network that they've established in the course of that hundred years will support them. I don't know whether the State might re-float them, or whether his son-in-law will be accepted as Secretary of State, he's a very decent chap with a good knowledge of economics, and a good speaker into the bargain."

"Quite. You've got a grasp of public affairs."

"So Holub and Company needn't be ruined," the Town Clerk went on with a little more self-control. "Although as far as my information goes, superficially it's rather a question of saving face. But the way out for him isn't to send people to City Hall to copy out competitive tenders that have been submitted so as to undercut them... That's not the way, Your Worship, because if he's here now he isn't a stranger, but a relation, if not by blood then on a financial basis. Please find such a way of winding up the Pig Farm."

"Perhaps you've got such a solution. I mean, you've got an excellent head on you, my dear chap, and you seem perfectly capable of averting difficulties with big plans. If I'm not mistaken that's the third idea for pouring oil on troubled waters that you've thrown out in this short conversation."

"Yes, I had a sort of plan for this that I mentioned to Kardics bácsi last evening, I'm sorry he didn't mention it to you..."

"So," the Mayor looked at him with infinite softness and affection.

"I think that, on the one hand, in its present form the Pig Farm has lost its viability, because the people that were in command have become exhausted materially, and therefore spiritually, and on the other hand it's inappropriate for a company established by the city to enter into negotiations with the city. Therefore a syndicate has to be set up to acquire the Pig Farm shares. It'll pay a modest amount for them, and will in turn take over, in exchange for value in kind, such part of the indebtedness as may be transferable. In this way perhaps it might be possible to save Szentkálnay long enough for him to stay in business and be able to re-schedule the Holub debt that he's liable for."

"Very interesting," and the Mayor shifted in his seat. "Of course, of course... You could make a private purchase of the Pig Farm in the same way as the Boronkay villa. Isn't that the idea?"

Pista said nothing. What was this? Open ridicule now? His nerves were stretched to breaking-point.

"The only question is whether you've got enough money to afford your portion of the shares."

Pista said nothing.

"Of course, of course. As far as I'm aware, you've got a balance of fifteen thousand pengős in the Bank."

Pista thought for a moment.

"Yes," he said, "and the expectation of twenty thousand. But that would amount to a third of the hundred thousand pengős."

"And a bit to spare," the Mayor gave a cheery though involuntary laugh. "Thirty three and a third. So you'd have something like one thousand seven hundred left."

"That's right."

"Very well. That's good... That'd be all right... So the only trouble is that Berci bácsi's coal..."

The Town Clerk's head swam.

"Well, of course, only in the event of Berci bácsi being able to provide top quality coal," he said.

"Yes, yes, yes. Yes to that. Berci bácsi has been able to provide top-quality coal..."

"Has been?... So the coal's here?"

"Of course. Berci bácsi's a very industrious man. The coal arrived surprisingly quickly. In fact, it came today. They've just phoned to say it's arrived and it's first-class."

"Well, that's marvellous. So things are going like clockwork."

The Mayor laughed loudly. All his false teeth gleamed.

"Hahaha, very good, ve-ery good, everything's going like clockwork... Clockwork, that's brilliantly put, my dear chap. So, you've proposed to me three first-grade plans: firstly, that we should reconsider the business of setting up 'bush-farms' so as to get our hands on the smallholders more easily. Quite brilliant, but not very popular... Because, look here, if I were to say that we must put the farm-village system into effect out of modern social considerations, that would be in order; but that the Town Clerk should come forward with such an idea, not for the sake of hygiene or culture or the well-being of the people, but just so that we can lay our hands on the whole pack more easily, those thousand or two families that rent smallholdings from the city... No, I don't think that it would be very popular, that is too say, this point of view..."

The Town Clerk gave the Mayor a hostile look.

"The second plan you proposed, to save the Szentkálnays in such a way that the State might take the boy as, shall we say, an Under-Secretary of State... Here too the problem's just a question of attitude. Because if this really happens, my God, at least the government is wise and the government can pick the man for the job... That's the government's business; but that this plan should be put into position from below, that doesn't seem sufficiently popular... At this point I'm placing emphasis only on popularity."

A further painful interval. Pista couldn't imagine where the Mayor was leading with his smooth smile...

"The third plan. The most colossal of all... That a consortium should acquire the Pig Farm for, say seven hundred thousand pengős gross... Because what you have in mind, if I'm right, is a hundred thousand for the share package, six hundred thousand for the transferred debt. And then to foist this rubbish on the city for, say, a million. By which the three members of the consortium will each make a cool hundred thousand pengős... The least popular of the lot... Profitable, I don't deny, especially for the three entrepreneurs, but public opinion will smell a rat at once... Oh, I know public opinion. The leader of the Opposition, my dear chap, is only leader of the Opposition until he's made some money. The moment he does... At that moment, he's a lost man in the eyes of the public.

The Town Clerk went pale at this.

"I don't understand you, Your Worship," he mumbled.

"Let's just look at the business closely. This won't just go through in secret. Public opinion will have a word to say. And what a lot of words, my dear Kopjáss. They'll say that they'll look into it... But never mind, never mind, there's just the coal, that coal..."

"What coal?"

"Berci bácsi's, of course... That is to say, Berci bácsi was so afraid that the coal from his little mine might not be up to standard – it's lignite, soft brown stuff, which won't burn in our furnaces, or if we do use it, it'll block the flues after one stoking and we'll have to clean them out – anyway, Berci bácsi's bought two truck-loads of Salgótarján coal and delivered those."

It was as if the whole huge building had fallen in on the Town Clerk's head. All at once he couldn't breathe, he turned deathly pale and broke out in a cold sweat.

After a lengthy pause he could only say:

"Has this been checked?"

"Yes, my dear chap, Máté from Goods Inwards went out to your Uncle Berci's mine, brought back a sample of coal that was actually mined there and escorted the Salgótarján coal back here and accepted it... The Salgótarján dispatch-notes are still on the trucks, they forgot to take 'em off..."

The Town Clerk clasped his head in his hands.

Dimly there came to him the recollection of Menyhért telling him to beware of Berci bácsi, that Berci bácsi had never made an honest go of anything... Something of the sort. The room was spinning, and he could see that this was the end, the end of everything.

He was no longer listening to what the Mayor was saying, but heard only:

"Huh, relations, relations..."

Now what?

Suddenly he jumped up and in exasperation exclaimed:

"My office was broken into last night. The safe was opened with a skeleton key and the Pig Farm documents were gone through."

The Mayor looked at him coolly and contemptuously.

"Broken into? Opened? Gone through? A check took place, on my orders..."

"I had the keys."

"The duplicate set! Because I have the master-keys."

And from his desk he picked up two Wertheim keys. "That's my safe, Town Clerk, it's only kept in the Town Clerk's office."

"There's nothing to that effect in orders."

"A trifling point... There was nothing in the arrangements about Berci bácsi sending Salgótarján coal from Kalácsbánya!"

He was felled, like an ox, with a deadly blow. He sank back and couldn't move, couldn't breathe. His world had collapsed. No more head held high, no more plans and hope. No more life.

He felt that there were wild beasts around him, and he, fool that he was, had thought that he more of a wolf than the wolves... He'd felt that he held the whole city in his hand... but now he was down on the ground, in the mud, his honourable name in the dirt. He'd deserved it... Had he acted hastily?... There were things with which one has to hurry, or nothing will come of them... Had he been lured into a trap? Possibly... he hadn't been cautious... wasn't accustomed to fighting duels with the unscrupulous...

He looked up but did not raise his head. The Mayor was not

looking at him, his big round spectacles were on his nose and he was examining a document.

Perhaps it was something about him? Or perhaps he had by now been dealt with, and it didn't matter any more whether he was there or not...

And what was to happen now?... He felt for Lina in that moment. Should he go home and tell her everything?... Or nothing, or just say 'Berci bácsi', and Lina would know everything... It was his fault that Berci bácsi...

An honest, innocent man had fallen among thieves, and it had turned out to be him or them... Didn't life tolerate honourable men?...

And was he in fact an honourable man?... Hadn't he wanted what they did?... How well this old man had seen through him... he'd recognised such thoughts... been on the scent like a fox... understood everything in a flash, sniffed it all out. He was truly impressive. To be able to sit there thirty-eight years...

Now he'd gathered his thoughts, and he was going to do it. He had to, there was no other way out... It didn't worry him, it was all the same to him... He was dead already...

He was exposed... mercilessly, pitilessly. He'd mounted a horse and been thrown; got on a train and fallen off, and now the wheels were crushing him. He could feel the machinery snapping, grinding his bones... And he went on sitting. His sons. They'd start as he'd done, in poverty, adversity, perhaps one of them would make good... drag himself back up... then the rest would be a burden to him: 'God's given you good fortune, help me...'

He sat helpless in the big armchair, lost, just as he'd sat, a sick child, in his mother's arms. He leaned his head against the leather upholstery and the room swam slowly around him...

Was this all that one was? Was this all that life was? A man could be finished off as quickly as this...

Well, let them trample him to death. Bury him. Kick his grave...

Lina was a qualified teacher, perhaps she'd be able to get a bit of a job. They could do without the corner room. She could take in students... do their washing. Lina had strength of will, and having to think of the children would stiffen her resolve. 'Take care of yourself, my love'. How had she thought, how had she sensed, why had she been terrified that there was something wrong, that he was swimming in troubles, when he himself hadn't even suspected...

He glanced again at the Mayor's face. He was hard at it; pencilling notes on something. The way he worked! How could he stand it! With his silver head... It crossed his mind that he'd had one thought, that the Mayor was old, very old... it wouldn't be long before they needed another... and he'd have had such great wealth, importance, influence, popularity... That this old man had been able to twist everything... Face to face he'd so contrived things that everything was 'dead unpopular': that is to say, his every thought was evil... Perhaps... But their mouths wanted to have everything to their taste, because how else would they have understood... and how well he had understood... It was unthinkable for him to be shown up as a swindler and exploiter of the people...

Pista sat on, looking at the floor, listening to the pulsing of his blood. He ought to get up. He ought to bang on the desk. He ought to shout in their faces...

But so what.

Everything was against him... and above all Berci bácsi...

Red lights...

Blackness...

the end of everything

no help to be found

and why indeed, when life was so loathsome

not worth living

vomit

When he was clean and honest

don't need honesty

must be born to evil

can't just suddenly become a villain

must have started years ago, in his childhood

oh, never mind

a hole had been burned in his life and Magdaléna would brush off even the memory of him...

a swindler didn't deserve...

Now the Mayor looked up. In his eyes was a sort of cold, alien quality. He looked at Pista in surprise at finding him still there...

Pista stood up.

He wanted to say something, but nothing came to mind.

He bowed and went out.

The Mayor did not speak, did not say goodbye, no kind word, did not say 'goodbye, my dear chap'.

It was as if he were walking on someone else's legs. Yes, since he'd been in here, he'd been walking on someone else's legs...

He went out and closed the door behind him.

A moment later Kardics bácsi came through from the other room.

"By the way," he said, "dinner at the Szentkálnays', don't forget."

"Ah, how could I forget. As if I could forget."

Kardics bácsi held out his hand.

"You were brilliant," he said.

The Mayor took his glasses off his nose, put them down and held out his thin, fleshless, dry hand in response.

"You were superb, my dear fellow," said Kardics bácsi, and his greasy face was warm with flattery.

"What I think is that we..." said the Mayor, leaving his one hand in Kardics's, who would not release it, and stroking his beard with the other, "what I think is that if that man comes back tomorrow, then he'll be a very useful man: because, do you know, in all my long career I've scarcely met anybody that's picked up the threads so quickly and so very well. That... that syndicate idea might be a very good solution of the problem. It's... it's a stroke of genius... And naturally... naturally, it couldn't be achieved without him... because, well, he sees things so clearly, don't you agree, that he'd be indispensable... It's very good... I can tell you, the business is well and truly settled..."

Kardics released the Mayor's hand.

"Yes. Yes. And really, three people are enough... Let's say, your son-in-law... and myself, not personally, but perhaps acting through my Henrik, and... and him."

At that moment in rushed Dr. Péterfi, frantic.

25.

"Your Worship," he stammered, "the Town Clerk, it's the Town Clerk..."

"Well, well, what's the matter?"

"He's shot himself."

"Ah, ah, why?"

He looked at the man so indignantly that he gaped in alarm.

"I don't know."

"And what was this revolver? Where did he get it?"

"Your Worship, Makróczy's revolver was left in the office, that's the one."

"Oh... oh... but this is awful... Well, call a doctor at once... we must save the poor man... Is he dead?"

"He's in a bad way."

"Well, why are we wasting time, damn it! He's the most outstanding man in the city! Call out the whole hospital at once!"

"Very good."

Dr. Péterfi rushed out as he had come in, and the Mayor took his hat and coat, because the corridors were draughty.

"You don't mean to go to him?" exclaimed Kardics in alarm.

"I certainly do. This is terrible. He must be saved. He must have medical attention."

He spoke to his secretary as he came in:

"Send a thousand pengős to the widow right away... That is, to his poor wife... Five hundred. Send her five hundred pengős immediately."

"I'll put a hundred to that," said Kardics bácsi, reaching for his wallet. "One needs money at a time like this."

And they hurried away to save the poor man's life.

Translator's notes

I offer a few comments on my attempts to deal with some of the problems involved in the translation of Hungarian and to offer explanations of certain details.

Hungarian words in the text. These comprise:
a) personal and place-names;
b) words such as *úr, hajdú, ferbli*, which are explained in notes;
c) coinage. From 1858–1892 the Austro-Hungarian Empire used the *forint* (=100 *fillér*); in 1892 the *forint* was replaced by the *korona* (=100 *krajcár*), which in 1927 became the *pengő* (=100 *fillér*) at a rate of 12.5K=1P. The word *krajcár* remains in colloquial use at the time of this book to denote the smallest (fillér) coin. The modern Hungarian *forint* dates from 1946.

Modes of address. In Hungarian a complex system of address is used – the familiar second person *te* (plural *ti*), the honorific *Maga* or *Ön* (plurals *Maguk, Önök*) with the third person of the verb, the now old-fashioned *kend*, used to a social inferior, and the very formal *tetszik* 'it pleases' followed by the infinitive, all of which are alien to modern English. All these forms have been rendered by the second person. The reader should know that Pista and his wife, for example, spend most of the text addressing one another in the honorific form, while colleagues in the City Hall, irrespective of status, are almost always *te*.

The words *bácsi* 'uncle' (*bátyám* 'my uncle'), *öcs* 'nephew, younger brother' (*öcsém* 'my nephew') and *néni* 'aunt' are frequently used. *Bácsi* and *néni* are used for persons older than the speaker, male and female respectively, while *öcsém* is used for younger males. These terms imply a degree of kinship or familiarity. Also to be found is *fiam* 'my son'.

Úr 'lord, gentleman' after a surname is the equivalent of the English 'Mister' (there is no equivalent word for 'Mrs'); *úr* (plural *urak*) alone denotes a member of the decadent (former) land-owning class. The author's dislike of these people is succinctly expressed in the book.

Geography. The Treaty of Trianon (1920), in breaking up the Austro-Hungarian Empire, assigned Erdély (Transylvania) to Romania and a considerable area of northern Hungary to what are now the Czech Republic and Slovakia. A number of places referred to in the book are in these 'lost' territories. It may be noted that these are in the main correctly named, whereas towns remaining in Hungary are usually named in Hardyesque fashion, unless they are places of importance.

257

The city of Zsarátnok itself is not to be found on the map; the name is allegorical, meaning 'embers' – dull on the surface but red-hot underneath. Enough details emerge in the course of the book for the reader to make a shrewd guess at where Móricz might actually intend it to be.

Hungarian pronunciation. The reader may find it helpful to have one or two features of Hungarian orthography and pronunciation made clear.

All Hungarian words are stressed on the initial syllable. Double consonants are pronounced twice as long as single consonants. Vowels written with accents (and double accents) are long. Vowels are not quite the same as their English equivalents. The most conspicuous departures are:

Hungarian *a*: as the vowel in English <u>hot</u>: <u>hat</u> 'six'; <u>ma</u> 'today';

         á: the vowel in English <u>cat</u> – but long; <u>kár</u> 'damage' is not unlike the American <u>car</u>, but without the nasal quality! <u>lát</u> 'sees'.

         é: as French <u>é</u>; <u>Béla</u> (man's name).

         ö: as German <u>ö</u>; <u>Ön</u> 'you'; <u>öt</u> 'five'.

         ő: the same but long; <u>bőgő</u> 'cello'; <u>őt</u> 'him', 'her'.

         ü: as German <u>ü</u>; <u>ül</u> 'sits'; sün 'hedgehog'.

         ű: the same but long; <u>űz</u> 'drives'; <u>tűz</u> 'fire'.

Consonants too do not always indicate the sounds that one might expect:

Hungarian *c/cz:* English <u>ts</u>; Kuruc.

         cs: <u>ch</u>; kocsma, csinál 'make'.

         gy: <u>dy</u>; egy 'one', Magyar.

         j and *ly:* consonantal <u>y</u>; Károly, Kopjáss.

         ny: <u>ny</u>; nyir 'mows', lány 'girl'.

         s: <u>sh</u>: tessék 'come in', István.

         sz: <u>s</u>; csusza, tetszik.

         ty: <u>ty</u>; tyúk 'chicken', ponty 'carp'.

---

[1] The Hungarian word *főügyész* means 'head lawyer'. 'Town Clerk' is the nearest English approximation in a civic context.

[2] Mayor: The Hungarian *polgármester* is more akin to the French *Maire* than to his English counterpart.

[3] The *Főispán* was the appointed representative of the Crown in a pre-

war Hungarian county. Unlike the modern English Lord Lieutenant he was politically active.

4 boom: Hungary experienced a period of prosperity under the influence of League of Nations assistance from 1924 on, but suffered severely from the collapse of world wheat prices in 1929. The 'boom' was at its height in the early months of 1927.

5 Turkish times: Much of Hungary was overrun by the expanding Ottoman Empire. The Turkish era is usually reckoned as beginning with the defeat at Mohács (1526) and ending with the Peace of Karlowitz (1699).

6 Kálmán Tisza: Hungarian statesman (1830–1902) and great landowner.

7 Beszteréd: Possibly out of *Beszterce* in Transylvania by *Geszteréd* in Szabolcs county!

8 Ferenc József: The Hungarian form of Franz Josef, Habsburg Emperor 1848–1916.

9 *hajdú*: A liveried attendant of county dignitaries.

10 *Schadenfreude*: delight in misfortune.

11 Balázs Hübele: A nursery-rhyme character, always in a mess, who acts without thinking.

12 Consolidation: The change and revaluation of coinage from *korona* to *pengő* in 1927.

13 *puszta*: Areas of treeless steppe terrain on the Great Plain (Alföld), mainly devoted to animal husbandry.

14 *csikós*: The Hungarian equivalent of the cowboy.

15 Kőszén and Rimamurányi: Mining and ironmaking concerns at Salgótarján in the Rima valley.

16 Kishegyes: "Little Hill", a *puszta* west of Debrecen.

17 revolutions: A period of unrest following the Great War.

[18] Székely: The Hungarian-speaking inhabitants of the eastern parts of Transylvania.

[19] Kuruc: The Hungarian irregulars under Thököly and Ferenc Rákóczy that opposed the Labanc Austrian Imperial forces in the late 17th-century fight for independence from the House of Habsburg.

[20] Borsod is a real county, but Köleser seems to be imaginary.

[21] boss: Count István Bethlen was Prime Minister 1921–31.

[22] The *Alispán* was the senior elected officier of a pre-war Hungarian county, and its principal representative to central government. He was the deputy of the *Főispán*.

[23] King Károly: Successor to the throne of Emperor Francis Joseph who, as king of Hungary, was known as Charles IV (1916–20).

[24] St. Sephen's Day: August 20th, the celebration of the new bread, named in honour of Hungary's first king.

[25] Romanians: Romanian forces entered Hungary in 1919, occupying Budapest in August, and leaving the country in November.

[26] Lequeitio: Following the death in 1922 of the deposed King Károly, Queen Zita and their numerous children moved to Lequeitio, on the north coast of Spain.

[27] Conquest period: The entry of the Magyars to the territory of Hungary, traditionally dated 896 AD.

[28] *protekció*: The exercise of personal influence on behalf of another.

[29] *Iam vidi ventos alienos:* This misquotation is from Cicero *In Pisonem* 9.21: *Alios ego vidi ventos; alias prospexi animo procellas* – "I have seen other winds; in my mind I have contemplated other storms".

[30] district administrator: The Hungarian *szolgabíró* was the lowest of the ranks of the judiciary.

[31] *ferbli*: A card game akin to poker, played with the traditional Hungarian pack of 32 cards.

[32] Castle: The castle area of Buda, where many government offices were located.

[33] Pilis: A range of mountains north-west of Budapest.

[34] Hortobágy: An area of the Great Plain near Debrecen.

[35] *suba*: A full-length fur coat, usually of sheep-skin, worn with the fur inside, often serving the poor for bed and blanket as well as outerwear.

[36] *járásbíró:* A legal office similar to the English district judge.

[37] Fisherman's Bastion: A notable feature and tourist attraction of the ramparts of the Castle area in Buda, built for the millennial celebrations of 1896.

[38] AKT: 'Motor Trading/Transport Company'.

[39] Nagykároly: A town formerly in Szatmár county, Transylvania, now Carei in Romania.

[40] Sándor Rózsa: An outlaw leader (1813–78) of eastern Hungary and leader of the guerrillas against the Serbs in 1848–49 who became a later-day Robin Hood figure. Móricz was interested in this man and his last two novels were biographical of him.

[41] Bakony: A wild, hilly area of Transdanubia (the Dunántúl) in western Hungary, historiclaly the refuge of outlaws.

[42] Szepes: A county of northern Hungary, now in Slovakia.

[43] Szabolcs: A county of north-eastern Hungary.

[44] Gömör: a county of northern Hungary, now in Slovakia.

[45] the old Hungary: The jingle ran *Teljes Magyarország mennyország, csonka Magyarország nem ország* – A whole Hungary is heaven, mutilated Hungary is not even a country.

[46] Podolinec: Formerly in Szepes county, now Podolinec in Slovakia.

[47] Nagy-Sándor: József Nagy-Sándor was a general in the war of 1848–49.

[48] *főbíró*: Chief Justice, a high legal office.

[49] Ferenc Deák: 1803–76, Hungarian statesman, the force behind the Compromise of 1867 with the Habsburgs, known as the "Wise Man of the Nation".

[50] Queen of England: A central Budapest hotel.

[51] Menyhért Lónyay: Land-owner and influential politician, 1822–84.

[52] Tatárdomb: 'Tatar Hill'.

[53] *mázsa*: Pre-metric unit of weight (equivalent of 100 kilograms).

[54] Mangalicas: A breed of pig of Balkan origin, extremely fat and with very curly bristles. Recently introduced to UK as a rare breed.

[55] Kellerman Tunnel: A reference to the novel *The Tunnel* (1913) by Bernhard Kellerman.

[56] Nyíregyháza: A large town in north-eastern Hungary.

[57] Allusion to the last line of Imre Madách's famous epic, *The Tragedy of Man* – "Man, I have spoken: strive on , trust, have faith!" (trans. George Szirtes, Corvina, 1988).

[58] Treaty of Westphalia: 1648.

[59] Rimaszombat: now Rimavská Sobota, formerly in Gömör-Kishont county, now in Slovakia.

[60] *csárdás*: A vigorous Hungarian dance.

[61] Election of the king was a medieval Hungarian tradition, replaced under the Habsburgs by western-style succession. On the deposition of Károly IV in 1921, the right of the people to elect the monarch was in principle restored, but was never in fact exercised. Admiral Horthy ruled as Regent until 1944.

[62] Árpád: The leader who brought the Magyar tribes to the territory of latter-day Hungary.

Printed in Hungary, 2007